THE ADVENTURES OF TOM SWIFT

VOLUME ONE

TOM SWIFT AND HIS MOTOR-CYCLE

TOM SWIFT AND HIS MOTOR BOAT

TOM SWIFT AND HIS AIRSHIP

TOM SWIFT AND HIS SUBMARINE BOAT

THE ADVENTURES OF TOM SWIFT

VOLUME ONE

VICTOR APPLETON

Brownstone Books

THE ADVENTURES OF TOM SWIFT, VOLUME ONE

CONTENTS

TOM SWIFT AND HIS MOTOR-CYCLE

CHAPTER I

A NARROW ESCAPE

"That's the way to do it! Whoop her up, Andy! Shove the spark lever over, and turn on more gasolene! We'll make a record this trip."

Two lads in the tonneau of a touring car, that was whirling along a country road, leaned forward to speak to the one at the steering wheel. The latter was a red-haired youth, with somewhat squinty eyes, and not a very pleasant face, but his companions seemed to regard him with much favor. Perhaps it was because they were riding in his automobile.

"Whoop her up, Andy!" added the lad on the seat beside the driver. "This is immense!"

"I rather thought you'd like it," remarked Andy Foger, as he turned the car to avoid a stone in the road. "I'll make things hum around Shopton!"

"You have made them hum already, Andy," commented the lad beside him. "My ears are ringing. Wow! There goes my cap!"

As the boy spoke, the breeze, created by the speed at which the car was traveling, lifted off his cap, and sent it whirling to the rear.

Andy Foger turned for an instant's glance behind. Then he opened the throttle still wider, and exclaimed:

"Let it go, Sam. We can get another. I want to see what time I can make to Mansburg! I want to break a record, if I can."

"Look out, or you'll break something else!" cried a lad on the rear seat. "There's a fellow on a bicycle just ahead of us. Take care, Andy!"

"Let him look out for himself," retorted Foger, as he bent lower over the steering wheel, for the car was now going at a terrific rate. The youth on the bicycle was riding slowly along, and did not see the approaching automobile until it was nearly upon him. Then, with a mean grin, Andy Foger pressed the rubber bulb of the horn with sudden energy, sending out a series of alarming blasts.

"It's Tom Swift!" cried Sam Snedecker. "Look out, or you'll run him down!"

"Let him keep out of my way," retorted Andy savagely.

The youth on the wheel, with a sudden spurt of speed, tried to cross the highway. He did manage to do it, but by such a narrow margin that in very terror Andy Foger shut off the power, jammed down the brakes and steered to one side. So suddenly was he obliged to swerve over that the ponderous machine skidded and went into the ditch at the side of the road, where it brought up, tilting to one side.

Tom Swift, his face rather pale from his narrow escape, leaped from his bicycle, and stood regarding the automobile. As for the occupants of that machine, from Andy Foger, the owner, to the three cronies who were riding with him, they all looked very much astonished.

"Are we—is it damaged any, Andy?" asked Sam Snedecker.

"I hope not," growled Andy. "If my car's hurt it's Tom Swift's fault!"

He leaped from his seat and made a hurried inspection of the machine. He found nothing the matter, though it was more from good luck than good management. Then Andy turned and looked savagely at Tom Swift. The latter, standing his wheel up against the fence, walked forward.

"What do you mean by getting in the way like that?" demanded Andy with a scowl. "Don't you see that you nearly upset me?"

"Well, I like your nerve, Andy Foger!" cried Tom. "What do you mean by nearly running me down? Why didn't you sound your horn? You automobilists take too much for granted! You were going faster than the legal rate, anyhow!"

"I was, eh?" sneered Andy.

"Yes, you were, and you know it. I'm the one to make a kick, not you. You came pretty near hitting me. Me getting in your way! I guess I've got some rights on the road!"

"Aw, go on!" growled Andy, for he could think of nothing else to say. "Bicycles are a back number, anyhow."

"It isn't so very long ago that you had one," retorted Tom. "First you fellows know, you'll be pulled in for speeding."

"I guess we had better go slower, Andy," advised Sam in a low voice. "I don't want to be arrested."

"Leave this to me," retorted Andy. "I'm running this tour. The next time you get in my way I'll run you down!" he threatened Tom. "Come on, fellows, we're late now, and can't make a record run, all on account of him," and Andy got back into the car, followed by his cronies, who had hurriedly alighted after their thrilling stop.

"If you try anything like this again you'll wish you hadn't," declared Tom, and he watched the automobile party ride off.

"Oh, forget it!" snapped back Andy, and he laughed, his companions joining.

Tom Swift said nothing in reply. Slowly he remounted his wheel and rode off, but his thoughts toward Andy Foger were not very pleasant ones. Andy was the son of a wealthy man of the town, and his good fortune in the matter of money seemed to have spoiled him, for he was a bully and a coward. Several times he and Tom Swift had clashed, for Andy was overbearing. But this was the first time Andy had shown such a vindictive spirit.

"He thinks he can run over everything since he got his new auto," commented Tom aloud as he rode on. "He'll have a smash-up some day, if he isn't careful. He's too fond of speeding. I wonder where he and his crowd are going?"

Musing over his narrow escape Tom rode on, and was soon at his home, where he lived with his widowed father, Barton Swift, a wealthy inventor, and the latter's housekeeper, Mrs. Baggert. Approaching a machine shop, one of several built near his house by Mr. Swift, in which he conducted experiments and constructed apparatus. Tom was met by his parent.

"What's the matter, Tom?" asked Mr. Swift. "You look as if something had happened."

"Something very nearly did," answered the youth, and related his experience on the road.

"Humph," remarked the inventor; "your little pleasure-jaunt might have ended disastrously. I suppose Andy and his chums are off on their trip. I remember Mr. Foger speaking to me about it the other day. He said Andy and some companions were going on a tour, to be gone a week or more. Well, I'm glad it was no worse. But have you anything special to do, Tom?"

"No; I was just riding for pleasure, and if you want me to do anything, I'm ready."

"Then I wish you'd take this letter to Mansburg for me. I want it registered, and I don't wish to mail it in the Shopton post-office. It's too important, for it's about a valuable invention."

"The new turbine motor, dad?"

"That's it. And on your way I wish you'd stop in Merton's machine shop and get some bolts he's making for me."

"I will. Is that the letter?" and Tom extended his hand for a missive his father held.

"Yes. Please be careful of it. It's to my lawyers in Washington regarding the final steps in getting a patent for the turbine. That's why I'm so particular about not wanting it mailed here. Several times before I have posted letters here, only to have the information contained in them leak out before my attorneys received them. I do not want that to happen in this case. Another thing; don't speak about my new invention in Merton's shop when you stop for the bolts."

"Why, do you think he gave out information concerning your work?"

"Well, not exactly. He might not mean to, but he told me the other day that some strangers were making inquiries of him, about whether he ever did any work for me."

"What did he tell them?"

"He said that he occasionally did, but that most of my inventive work was done in my own shops, here. He wanted to know why the men were asking such questions, and one of them said they expected to open a machine shop soon, and wanted to ascertain if they might figure on getting any of my trade. But I don't believe that was their object."

"What do you think it was?"

"I don't know, exactly, but I was somewhat alarmed when I heard this from Merton. So I am going to take no risks. That's why I send this letter to Mansburg. Don't lose it, and don't forget about the bolts. Here is a blue-print of them, so you can see if they come up to the specifications."

Tom rode off on his wheel, and was soon spinning down the road.

"I wonder if I'll meet Andy Foger and his cronies again?" he thought. "Not very likely to, I guess, if they're off on a tour. Well, I'm just as well satisfied. He and I always seem to get into trouble when we meet." Tom was not destined to meet Andy again that day, but the time was to come when the red-haired bully was to cause Tom Swift no little trouble, and get him into danger besides. So Tom rode along, thinking over what his father had said to him about the letter he carried.

Mr. Barton Swift was a natural inventor. From a boy he had been interested in things mechanical, and one of his first efforts had been to arrange a system of pulleys, belts and gears so that the wind-mill would operate the churn in the old farmhouse where he was born. The fact that the mill went so fast that it broke the churn all to pieces did not discourage him, and he at once set to work, changing the gears. His father had to buy a new churn, but the young inventor made his plan work on the second trial, and thereafter his mother found butter-making easy.

From then on Barton Swift lived in a world of inventions. People used to say he would never amount to anything, that inventors never did, but Mr. Swift proved them all wrong by amassing a considerable fortune out of his many patents. He grew up, married and had one son, Tom. Mrs. Barton died when Tom was three years old, and since then he had lived with his father and a succession of nurses and housekeepers. The last woman to have charge of the household was a Mrs. Baggert, a motherly widow, and she succeeded so well, and Tom and his father formed such an attachment for her, that she was regarded as a fixture, and had now been in charge ten years.

Mr. Swift and his son lived in a handsome house on the outskirts of the village of Shopton, in New York State. The village was near a large body of water, which I shall call Lake Carlopa, and there Tom and his father used to spend many pleasant days boating, for Tom and the inventor were better chums than many boys are, and they were often seen together in a craft rowing about, or fishing. Of course Tom had some boy friends, but he went with his father more often than he did with them.

Though many of Mr. Swift's inventions paid him well, he was constantly seeking to perfect others. To this end he had built near his home several machine shops, with engines, lathes and apparatus for various kinds of work. Tom, too, had the inventive fever in his veins, and had planned some useful implements and small machines.

Along the pleasant country roads on a fine day in April rode Tom Swift on his way to Mansburg to register the letter. As he descended a little hill he saw, some distance away, but coming toward him, a great cloud of dust.

"Somebody must be driving a herd of cattle along the road," thought Tom. "I hope they don't get in my way, or, rather, I hope I don't get in theirs. Guess I'd better keep to one side, yet there isn't any too much room."

The dust-cloud came nearer. It was so dense that whoever or whatever was making it could not he distinguished.

"Must be a lot of cattle in that bunch," mused the young inventor, "but I shouldn't think they'd trot them so on a warm day like this. Maybe they're stampeded. If they are I've got to look out." This idea caused him some alarm.

He tried to peer through the dust-cloud, but could not. Nearer and nearer it came. Tom kept on, taking care to get as far to the side of the road as he could. Then from the midst of the enveloping mass came the sound of a steady "chug-chug."

"It's a motor-cycle!" exclaimed Tom. "He must have his muffler wide open, and that's kicking up as much dust as the wheels do. Whew! But whoever's on it will look like a clay image at the end of the line!"

Now that he knew it was a fellow-cyclist who was raising such a disturbance, Tom turned more toward the middle of the road. As yet he had not had a sight of the rider, but the explosions of the motor were louder. Suddenly, when the first advancing particles of dust reached him, almost making him sneeze, Tom caught sight of the rider. He was a man of middle age, and he was clinging to the handle-bars of the machine. The motor was going at full speed.

Tom quickly turned to one side, to avoid the worst of the dust. The motor-cyclist glanced at the youth, but this act nearly proved disastrous for him. He took his eyes from the road ahead for just a moment, and he did not see a large stone directly in his path. His front wheel hit it, and the heavy machine, which he could not control very well, skidded over toward the lad on the bicycle. The motor-cyclist bounced up in the air from the saddle, and nearly lost his hold on the handle-bars.

"Look out!" cried Tom. "You'll smash into me!"

"I'm—I'm—try—ing—not—to!" were the words that were rattled out of the middle-aged man.

Tom gave his wheel a desperate twist to get out of the way. The motor-cyclist tried to do the same, but the machine he was on appeared to want matters its own way. He came straight for Tom, and a disastrous collision might have resulted had not another stone been in the way. The front wheel hit this, and was swerved to one side. The motor-cycle flashed past Tom, just grazing his wheel, and then was lost to sight beyond in a cloud of dust that seemed to follow it like a halo.

"Why don't you learn to ride before you come out on the road!" cried Tom somewhat angrily.

Like an echo from the dust-cloud came floating back these words:

"I'm—try—ing—to!" Then the sound of the explosions became fainter.

"Well, he's got lots to learn yet!" exclaimed Tom. "That's twice today I've nearly been run down. I expect I'd better look out for the third time. They say that's always fatal," and the lad leaped from his wheel. "Wonder if he bent any of my spokes?" the young inventor continued as he inspected his bicycle.

CHAPTER II

TOM OVERHEARS SOMETHING

"Everything seems to be all right," Tom remarked, "but another inch or so and he'd have crashed into me. I wonder who he was? I wish I had a machine like that. I could make better time than I can on my bicycle. Perhaps I'll get one some day. Well, I might as well ride on."

Tom was soon at Mansburg, and going to the post-office handed in the letter for registry. Bearing in mind his father's words, he looked about to see if there were any suspicious characters, but the only person he noticed was a well-dressed man, with a black mustache, who seemed to be intently studying the schedule of the arrival and departure of the mails.

"Do you want the receipt for the registered, letter sent to you here or at Shopton?" asked the clerk of Tom. "Come to think of it, though, it will have to come here, and you can call for it. I'll have it returned to Mr. Barton Swift, care of general delivery, and you can get it the next time you are over," for the clerk knew Tom.

"That will do," answered our hero, and as he turned away from the window he saw that the man who had been inquiring about the mails was regarding him curiously. Tom thought nothing of it at the time, but there came an occasion when he wished that he had taken more careful note of the well-dressed individual. As the youth passed out of the outer door he saw the man walk over to the registry window.

"He seems to have considerable mail business," thought Tom, and then the matter passed from his mind as he mounted his wheel and hurried to the machine shop.

"Say, I'm awfully sorry," announced Mr. Merton when Tom said he had come for the bolts, "but they're not quite done. They need polishing. I know I promised them to your father today, and he can have them, but he was very particular about the polish, and as one of my best workers was taken sick, I'm a little behind."

"How long will it take to polish them?" asked Tom.

"Oh, about an hour. In fact, a man is working on them now. If you could call this afternoon they'll be ready. Can you?"

"I s'pose I've got to," replied Tom good-naturedly. "Guess I'll have to stay in Mansburg for dinner. I can't get back to Shopton in time now."

"I'll be sure to have them for you after dinner," promised Mr.

Merton. "Now, there's a matter I want to speak to you about, Tom. Has your father any idea of giving the work he has been turning over to me to some other firm?"

"Not that I know of. Why?" and the lad showed his wonder.

"Well, I'll tell you why. Some time ago there was a stranger in here, asking about your father's work. I told Mr. Swift of it at the time. The stranger said then that he and some others were thinking of opening a machine shop, and he wanted to find out whether they would be likely to get any jobs from your father. I told the man I knew nothing about Mr. Swift's business, and he went away. I didn't hear any more of it, though of course I didn't want to lose your father's trade. Now a funny thing happened. Only this morning the same man was back here, and he was making particular inquiries about your father's private machine shops."

"He was?" exclaimed Tom excitedly.

"Yes. He wanted to know where they were located, how they were laid out, and what sort of work he did in them."

"What did you tell him?"

"Nothing at all. I suspected something, and I said the best way for him to find out would be to go and see your father. Wasn't that right?"

"Sure. Dad doesn't want his business known any more than he can help. What do you suppose they wanted?"

"Well, the man talked as though he and his partners would like to buy your father's shops."

"I don't believe he'd sell. He has them arranged just for his own use in making patents, and I'm sure he would not dispose of them."

"Well, that's what I thought, but I didn't tell the man so. I judged it would be best for him to find out for himself."

"What was the man's name?"

"He didn't tell me, and I didn't ask him."

"How did he look?"

"Well, he was well dressed, wore kid gloves and all that, and he had a little black mustache."

Tom started, and Mr. Merton noticed it.

"Do you know him?" he asked.

"No," replied Tom, "but I saw—" Then he stopped. He recalled the man he had seen in the post-office. He answered this description, but it was too vague to be certain.

"Did you say you'd seen him?" asked Mr. Merton, regarding Tom curiously.

"No—yes—that is—well, I'll tell my father about it," stammered Tom, who concluded that it would be best to say nothing of his suspicions. "I'll be back right after dinner, Mr. Merton. Please have the bolts ready for me, if you can."

"I will. Is your father going to use them in a new machine?"

"Yes; dad is always making new machines," answered the youth, as the most polite way of not giving the proprietor of the shop any information. "I'll be back right after dinner," he called as he went out to get on his wheel.

Tom was much puzzled. He felt certain that the man in the postoffice and the one who had questioned Mr. Merton were the same.

"There is something going on, that dad should know about," reflected Tom. "I must tell him. I don't believe it will be wise to send any more of his patent work over to Merton. We must do it in the shops at home, and dad and I will have to keep our eyes open. There may be spies about seeking to discover something about his new turbine motor. I'll hurry back with those bolts and tell dad. But first I must get lunch. I'll go to the restaurant and have a good feed while I'm at it."

Tom had plenty of spending money, some of which came from a small patent he had marketed himself. He left his wheel outside the restaurant, first taking the precaution to chain the wheels, and then went inside. Tom was hungry and ordered a good meal. He was about half way through it when some one called his name.

"Hello, Ned!" he answered, looking up to see a youth about his own age. "Where did you blow in from?"

"Oh, I came over from Shopton this morning," replied Ned Newton, taking a seat at the table with Tom. The two lads were chums, and in their younger days had often gone fishing, swimming and hunting together. Now Ned worked in the Shopton bank, and Tom was so busy helping his father, so they did not see each other so often.

"On business or pleasure?" asked Tom, putting some more sugar in his coffee.

"Business. I had to bring some papers over from our bank to the First National here. But what about you?"

"Oh, I came on dad's account."

"Invented anything new?" asked Ned as he gave his order to the waitress.

"No, nothing since the egg-beater I was telling you about. But I'm working on some things."

"Why don't you invent an automobile or an airship?"

"Maybe I will some day, but, speaking of autos, did you see the one Andy Foger has?"

"Yes; it's a beaut! Have you seen it?"

"Altogether at too close range. He nearly ran over me this morning," and the young inventor related the occurrence.

"Oh, Andy always was too fresh," commented Ned; "and since his father let him get the touring car I suppose he'll be worse than ever."

"Well, if he tries to run me down again he'll get into trouble," declared Tom, calling for a second cup of coffee.

The two chums began conversing on more congenial topics, and Ned was telling of a new camera he had, when, from a table directly behind him, Tom heard some one say in rather loud tones:

"The plant is located in Shopton, all right, and the buildings are near Swift's house."

Tom started, and listened more intently.

"That will make it more difficult," one man answered. "But if the invention is as valuable as—"

"Hush!" came a caution from another of the party. "This is too public a place to discuss the matter. Wait until we get out. One of us will have to see Swift, of course, and if he proves stubborn—"

"I guess you'd better hush yourself," retorted the man who had first spoken, and then the voices subsided.

But Tom Swift had overheard something which made him vaguely afraid. He started so at the sound of his father's name that he knocked a fork from the table.

"What's the matter; getting nervous?" asked Ned with a laugh.

"I guess so," replied Tom, and when he stooped to pick the fork up, not waiting for the girl who was serving at his table, he stole a look at the strangers who had just entered. He was startled to note that one of the men was the same he had seen in the post-office—the man who answered the description of the one who had been inquiring of Mr. Merton about the Swift shops.

"I'm going to keep my ears open," thought Tom as he went on eating his dinner.

CHAPTER III

IN A SMASH-UP

Though the young inventor listened intently, in an endeavor to hear the conversation of the men at the table behind him, all he could catch was an indistinct murmur. The strangers appeared to have heeded the caution of one of their number and were speaking in low tones.

Tom and Ned finished their meal, and started to leave the restaurant. As Mr. Swift's son passed the table where the men sat they looked up quickly at him. Two of them gave Tom but a passing glance, but one—he whom the young inventor had noticed in the postoffice —stared long and intently.

"I think he will know me the next time he sees me," thought Tom, and he boldly returned the glance of the stranger.

The bolts were ready when the inventor's son called at the machine shop a second time, and making a package of them Tom fastened it to the saddle of his bicycle. He started for home at a fast pace, and was just turning from a cross road into the main highway when he saw ahead of him a woman driving a light wagon. As the sun flashed on Tom's shining wheel the horse gave a sudden leap, swerved to one side, and then bolted down the dusty stretch, the woman screaming at the top of her voice.

"A runaway!" cried Tom; "and partly my fault, too!"

Waiting not an instant the lad bent over his handle-bars and pedaled with all his force. His bicycle seemed fairly to leap forward after the galloping horse.

"Sit still! Don't jump out! Don't jump!" yelled the young inventor. "I'll try to catch him!" for the woman was standing up in front of the seat and leaning forward, as if about to leap from the wagon.

"She's lost her head," thought Tom. "No wonder! That's a skittish horse."

Faster and faster he rode, bending all his energies to overtake the animal. The wagon was swaying from side to side, and more than once the woman just saved herself from being thrown out by grasping the edge of the seat. She found that her standing position was a dangerous one and crouched on the bottom of the swaying vehicle.

"That's better!" shouted Tom, but it is doubtful if she heard him, for the rattling of the wagon and the hoofbeats of the horse drowned all other sounds. "Sit still!" he shouted. "I'll stop the horse for you!"

Trying to imagine himself in a desperate race, in order to excite himself to greater speed, Tom continued on. He was now even with the tail-board of the wagon, and slowly creeping up. The woman was all huddled up in a lump.

"Grab the reins! Grab the reins!" shouted Tom. "Saw on the bit! That will stop him!"

The occupant of the wagon turned to look at the lad. Tom saw that she was a handsome young lady. "Grab the reins!" he cried again. "Pull hard!"

"I—I can't!" she answered frightenedly. "They have dropped down! Oh, do please stop the horse! I'm so—so frightened!"

"I'll stop him!" declared the youth firmly, and he set his teeth hard. Then he saw the reason the fair driver could not grasp the lines. They had slipped over the dashboard and were trailing on the ground.

The horse was slacking speed a bit now, for the pace was telling on his wind. Tom saw his opportunity, and with a sudden burst of energy was at the animal's head. Steering his wheel with one hand, with the other the lad made a grab for the reins near the bit. The horse swerved frightenedly to one side, but Tom swung in the same direction. He grasped the leather and then, with a kick, he freed himself from the bicycle, giving it a shove to one side. He was now clinging to the reins with both hands, and, being a muscular lad and no lightweight, his bulk told.

"Sit—still!" panted our hero to the young woman, who had arisen to the seat. "I'll have him stopped in half a minute now!"

It was in less time than that, for the horse, finding it impossible to shake off the grip of Tom, began to slow from a gallop to a trot, then to a canter, and finally to a slow walk. A moment later the horse had stopped, breathing heavily from his run.

"There, there, now!" spoke Tom soothingly. "You're all right, old fellow. I hope you're not hurt"—this to the young lady—and Tom made a motion to raise his cap, only to find that it had blown off.

"Oh, no—no; I'm more frightened than hurt."

"It was all my fault," declared the young inventor. "I should not have swung into the road so suddenly. My bicycle alarmed your horse."

"Oh, I fancy Dobbin is easily disturbed," admitted the fair driver. "I can't thank you enough for stopping him. You saved me from a bad accident."

"It was the least I could do. Are you all right now?" and he handed up the dangling reins. "I think Dobbin, as you call him, has had enough of running," went on Tom, for the horse was now quiet.

"I hope so. Yes, I am all right. I trust your wheel is not damaged. If it is, my father, Mr. Amos Nestor, of Mansburg, will gladly pay for its repair."

This reminded the young inventor of his bicycle, and making sure that the horse would not start up again, he went to where his wheel and his cap lay. He found that the only damage to the bicycle was a few bent spokes, and, straightening them and having again apologized to the young woman, receiving in turn her pardon and thanks, and learning that her name was Mary Nestor, Tom once more resumed his trip. The wagon followed him at a distance, the horse evincing no desire now to get out of a slow amble.

"Well, things are certainly happening to me today," mused Tom as he pedaled on. "That might have been a serious runaway if there'd been anything in the road."

Tom did not stop to think that he had been mainly instrumental in preventing a bad accident, as he had been the innocent cause of starting the runaway, but Tom was ever a modest lad. His arms were wrenched from jerking on the bridle, but he did not mind that much, and bent over the handle-bars to make up for lost time.

Our hero was within a short distance of his house and was coasting easily along when, just ahead of him, he saw a cloud of dust, very similar to the one that had, some time before, concealed the inexperienced motor-cyclist.

"I wonder if that's him again?" thought Tom. "If it is I'm going to hang back until I see which way he's headed. No use running any more risks."

Almost at that moment a puff of wind blew some of the dust to one side. Tom had a glimpse of the man on the puffing machine.

"It's the same chap!" he exclaimed aloud; "and he's going the same way I am. Well, I'll not try to catch up to him. I wonder what he's been doing all this while, that he hasn't gotten any farther than this? Either he's been riding back and forth, or else he's been resting. My, but he certainly is scooting along!"

The wind carried to Tom the sound of the explosions of the motor, and he could see the man clinging tightly to the handle-bars. The rider was almost in front of Tom's house now, when, with a suddenness that caused the lad to utter an exclamation of alarm, the stranger turned his machine right toward a big oak tree.

"What's he up to?" cried Tom excitedly. "Does he think he can climb that, or is he giving an exhibition by showing how close he can come and not hit it?"

A moment later the motor-cyclist struck the tree a glancing blow. The man went flying over the handle-bars, the machine was shunted to the ditch along the road, and falling over on one side the motor raced furiously. The rider lay in a heap at the foot of the tree.

"My, that was a smash!" cried Tom. "He must be killed!" and bending forward, he raced toward the scene of the accident.

CHAPTER IV

TOM AND A MOTOR-CYCLE

When Tom reached the prostrate figure on the grass at the foot of the old oak tree, the youth bent quickly over the man. There was an ugly cut on his head, and blood was flowing from it. But Tom quickly noticed that the stranger was breathing, though not very strongly.

"Well, he's not dead—just yet!" exclaimed the youth with a sigh of relief. "But I guess he's pretty badly hurt. I must get help—no, I'll take him into our house. It's not far. I'll call dad."

Leaning his wheel against the tree Tom started for his home, about three hundred feet away, and then he noticed that the stranger's motor-cycle was running at full speed on the ground.

"Guess I'd better shut off the power!" he exclaimed. "No use letting the machine be ruined." Tom had a natural love for machinery, and it hurt him almost as much to see a piece of fine apparatus abused as it did to see an animal mistreated. It was the work of a moment to shut off the gasolene and spark, and then the youth raced on toward his house.

"Where's dad?" he called to Mrs. Baggert, who was washing the dishes.

"Out in one of the shops," replied the housekeeper. "Why, Tom," she went on hurriedly as she saw how excited he was, "whatever has happened?"

"Man hurt—out in front—motor-cycle smash—I'm going to bring him in here—get some things ready—I'll find dad!"

"Bless and save us!" cried Mrs. Baggert. "Whatever are we coming to? Who's hurt? How did it happen? Is he dead?"

"Haven't time to talk now!" answered Tom, rushing from the house. "Dad and I will bring him in here."

Tom found his father in one of the three small machine shops on the grounds about the Swift home. The youth hurriedly told what had happened.

"Of course we'll bring him right in here!" assented Mr. Swift, putting aside the work upon which he was engaged. "Did you tell Mrs. Baggert?"

"Yes, and she's all excited."

"Well, she can't help it, being a woman, I suppose. But we'll manage. Do you know the man?"

"Never saw him before today, when he tried to run me down.

Guess he doesn't know much about motor-cycles. But come on, dad. He may bleed to death."

Father and son hurried to where the stranger lay. As they bent over him he opened his eyes and asked faintly:

"Where am I? What happened?"

"You're all right—in good hands," said Mr. Swift. "Are you much hurt?"

"Not much—mostly stunned, I guess. What happened?" he repeated.

"You and your motor-cycle tried to climb a tree," remarked Tom with grim humor.

"Oh, yes, I remember now. I couldn't seem to steer out of the way. And I couldn't shut off the power in time. Is the motor-cycle much damaged?"

"The front wheel is," reported Tom, after an inspection, "and there are some other breaks, but I guess—"

"I wish it was all smashed!" exclaimed the man vigorously. "I never want to see it again!"

"Why, don't you like it?" asked Tom eagerly.

"No, and I never will," the man spoke faintly but determinedly.

"Never mind now," interposed Mr. Swift. "Don't excite yourself. My son and I will take you to our house and send for a doctor."

"I'll bring the motor-cycle, after we've carried you in," added Tom.

"Don't worry about the machine. I never want to see it again!" went on the man, rising to a sitting position. "It nearly killed me twice to day. I'll never ride again."

"You'll feel differently after the doctor fixes you up," said Mr. Swift with a smile.

"Doctor! I don't need a doctor," cried the stranger. "I am only bruised and shaken up."

"You have a bad cut on your head," said Tom.

"It isn't very deep," went on the injured man, placing his fingers on it. "Fortunately I struck the tree a glancing blow. If you will allow me to rest in your house a little while and give me some plaster for the cut I shall be all right again."

"Can you walk, or shall we carry you?" asked Tom's father.

"Oh, I can walk, if you'll support me a little." And the stranger proved that he could do this by getting to his feet and taking a few steps. Mr. Swift and his son took hold of his arms and led him to the house. There he was placed on a lounge and given some simple restoratives by Mrs. Baggert, who, when she found the accident was not serious, recovered her composure.

"I must have been unconscious for a few minutes," went on the man.

"You were," explained Tom. "When I got up to you I thought you were dead, until I saw you breathe. Then I shut off the power of your machine and ran in for dad. I've got the motor-cycle outside. You can't ride it for some time, I'm afraid, Mr.—er—" and Tom stopped in some confusion, for he realized that he did not know the man's name.

"I beg your pardon for not introducing myself before," went on the stranger. "I'm Wakefield Damon, of Waterfield. But don't worry about me riding that machine again. I never shall."

"Oh, perhaps—" began Mr. Swift.

"No, I never shall," went on Mr. Damon positively. "My doctor told me to get it, as he thought riding around the country would benefit my health I shall tell him his prescription nearly killed me."

"And me too," added Tom with a laugh.

"How—why—are you the young man I nearly ran down this morning?" asked Mr. Damon, suddenly sitting up and looking at the youth.

"I am," answered our hero.

"Bless my soul! So you are!" cried Mr. Damon. "I was wondering who it could be. It's quite a coincidence. But I was in such a cloud of dust I couldn't make out who it was."

"You had your muffler open, and that made considerable dust," explained Tom.

"Was that it? Bless my existence! I thought something was wrong, but I couldn't tell what. I went over all the instructions in the book and those the agent told me, but I couldn't think of the right one. I tried all sorts of things to make less dust, but I couldn't. Then, bless my eyelashes, if the machine didn't stop just after I nearly ran into you. I tinkered over it for an hour or more before I could get it to going again. Then I ran into the tree. My doctor told me the machine would do my liver good, but, bless my happiness, I'd as soon be without a liver entirely as to do what I've done today. I am done with motor-cycling!"

A hopeful look came over Tom's face, but he said nothing, that is, not just then. In a little while Mr. Damon felt so much better that he said he would start for home. "I'm afraid you'll have to leave your machine here," said Tom.

"You can send for it any time you want to," added Mr. Swift.

"Bless my hatband!" exclaimed Mr. Damon, who appeared to be very fond of blessing his various organs and his articles of wearing apparel. "Bless my hatband! I never want to see it again! If you will be so kind as to keep it for me, I will send a junk man after it. I will never spend anything on having it repaired. I am done with that form of exercise—liver or no liver—doctor or no doctor."

He appeared very determined. Tom quickly made up his mind. Mr. Damon had gone to the bathroom to get rid of some of the mud on his hands and face.

"Father," said Tom earnestly, "may I buy that machine of him?"

"What? Buy a broken motor-cycle?"

"I can easily fix it. It is a fine make, and in good condition. I can repair it. I've wanted a motor-cycle for some time, and here's a chance to get a good one cheap."

"You don't need to do that," replied Mr. Swift. "You have money enough to buy a new one if you want it. I never knew you cared for them."

"I didn't, until lately. But I'd rather buy this one and fix it up than get a new one. Besides, I have an idea for a new kind of transmission, and perhaps I can work it out on this machine."

"Oh, well, if you want it for experimental purposes, I suppose it will be as good as any. Go ahead, get it if you wish, but don't give too much for it."

"I'll not. I fancy I can get it cheap."

Mr. Damon returned to the living-room, where he had first been carried.

"I cannot thank you enough for what you have done for me," he said. "I might have lain there for hours. Bless my very existence! I have had a very narrow escape. Hereafter when I see anyone on a motor-cycle I shall turn my head away. The memory will be too painful," and he touched the plaster that covered a cut on his head.

"Mr. Damon," said Tom quickly, "will you sell me that motor-cycle?"

"Bless my finger rings! Sell you that mass of junk?"

"It isn't all junk," went on the young inventor. "I can easily fix it; though, of course," he added prudently, "it will cost something. How much would you want for it?"

"Well," replied Mr. Damon, "I paid two hundred and fifty dollars last week. I have ridden a hundred miles on it. That is at the rate of two dollars and a half a mile—pretty expensive riding. But if you are in earnest I will let you have the machine for fifty dollars, and then I fear that I will be taking advantage of you."

"I'll give you fifty dollars," said Tom quickly, and Mr. Damon exclaimed:

"Bless my liver—that is, if I have one. Do you mean it?"

Tom nodded. "I'll fetch you the money right away," he said,

starting for his room. He got the cash from a small safe he had arranged, which was fitted up with an ingenious burglar alarm, and was on his way downstairs when he heard his father call out:

"Here! What do you want? Go away from that shop! No one is allowed there!" and looking from an upper window, Tom saw his father running toward a stranger, who was just stepping inside the shop where Mr. Swift was constructing his turbine motor. Tom started as he saw that the stranger was the same black-mustached man whom he had noticed in the post-office, and, later, in the restaurant at Mansburg.

CHAPTER V

MR. SWIFT IS ALARMED

Stuffing the money which he intended to give to Mr. Damon in his pocket, Tom ran downstairs. As he passed through the living-room, intending to see what the disturbance was about, and, if necessary, aid his father, the owner of the broken motor-cycle exclaimed:

"What's the matter? What has happened? Bless my coat-tails, but is anything wrong?"

"I don't know," answered Tom. "There is a stranger about the shop, and my father never allows that. I'll be back in a minute."

"Take your time," advised the somewhat eccentric Mr. Damon. "I find my legs are a bit weaker than I suspected, and I will be glad to rest a while longer. Bless my shoelaces, but don't hurry!"

Tom went into the rear yard, where the shops, in a small cluster of buildings, were located. He saw his father confronting the man with the black mustache, and Mr. Swift was saying:

"What do you want? I allow no people to come in here unless I or my son invites them. Did you wish to see me?"

"Are you Mr. Barton Swift?" asked the man.

"Yes, that is my name."

"The inventor of the Swift safety lamp, and the turbine motor?"

At the mention of the motor Mr. Swift started.

"I am the inventor of the safety lamp you mention," he said stiffly, "but I must decline to talk about the motor. May I ask where you obtained your information concerning it?"

"Why, I am not at liberty to tell," went on the man. "I called to see if we could negotiate with you for the sale of it. Parties whom I represent—"

At that moment Tom plucked his father by the sleeve.

"Dad," whispered the youth, "I saw him in Mansburg. I think he is one of several who have been inquiring in Mr. Merton's shop about you and your patents. I wouldn't have anything to do with him until I found out more about him."

"Is that so?" asked Mr. Swift quickly. Then, turning to the stranger, he said: "My son tells me—"

But Mr. Swift got no further, for at that moment the stranger caught sight of Tom, whom he had not noticed before.

"Ha!" exclaimed the man. "I have forgotten something—an important engagement—will be back directly—will see you again,

Mr. Swift— excuse the trouble I have put you to—I am in a great hurry," and before father or son could stop him, had they any desire to, the man turned and walked quickly from the yard.

Mr. Swift stood staring at him, and so did Tom. Then the inventor asked:

"Do you know that man? What about him, Tom? Why did he leave so hurriedly?"

"I don't know his name," replied Tom, "but I am suspicious regarding him, and I think he left because he suddenly recognized me." Thereupon he told his father of seeing the man in the post-office, and hearing the talk of the same individual and two companions in the restaurant.

"And so you think they are up to some mischief, Tom?" asked the parent when the son had finished.

"Well, I wouldn't go quite as far as that, but I think they are interested in your patents, and you ought to know whether you want them to be, or not."

"I most certainly do not—especially in the turbine motor. That is my latest invention, and, I think, will prove very valuable. But, though I have not mentioned it before, I expect to have trouble with it. Soon after I perfected it, with the exception of some minor details, I received word from a syndicate of rich men that I was infringing on a motor, the patent of which they controlled."

"This surprised me for two reasons. One was because I did not know that any one knew I had invented the motor. I had kept the matter secret, and I am at a loss to know how it leaked out. To prevent any further information concerning my plans becoming public, I sent you to Mansburg today. But it seems that the precaution was of little avail. Another matter of surprise was the information that I was infringing on the patent of some one else. I had a very careful examination made, and I found that the syndicate of rich men was wrong. I was not infringing. In fact, though the motor they have is somewhat like mine, there is one big difference—theirs does not work, while mine does. Their patents are worthless."

"Then what do you think is their object?"

"I think they want to get control of my invention of the turbine motor, Tom. That is what has been worrying me lately. I know these men to be unscrupulous, and, with plenty of money, they may make trouble for me."

"But can't you fight them in the courts?"

"Yes, I could do that. It is not as if I was a poor man, but I do not like lawsuits. I want to live quietly and invent things. I dislike litigation. However, if they force it on me I will fight!" exclaimed Mr.

Swift determinedly.

"Do you think this man was one of the crowd of financiers?" asked Tom.

"It would be hard to say. I did not like his actions, and the fact that he sneaked in here, as if he was trying to get possession of some of my models or plans, makes it suspicious."

"It certainly does," agreed Tom. "Now, if we only knew his name we could—"

He suddenly paused in his remark and sprang forward. He picked up an envelope that had dropped where the stranger had been standing.

"The man lost this from his pocket, dad," said Tom eagerly. "It's a telegram. Shall we look at it?"

"I think we will be justified in protecting ourselves. Is the envelope open?"

"Yes."

"Then read the telegram."

Tom drew out a folded yellow slip of paper. It was a short message. He read:

"'Anson Morse, Mansburg. See Swift today. Make offer. If not accepted do the best you can. Spare no effort. Don't give plans away.'"

"Is that all?" asked Mr. Swift.

"All except the signature."

"Who is the telegram signed by?"

"By Smeak & Katch," answered Tom.

"Those rascally lawyers!" exclaimed his father. "I was beginning to suspect this. That is the firm which represents the syndicate of wealthy men who are trying to get my turbine motor patents away from me. Tom, we must be on our guard! They will wage a fierce fight against me, for they have sunk many thousands of dollars in a worthless machine, and are desperate."

"We'll fight 'em!" cried Tom. "You and I, dad! We'll show 'em that the firm of Swift & Son is swift by name and swift by nature!"

"Good!" exclaimed the inventor. "I'm glad you feel that way about it, Tom. But we are going to have no easy task. Those men are rich and unscrupulous. We shall have to be on guard constantly. Let me have that telegram. It may come in useful. Now I must send word to Reid & Crawford, my attorneys in Washington, to be on the lookout. Matters are coming to a curious pass."

As Mr. Swift and his son started for the house, they met Mr. Damon coming toward them.

"Bless my very existence!" cried the eccentric man. "I was

beginning to fear something had happened to you. I am glad that you are all right. I heard voices, and I imagined—"

"It's all right," Mr. Swift reassured him. "There was a stranger about my shop, and I never allow that. Do you feel well enough to go? If not we shall be glad to have you remain with us. We have plenty of room."

"Oh, thank you very much, but I must be going. I feel much better. Bless my gaiters, but I never will trust myself in even an automobile again! I will renounce gasolene from now on."

"That reminds me," spoke Tom. "I have the money for the motor-cycle," and he drew out the bills. "You are sure you will not regret your bargain, Mr. Damon? The machine is new, and needs only slight repairs. Fifty dollars is—"

"Tut, tut, young man! I feel as if I was getting the best of you. Bless my handkerchief! I hope you have no bad luck with it."

"I'll try and be careful," promised Tom with a smile as he handed over the money. "I am going to gear it differently and put some improvements on it. Then I will use it instead of my bicycle."

"It would have to be very much improved before I trusted myself on it again," declared Mr. Damon. "Well, I appreciate what you have done for me, and if at any time I can reciprocate the favor, I will only be too glad to do so. Bless my soul, though, I hope I don't have to rescue you from trying to climb a tree," and with a laugh, which showed that he had fully recovered from his mishap, he shook hands with father and son and left.

"A very nice man, Tom," commented Mr. Swift. "Somewhat odd and out of the ordinary, but a very fine character, for all that."

"That's what I say," added the son. "Now, dad, you'll see me scooting around the country on a motor-cycle. I've always wanted one, and now I have a bargain."

"Do you think you can repair it?"

"Of course, dad. I've done more difficult things than that. I'm going to take it apart now, and see what it needs."

"Before you do that, Tom, I wish you would take a telegram to town for me. I must wire my lawyers at once."

"Dad looks worried," thought Tom as he wheeled the broken motor-cycle into a machine shop, where he did most of his work. "Well, I don't blame him. But we'll get the best of those scoundrels yet!"

CHAPTER VI

AN INTERVIEW IN THE DARK

While Mr. Swift was writing the message he wished his son to take to the village, the young mechanic inspected the motor-cycle he had purchased. Tom found that a few repairs would suffice to put it in good shape, though an entire new front wheel would be needed. The motor had not been damaged, as he ascertained by a test. Tom rode into town on his bicycle, and as he hurried along he noticed in the west a bank of ugly-looking clouds that indicated a shower.

"I'm in for a wetting before I get back," he mused, and he increased his speed, reaching the telegraph office shortly before seven o'clock.

"Think this storm will hold off until I get home?" asked Tom.

"I'm afraid not," answered the agent. "You'd better get a hustle on."

Tom sprinted off. It was getting dark rapidly, and when he was about a mile from home he felt several warm drops on his face.

"Here it comes!" exclaimed the youth. "Now for a little more speed!"

Tom pressed harder on the pedals, too hard, in fact, for an instant later something snapped, and the next he knew he was flying over the handlebars of the bicycle. At the same time there was a metallic, clinking sound.

"Chain's busted!" exclaimed the lad as he picked himself up out of the dust. "Well, wouldn't that jar you!" and he walked back to where, in the dusk, he could dimly discern his wheel.

The chain had come off the two sprockets and was lying to one side. Tom picked it up and ascertained by close observation that the screw and nut holding the two joining links together was lost.

"Nice pickle!" he murmured. "How am I going to find it in all this dust and darkness?" he asked himself disgustedly. "I'll carry an extra screw next time. No, I won't, either. I'll ride my motor-cycle next time. Well, I may as well give a look around. I hate to walk, if I can fix it and ride."

Tom had not spent more than two minutes looking about the dusty road, with the aid of matches, for the screw, when the rain suddenly began falling in a hard shower.

"Guess there's no use lingering here any longer," he remarked. "I'll push the wheel and run for home."

He started down the road in the storm and darkness. The highway soon became a long puddle of mud, through which he splashed, finding it more and more difficult every minute to push the bicycle in the thick, sticky clay.

Above the roar of the wind and the swishing of the rain he heard another sound. It was a steady "puff-puff," and then the darkness was cut by a glare of light.

"An automobile," said Tom aloud. "Guess I'd better get out of the way."

He turned to one side, but the auto, instead of passing him when it got to the place where he was, made a sudden stop.

"Want a ride?" asked the chauffeur, peering out from the side curtains which somewhat protected him from the storm. Tom saw that the car was a large, touring one. "Can I give you a lift?" went on the driver.

"Well, I've got my bicycle with me," explained the young inventor. "My chain's broken, and I've got a mile to go."

"Jump up in back," invited the man. "Leave your wheel here; I guess it will be safe."

"Oh, I couldn't do that," said Tom. "I don't mind walking. I'm wet through now, and I can't get much wetter. I'm much obliged, though."

"Well, I'm sorry, but I can hardly take you and the bicycle, too," continued the chauffeur.

"Certainly not," added a voice from the tonneau of the car. "We can't have a muddy bicycle in here. Who is that person, Simpson?"

"It's a young man," answered the driver.

"Is he acquainted around here?" went on the voice from the rear of the car. "Ask him if he is acquainted around here, Simpson."

Tom was wondering where he had heard that voice before. He had a vague notion that it was familiar.

"Are you acquainted around here?" obediently asked the man at the wheel.

"I live here," replied Tom.

"Ask him if he knows any one named Swift?" continued the voice from the tonneau, and the driver started to repeat it.

"I heard him," interrupted Tom. "Yes, I know a Mr. Swift;" but Tom, with a sudden resolve, and one he could hardly explain, decided that, for the present, he would not betray his own identity.

"Ask him if Mr. Swift is an inventor." Once more the unseen person spoke in the voice Tom was trying vainly to recall.

"Yes, he is an inventor," was the youth's answer.

"Do you know much about him? What are his habits? Does he

live near his workshops? Does he keep many servants? Does he—"

The unseen questioner suddenly parted the side curtains and peered out at Tom, who stood in the muddy road, close to the automobile. At that moment there came a bright flash of lightning, illuminating not only Tom's face, but that of his questioner as well. And at the sight Tom started, no less than did the man. For Tom had recognized him as one of the three mysterious persons in the restaurant, and as for the man, he had also recognized Tom.

"Ah—er—um—is—Why, it's you, isn't it?" cried the questioner, and he thrust his head farther out from between the curtains. "My, what a storm!" he exclaimed as the rain increased. "So you know Mr. Swift, eh? I saw you today in Mansburg, I think. I have a good memory for faces. Do you work for Mr. Swift? If you do I may be able to—"

"I'm Tom Swift, son of Mr. Barton Swift," said Tom as quietly as he could.

"Tom Swift! His son!" cried the man, and he seemed much agitated. "Why, I thought—that is, Morse said—Simpson, hurry back to Mansburg!" and with that, taking no more notice of Tom, the man in the auto hastily drew the curtains together.

The chauffeur threw in the gears and swung the ponderous machine to one side. The road was wide, and he made the turn skilfully. A moment later the car was speeding back the way it had come, leaving Tom standing on the highway, alone in the mud and darkness, with the rain pouring down in torrents.

CHAPTER VII

OFF ON A SPIN

Tom's first impulse was to run after the automobile, the red tail-light of which glowed through the blackness like a ruby eye. Then he realized that it was going from him at such a swift pace that it would be impossible to get near it, even if his bicycle was in working order.

"But if I had my motor-cycle I'd catch up to them," he murmured. "As it is, I must hurry home and tell dad. This is another link in the queer chain that seems to be winding around us. I wonder who that man was, and what he wanted by asking so many personal questions about dad?"

Trundling his wheel before him, with the chain dangling from the handle-bar, Tom splashed on through the mud and rain. It was a lonesome, weary walk, tired as he was with the happenings of the day, and the young inventor breathed a sigh of thankfulness as the lights of his home shone out in the mist of the storm. As he tramped up the steps of the side porch, his wheel bumping along ahead of him, a door was thrown open.

"Why, it's Tom!" exclaimed Mrs. Baggert. "Whatever happened to you?" and she hurried forward with kindly solicitude, for the housekeeper was almost a second mother to the youth.

"Chain broke," answered the lad laconically. "Where's dad?"

"Out in the shop, working at his latest invention, I expect. But are you hurt?"

"Oh, no. I fell easily. The mud was like a feather-bed, you know, except that it isn't so good for the clothes," and the young inventor looked down at his splashed and bedraggled garments.

Mr. Swift was very much surprised when Tom told him of the happening on the road, and related the conversation and the subsequent alarm of the man on learning Tom's identity.

"Who do you suppose he could have been?" asked Tom, when he had finished.

"I am pretty certain he was one of that crowd of financiers of whom Anson Morse seems to be a representative," said Mr. Swift. "Are you sure the man was one of those you saw in the restaurant?"

"Positive. I had a good look at him both times. Do you think he imagined he could come here and get possession of some of your secrets?"

"I hardly know what to think, Tom. But we will take every precaution. We will set the burglar alarm wires, which I have neglected for some time, as I fancied everything would be secure here. Then I will take my plans and the model of the turbine motor into the house. I'll run no chances tonight."

Mr. Swift, who was adjusting some of the new bolts that Tom had brought home that day; began to gather up his tools and material.

"I'll help you, dad," said Tom, and he began connecting the burglar alarm wires, there being an elaborate system of them about the house, shops and grounds.

Neither Tom nor his father slept well that night. Several times one or the other of them arose, thinking they heard unusual noises, but it was only some disturbance caused by the storm, and morning arrived without anything unusual having taken place. The rain still continued, and Tom, looking from his window and seeing the downpour, remarked:

"I'm glad of it!"

"Why?" asked his father, who was in the next room.

"Because I'll have a good excuse for staying in and working on my motor-cycle."

"But you must do some studying," declared Mr. Swift. "I will hear you in mathematics right after breakfast."

"All right, dad. I guess you'll find I have my lessons."

Tom had graduated with honors from a local academy, and when it came to a question of going further in his studies, he had elected to continue with his father for a tutor, instead of going to college. Mr. Swift was a very learned man, and this arrangement was satisfactory to him, as it allowed Tom more time at home, so he could aid his father on the inventive work and also plan things for himself. Tom showed a taste for mechanics, and his father wisely decided that such training as his son needed could be given at home to better advantage than in a school or college.

Lessons over, Tom hurried to his own particular shop, and began taking apart the damaged motor-cycle.

"First I'll straighten the handle-bars, and then I'll fix the motor and transmission," he decided. "The front wheel I can buy in town, as this one would hardly pay for repairing." Tom was soon busy with wrenches, hammers, pliers and screw-driver. He was in his element, and was whistling over his task. The motor he found in good condition, but it was not such an easy task as he had hoped to change the transmission. He had finally to appeal to his father, in order to get the right proportion between the back and front gears, for the motor-cycle was operated by a sprocket chain, instead of a belt drive, as is the case with some.

Mr. Swift showed Tom how to figure out the number of teeth needed on each sprocket, in order to get an increase of speed, and as there was a sprocket wheel from a disused piece of machinery available, Tom took that. He soon had it in place, and then tried the motor. To his delight the number of revolutions of the rear wheel were increased about fifteen per cent.

"I guess I'll make some speed," he announced to his father.

"But it will take more gasolene to run the motor; don't forget that. You know the great principle of mechanics—that you can't get out of a machine any more than you put into it, nor quite as much, as a matter of fact, for considerable is lost through friction."

"Well, then, I'll enlarge the gasolene tank," declared Tom. "I want to go fast when I'm going."

He reassembled the machine, and after several hours of work had it in shape to run, except that a front wheel was lacking.

"I think I'll go to town and get one," he remarked. "The rain isn't quite so hard now."

In spite of his father's mild objections Tom went, using his bicycle, the chain of which he had quickly repaired. He found just the front wheel needed, and that night his motor-cycle was ready to run. But it was too dark to try it then, especially as he had no good lantern, the one on the cycle having been smashed, and his own bicycle light not being powerful enough. So he had to postpone his trial trip until the next day.

He was up early the following morning, and went out for a spin before breakfast. He came back, with flushed cheeks and bright eyes, just as Mr. Swift and Mrs. Baggert were sitting down to the table.

"To Reedville and back," announced Tom proudly.

"What, a round trip of thirty miles!" exclaimed Mr. Swift.

"That's what!" declared his son. "I went like a greased pig most of the way. I had to slow up going through Mansburg, but the rest of at time I let it out for all it was worth."

"You must be careful," cautioned his father. "You are not an expert yet."

"No, I realize that. Several times, when I wanted to slow up, I began to back-pedal, forgetting that I wasn't on my bicycle. Then I thought to shut off the power and put on the brake. But it's glorious fun. I'm going out again as soon as I have something to eat. That is, unless you want me to help you, dad."

"No, not this morning. Learn to ride the motor-cycle. It may come in handy."

Neither Tom nor his father realized what an important part the machine was soon to play in their lives.

Tom went out for another spin after breakfast, and in a different direction. He wanted to see what the machine would do on a hill, and there was a long, steep one about five miles from home. The roads were in fine shape after the rain, and he speeded up the incline at a rapid rate.

"It certainly does eat up the road," the lad murmured. "I have improved this machine considerably. Wish I could take out a patent on it."

Reaching the crest of the slope, he started down the incline. He turned off part of the power, and was gliding along joyously, when from a cross-road he suddenly saw turn into the main highway a mule, drawing a ramshackle wagon, loaded with fence posts. Beside the animal walked an old colored man.

"I hope he gets out of the way in time," thought Tom. "He's moving as slow as molasses, and I'm going a bit faster than I like. Guess I'll shut off and put on the brakes."

The mule and wagon were now squarely across the road. Tom was coming nearer and nearer. He turned the handle-grip, controlling the supply of gasolene, and to his horror he found that it was stuck. He could not stop the motor-cycle!

"Look out! Look out!" cried Tom to the negro. "Get out of the way! I can't stop! Let me pass you!"

The darky looked up. He saw the approaching machine, and he seemed to lose possession of his senses.

"Whoa, Boomerang!" cried the negro. "Whoa! Suffin's gwine t' happen!"

"That's what!" muttered Tom desperately, as he saw that there was not room for him to pass without going into the ditch, a proceeding that would mean an upset. "Pull out of the way!" he yelled again.

But either the driver could not understand, or did not appreciate the necessity. The mule stopped and reared up. The colored man hurried to the head of the animal to quiet it.

"Whoa, Boomerang! Jest yo' stand still!" he said.

Tom, with a great effort, managed to twist the grip and finally shut off the gasolene. But it was too late. He struck the darky with the front wheel. Fortunately the youth had managed to somewhat reduce his speed by a quick application of the brake, or the result might have been serious. As it was, the colored man was gently lifted away from the mule's head and tossed into the long grass in the ditch. Tom, by a great effort, succeeded in maintaining his seat in the saddle, and then, bringing the machine to a stop, he leaped off and turned back.

The colored man was sitting up, looking dazed.

"Whoa, Boomerang!" he murmured. "Suffin's happened!"

But the mule, who had quieted down, only waggled his ears lazily, and Tom, ready to laugh, now that he saw he had not committed manslaughter, hurried to where the colored man was sitting.

CHAPTER VIII

SUSPICIOUS ACTIONS

"Are you hurt?" asked Tom as he leaned his motor-cycle against the fence and stood beside the negro.

"Hurt?" repeated the darky. "I'se killed, dat's what I is! I ain't got a whole bone in mah body! Good landy, but I suttinly am in a awful state! Would yo' mind tellin' me if dat ar' mule am still alive?"

"Of course he is," answered Tom. "He isn't hurt a bit. But why can't you turn around and look for yourself?"

"No, sah! No, indeedy, sah!" replied the colored man. "Yo' doan't catch dis yeah nigger lookin' around!"

"Why not?"

"Why not? 'Cause I'll tell yo' why not. I'm so stiff an' I'm so nearly broke t' pieces, dat if I turn mah head around it suah will twist offen mah body. No, sah! No, indeedy, sah, I ain't gwine t' turn 'round. But am yo' suah dat mah mule Boomerang ain't hurted?"

"No, he's not hurt a bit, and I'm sure you are not. I didn't strike you hard, for I had almost stopped my machine. Try to get up. I'm positive you'll find yourself all right. I'm sorry it happened."

"Oh, dat's all right. Doan't mind me," went on the colored man. "It was mah fault fer gittin in de road. But dat mule Boomerang am suttinly de most outrageous quadruped dat ever circumlocuted."

"Why do you call him Boomerang?" asked Tom, wondering if the negro really was hurt.

"What fo' I call him Boomerang? Did yo' eber see dem Australian black mans what go around wid a circus t'row dem crooked sticks dey calls boomerangs?"

"Yes, I've seen them."

"Well, Boomerang, mah mule, am jest laik dat. He's crooked, t' begin wid, an' anudder t'ing, yo' can't never tell when yo' start him whar he's gwine t' land up. Dat's why I calls him Boomerang."

"I see. It's a very proper name. But why don't you try to get up?"

"Does yo' t'ink I can?"

"Sure. Try it. By the way, what's your name?"

"My name? Why I was christened Eradicate Andrew Jackson Abraham Lincoln Sampson, but folks most ginnerally calls me Eradicate Sampson, an' some doan't eben go to dat length. Dey jest calls me Rad, fo' short."

"Eradicate," mused Tom. "That's a queer name, too. Why were you called that?"

"Well, yo' see I eradicates de dirt. I'm a cleaner an' a white-washer by profession, an' somebody gib me dat name. Dey said it were fitten an' proper, an' I kept it eber sence. Yais, sah, I'se Eradicate Sampson, at yo' service. Yo' ain't got no chicken coops yo' wants cleaned out, has yo'? Or any stables or fences t' whitewash? I guarantees satisfaction."

"Well, I might find some work for you to do," replied the young inventor, thinking this would be as good a means as any of placating the darky. "But come, now, try and see if you can't stand. I don't believe I broke any of your legs."

"I guess not. I feels better now. Where am dat work yo' was speakin' ob?" and Eradicate Sampson, now that there seemed to be a prospect of earning money, rose quickly and easily.

"Why, you're all right!" exclaimed Tom, glad to find that the accident had had no serious consequences.

"Yais, sah, I guess I be. Whar did yo' say, yo' had some white-washin' t' do?"

"No place in particular, but there is always something that needs doing at our house. If you call I'll give you a job."

"Yais, sah, I'll be sure to call," and Eradicate walked back to where Boomerang was patiently waiting.

Tom told the colored man how to find the Swift home, and was debating with himself whether he ought not to offer Eradicate some money as compensation for knocking him into the air, when he noticed that the negro was tying one wheel of his wagon fast to the body of the vehicle with a rope.

"What are you doing that for?" asked Tom.

"Got to, t' git downhill wid dis load ob fence posts," was the answer. "Ef I didn't it would he right on to de heels ob Boomerang, an' wheneber he feels anyt'ing on his heels he does act wuss dan a circus mule."

"But why don't you use your brake? I see you have one on the wagon. Use the brake to hold back going downhill."

"'Scuse me, Mistah Swift, 'scuse me!" exclaimed Eradicate quickly. "But yo' doan't know dat brake. It's wuss dan none at all. It doan't work, fer a fact. No, indeedy, sah. I'se got to rope de wheel."

Tom was interested at once. He made an examination of the brake, and soon saw why it would not hold the wheels. The foot lever was not properly connected with the brake bar. It was a simple matter to adjust it by changing a single bolt, and this Tom did with tools he took from the bag on his motor-cycle. The colored man looked on in open-mouthed amazement, and even Boomerang peered lazily around, as if taking an interest in the proceedings.

"There," said Tom at length, as he tightened the nut. "That brake will work now, and hold the wagon on any hill. You won't need to rope the wheel. You didn't have the right leverage on it."

"'Scuse me, Mistah Swift, but what's dat yo' said?" and Eradicate leaned forward to listen deferentially.

"I said you didn't have the right leverage."

"No, sah, Mistah Swift, 'scuse me, but yo' made a slight mistake. I ain't never had no liverage on dis yeah wagon. It ain't dat kind ob a wagon. I onct drove a livery rig, but dat were some years ago. I ain't worked fo' de livery stable in some time now. Dat's why I know dere ain't no livery on dis wagon. Yo'll 'scuse me, but yo' am slightly mistaken."

"All right," rejoined Tom with a laugh, not thinking it worth while to explain what he meant by the lever force of the brake rod. "Let it go at that. Livery or no livery, your brake will work now. I guess you're all right. Now don't forget to come around and do some whitewashing," and seeing that the colored man was able to mount to the seat and start off Boomerang, who seemed to have deep-rooted objections about moving, Tom wheeled his motorcycle back to the road.

Eradicate Sampson drove his wagon a short distance and then suddenly applied the brake. It stopped short, and the mule looked around as if surprised.

"It suah do work, Mistah Swift!" called the darky to Tom, who was waiting the result of his little repair job. "It suah do work!"

"I'm glad of it."

"Mah golly! But yo' am suttinly a conjure-man when it comes t' fixin' wagons! Did yo' eber work fer a blacksmith?"

"No, not exactly. Well, good-by, Eradicate. I'll look for you some day next week."

With that Tom leaped on his machine and speeded off ahead of the colored man and his rig. As he passed the load of fence posts the youth heard Eradicate remark in awestricken tones:

"Mah golly! He suttinly go laik de wind! An' t' t'ink dat I were hit by dat monstrousness machine, an' not hurted! Mah golly! T'ings am suttinly happenin'! G'lang, Boomerang!"

"This machine has more possibilities in it than I suspected," mused Tom. "But one thing I've got to change, and that is the gasolene and spark controls. I don't like them the way they are. I want a better leverage, just as Eradicate needed on his wagon. I'll fix them, too, when I get home."

He rode for several hours, until he thought it was about dinner time, and then, heading the machine toward home, he put on all the speed possible, soon arriving where his father was at work in the shop.

"Well, how goes it?" asked Mr. Swift with a smile as he looked at the flushed face of his son.

"Fine, dad! I scooted along in great shape. Had an adventure, too."

"You didn't meet any more of those men, did you? The men who are trying to get my invention?" asked Mr. Swift apprehensively.

"No, indeed, dad. I simply had a little run-in with a chap named Eradicate Andrew Jackson Abraham Lincoln Sampson, otherwise known as Rad Sampson, and I engaged him to do some whitewashing for us. We do need some white washing done, don't we, dad?"

"What's that?" asked Mr. Swift, thinking his son was joking.

Then Tom told of the happening.

"Yes, I think I can find some work for Eradicate to do," went on Mr. Swift. "There is some dirt in the boiler shop that needs eradicating, and I think he can do it. But dinner has been waiting some time. We'll go in now, or Mrs. Baggert will be out after us."

Father and son were soon at the table, and Tom was explaining what he meant to do to improve his motor-cycle. His father offered some suggestions regarding the placing of the gasolene lever.

"I'd put it here," he said, and with his pencil he began to draw a diagram on the white table cloth.

"Oh, my goodness me, Mr. Swift!" exclaimed Mrs. Baggert. "Whatever are you doing?" and she sprang up in some alarm.

"What's the matter? Did I upset my tea?" asked the inventor innocently.

"No; but you are soiling a clean tablecloth. Pencil-marks are so hard to get out. Take a piece of paper, please."

"Oh, is that all?" rejoined Mr. Swift with a smile. "Well, Tom, here is the way I would do that," and substituting the back of an envelope for the tablecloth, he continued the drawing.

Tom was looking over his father's shoulder interestedly, when Mrs. Baggert, who was taking off some of the dinner dishes, suddenly asked:

"Are you expecting a visitor, Mr. Swift?"

"A visitor? No. Why?" asked the inventor quickly.

"Because I just saw a man going in the machine shop," went on the housekeeper.

"A man! In the machine shop!" exclaimed Tom, rising from his chair. Mr. Swift also got up, and the two hurried from the house. As they reached the yard they saw a man emerging from the building where Mr. Swift was constructing his turbine motor. The man had his back turned toward them and seemed to be sneaking around, as though desirous of escaping observation.

"What do you want?" called Mr. Swift.

The man turned quickly. At the sight of Mr. Swift and Tom he made a jump to one side and got behind a big packing-box.

"That's queer," spoke Tom. "I wonder what he wants?"

"I'll soon see," rejoined Mr. Swift, and he started on a run toward where the man was hiding. Tom followed his father, and as the two inventors reached the box the man sprang from behind it and down the yard to a lane that passed in back of the Swift house. As he ran he was seen to stuff some papers in his pocket.

"My plans! He's stolen some of my plans!" cried Mr. Swift. "Catch him, Tom!"

Tom ran after the stranger, whose curious actions had roused their suspicions, while Mr. Swift entered the motor shop to ascertain whether anything had been stolen.

CHAPTER IX

A FRUITLESS PURSUIT

Down through the yard Tom speeded, in and out among the buildings, looking on every side for a sight of the bold stranger. No one was to be seen.

"He can't be very far ahead." thought Tom. "I ought to catch him before he gets to the woods. If he reaches there he has a good chance of getting away."

There was a little patch of trees just back of the inventor's house, not much of a woods, perhaps, but that is what they were called.

"I wonder if he was some ordinary tramp, looking for what he could steal, or if he was one of the gang after dad's invention?" thought Tom as he sprinted ahead.

By this time the youth was clear of the group of buildings and in sight of a tall, board fence, which surrounded the Swift estate on three sides. Here and there, along the barrier, were piled old packing-cases, so that it would be easy for a fugitive to leap upon one of them and so get over the fence. Tom thought of this possibility in a moment.

"I guess he got over ahead of me," the lad exclaimed, and he peered sharply about. "I'll catch him on the other side!"

At that instant Tom tripped over a plank and went down full length, making quite a racket. When he picked himself up he was surprised to see the man he was after dart from inside a big box and start for the fence, near a point where there were some packing-cases piled up, making a good approach to the barrier. The fugitive had been hiding, waiting for a chance to escape, and Tom's fall had alarmed him.

"Here! Hold on there! Come back!" cried the youth as he recovered his wind and leaped forward.

But the man did not stay. With a bound he was up on the pile of boxes, and the next moment he was poised on top of the fence. Before leaping down on the other side, a jump at which even a practiced athlete might well hesitate, the fleeing stranger paused and looked back. Tom gazed at him and recognized the man in an instant. He was the third of the mysterious trio whom the lad had seen in the Mansburg restaurant.

"Wait a minute! What do you want sneaking around here?" shouted Tom as he ran forward. The man returned no answer, and an instant later disappeared from view on the other side of the fence.

"He jumped down!" thought Tom. "A big leap, too. Well, I've got to follow. This is a queer proceeding. First one, then the second, and now the third of those men seem determined to get something here. I wonder if this one succeeded? I'll soon find out."

The lad was up on the pile of packing-cases and over the fence in almost record time. He caught a glimpse of the fugitive running toward the woods. Then the boy leaped down, jarring himself considerably, and took after the man.

But though Tom was a good runner he was handicapped by the fact that the man had a start of him, and also by the fact that the stranger had had a chance to rest while hiding for the second time in the big box, while Tom had kept on running. So it is no great cause for wonder that Mr. Swift's son found himself being distanced.

Once, twice he called on the fleeing one to halt, but the man paid no attention, and did not even turn around. Then the youth wisely concluded to save his wind for running. He did his best, but was chagrined to see the man reach the woods ahead of him.

"I've lost him now," thought Tom. "Well, there's no help for it."

Still he did not give up, but kept on through the patch of trees. On the farther side was Lake Carlopa, a broad and long sheet of water.

"If he doesn't know the lake's there," thought our hero, "he may keep straight on. The water will be sure to stop him, and I can catch him. But what will I do with him after I get him? That's another question. I guess I've got a right to demand to know what he was doing around our place, though."

But Tom need not have worried on this score. He could hear the fugitive ahead of him, and marked his progress by the crackling of the underbrush.

"I'm almost up to him," exulted the young inventor. Then, at the same moment, he caught sight of the man running, and a glimpse of the sparkling water of Lake Carlopa. "I've got him! I've got him!" Tom almost cried aloud in his excitement. "Unless he takes to the water and swims for it, I've got him!"

But Tom did not reckon on a very simple matter, and that was the possibility of the man having a boat at hand. For this is just what happened. Reaching the lake shore the fugitive with a final spurt managed to put considerable distance between himself and Tom. Drawn up on the beach was a little motor-boat. In this, after he had pushed it from shore, the stranger leaped. It was the work of but a second to set the engine in motion, and as Tom reached the edge of the woods and started across the narrow strip of sand and gravel that was between the water and the trees, he saw the man steering his craft toward the middle of the lake.

"Well—I'll—be—jiggered!" exclaimed the youth. "Who would have thought he'd have a motor-boat waiting for him? He planned this well."

There was nothing to do but turn back. Tom had a small row-boat and a sailing skiff on the lake, but his boathouse was some distance away, and even if he could get one of his craft out, the motor-boat would soon distance it.

"He's gone!" thought the searcher regretfully.

The man in the motor-boat did not look back. He sat in the bow, steering the little craft right across the broadest part of Lake Carlopa.

"I wonder where he came from, and where he's going?" mused Tom. "That's a boat I never saw on this lake before. It must be a new one. Well, there's no help for it, I've got to go back and tell dad I couldn't catch him." And with a last look at the fugitive, who, with his boat, was becoming smaller and smaller every minute, Tom turned and retraced his steps.

CHAPTER X

OFF TO ALBANY

"Did you catch him, Tom?" asked Mr. Swift eagerly when his son returned, but the inventor needed but a glance at the lad's despondent face to have his question answered without words, "Never mind," he added, "there's not much harm done, fortunately."

"Did he get anything? Any of your plans or models, dad?"

"No; not as far as I can discover. My papers in the shop were not disturbed, but it looked as if the turbine model had been moved. The only thing missing seems to be a sheet of unimportant calculations. Luckily I had my most valuable drawings in the safe in the house."

"Yet that man seemed to be putting papers in his pocket, dad. Maybe he made copies of some of your drawings."

"That's possible, Tom, and I admit it worries me. I can't imagine who that man is, unless—"

"Why, he's one of the three men I saw in Mansburg in the restaurant," said Tom eagerly. "Two of them tried to get information here, and now the third one comes. He got away in a motor-boat," and Tom told how the fugitive escaped.

Mr. Swift looked worried. It was not the first time attempts had been made to steal his inventions, but on this occasion a desperate and well-organized plan appeared to be on foot.

"What do you think they are up to, dad?" asked Tom.

"I think they are trying to get hold of my turbine motor, Tom. You know I told you that the financiers were disappointed in the turbine motor they bought of another inventor. It does not work. To get back the money they spent in building an expensive plant they must have a motor that is successful. Hence their efforts to get control of mine. I don't know whether I told you or not, but some time ago I refused a very good offer for certain rights in my invention. I knew it was worth more. The offer came through Smeak & Katch, the lawyers, and when I refused it they seemed much disappointed. I think now that this same firm, and the financiers who have employed them, are trying by all the means in their power to get possession of my ideas, if not the invention and model itself."

"What can you do, dad?"

"Well, I must think. I certainly must take some means to protect myself. I have had trouble before, but never any like this. I did not think those men would be so unscrupulous."

"Do you know their names?"

"No, only from that telegram we found; the one which the first stranger dropped. One of them must be Anson Morse. Who the others are I don't know. But now I must make some plans to foil these sharpers. I may have to call on you for help, Tom."

"And I'll be ready any time you call on me, dad," responded Tom, drawing himself up. "Can I do anything for you right away?"

"No; I must think out a plan."

"Then I am going to change my motor-cycle a bit. I'll put some more improvements on it."

"And I will write some letters to my lawyers in Washington and ask their advice." It took Tom the remainder of that day, and part of the next, to arrange the gasolene and spark control of his machine to his satisfaction. He had to make two small levers and some connecting rods. This he did in his own particular machine shop, which was fitted up with a lathe and other apparatus. The lathe was run by power coming from a small engine, which was operated by an engineer, an elderly man to whom Mr. Swift had given employment for many years. He was Garret Jackson, and he kept so close to his engine and boiler-room that he was seldom seen outside of it except when the day's work was done.

One afternoon, a few days after the unsuccessful chase after the fugitive had taken place, Tom went out for a spin on his motor-cycle. He found that the machine worked much better, and was easier to control. He rode about fifteen miles away from home, and then returned. As he entered the yard he saw, standing on the drive, a ramshackle old wagon, drawn by a big mule, which seemed, at the time Tom observed him, to be asleep.

"I'll wager that's Boomerang," said Tom aloud, and the mule opened its eyes, wiggled its ears and started forward.

"Whoa dar, Boomerang!" exclaimed a voice, and Eradicate Sampson hurried around the corner of the house. "Dat's jest lake yo'," went on the colored man. "Movin' when yo' ain't wanted to." Then, as he caught sight of Tom, he exclaimed, "Why, if it ain't young Mistah Swift! Good lordy! But dat livery brake yo' done fixed on mah wagon suttinly am fine. Ah kin go down de steepest hill widout ropin' de wheel."

"Glad of it," replied Tom. "Did you come to do some work?"

"Yais, sah, I done did. I found I had some time t' spah, an' thinks I dere might be some whitewashin' I could do. Yo' see, I lib only 'bout two mile from heah."

"Well, I guess you can do a few jobs," said Tom. "Wait here."

He hunted up his father, and obtained permission to set Eradicate at work cleaning out a chicken house and whitewashing it. The darky was soon at work. A little later Tom passing saw him putting the whitewash on thick. Eradicate stopped at the sight of Tom, and made some curious motions.

"What's the matter, Rad?" asked the young inventor.

"Why, de whitewash done persist in runnin' down de bresh handle an' inter mah sleeve. I'm soakin' wet from it now, an' I has t' stop ebery onct in a while 'case mah sleeve gits full."

Tom saw what the trouble was. The white fluid did run down the long brush handle in a small rivulet. Tom had once seen a little rubber device on a window-cleaning brush that worked well, and he decided to try it for Eradicate.

"Wait a minute," Tom advised. "I think I can stop that for you."

The colored man was very willing to take a rest, but it did not last long, for Tom was soon back at the chicken coop. He had a small rubber disk, with a hole in the center, the size of the brush handle. Slipping the disk over the wood, he pushed it about half way along, and then, handing the brush back to the negro, told him to try it that way.

"Did yo' done put a charm on mah bresh?" asked Eradicate somewhat doubtfully.

"Yes, a sort of hoodoo charm. Try it now."

The darky dipped his brush in the pail of whitewash, and then began to spread the disinfectant on the sides of the coop near the top. The surplus fluid started to run down the handle, but, meeting the piece of rubber, came no farther, and dripped off on the ground. It did not run down the sleeve of Eradicate.

"Well, I 'clar t' goodness! That suttinly am a mighty fine charm!" cried the colored man. "Yo' suah am a pert gen'men, all right. Now I kin work widout stoppin' t' empty mah sleeve ob lime juice ebery minute. I'se suttinly obliged t' yo'."

"You're welcome, I'm sure," replied Tom. "I think some day I'll invent a machine for whitewashing, and then—"

"Doan't do dat! Doan't do dat!" begged Eradicate earnestly. "Dis, an' makin' dirt disappear, am de only perfessions I got. Doan't go 'ventin' no machine, Mistah Swift."

"All right. I'll wait until you get rich."

"Ha, ha! Den yo' gwine t' wait a pow'ful long time," chuckled Eradicate as he went on with his whitewashing.

Tom went into the house. He found his father busy with some papers at his desk.

"Ah, it's you, is it, Tom?" asked the inventor, looking up. "I was just wishing you would come in."

"What for, dad?"

"Well, I have quite an important mission for you. I want you to go on a journey."

"A journey? Where?"

"To Albany. You see, I've been thinking over matters, and I have been in correspondence with my lawyers in regard to my turbine motor. I must take measures to protect myself. You know I have not yet taken out a complete patent on the machine. I have not done so because I did not want to put my model on exhibition in Washington. I was afraid some of those unscrupulous men would take advantage of me. Another point was that I had not perfected a certain device that goes on the motor. That objection is now removed, and I am ready to send my model to Washington, and take out the complete patent."

"But I thought you said you wanted me to go to Albany."

"So I do. I will explain. I have just had a letter from Reid & Crawford, my Washington attorneys. Mr. Crawford, the junior member of the firm, will be in Albany this week on some law business. He agrees to receive my model and some papers there, and take them back to Washington with him. In this way they will be well protected. You see, I have to be on my guard, and if I send the model to Albany, instead of the national capital, I may throw the plotters off the track, for I feel that they are watching every move I make. As soon as you or I should start for Washington they would be on our trail. But you can go to Albany unsuspected. Mr. Crawford will wait for you there. I want you to start day after tomorrow."

"All right, dad. I can start now, if you say so."

"No, there is no special need for haste. I have some matters to arrange. You might go to the station and inquire about trains to the State capital."

"Am I going by train?"

"Certainly. How else could you go?"

There was a look of excitement in Tom's eyes. He had a sudden idea.

"Dad," he exclaimed, "why couldn't I go on my motor-cycle?"

"Your motor-cycle?"

"Yes. I could easily make the trip on it in one day. The roads are good, and I would enjoy it. I can carry the model back of me on the saddle. It is not very large."

"Well," said Mr. Swift slowly, for the idea was a new one to him, "I suppose that part would be all right. But you have not had much experience riding a motor-cycle. Besides, you don't know the roads."

"I can inquire. Will you let me go, dad?"

Mr. Swift appeared to hesitate.

"It will be fine!" went on Tom. "I would enjoy the trip, and there's another thing. If we want to keep this matter secret the best plan would be to let me go on my machine. If those men are on the watch, they will not think that I have the model. They will think I'm just going for a pleasure jaunt."

"There's something in that," admitted Mr. Swift, and Tom, seeing that his father was favorably inclined, renewed his arguments, until the inventor finally agreed.

"It will be a great trip!" exclaimed Tom. "I'll go all over my machine now, to see that it's in good shape. You get your papers and model ready, dad, and I'll take them to Albany for you. The motor-cycle will come in handy."

But had Tom only known the dangers ahead of him, and the risks he was to run, he would not have whistled so light heartedly as he went over every nut and bolt on his machine.

Two days later, the valuable model, having been made into a convenient package, and wrapped in water-proof paper, was fastened back of the saddle on the motor-cycle. Tom carefully pinned in an inside pocket the papers which were to be handed to Mr. Crawford. He was to meet the lawyer at a hotel in Albany.

"Now take care of yourself, Tom," cautioned his father as he bade him good-by. "Don't try to make speed, as there is no special rush. And, above all, don't lose anything."

"I'll not, dad," and with a wave of his hand to Mr. Swift and the housekeeper, who stood in the door to see him off, Tom jumped into the saddle, started the machine, and then, after sufficient momentum had been attained, he turned on the gasolene and set the spark lever. With rattles and bangs, which were quickly subdued by the muffler, the machine gathered speed. Tom was off for Albany.

CHAPTER XI

A VINDICTIVE TRAMP

Though Tom's father had told him there was no necessity for any great speed, the young inventor could not resist the opportunity for pushing his machine to the limit. The road was a level one and in good condition, so the motor-cycle fairly flew along. The day was pleasant, a warm sun shining overhead, and it was evident that early summer was crowding spring rather closely.

"This is glorious!" exclaimed Tom aloud as he spun along. "I'm glad I persuaded dad to let me take this trip. It was a great idea. Wish Ned Newton was along, though. He'd be company for me, but, as Ned would say, there are two good reasons why he can't come. One is he has to work in the bank, and the other is that he has no motor-cycle."

Tom swept past house after house along the road, heading in the opposite direction from that in which lay the town of Shopton and the city of Mansburg. For several miles Tom's route would lie through a country district. The first large town he would reach would be Centreford. He planned to get lunch there, and he had brought a few sandwiches with him to eat along the road in case he became hungry before he reached the place.

"I hope the package containing the model doesn't jar off," mused the lad as he reached behind to make sure that the precious bundle was safe. "Dad would be in a bad way if that should disappear. And the papers, too." He put his hand to his inner pocket to feel that they were secure. Coming to a little down-grade, Tom shut off some of the power, the new levers he had arranged to control the gasolene and spark working well.

"I think I'll take the old wood road and pass through Pompville," Tom decided, after covering another mile or two. He was approaching a division in the highway. "It's a bit sandy," he went on, "and the going will be heavy, but it will be a good chance to test my machine. Besides, I'll save five miles, and, while I don't have to hurry, I may need time on the other end. I'd rather arrive in Albany a little before dusk than after dark. I can deliver the model and papers and have a good night's sleep before starting back. So the old wood road it will be."

The wood road, as Tom called it, was a seldom used highway, which, originally, was laid out for just what the name indicated, to bring wood from the forest. With the disappearance of most of the trees the road became more used for ordinary traffic between the towns of Pompville and Edgefield. But when the State built a new highway connecting these two places the old road fell into disuse, though it was several miles shorter than the new turnpike.

He turned from the main thoroughfare, and was soon spinning along the sandy stretch, which was shaded with trees that in some places met overhead, forming a leafy arch. It was cool and pleasant, and Tom liked it.

"It isn't as bad as I thought," he remarked. "The sand is pretty thick, but this machine of mine appears to be able to crawl through it."

Indeed, the motor-cycle was doing remarkably well, but Tom found that he had to turn on full power, for the big rubber wheels went deep into the soft soil. Along Tom rode, picking out the firmest places in the road. He was so intent on this that he did not pay much attention to what was immediately ahead of him, knowing that he was not very likely to meet other vehicles or pedestrians. He was considerably startled therefore when, as he went around a turn in the highway where the bushes grew thick, right down to the edge of the road, to see a figure emerge from the underbrush and start across the path. So quickly did the man appear that Tom was almost upon him in an instant, and even though the young inventor shut off the power and applied the brake, the front wheel hit the man and knocked him down.

"What's the matter with you? What are you trying to do—kill me? Why don't you ring a bell or blow a horn when you're coming?" The man had sprung up from the soft sand where the wheel from the motor-cycle had sent him and faced Tom angrily. Then the rider, who had quickly dismounted, saw that his victim was a ragged tramp.

"I'm sorry," began Tom. "You came out of the bushes so quickly that I didn't have a chance to warn you. Did I hurt you much?"

"Well, youse might have. 'Tain't your fault dat youse didn't," and the tramp began to brush the dirt from his ragged coat. Tom was instantly struck by a curious fact. The tramp in his second remarks used language more in keeping with his character, whereas, in his first surprise and anger, he had talked much as any other person would. "Youse fellers ain't got no right t' ride dem machines like lightnin' along de roads," the ragged chap went on, and he still clung to the use of words and expressions current among his fraternity. Tom wondered at it, and then, ascribing the use of the better language to the fright caused by being hit by the machine, the lad thought no more about it at the time. There was occasion, however, when he attached more meaning to it.

"I'm very sorry," went on Tom. "I'm sure I didn't mean to. You see, I was going quite slowly, and—"

"You call dat slow, when youse hit me an' knocked me down?" demanded the tramp. "I'd oughter have youse arrested, dat's what, an' I would if dere was a cop handy."

"I wasn't going at all fast," said Tom, a little nettled that his conciliatory words should be so rudely received. "If I had been going full speed I'd have knocked you fifty feet."

"It's a good thing. Cracky, den I'm glad dat youse wasn't goin' like dat," and the tramp seemed somewhat confused. This time Tom looked at him more closely, for the change in his language had been very plain. The fellow seemed uneasy, and turned his face away. As he did so Tom caught a glimpse of what he was sure was a false beard. It was altogether too well-kept a beard to be a natural one for such a dirty tramp as this one appeared to be.

"That fellow's disguised!" Tom thought. "He's playing a part. I wonder if I'd better take chances and spring it on him that I'm on to his game?"

Then the ragged man spoke again:

"I s'pose it was part my fault, cully. I didn't know dat any guy was comin' along on one of dem buzz-machines, or I'd been more careful. I don't s'pose youse meant to upset me?" and he looked at Tom more boldly. This time his words seemed so natural, and his beard, now that Tom took a second look at it, so much a part of himself, that the young inventor wondered if he could have been mistaken in his first surmise.

"Perhaps he was once a gentleman, and has turned tramp because of hard luck," thought Tom. "That would account for him using good language at times. Guess I'd better keep still." Then to the tramp he said: "I'm sure I didn't mean to hit you. I admit I wasn't looking where I was going, but I never expected to meet any one on this road. I certainly didn't expect to see a—"

He paused in some confusion. He was about to use the term "tramp," and he hesitated, not knowing how it would be received by his victim.

"Oh, dat's all right, cully. Call me a tramp—I know dat's what youse was goin' t' say. I'm used t' it. I've been a hobo so many years now dat I don't mind. De time was when I was a decent chap, though. But I'm a tramp now. Say, youse couldn't lend me a quarter, could youse?"

He approached closer to Tom, and looked quickly up and down the road. The highway was deserted, nor was there any likelihood that any one would come along. Tom was somewhat apprehensive, for the tramp was a burly specimen. The young inventor, however, was not so much alarmed at the prospect of a personal encounter, as that he feared he might be robbed, not only of his money, but the valuable papers and model he carried. Even if the tramp was content with taking his money, it would mean that Tom would have to go back home for more, and so postpone his trip.

So it was with no little alarm that he watched the ragged man coming nearer to him. Then a bright idea came into Tom's head. He quickly shifted his position so that he brought the heavy motor-cycle between the man and himself. He resolved, if the tramp showed a disposition to attack him, to push the machine over on him, and this would give Tom a chance to attack the thief to better advantage. However, the "hobo" showed no evidence of wanting to resort to highwayman methods. He paused a short distance from the machine, and said admiringly:

"Dat's a pretty shebang youse has."

"Yes, it's very fair," admitted Tom, who was not yet breathing easily.

"Kin youse go far on it?"

"Two hundred miles a day, easily."

"Fer cats' sake! An' I can't make dat ridin' on de blind baggage; but dat's 'cause I gits put off so much. But say, is youse goin' to let me have dat quarter? I need it, honest I do. I ain't had nuttin' t' eat in two days."

The man's tone was whining. Surely he seemed like a genuine tramp, and Tom felt a little sorry for him. Besides, he felt that he owed him something for the unceremonious manner in which he had knocked the fellow down. Tom reached his hand in his pocket for some change, taking care to keep the machine between himself and the tramp.

"Are youse goin' far on dat rig-a-ma-jig?" went on the man as he looked carefully over the motor-cycle.

"To Albany," answered Tom, and the moment the words were out of his mouth he wished he could recall them. All his suspicions regarding the tramp came back to him. But the ragged chap appeared to attach no significance to them.

"Albany? Dat's in Jersey, ain't it?" he asked.

"No, it's in New York," replied Tom, and then, to change the subject, he pulled out a half-dollar and handed it to the man. As he did so Tom noticed that the tramp had tattooed on the little finger of his left hand a blue ring.

"Dat's de stuff! Youse is a reg'lar millionaire, youse is!"

exclaimed the tramp, and his manner seemed in earnest. "I'll remember youse, I will. What's your name, anyhow, cully?"

"Tom Swift," replied our hero, and again he wished he had not told. This time he was sure the tramp started and glanced at him quickly, but perhaps it was only his imagination.

"Tom Swift," repeated the man musingly, and his tones were different from the whining ones in which he had asked for money. Then, as if recollecting the part he was playing, he added: "I s'pose dey calls youse dat because youse rides so quick on dat machine. But I'm certainly obliged to youse—Tom Swift, an' I hopes youse gits t' Albany, in Jersey, in good time."

He turned away, and Tom was beginning to breathe more easily when the ragged man, with a quick gesture, reached out and grabbed hold of the motor-cycle. He gave it such a pull that it was nearly torn from Tom's grasp. The lad was so startled at the sudden exhibition of vindictiveness an the part of the tramp that he did not know what to do. Then, before he could recover himself, the tramp darted into the bushes.

"I guess Happy Harry—dat's me—has spoiled your ride t' Albany!" the tramp cried. "Maybe next time youse won't run down poor fellers on de road," and with that, the ragged man, shaking his fist at Tom, was lost to sight in the underbrush.

"Well, if that isn't a queer end up," mused Tom. "He must be crazy. I hope I don't meet you again, Happy Harry, or whatever your name is. Guess I'll get out of this neighborhood."

CHAPTER XII

THE MEN IN THE AUTO

Tom first made sure that the package containing the model was still safely in place back of his saddle on the motor-cycle. Finding it there he next put his hand in his pocket to see that he had the papers.

"They're all right," spoke Tom aloud. "I didn't know but what that chap might have worked a pickpocket game on me. I'm glad I didn't meet him after dark. Well, it's a good thing it's no worse. I wonder if he tried to get my machine away from me? Don't believe he'd know how to ride it if he did."

Tom wheeled his motor-cycle to a hard side-path along the old road, and jumped into the saddle. He worked the pedals preparatory to turning on the gasolene and spark to set the motor in motion. As he threw forward the levers, having acquired what he thought was the necessary momentum, he was surprised that no explosion followed. The motor seemed "dead."

"That's queer," he thought, and he began to pedal more rapidly. "It always used to start easily. Maybe it doesn't like this sandy road."

It was hard work sending the heavy machine along by "leg power," and once more, when he had acquired what he thought was sufficient speed, Tom turned on the power. But no explosions followed, and in some alarm he jumped to the ground.

"Something's wrong," he said aloud. "That tramp must have damaged the machine when he yanked it so." Tom went quickly over the different parts. It did not take him long to discover what the trouble was. One of the wires, leading from the batteries to the motor, which wire served to carry the current of electricity that exploded the mixture of air and gasolene, was missing. It had been broken off close to the battery box and the spark plug.

"That's what Happy Harry did!" exclaimed Tom. "He pulled that wire off when he yanked my machine. That's what he meant by hoping I'd get to Albany. That fellow was no tramp. He was disguised, and up to some game. And he knows something about motor-cycles, too, or he never would have taken that wire. I'm stalled, now, for I haven't got another piece. I ought to have brought some. I'll have to push this machine until I get to town, or else go back home."

The young inventor looked up and down the lonely road, undecided what to do. To return home meant that he would be delayed in getting to Albany, for he would lose a day. If he pushed on to Pompville he might be able to get a bit of wire there.

Tom decided that was his best plan, and plodded on through the thick sand. He had not gone more than a quarter of a mile, every step seeming harder than the preceding one, when he heard, from the woods close at his left hand, a gun fired. He jumped so that he nearly let the motor-cycle fall over, for a wild idea came into his head that the tramp had shot at him. With a quickly-beating heart the lad looked about him.

"I wonder if that was Happy Harry?" he mused.

There was a crackling in the bushes and Tom, wondering what he might do to protect himself, looked toward the place whence the noise proceeded. A moment later a hunter stepped into view. The man carried a gun and wore a canvas suit, a belt about his waist being filled with cartridges.

"Hello!" he exclaimed pleasantly, Then, seeing a look of alarm on the lad's face, he went on:

"I hope I didn't shoot in your direction, young man; did I?"

"No—no, sir," replied the youthful inventor, who had hardly recovered his composure. "I heard your gun, and I imagined—"

"Did you think you had been shot? You must have a very vivid imagination, for I fired in the air."

"No, I didn't exactly think that," replied Tom, "but I just had an encounter with an ugly tramp, and I feared he might be using me for a target."

"Is that so. I hadn't noticed any tramps around here, and I've been in these woods nearly all day. Did he harm you?"

"No, not me, but my motor-cycle," and the lad explained.

"Pshaw! That's too bad!" exclaimed the hunter. "I wish I could supply you with a bit of wire, but I haven't any. I'm just walking about, trying my new gun."

"I shouldn't think you'd find anything to shoot this time of year," remarked Tom.

"I don't expect to," answered the hunter, who had introduced himself as Theodore Duncan. "But I have just purchased a new gun, and I wanted to try it. I expect to do considerable hunting this fall, and so I'm getting ready for it."

"Do you live near here?"

"Well, about ten miles away, on the other side of Lake Carlopa, but I am fond of long walks in the woods. If you ever get to Waterford I wish you'd come and see me, Mr. Swift. I have heard of your father."

"I will, Mr. Duncan; but if I don't get something to repair my machine with I'm not likely to get anywhere right away."

"Well, I wish I could help you, but I haven't the least ingenuity when it comes to machinery. Now if I could help you track down that tramp—"

"Oh, no, thank you, I'd rather not have anything more to do with him."

"If I caught sight of him now," resumed the hunter, "I fancy I could make him halt, and, perhaps, give you back the wire. I'm a pretty good shot, even if this is a new gun. I've been practicing at improvised targets all day."

"No; the less I have to do with him, the better I shall like it," answered Tom, "though I'm much obliged to you. I'll manage somehow until I get to Pompville."

He started off again, the hunter disappearing in the woods, whence the sound of his gun was again heard.

"He's a queer chap," murmured Tom, "but I like him. Perhaps I may see him when I go to Waterford, if I ever do."

Tom was destined to see the hunter again, at no distant time, and under strange circumstances. But now the lad's whole attention was taken up with the difficulty in which he found himself. Vainly musing on what object the tramp could have had in breaking off the wire, the young inventor trudged on.

"I guess he was one of the gang after dad's invention," thought Tom, "and he must have wanted to hinder me from getting to Albany, though why I can't imagine." With a dubious shake of his head Tom proceeded. It was hard work pushing the heavy machine through the sand, and he was puffing before he had gone very, far.

"I certainly am up against it," he murmured. "But if I can get a bit of wire in Pompville I'll be all right. If I can't—"

Just then Tom saw something which caused him to utter an exclamation of delight.

"That's the very thing!" he cried. "Why didn't I think of it before?"

Leaving his motor-cycle standing against a tree Tom hurried to a fence that separated the road from a field. The fence was a barbedwire one, and in a moment Tom had found a broken strand.

"Guess no one will care if I take a piece of this," he reasoned. "It will answer until I can get more. I'll have it in place in a jiffy!"

It did not take long to get his pliers from his toolbag and snip off a piece of the wire. Untwisting it he took out the sharp barbs, and then was ready to attach it to the binding posts of the battery box and the spark plug.

"Hold on, though!" he exclaimed as he paused in the work. "It's got to be insulated, or it will vibrate against the metal of the machine and short circuit. I have it! My handkerchief! I s'pose Mrs. Baggert will kick at tearing up a good one, but I can't help it."

Tom took a spare handkerchief from the bundle in which he had a few belongings carried with the idea of spending the night at an Albany hotel, and he was soon wrapping strips of linen around the wire, tying them with pieces of string.

"There!" he exclaimed at length. "That's insulated good enough, I guess. Now to fasten it on and start."

The young inventor, who was quick with tools, soon had the improvised wire in place. He tested the spark and found that it was almost as good as when the regular copper conductor was in place. Then, having taken a spare bit of the barbed-wire along in case of another emergency, he jumped on the motor-cycle, pedaled it until sufficient speed was attained, and turned on the power.

"That's the stuff!" he cried as the welcome explosions sounded. "I guess I've fooled Happy Harry! I'll get to Albany pretty nearly on time, anyhow. But that tramp surely had me worried for a while."

He rode into Pompville, and on inquiring in a plumbing shop managed to get a bit of copper wire that answered better than did the galvanized piece from the fence. The readjustment was quickly made, and he was on his way again. As it was getting close to noon he stopped near a little spring outside of Pompville and ate a sandwich, washing it down with the cold water. Then he started for Centreford.

As he was coming into the city he heard an automobile behind him. He steered to one side of the road to give the big car plenty of room to pass, but it did not come on as speedily as he thought it would. He looked back and saw that it was going to stop near him. Accordingly he shut off the power of his machine.

"Is this the road to Centreford?" asked one of the travelers in the auto.

"Straight ahead," answered the lad.

At the sound of his voice one of the men in the big touring car leaned forward and whispered something to one on the front seat. The second man nodded, and looked closely at Tom. The youth, in turn, stared at the men. He could not distinguish their faces, as they had on auto goggles.

"How many miles is it?" asked the man who had whispered, and at the sound of his voice Tom felt a vague sense that he had heard it before.

"Three," answered the young inventor, and once more he saw the men whisper among themselves.

"Thanks," spoke the driver of the car, and he threw in the gears. As the big machine darted ahead the goggles which one of the men wore slipped off. Tom had a glimpse of his face.

"Anson Morse!" he exclaimed. "If that isn't the man who was sneaking around dad's motor shop he's his twin brother! I wonder if those aren't the men who are after the patent model? I must be on my guard!" and Tom, watching the car fade out of sight on the road ahead of him, slowly started his motor-cycle. He was much puzzled and alarmed.

CHAPTER XIII

CAUGHT IN A STORM

The more Tom tried to reason out the cause of the men's actions, the more he dwelt upon his encounter with the tramp, and the harder he endeavored to seek a solution of the queer puzzle, the more complicated it seemed. He rode on until he saw in a valley below him the buildings of the town of Centreford, and, with a view of them, a new idea came into his mind.

"I'll go get a good dinner," he decided, "and perhaps that will help me to think more clearly. That's what dad always does when he's puzzling over an invention." He was soon seated in a restaurant, where he ate a substantial dinner. "I'm just going to stop puzzling over this matter," he decided. "I'll push an to Albany and tell the lawyer, Mr. Crawford. Perhaps he can advise me."

Once this decision was made Tom felt better.

"That's just what I needed," he thought; "some one to shift the responsibility upon. I'll let the lawyers do the worrying. That's what they're paid for. Now for Albany, and I hope I don't have to stop, except for supper, until I get there. I've got to do some night riding, but I've got a powerful lamp, and the roads from now on are good."

Tom was soon on his way again. The highway leading to Albany was a hard, macadam one, and he fairly flew along the level stretches.

"This is making good time," he thought. "I won't be so very late, after all; that is, if nothing delays me."

The young inventor looked up into the sky. The sun, which had been shining brightly all day, was now hidden behind a mass of hazy clouds, for which the rider was duly grateful, as it was becoming quite warm.

"It's more like summer than I thought," said Tom to himself. "I shouldn't be surprised if we got rain tomorrow."

Another look at the sky confirmed him in this belief, and he had not gone on many miles farther when his opinion was suddenly changed. This was brought about by a dull rumble in the west, and Tom noticed that a bank of low-lying clouds had formed, the black, inky masses of vapor being whirled upward as if by some powerful blast.

"Guess my storm is going to arrive ahead of time," he said. "I'd better look for shelter."

With a suddenness that characterizes summer showers, the

whole sky became overcast. The thunder increased, and the flashes of lightning became more frequent and dazzling. A wind sprang up and blew clouds of dust in Tom's face.

"It certainly is going to be a thunder storm," he admitted. "I'm bound to be delayed now, for the roads will be mucky. Well, there's no help for it. If I get to Albany before midnight I'll he doing well."

A few drops of rain splashed on his hands, and as he looked up to note the state of the sky others fell in his face. They were big drops, and where they splashed on the road they formed little globules of mud.

"I'll head for that big tree," thought Tom "It will give me some shelter. I'll wait there—" His words were interrupted by a deafening crash of thunder which followed close after a blinding flash. "No tree for mine!" murmured Tom. "I forgot that they're dangerous in a storm. I wonder where I can stay?"

He turned on all the power possible and sprinted ahead. Around a curve in the road he went, leaning over to preserve his balance, and just as the rain came pelting down in a torrent he saw just ahead of him a white church on the lonely country road. To one side was a long shed, where the farmers were in the habit of leaving their teams when they came to service.

"Just the thing!" cried the boy; "and just in time!"

He turned his motor-cycle into the yard surrounding the church, and a moment later had come to a stop beneath the shed. It was broad and long, furnishing a good protection against the storm, which had now burst in all its fury.

Tom was not very wet, and looking to see that the model, which was partly of wood, had suffered no damage, the lad gave his attention to his machine.

"Seems to be all right," he murmured. "I'll just oil her up while I'm waiting. This can't last long; it's raining too hard."

He busied himself over the motor-cycle, adjusting a nut that had been rattled loose, and putting some oil on the bearings. The rain kept up steadily, and when he had completed his attentions to his machine Tom looked out from under the protection of the shed.

"It certainly is coming down for keeps," he murmured. "This trip is a regular hoodoo so far. Hope I have it better coming back."

As he looked down the road he espied an automobile coming through the mist of rain. It was an open car, and as he saw the three men in it huddled up under the insufficient protection of some blankets, Tom said:

"They'd ought to come in here. There's lots of room. Maybe they don't see it. I'll call to them."

The car was almost opposite the shed which was dose to the roadside. Tom was about to call when one of the men in the auto looked up. He saw the shelter and spoke to the chauffeur. The latter was preparing to steer up into the shed when the two men on the rear seat caught sight of Tom.

"Why, that's the same car that passed me a while ago," said the young inventor half aloud. "The one that contained those men whom I suspected might be after dad's patent. I hope they—"

He did not finish his sentence, for at that instant the chauffeur quickly swung the machine around and headed it back into the road. Clearly the men were not going to take advantage of the shelter of the shed.

"That's mighty strange," murmured Tom. "They certainly saw me, and as soon as they did they turned away. Can they be afraid of me?"

He went to the edge of the shelter and peered out. The auto had disappeared down the road behind a veil of rain, and, shaking his head over the strange occurrence, Tom went back to where he had left his motor-cycle.

"Things are getting more and more muddled," he said. "I'm sure those were the same men, and yet—"

He shrugged his shoulders. The puzzle was getting beyond him.

CHAPTER XIV

ATTACKED FROM BEHIND

Steadily the rain came down, the wind driving it under the shed until Tom was hard put to find a place where the drops would not reach him. He withdrew into a far corner, taking his motor-cycle with him, and then, sitting on a block of wood, under the rough mangers where the horses were fed while the farmers attended church, the lad thought over the situation. He could make little of it, and the more he tried the worse it seemed to become. He looked out across the wet landscape.

"I wonder if this is ever going to stop?" he mused. "It looks as if it was in for an all-day pour, yet we ought only to have a summer shower by rights."

"But then I guess what I think about it won't influence the weather man a bit. I might as well make myself comfortable, for I can't do anything. Let's see. If I get to Fordham by six o'clock I ought to be able to make Albany by nine, as it's only forty miles. I'll get supper in Fordham, and push on. That is, I will if the rain stops."

That was the most necessary matter to have happen first, and Tom arising from his seat strolled over to the front of the shed to look out.

"I believe it is getting lighter in the west," he told himself. "Yes, the clouds are lifting. It's going to clear. It's only a summer shower, after all."

But just as he said that there came a sudden squall of wind and rain, fiercer than any which had preceded. Tom was driven back to his seat on the log. It was quite chilly now, and he noticed that near where he sat there was a big opening in the rear of the shed, where a couple of boards were off.

"This must be a draughty place in winter," he observed. "If I could find a drier spot I'd sit there, but this seems to be the best," and he remained there, musing on many things. Suddenly in the midst of his thoughts he imagined he heard the sound of an automobile approaching. "I wonder if those men are coming back here?" he exclaimed. "If they are—"

The youth again arose, and went to the front of the shed. He could see nothing, and came back to escape the rain. There was no doubt but that the shower would soon be over, and looking at his watch, Tom began to calculate when he might arrive in Albany.

He was busy trying to figure out the best plan to pursue, and was hardly conscious of his surroundings. Seated on the log, with his back to the opening in the shed, the young inventor could not see a figure stealthily creeping up through the wet grass. Nor could he see an automobile, which had come to a stop back of the horse shelter—an automobile containing two rain-soaked men, who were anxiously watching the one stealing through the grass.

Tom put his watch back into his pocket and looked out into the storm. It was almost over. The sun was trying to shine through the clouds, and only a few drops were falling. The youth stretched with a yawn, for he was tired of sitting still. At the moment when he raised his arms to relieve his muscles something was thrust through the opening behind him. It was a long club, and an instant later it descended on the lad's head. He went down in a heap, limp and motionless.

Through the opening leaped a man. He bent over Tom, looked anxiously at him, and then, stepping to the place where the boards were off the shed, he motioned to the men in the automobile.

They hurried from the machine, and were soon beside their companion.

"I knocked him out, all right," observed the man who had reached through and dealt Tom the blow with the club.

"Knocked him out! I should say you did, Featherton!" exclaimed one who appeared better dressed than the others. "Have you killed him?"

"No; but I wish you wouldn't mention my name, Mr. Appleson. I—I don't like—"

"Nonsense, Featherton. No one can hear us. But I'm afraid you've done for the chap. I didn't want him harmed."

"Oh, I guess Featherton knows how to do it, Appleson," commented the third man. "He's had experience that way, eh, Featherton?"

"Yes, Mr. Morse; but if you please I wish you wouldn't mention—"

"All right, Featherton, I know what you mean," rejoined the man addressed as Morse. "Now let's see if we have drawn a blank or not. I think he has with him the very thing we want,"

"Doesn't seem to be about his person," observed Appleson, as he carefully felt about the clothing of the unfortunate Tom.

"Very likely not. It's too bulky. But there's his motor-cycle over there. It looks as if what we wanted was on the back of the saddle. Jove, Featherton, but I think he's coming to!"

Tom stirred uneasily and moved his arms, while a moan came from between his parted lips.

"I've got some stuff that will fix him!" exclaimed the man addressed as Featherton, and who had been operating the automobile. He took something from his pocket and leaned over Tom. In a moment the young inventor was still again.

"Quick now, see if it's there," directed Morse, and Appleson hurried over to the machine.

"Here it is!" he called. "I'll take it to our car, and we can get away."

"Are you going to leave him here like this?" asked Morse.

"Yes; why not?"

"Because some one might have seen him come in here, and also remember that we, too, came in this direction."

"What would you do?"

"Take him down the road a way and leave him. We can find some shed near a farmhouse where he and his machine will be out of sight until we get far enough away. Besides, I don't like to leave him so far from help, unconscious as he is."

"Oh, you're getting chicken-hearted," said Appleson with a sneer. "However, have your way about it. I wonder what has become of Jake Burke? He was to meet us in Centreford, but he did not show up."

"Oh, I shouldn't be surprised if he had trouble in that tramp rig he insisted on adopting. I told him he was running a risk, but he said he had masqueraded as a tramp before."

"So he has. He's pretty good at it. Now, Simpson, if you will—"

"Not Simpson! I thought you agreed to call me Featherton," interrupted the chauffeur, turning to Morse and Appleson.

"Oh, so we did. I forgot that this lad met us one day, and heard me call you Simpson," admitted Morse. "Well, Featherton it shall be. But we haven't much time. It's stopped raining, and the roads will soon be well traveled. We must get away, and if we are to take the lad and his machine to some secluded place, we'd better be at it. No use waiting for Burke. He can look out after himself. Anyhow, we have the model now, and there's no use in him hanging around Swift's shop, as he intended to do, waiting for a chance to sneak in after it. Appleson, if you and Simpson—I mean Featherton—will carry young Swift, I'll shove his wheel along to the auto, and we can put it and him in."

The two men, first looking through the hole in the shed to make sure they were not observed, went out, carrying Tom, who was no light load. Morse followed them, pushing the motor-cycle, and carrying under one arm the bundle containing the valuable model, which he had detached.

"I think this is the time we get ahead of Mr. Swift," murmured Morse, pulling his black mustache, when he and his companions had reached the car in the field. "We have just what we want now."

"Yes, but we had hard enough work getting it," observed Appleson. "Only by luck we saw this lad come in here, or we would have had to chase all over for him, and maybe then we would have missed him. Hurry, Simpson—I mean Featherton. It's getting late, and we've got lots to do."

The chauffeur sprang to his seat, Appleson taking his place beside him. The motor-cycle was tied on behind the big touring car, and with the unconscious form of Tom in the tonneau, beside Morse, who stroked his mustache nervously, the auto started off. The storm had passed, and the sun was shining brightly, but Tom could not see it.

CHAPTER XV

A VAIN SEARCH

Several hours later Tom had a curious dream. He imagined he was wandering about in the polar regions, and that it was very cold. He was trying to reason with himself that he could not possibly be on an expedition searching for the North Pole, still he felt such a keen wind blowing over his scantily-covered body that he shivered. He shivered so hard, in fact, that he shivered himself awake, and when he tried to pierce the darkness that enveloped him he was startled, for a moment, with the idea that perhaps, after all, he had wandered off to some unknown country.

For it was quite dark and cold. He was in a daze, and there was a curious smell about him—an odor that he tried to recall. Then, all at once, it came to him what it was—chloroform. Once his father had undergone an operation, and to deaden his pain chloroform had been used.

"I've been chloroformed!" exclaimed the young inventor, and his words sounded strange in his ears. "That's it. I've met with an accident riding my motor-cycle. I must have hit my head, for it hurts fearful. They picked me up, carried me to a hospital and have operated on me. I wonder if they took off an arm or leg? I wonder what hospital I'm in? Why is it so dark and cold?"

As he asked himself these questions his brain gradually cleared from the haze caused by the cowardly blow, and from the chloroform that had been administered by Featherton.

Tom's first act was to feel first of one arm, then the other. Having satisfied himself that neither of these members were mutilated he reached down to his legs.

"Why, they're all right, too," he murmured. "I wonder what they did to me? That's certainly, chloroform I smell, and my head feels as if some one had sat on it. I wonder—"

Quickly he put up his hands to his head. There appeared to be nothing the matter with it, save that there was quite a lump on the back, where the club had struck.

"I seem to be all here," went on Tom, much mystified. "But where am I? That's the question. It's a funny hospital, so cold and dark—"

Just then his hands came in contact with the cold ground on which he was lying.

"Why, I'm outdoors!" he exclaimed. Then in a flash it all came back to him—how he had gone to wait under the church shed until the rain was over.

"I fell asleep, and now it's night," the youth went on. "No wonder I am sore and stiff. And that chloroform—" He could not account for that, and he paused, puzzled once more. Then he struggled to a sitting position. His head was strangely dizzy, but he persisted, and got to his feet. He could see nothing, and groped around In the dark, until he thought to strike a match. Fortunately he had a number in his pocket. As the little flame flared up Tom started in surprise.

"This isn't the church shed!" he exclaimed. "It's much smaller! I'm in a different place! Great Scott! but what has happened to me?"

The match burned Tom's fingers and he dropped it. The darkness closed in once more, but Tom was used to it by this time, and looking ahead of him he could make out that the shed was an open one, similar to the one where he had taken shelter. He could see the sky studded with stars, and could feel the cold night wind blowing in.

"My motor-cycle!" he exclaimed in alarm. "The model of dad's invention—the papers!"

Our hero thrust his hand into his pocket. The papers were gone! Hurriedly he lighted another match. It took but an instant to glance rapidly about the small shed. His machine was not in sight!

Tom felt his heart sink. After all his precautions he had been robbed. The precious model was gone, and it had been his proposition to take it to Albany in this manner. What would his father say?

The lad lighted match after match, and made a rapid tour of the shed. The motor-cycle was not to be seen. But what puzzled Tom more than anything else was how he had been brought from the church shed to the one where he had awakened from his stupor.

"Let me try to think," said the boy, speaking aloud, for it seemed to help him. "The last I remember is seeing that automobile, with those mysterious men in, approaching. Then it disappeared in the rain. I thought I heard it again, but I couldn't see it. I was sitting on the log, and—and—well, that's all I can remember. I wonder if those men—"

The young inventor paused. Like a flash it came to him that the men were responsible for his predicament. They had somehow made him insensible, stolen his motor-cycle, the papers and the model, and then brought him to this place, wherever it was. Tom was a shrewd reasoner, and he soon evolved a theory which he afterward learned was the correct one. He reasoned out almost every step in the crime of which he was the victim, and at last came to the conclusion that the men had stolen up behind the shed and attacked him.

"Now, the next question to settle," spoke Tom, "is to learn where I am. How far did those scoundrels carry me, and what has become of my motor-cycle?"

He walked toward the point of the shed where he could observe the stars gleaming, and there he lighted some more matches, hoping he might see his machine. By the gleam of the little flame he noted that he was in a farmyard, and he was just puzzling his brain over the question as to what city or town he might be near when he heard a voice shouting:

"Here, what you lightin' them matches for? You want to set the place afire? Who be you, anyhow—a tramp?"

It was unmistakably the voice of a farmer, and Tom could hear footsteps approaching on the run.

"Who be you, anyhow?" the voice repeated. "I'll have the constable after you in a jiffy if you're a tramp."

"I'm not a tramp," called Tom promptly. "I've met with an accident. Where am I?"

"Humph! Mighty funny if you don't know where you are," commented the farmer. "Jed, bring a lantern until I take a look at who this is."

"All right, pop," answered another voice, and a moment later Tom saw a tall man standing in front of him.

"I'll give you a look at me without waiting for the lantern," said Tom quickly, and he struck a match, holding it so that the gleam fell upon his face.

"Salt mackerel! It's a young feller!" exclaimed the farmer. "Who be you, anyhow, and what you doin' here?"

"That's just what I would like to know," said Tom, passing his hand over his head, which was still paining him. "Am I near Albany? That's where I started for this morning."

"Albany? You're a good way from Albany," replied the farmer. "You're in the village of Dunkirk."

"How far is that from Centreford?"

"About seventy miles."

"As far as that?" cried Tom. "They must have carried me a good way in their automobile."

"Was you in that automobile?" demanded the farmer.

"Which one?" asked Tom quickly.

"The one that stopped down the road just before supper. I see it, but I didn't pay no attention to it. If I'd 'a' knowed you fell out, though, I'd 'a' come to help you."

"I didn't fall out, Mr.—er—" Tom paused.

"Blackford is my name; Amos Blackford."

"Well, Mr. Blackford, I didn't fall out. I was drugged and brought here."

"Drugged! Salt mackerel! But there's been a crime committed, then. Jed, hurry up with that lantern an' git your deputy sheriff's badge on. There's been druggin' an' all sorts of crimes committed. I've caught one of the victims. Hurry up! My son's a deputy sheriff," he added, by way of an explanation.

"Then I hope he can help me catch the scoundrels who robbed me," said Tom.

"Robbed you, did they? Hurry up, Jed. There's been a robbery! We'll rouse the neighborhood an' search for the villains. Hurry up, Jed!"

"I'd rather find my motor-cycle, and a valuable model which was on it, than locate those men," went on Tom. "They also took some papers from me."

Then he told how he had started for Albany, adding his theory of how he had been attacked and carried away in the auto. The latter part of it was borne out by the testimony of Mr. Blackford.

"What I know about it," said the farmer, when his son Jed had arrived on the scene with a lantern and his badge, "is that jest about supper time I saw an automobile stop down the road a bit, It was gittin' dusk, an' I saw some men git out. I didn't pay no attention to them, 'cause I was busy about the milkin'. The next I knowed I seen some one strikin' matches in my wagon shed, an' I come out to see what it was."

"The men must have brought me all the way from the church shed near Centreford to here," declared Tom. "Then they lifted me out and put me in your shed. Maybe they left my motor-cycle also."

"I didn't see nothin' like that," said the farmer. "Is that what you call one of them two-wheeled lickity-split things that a man sits on the middle of an' goes like chain-lightning?"

"It is," said Tom. "I wish you'd help me look for it."

The farmer and his son agreed, and other lanterns having been secured, a search was made. After about half an hour the motor-cycle was discovered in some bushes at the side of the road, near where the automobile had stopped. But the model was missing from it, and a careful search near where the machine had been hidden did not reveal it. Nor did as careful a hunt as they could make in the darkness disclose any dues to the scoundrels who had drugged and robbed Tom.

CHAPTER XVI

BACK HOME

"We've got to organize a regular searchin' party," declared Jed Blackford, after he and his father, together with Tom and the farmer's hired man, had searched up and down the road by the light of lanterns. "We'll organize a posse an' have a regular hunt. This is the worst crime that's been committed in this deestrict in many years, an' I'm goin' to run the scoundrels to earth."

"Don't be talkin' nonsense, Jed," interrupted his father. "You won't catch them fellers in a hundred years. They're miles an' miles away from here by this time in their automobile. All you can do is to notify the sheriff. I guess we'd better give this young man some attention. Let's see, you said your name was Quick, didn't you?"

"No, but it's very similar," answered Tom with a smile. "It's Swift."

"I knowed it was something had to do with speed," went on Mr. Blackford. "Wa'al, now, s'pose you come in the house an' have a hot cup of tea. You look sort of draggled out."

Tom was glad enough to avail himself of the kind invitation, and he was soon in the comfortable kitchen, relating his story, with more detail, to the farmer and his family. Mrs. Blackford applied some home-made remedies to the lump on the youth's head, and it felt much better.

"I'd like to take a look at my motor-cycle," he said, after his second cup of tea. "I want to see if those men damaged it any. If they have I'm going to have trouble getting back home to tell my father of my bad luck. Poor dad! He will be very much worried when I tell him the model and his patent papers have been stolen."

"It's too bad!" exclaimed Mrs. Blackford. "I wish I had hold of them scoundrels!" and her usually gentle face bore a severe frown. "Of course you can have your thing-a-ma-bob in to see if it's hurt, but please don't start it in here. They make a terrible racket."

"No, I'll look it over in the woodshed," promised Tom. "If it's all right I think I'll start back home at once."

"No, you can't do that," declared Mr. Blackford. "You're in no condition to travel. You might fall off an' git hurt. It's nearly ten o'clock now. You jest stay here all night, an' in the mornin', if you feel all right, you can start off. I couldn't let you go tonight."

Indeed, Tom did not feel very much like undertaking the journey, for the blow on his head had made him dazed, and the chloroform caused a sick feeling. Mr. Blackford wheeled the motor-cycle into the woodhouse, which opened from the kitchen, and there the youth went over the machine. He was glad to find that it had sustained no damage. In the meanwhile Jed had gone off to tell the startling news to near-by farmers. Quite a throng, with lanterns, went up and down the road, but all the evidence they could find were the marks of the automobile wheels, which clues were not very satisfactory.

"But we'll catch them in the mornin'," declared the deputy sheriff. "I'll know that automobile again if I see it. It was painted red."

"That's the color of a number of automobiles," said Tom with a smile. "I'm afraid you'll have trouble identifying it by that means. I am surprised, though, that they did not carry my motor-cycle away with them. It is a valuable machine."

"They were afraid to," declared Jed. "It would look queer to see a machine like that in an auto. Of course when they were going along country roads in the evening it didn't much matter, but when they headed for the city, as they probably did, they knew it would attract suspicion to 'em. I know, for I've been a deputy sheriff 'most a year."

"I believe you're right," agreed Tom. "They didn't dare take the motor-cycle with them, but they hid it, hoping I would not find it. I'd rather have the model and the papers, though, than half a dozen motor-cycles."

"Maybe the police will help you find them," said Mrs. Blackford. "Jed, you must telephone to the police the first thing in the morning. It's a shame the way criminals are allowed to go on. If honest people did those things, they'd be arrested in a minute, but it seems that scoundrels can do as they please."

"You wait; I'll catch 'em!" declared Jed confidently. "I'll organize another posse in the mornin'."

"Well, I know one thing, and that is that the place for this young man is in bed!" exclaimed motherly Mrs. Blackford, and she insisted on Tom retiring. He was somewhat restless at first, and the thought of the loss of the model and the papers preyed on his mind. Then, utterly exhausted, he sank into a heavy slumber, and did not awaken until the sun was shining in his window the next morning. A good breakfast made him feel somewhat better, and he was more like the resourceful Tom Swift of old when he went to get his motor-cycle in shape for the ride back to Shopton.

"Well, I hope you find those criminals," said Mr. Blackford, as he watched Tom oiling the machine. "If you're ever out this way again, stop off and see us."

"Yes, do," urged Mrs. Blackford, who was getting ready to churn. Her husband looked at the old-fashioned barrel and dasher arrangement, which she was filling with cream.

"What's the matter with the new churn?" he asked in some surprise.

"It's broken," she replied. "It's always the way with those newfangled things. It works ever so much nicer than this old one, though," she went on to Tom, "but it gets out of order easy."

"Let me look at it," suggested the young inventor. "I know something about machinery."

The churn, which worked by a system of cogs and a handle, was brought from the woodshed. Tom soon saw what the trouble was. One of the cogs had become displaced. It did not take him five minutes, with the tools he carried on his motor-cycle, to put it back, and the churn was ready to use.

"Well, I declare!" exclaimed Mrs. Blackford. "You are handy at such things!"

"Oh, it's just a knack," replied Tom modestly. "Now I'll put a plug in there, and the cog wheel won't come loose again. The manufacturers of it ought to have done that. I imagine lots of people have this same trouble with these churns."

"Indeed they do," asserted Mrs. Blackford. "Sallie Armstrong has one, and it got out of order the first week they had it. I'll let her look at mine, and maybe her husband can fix it."

"I'd go and do it myself, but I want to get home," said Tom, and then he showed her how, by inserting a small iron plug in a certain place, there would be no danger of the cog coming loose again.

"That's certainly slick!" exclaimed Mr. Blackford. "Well, I wish you good luck, Mr. Swift, and if I see those scoundrels around this neighborhood again I'll make 'em wish they'd let you alone."

"That's what," added Jed, polishing his badge with his big, red handkerchief.

Mrs. Blackford transferred the cream to the new churn which Tom had fixed, and as he rode off down the highway on his motorcycle, she waved one hand to him, while with the other she operated the handle of the apparatus.

"Now for a quick run to Shopton to tell dad the bad news," spoke Tom to himself as he turned on full speed and dashed away. "My trip has been a failure so far."

CHAPTER XVII

MR. SWIFT IN DESPAIR

Tom was thinking of many things as his speedy machine carried him mile after mile nearer home. By noon he was over half way on his journey, and he stopped in a small village for his dinner.

"I think I'll make inquiries of the police here, to see if they caught sight of those men," decided Tom as he left the restaurant. "Though I am inclined to believe they kept on to Albany, or some large city, where they have their headquarters. They will want to make use of dad's model as soon as possible, though what they will do with it I don't know." He tried to telephone to his father, but could get no connection, as the wire was being repaired.

The police force of the place where Tom had stopped for lunch was like the town itself—small and not of much consequence. The chief constable, for he was not what one could call a chief of police, had heard of the matter from the alarm sent out in all directions from Dunkirk, where Mr. Blackford lived.

"You don't mean to tell me you're the young man who was chloroformed and robbed!" exclaimed the constable, looking at Tom as if he doubted his word.

"I'm the young man," declared our hero. "Have you seen anything of the thieves?"

"Not a thing, though I've instructed all my men to keep a sharp lookout for a red automobile, with three scoundrels in it. My men are to make an arrest on sight."

"How many men have you?"

"Two," was the rather surprising answer; "but one has to work on a farm daytimes, so I ain't really got but one in what you might call active service."

Tom restrained a desire to laugh. At any rate, the aged constable meant well.

"One of my men seen a red automobile, a little while before you come in my office," went on the official, "but it wasn't the one wanted, 'cause a young woman was running it all alone. It struck me as rather curious that a woman would trust herself all alone in one of them things; wouldn't it you?"

"Oh, no, women and young ladies often operate them," said Tom.

"I should think you'd find one handier than the two-wheeled apparatus you have out there," went on the constable, indicating the motor-cycle, which Tom had stood up against a tree.

"I may have one some day," replied the young inventor. "But I guess I'll be moving on now. Here's my address, in case you hear anything of those men, but I don't imagine you will."

"Me either. Fellows as slick as them are won't come back this way and run the chance of being arrested by my men. I have two on duty nights," he went on proudly, "besides myself, so you see we're pretty well protected."

Tom thanked him for the trouble he had taken, and was soon on his way again. He swept on along the quiet country roads anxious for the time when he could consult with his father over what would be the best course to take.

When Tom was about a mile away from his house he saw in the road ahead of him a rickety old wagon, and a second glance at it told him the outfit belonged to Eradicate Sampson, for the animal drawing the vehicle was none other than the mule, Boomerang.

"But what in the world is Rad up to?" mused Tom, for the colored man was out of the wagon and was going up and down in the grass at the side of the highway in a curious fashion. "I guess he's lost something," decided Tom.

When he got nearer he saw what Eradicate was doing. The colored man was pushing a lawn-mower slowly to and fro in the tall, rank grass that grew beside the thoroughfare, and at the sound of Tom's motor-cycle the negro looked up. There was such a woe-begone expression on his face that Tom at once stopped his machine and got off.

"What's the matter, Rad?" Tom asked.

"Mattah, Mistah Swift? Why, dere's a pow'ful lot de mattah, an' dat's de truff. I'se been swindled, dat's what I has."

"Swindled? How?"

"Well, it's dis-a-way. Yo' see dis yeah lawn-moah?"

"Yes; it doesn't seem to work," and Tom glanced critically at it. As Eradicate pushed it slowly to and fro, the blades did not revolve, and the wheels slipped along on the grass.

"No, sah, it doan't work, an' dat's how I've been swindled, Mistah Swift. Yo' see, I done traded mah ole grindstone off for dis yeah lawn-moah, an' I got stuck."

"What, that old grindstone that was broken in two, and that you fastened together with concrete?" asked Tom, for he had seen the outfit with which Eradicate, in spare times between cleaning and whitewashing, had gone about the country, sharpening knives and scissors. "You don't mean that old, broken one?"

"Dat's what I mean, Mistah Swift. Why, it was all right. I

mended it so dat de break wouldn't show, an' it would sharpen things if yo' run it slow. But dis yeah lawn-moah won't wuk slow ner fast."

"I guess it was an even exchange, then," went on Tom. "You didn't get bitten any worse than the other fellow did."

"Yo' doan't s'pose yo' kin fix dis yeah moah so's I kin use it, does yo', Mistah Swift?" asked Eradicate, not bothering to go into the ethics of the matter. "I reckon now with summah comin' on I kin make mo' with a lawn-moah than I kin with a grindstone—dat is, ef I kin git it to wuk. I jest got it a while ago an' decided to try it, but it won't cut no grass."

"I haven't much time," said Tom, "for I'm anxious to get home, but I'll take a look at it."

Tom leaned his motor-cycle against the fence. He could no more pass a bit of broken machinery, which he thought he could mend, than some men and boys can pass by a baseball game without stopping to watch it, no matter how pressed they are for time. It was Tom's hobby, and he delighted in nothing so much as tinkering with machines, from lawn-mowers to steam engines.

Tom took hold of the handle, which Eradicate gladly relinquished to him, and his trained touch told him at once what was the trouble.

"Some one has had the wheels off and put them on wrong, Rad," he said. "The ratchet and pawl are reversed. This mower would work backwards, if that were possible."

"Am dat so, Mistah Swift?"

"That's it. All I have to do is to take off the wheels and reverse the pawl."

"I—I didn't know mah lawn-moah was named Paul," said the colored man. "Is it writ on it anywhere?"

"No, it's not the kind of Paul you mean," said Tom with a laugh. "It's spelled differently. A pawl is a sort of catch that fits into a ratchet wheel and pushes it around, or it may be used as a catch to prevent the backward motion of a windlass or the wheel on a derrick. I'll have it fixed in a jiffy for you."

Tom worked rapidly. With a monkey-wrench he removed the two big wheels of the lawn-mower and reversed the pawl in the cogs. In five minutes he had replaced the wheels, and the machine, except for needed sharpening, did good work.

"There you are, Rad!" exclaimed Tom at length.

"Yo' suah am a wonder at inventin'!" cried the colored man gratefully. "I'll cut yo' grass all summah fo' yo' to pay fo' this, Mistah Swift."

"Oh, that's too much. I didn't do a great deal, Rad."

"Well, yo' saved me from bein' swindled, Mistah Swift, an' I suah does 'preciate dat."

"How about the fellow you traded the cracked grindstone to, Rad?"

"Oh, well, ef he done run it slow it won't fly apart, an' he'll do dat, anyhow, fo' he suah am a lazy coon. I guess we am about even there, Mistah Swift."

"All right," spoke Tom with a laugh. "Sharpen it up, Rad, and start in to cut grass. It will soon be summer," and Tom, leaping upon his motor-cycle, was off like a shot.

He found his father in his library, reading a book on scientific matters. Mr. Swift looked up in surprise at seeing his son.

"What! Back so soon?" he asked. "You did make a flying trip. Did you give the model and papers to Mr. Crawford?"

"No, dad, I was robbed yesterday. Those scoundrels got ahead of us, after all. They have your model. I tried to telephone to you, but the wires were down, or something."

"What!" cried Mr. Swift. "Oh, Tom! That's too bad! I will lose ten thousand dollars if I can't get that model and those papers back!" and with a despairing gesture Mr. Swift rose and began to pace the floor.

CHAPTER XVIII

HAPPY HARRY AGAIN

Tom watched his father anxiously. The young inventor knew the loss had been a heavy one, and he blamed himself for not having been more careful.

"Tell me all about it, Tom," said Mr. Swift at length. "Are you sure the model and papers are gone? How did it happen?"

Then Tom related what had befallen him.

"Oh, that's too bad!" cried Mr. Swift. "Are you much hurt, Tom? Shall I send for the doctor?" For the time being his anxiety over his son was greater than that concerning his loss.

"No, indeed, dad. I'm all right now. I got a bad blow on the head, but Mrs. Blackford fixed me up. I'm awfully sorry—-"

"There, there! Now don't say another word," interrupted Mr. Swift. "It wasn't your fault. It might have happened to me. I dare say it would, for those scoundrels seemed very determined. They are desperate, and will stop at nothing to make good the loss they sustained on the patent motor they exploited. Now they will probably try to make use of my model and papers."

"Do you think they'll do that, dad?"

"Yes. They will either make a motor exactly like mine, or construct one so nearly similar that it will answer their purpose. I will have no redress against them, as my patent is not fully granted yet. Mr. Crawford was to attend to that."

"Can't you do anything to stop them, dad? File an injunction, or something like that?"

"I don't know. I must see Mr. Crawford at once. I wonder if he could come here? He might be able to advise me. I have had very little experience with legal difficulties. My specialty is in other lines of work. But I must do something. Every moment is valuable. I wonder who the men were?"

"I'm sure one of them was the same man who came here that night—the man with the black mustache, who dropped the telegram," said Tom. "I had a pretty good look at him as the auto passed me, and I'm sure it was he. Of course I didn't see who it was that struck me down, but I imagine it was some one of the same gang."

"Very likely. Well, Tom, I must do something. I suppose I might telegraph to Mr. Crawford—he will be expecting you in Albany—" Mr. Swift paused musingly. "No, I have it!" he suddenly exclaimed. "I'll go to Albany myself."

"Go to Albany, dad?"

"Yes; I must explain everything to the lawyers and then he can advise me what to do. Fortunately I have some papers, duplicates of those you took, which I can show him. Of course the originals will be necessary before I can prove my claim. The loss of the model is the most severe, however. Without that I can do little. But I will have Mr. Crawford take whatever steps are possible. I'll take the night train, Tom. I'll have to leave you to look after matters here, and I needn't caution you to be on your guard, though, having got what they were after, I fancy those financiers, or their tools, will not bother us again."

"Very likely not," agreed Tom, "but I will keep my eyes open, just the same. Oh, but that reminds me, dad. Did you see anything of a tramp around here while I was away?"

"A tramp? No; but you had better ask Mrs. Baggert. She usually attends to them. She's so kind-hearted that she frequently gives them a good meal."

The housekeeper, when consulted, said that no tramps had applied in the last few days.

"Why do you ask, Tom?" inquired his father.

"Because I had an experience with one, and I believe he was a member of the same gang who robbed me." And thereupon Tom told of his encounter with Happy Harry, and how the latter had broken the wire on the motor-cycle.

"You had a narrow escape," commented Mr. Swift. "If I had known the dangers involved I would never have allowed you to take the model to Albany."

"Well, I didn't take it there, after all," said Tom with a grim smile, for he could appreciate a joke.

"I must hurry and pack my valise," went on Mr. Swift. "Mrs. Baggert, we will have an early supper, and I will start at once for Albany."

"I wish I could go with you, dad, to make up for the trouble I caused," spoke Tom.

"Tut, tut! Don't talk that way," advised his father kindly. "I will be glad of the trip. It will ease my mind to be doing something."

Tom felt rather lonesome after his father had left, but he laid out a plan of action for himself that he thought would keep him occupied until his father returned. In the first place he made a tour of the house and various machine shops to see that doors and windows were securely fastened.

"What's the matter? Do you expect burglars, Master Tom?" asked Garret Jackson, the aged engineer.

"Well, Garret, you never can tell," replied the young inventor, as he told of his experience and the necessity for Mr. Swift going to Albany. "Some of those scoundrels, finding how easy it was to rob me, may try it again, and get some at dad's other valuable models. I'm taking no chances."

"That's right, Master Tom. I'll keep steam up in the boiler tonight, though we don't really need it, as your father told me you would probably not run any machinery when he was gone. But with a good head of steam up, and a hose handy, I can give any burglars a hot reception. I almost wish they'd come, so I could get square with them."

"I don't, Garret. Well, I guess everything is in good shape. If you hear anything unusual, or the alarm goes off during the night, call me."

"I will, Master Tom," and the old engineer, who had a living-room in a shack adjoining the boiler-room, locked the door after Tom left.

The young inventor spent the early evening in attaching a new wire to his motor-cycle to replace the one he had purchased while on his disastrous trip. The temporary one was not just the proper thing, though it answered well enough. then, having done some work on a new boat propeller he was contemplating patenting, Tom felt that it was time to go to bed, as he was tired. He made a second round of the house, looking to doors and windows, until Mrs. Baggert exclaimed:

"Oh, Tom, do stop! You make me nervous, going around that way. I'm sure I shan't sleep a wink tonight, thinking of burglars and tramps."

Tom laughingly desisted, and went up to his room. He sat up a few minutes, writing a letter to a girl of his acquaintance, for, in spite of the fact that the young inventor was very busy with his own and his father's work, he found time for lighter pleasures. Then, as his eyes seemed determined to close of their own accord, if he did not let them, he tumbled into bed.

Tom fancied it was nearly morning when he suddenly awoke with a start. He heard a noise, and at first he could not locate it. Then his trained ear traced it to the dining-room.

"Why, Mrs. Baggert must be getting breakfast, and is rattling the dishes," he thought. "But why is she up so early?"

It was quite dark in Tom's room, save for a little gleam from the crescent moon, and by the light of this Tom arose and looked at his watch.

"Two o'clock," he whispered. "That can't be Mrs. Baggert,

unless she's sick, and got up to take some medicine."

He listened intently. Below, in the dining-room, he could hear stealthy movements.

"Mrs. Baggert would never move around like that," he decided. "She's too heavy. I wonder—it's a burglar—one of the gang has gotten in!" he exclaimed in tense tones. "I'm going to catch him at it!"

Hurriedly he slipped on some clothes, and then, having softly turned on the electric light in his room, he took from a corner a small rifle, which he made sure was loaded. Then, having taken a small electric flashlight, of the kind used by police men, and sometimes by burglars, he started on tiptoe toward the lower floor.

As Tom softly descended the stairs he could more plainly hear the movements of the intruder. He made out now that the burglar was in Mr. Swift's study, which opened from the dining-room.

"He's after dad's papers!" thought Tom. "I wonder which one this is?"

The youth had often gone hunting in the woods, and he knew how to approach cautiously. Thus he was able to reach the door of the dining-room without being detected. He had no need to flash his light, for the intruder was doing that so frequently with one he carried that Tom could see him perfectly. The fellow was working at the safe in which Mr. Swift kept his more valuable papers.

Softly, very softly Tom brought his rifle to bear on the back of the thief. Then, holding the weapon with one hand, for it was very light, Tom extended the electric flash, so that the glare would be thrown on the intruder and would leave his own person in the black shadows. Pressing the spring which caused the lantern to throw out a powerful glow, Tom focused the rays on the kneeling man.

"That will be about all!" the youth exclaimed in as steady a voice as he could manage.

The burglar turned like a flash, and Tom had a glimpse of his face. It was the tramp—Happy Harry—whom he had encountered on the lonely road.

CHAPTER XIX

TOM ON A HUNT

Tom held his rifle in readiness, though he only intended it as a means of intimidation, and would not have fired at the burglar except to save his own life. But the sight of the weapon was enough for the tramp. He crouched motionless. His own light had gone out, but by the gleam of the electric he carried Tom could see that the man had in his hand some tool with which he had been endeavoring to force the safe.

"I guess you've got me!" exclaimed the intruder, and there was in his tones no trace of the tramp dialect.

"It looks like it," agreed Tom grimly. "Are you a tramp now, or in some other disguise?"

"Can't you see?" asked the fellow sullenly, and then Tom did notice that the man still had on his tramp make-up.

"What do you want?" asked Tom.

"Hard to tell." replied the burglar calmly. "I hadn't got the safe open before you came down and disturbed me. I'm after money, naturally."

"No, you're not!" exclaimed Tom.

"What's that?" and the man seemed surprised.

"No, you're not!" went on Tom, and he held his rifle in readiness. "You're after the patent papers and the model of the turbine motor. But it's gone. Your confederates got it away from me. They probably haven't told you yet, and you're still on the hunt for it. You'll not get it, but I've got you."

"So I see," admitted Happy Harry, and he spoke with some culture. "If you don't mind," he went on, "would you just as soon move that gun a little? It's pointing right at my head, and it might go off."

"It is going off—very soon!" exclaimed Tom grimly, and the tramp started in alarm. "Oh, I'm not going to shoot you," continued the young inventor. "I'm going to fire this as an alarm, and the engineer will come in here and tie you up. Then I'm going to hand you over to the police. This rifle is a repeater, and I am a pretty good shot. I'm going to fire once now, to summon assistance, and if you try to get away I'll be ready to fire a second time, and that won't be so comfortable for you. I've caught you, and I'm going to hold on to you until I get that model and those papers back."

"Oh, you are, eh?" asked the burglar calmly. "Well, all I've got to say is that you have grit. Go ahead. I'm caught good and proper. I was foolish to come in here, but I thought I'd take a chance."

"Who are you, anyhow? Who are the men working with you to defraud my father of his rights?" asked Tom somewhat bitterly.

"I'll never tell you," answered the burglar. "I was hired to do certain work, and that's all there is to it. I'm not going to peach on my pals."

"We'll see about that!" burst out Tom. Then he noticed that a dining-room window behind where the burglar was kneeling was open. Doubtless the intruder had entered that way, and intended to escape in the same manner.

"I'm going to shoot," announced Tom, and, aiming his rifle at the open window, where the bullet would do no damage, he pressed the trigger. He noticed that the burglar was crouching low down on the floor, but Tom thought nothing of this at the time. He imagined that Happy Harry—or whatever his name was—might be afraid of getting hit.

There was a flash of fire and a deafening report as Tom fired. The cloud of smoke obscured his vision for a moment, and as the echoes died away Tom could hear Mrs. Baggert screaming in her room.

"It's all right!" cried the young inventor reassuringly. "No one is hurt, Mrs. Baggert!" Then he flashed his light on the spot where the burglar had crouched. As the smoke rolled away Tom peered in vain for a sight of the intruder.

Happy Harry was gone!

Holding his rifle in readiness, in case he should be attacked from some unexpected quarter, Tom strode forward. He flashed his light in every direction. There was no doubt about it. The intruder had fled. Taking advantage of the noise when the gun was fired, and under cover of the smoke, the burglar had leaped from the open window. Tom guessed as much. He hurried to the casement and peered out, at the same time noticing the cut wire of the burglar alarm. It was quite dark, and he fancied he could hear the noise of some one running rapidly. Aiming his rifle into the air, he fired again, at the same time crying out:

"Hold on!"

"All right, Master Tom, I'm coming!" called the voice of the engineer from his shack. "Are you hurt? Is Mrs. Baggert murdered? I hear her screaming."

"That's pretty good evidence that she isn't murdered," said Tom with a grim smile.

"Are you hurt?" again called Mr. Jackson.

"No, I'm all right," answered Tom. "Did you see any one running away as you came up?"

"No, Master Tom, I didn't. What happened?"

"A burglar got in, and I had him cornered, but he got away when I fired to arouse you."

By this time the engineer was at the stoop, on which the window opened. Tom unlocked a side door and admitted Mr. Jackson, and then, the incandescent light having been turned on, the two looked around the apartment. Nothing in it had been disturbed, and the safe had not been opened.

"I heard him just in time," commented Tom, telling the engineer what had happened. "I wish I had thought to get between him and the window. Then he couldn't have gotten away."

"He might have injured you, though," said Mr. Jackson. "We'll go outside now, and look—"

"Is any one killed? Are you both murdered?" cried Mrs. Baggert at the dining-room door. "If any one is killed I'm not coming in there. I can't bear the sight of blood."

"No one is hurt," declared Tom with a laugh. "Come on in, Mrs. Baggert," and the housekeeper entered, her hair all done up in curl papers.

"Oh, my goodness me!" she exclaimed. "When I heard that cannon go off I was sure the house was coming down. How is it some one wasn't killed?"

"That wasn't a cannon; it was only my little rifle," said Tom, and then he told again, for the benefit of the housekeeper, the story of what had happened.

"We'd better hurry and look around the premises," suggested Mr. Jackson. "Maybe he is hiding, and will come back, or perhaps he has some confederates on the watch."

"Not much danger of that," declared Tom. "Happy Harry is far enough away from here now, and so are his confederates, if he had any, which I doubt. Still, it will do no harm to take a look around."

A search resulted in nothing, however, and the Swift household had soon settled down again, though no one slept soundly during the remainder of the night.

In the morning Tom sent word of what had happened to the police of Shopton. Some officers came out to the house, but, beyond looking wisely at the window by which the burglar had entered and at some footprints in the garden, they could do nothing. Tom wanted to go off on his motor-cycle on a tour of the surrounding neighborhood to see if he could get any clues, but he did not think it would be wise in the absence of his father. He thought it would be better to remain at home, in case any further efforts were made to get possession of valuable models or papers.

"There's not much likelihood of that, though," said Tom to the old engineer. "Those fellows have what they want, and are not going to bother us again. I would like to get that model back for dad, though. If they file it and take out a patent, even if he can prove that it is his, it will mean a long lawsuit and he may be defrauded of his rights, after all. Possession is nine points of the law, and part of the tenth, too, I guess."

So Tom remained at home and busied himself as well as he could over some new machines he was constructing. He got a telegram from his father that afternoon, stating that Mr. Swift had safely arrived in Albany, and would return the following day.

"Did you have any luck, dad?" asked the young inventor, when his father, tired and worn from the unaccustomed traveling, reached home in the evening.

"Not much, Tom," was the reply. "Mr. Crawford has gone back to Washington, and he is going to do what he can to prevent those men taking advantage of me."

"Did you get any trace of the thieves? Does Mr. Crawford think he can?"

"No to both questions. His idea is that the men will remain in hiding for a while, and then, when the matter has quieted down, they will proceed to get a patent on the motor that I invented."

"But, in the meanwhile, can't you make another model and get a patent yourself?"

"No; there are certain legal difficulties in the way. Besides, those men have the original papers I need. As for the model, it will take me nearly a year to build a new one that will work properly, as it is very complicated. I am afraid, Tom, that all my labor on the turbine motor is thrown away. Those scoundrels will reap the benefit of it."

"Oh, I hope not, dad! I'm sure those fellows will be caught. Now that you are back home again, I'm going out on a hunt on my own account. I don't put much faith in the police. It was through me, dad, that you lost your model and the papers, and I'll get them back!"

"No, you must not think it was your fault, Tom," said his father. "You could not help it, though I appreciate your desire to recover the missing model."

"And I'll do it, too, dad. I'll start tomorrow, and I'll make a complete circuit of the country for a hundred miles around. I can easily do it on my motor-cycle. If I can't get on the trail of the three men who robbed me, maybe I can find Happy Harry."

"I doubt it, my son. Still, you may try. Now I must write to Mr. Crawford and tell him about the attempted burglary while I was away. It may give him a clue to work on. I'm afraid you ran quite a risk, Tom."

"I didn't think about that, dad. I only wish I had managed to keep that rascal a prisoner."

The next day Tom started off on a hunt. He planned to be gone overnight, as he intended to go first to Dunkirk, where Mr. Blackford lived, and begin his search from there.

CHAPTER XX

ERADICATE SAWS WOOD

The farmer's family, including the son who was a deputy sheriff, was glad to see Tom. Jed said he had "been on the job" ever since the mysterious robbery of Tom had taken place, but though he had seen many red automobiles he had no trace of the three men.

From Dunkirk Tom went back over the route he had taken in going from Pompville to Centreford, and made some inquiries in the neighborhood of the church shed, where he had taken shelter. The locality was sparsely settled, however, and no one could give any clues to the robbers.

The young inventor next made a trip over the lonely, sandy road, where he had met with the tramp, Happy Harry. But there were even fewer houses near that stretch than around the church, so he got no satisfaction there. Tom spent the night at a country inn, and resumed his search the next morning, but with no results. The men had apparently completely disappeared, leaving no traces behind them.

"I may as well go home," thought Tom, as he was riding his motor-cycle along a pleasant country road. "Dad may be worried, and perhaps something has turned up in Shopton that will aid me. If there isn't, I'm going to start out again in a few days in another direction."

There was no news in Shopton, however. Town found his father scarcely able to work, so worried was he over the loss of his most important invention.

Two weeks passed, the young machinist taking trips of several days' duration to different points near his home, in the hope of discovering something. But he was unsuccessful, and, in the meanwhile, no reassuring word was received from the lawyers in Washington. Mr. Crawford wrote that no move had yet been made by the thieves to take out patent papers, and while this, in a sense, was some aid to Mr. Swift, still he could not proceed on his own account to protect his new motor. All that could be done was to await the first movement on the part of the scoundrels.

"I think I'll try a new plan tomorrow, dad," announced Tom one night, when he and his father had talked over again, for perhaps the twentieth time, the happenings of the last few weeks.

"What is it, Tom?" asked the inventor.

"Well, I think I'll take a week's trip on my machine. I'll visit all the small towns around here, but, instead of asking in houses for news of the tramp or his confederates, I'll go to the police and constables. I'll ask if they have arrested any tramps recently, and, if they have, I'll ask them to let me see the 'hobo' prisoners."

"What good will that do?"

"I'll tell you. I have an idea that though the burglar who got in here may not be a regular tramp, yet he disguises himself like one at times, and may be known to other tramps. If I can get on the trail of Happy Harry, as he calls himself, I may locate the other men. Tramps would be very likely to remember such a peculiar chap as Happy Harry, and they will tell me where they had last seen him. Then I will have a starting point."

"Well, that may be a good plan," assented Mr. Swift. "At any rate it will do no harm to try. A tramp locked up in a country police station will very likely be willing to talk. Go ahead with that scheme, Tom, but don't get into any danger. How long will you be away?"

"I don't know. A week, perhaps; maybe longer. I'll take plenty of money with me, and stop at country hotels overnight."

Tom lost no time in putting his plan into execution. He packed some clothes in a grip, which he attached to the rear of his motorcycle, and then having said good-by to his father, started off. The first three days he met with no success. He located several tramps in country lock-ups, where they had been sent for begging or loitering, but none of them knew Happy Harry or had ever heard of a tramp answering his description.

"He ain't one of us, youse can make up your mind to dat," said one "hobo" whom Tom interviewed. "No real knight of de highway goes around in a disguise. We leaves dat for de story-book detectives. I'm de real article, I am, an' I don't know Happy Harry. But, fer dat matter, any of us is happy enough in de summer time, if we don't strike a burgh like dis, where dey jugs you fer panhandlin'."

In general, Tom found the tramp willing enough to answer his questions, though some were sullen, and returned only surly growls to his inquiries.

"I guess I'll have to give it up and go back home," he decided one night. But there was a small town, not many miles from Shopton, which he had not yet visited, and he resolved to try there before returning. Accordingly, the next morning found him inquiring of the police authorities in Meadton. But no tramps had been arrested in the last month, and no one had seen anything of a tramp like Happy Harry or three mysterious men in an automobile.

Tom was beginning to despair. Riding along a silent road, that passed through a strip of woods, he was trying to think of some new line of procedure, when the silence of the highway, that, hitherto, had resounded only with the muffled explosions of his machine, was broken by several exclamations.

"Now, Boomerang, yo' might jest as well start now as later," Tom heard a voice saying—a voice he recognized well. "Yo' hab got t' do dis yeah wuk, an' dere ain't no gittin' out ob it. Dis yeah wood am got to be sawed, an' yo' hab got to saw it. But it am jest laik yo' to go back on yo' ole friend Eradicate in dis yeah fashion. I neber could tell what yo' were gwine t' do next, an' I cain't now. G'lang, now, won't yo'? Let's git dis yeah sawmill started."

Tom shut off the power and leaped from his wheel. From the woods at his left came the protesting "hee-haw" of a mule.

"Boomerang and Eradicate Sampson!" exclaimed the young inventor. "What can they be doing here?"

He leaned his motor-cycle against the fence and advanced toward where he had heard the voice of the colored man. In a little clearing he saw him. Eradicate was presiding over a portable saw-mill, worked by a treadmill, on the incline of which was the mule, its ears laid back, and an unmistakable expression of anger on its face.

"Why, Rad, what are you doing?" cried Tom.

"Good land o' massy! Ef it ain't young Mistah Swift!" cried the darky. "Howdy, Mistah Swift! Howdy! I'm jest tryin' t' saw some wood, t' make a livin', but Boomerang he doan't seem t' want t' lib," and with that Eradicate looked reproachfully at the animal.

"What seems to be the trouble, and how did you come to own this sawmill?" asked Tom.

"I'll tell yo', Mistah Swift, I'll tell yo'," spoke Eradicate. "Sit right yeah on dis log, an' I'll explanation it to yo'."

"The last time I saw you, you were preparing to go into the grasscutting business," went on Tom.

"Yais, sah! Dat's right. So I was. Yo' has got a memory, yo' suah has. But it am dis yeah way. Grass ain't growin' quick enough, an' so I traded off dat lawn-moah an' bought dis yeah mill. But now it won't go, an' I suah am in trouble," and once more Eradicate Sampson looked indignantly at Boomerang.

CHAPTER XXI

ERADICATE GIVES A CLUE

"Tell me all about it," urged Tom sympathetically, for he had a friendly feeling toward the aged darky.

"Well," began Eradicate, "I suah thought I were gwine to make money cuttin' grass, 'specially after yo' done fixed mah moah. But 'peared laik nobody wanted any grass cut. I trabeled all ober, an' I couldn't git no jobs. Now me an' Boomerang has to eat, no mattah ef he is contrary, so I had t' look fo' some new wuk. I traded dat lawn-moah off fo' a cross-cut saw, but dat was such hard wuk dat I gib it up. Den I got a chance to buy dis yeah outfit cheap, an' I bought it."

Eradicate then went on to tell how he had purchased the portable sawmill from a man who had no further use for it, and how he had managed to transport it from a distant village to the spot where Tom had met him. There he had secured permission to work a piece of woodland on shares, sawing up the smaller trees into cord wood. He had started in well enough, cutting down considerable timber, for the colored man was a willing worker, but when he tried to start his mill he met with trouble.

"I counted on Boomerang helpin' me," he said to Tom. "All he has to do is walk on dat tread mill, an' keep goin'. Dat makes de saw go 'round, an' I saws de wood. But de trouble am dat I can't git Boomerang to move. I done tried ebery means I knows on, an' he won't go. I talked kind to him, an' I talked harsh. I done beat him wif a club, an' I rub his ears soft laik, an' he allers did laik dat, but he won't go. I fed him on carrots an' I gib him sugar, an' I eben starve him, but he won't go. Heah I been tryin' fo' three days now t' git him started, an' not a stick hab I sawed. De man what I'm wukin' wif on shares he git mad, an' he say ef I doan't saw wood pretty soon he gwine t' git annuder mill heah. Now I axes yo' fair, Mistah Swift, ain't I got lots ob trouble?"

"You certainly seem to have," agreed Tom "But why is Boomerang so obstinate? Usually on a treadmill a horse or a mule has to work whether they like it or not. If they don't keep moving the platform slides out from under them, and they come up against the back bar."

"Dat's what done happened to Boomerang," declared Eradicate. "He done back up against de bar, an' dere he stay."

Tom went over and looked at the mill. The outfit was an old

one, and had seen much service, but the trained eye of the young inventor saw that it could still be used effectively. Boomerang watched Tom, as though aware that something unusual was about to happen.

"Heah I done gone an' 'vested mah money in dis yeah mill," complained Eradicate, "an' I ain't sawed up a single stick. Ef I wasn't so kind-hearted I'd chastise dat mule wuss dan I has, dat's what I would."

Tom said nothing. He was stooping down, looking at the gearing that connected the tread mill with the shaft which revolved the saw. Suddenly he uttered an exclamation,

"Rad, have you been monkeying with this machinery?" he asked.

"Me? Good land, Mistah Swift, no, sah! I wouldn't tech it. It's jest as I got it from de man I bought it oh. It worked when he had it, but he used a hoss. It's all due to de contrariness ob Boomerang, an' if I—"

"No, it isn't the mule's fault at all!" exclaimed Tom. "The mill is out of gear, and tread is locked; that's all. The man you bought it off probably did it so you could haul it along the road. I'll have it fixed for you in a few minutes. Wait until I get some tools."

From the bag on his motor-cycle Tom got his implements. He first unlocked the treadmill, so that the inclined platform, on which the animal slowly walked, could revolve. No sooner had he done this than Boomerang, feeling the slats under his hoofs moving away, started forward. With a rattle the treadmill slid around.

"Good land o' massy! It's goin'!" cried Eradicate delightedly. "It suah am goin'!" he added as he saw the mule, with nimble feet, send the revolving, endless string of slats around and around. "But de saw doan't move, Mistah Swift. Yo' am pretty smart at fixin' it as much as yo' has, but I reckon it's too busted t' eber saw any wood. I'se got bad luck, dat's what I has."

"Nonsense!" exclaimed Tom. "The sawmill will be going in a moment. All I have to do is to throw it into gear. See here, Rad. When you want the saw to go you just throw this handle forward. That makes the gears mesh."

"What's dat 'bout mush?" asked Eradicate.

"Mesh—not mush. I mean it makes the cogs fit together. See," and Tom pressed the lever. In an instant, with a musical whirr, the saw began revolving.

"Hurrah! Dere it goes! Golly! see de saw move!" cried the delighted colored man. He seized a stick of wood, and in a trice it was sawed through.

"Whoop!" yelled Eradicate. "I'm sabed now! Bless yo', Mistah Swift, yo' suttinly am a wondah!"

"Now I'll show you how it works," went on Tom. "When you want to stop Boomerang, you just pull this handle. That locks the tread, and he can't move it," and, suiting the action to his words, Tom stopped the mill. "Then," he went on, "when you want him to move, you pull the handle this way," and he showed the darky how to do it. In a moment the mule was moving again. Then Tom illustrated how to throw the saw in and out of gear, and in a few minutes the sawmill was in full operation, with a most energetic colored man feeding in logs to be cut up into stove lengths.

"You ought to have an assistant, Rad," said Tom, after he had watched the work for a while. "You could get more done then, and move on to some other wood-patch."

"Dat's right, Mistah Swift, so I had. But I done tried, an' couldn't git any. I ast seberal colored men, but dey'd radder white-wash an' clean chicken coops. I guess I'll hab t' go it alone. I ast a white man yisterday ef he wouldn't like t' pitch in an' help, but he said he didn't like to wuk. He was a tramp, an' he had de nerve to ask me fer money—me, a hard-wukin' coon."

"You didn't give it to him, I hope."

"No, indeedy, but he come so close to me dat I was askeered he might take it from me, so I kept hold ob a club. He suah was a bad-lookin' tramp, an' he kept laffin' all de while, like he was happy."

"What's that?" cried Tom, struck by the words of the colored man. "Did he have a thick, brown beard?"

"Dat's what he had," answered Eradicate, pausing in the midst of his work. "He suah were a funny sort ob tramp. His hands done looked laik he neber wuked, an' he had a funny blue ring one finger, only it wasn't a reg'lar ring, yo' know. It was pushed right inter his skin, laik a man I seen at de circus once, all cobered wid funny figgers."

Tom leaped to his feet.

"Which finger was the blue ring tattooed on?" he asked, and he waited anxiously for the answer.

"Let me see, it were on de right—no, it were on de little finger ob de left hand."

"Are you sure, Rad?"

"Suah, Mistah Swift. I took 'tic'lar notice, 'cause he carried a stick in dat same hand."

"It must be my man—Happy Harry!" exclaimed Tom half aloud. "Which way did he go, Rad, after he left you?"

"He went up de lake shore," replied the colored man. "He asked me if I knowed ob an ole big house up dere, what nobody libed in, an' I said I did. Den he left, an' I were glad ob it."

"Which house did you mean, Rad?"

"Why, dat ole mansion what General Harkness used t' lib in befo' de wah. Dere ain't nobody libed in it fo' some years now, an' it's deserted. Maybe a lot ob tramps stays in it, an' dat's where dis man were goin'."

"Maybe," assented Tom, who was all excitement now. "Just where is this old house, Rad?"

"Away up at de head ob Lake Carlopa. I uster wuk dere befo' de wah, but it's been a good many years since quality folks libed dere. Why, did yo' want t' see dat man, Mistah Swift?"

"Yes, Rad, I did, and very badly, too. I think he is the very person I want. But don't say anything about it. I'm going to take a trip up to that strange mansion. Maybe I'll get on the trail of Happy Harry and the men who robbed me. I'm much obliged to you, Rad, for this information. It's a good clue, I think. Strange that you should meet the very tramp I've been searching for."

"Well, I suah am obliged to yo', Mistah Swift, fo' fixin' mah sawmill."

"That's all right. What you told me more than pays for what I did, Rad. Well, I'm going home now to tell dad, and then I'm going to start out. Yesterday, you said it was, you saw Happy Harry? Well, I'll get right after him," and leaving a somewhat surprised, but very much delighted, colored man behind him, Tom mounted his motor-cycle and started for home at a fast pace.

CHAPTER XXII

THE STRANGE MANSION

"Dad, I've got a clue!" exclaimed Tom, hurrying into the house late that afternoon, following a quick trip from where he had met Eradicate with his sawmill. "A good clue, and I'm going to start early in the morning to run it down."

"Wait a minute, now, Tom," cautioned his father slowly. "You know what happens when you get excited. Nothing good was ever done in a hurry."

"Well, I can't help being excited, dad. I think I'm on the trail of those scoundrels. I almost wish I could start tonight."

"Suppose you tell me all about it," and Mr. Swift laid aside a scientific book he was reading.

Whereupon Tom told of his meeting with the colored man, and what Eradicate had said about the tramp.

"But he may not be the same Happy Harry you are looking for," interposed Mr. Swift. "Tramps who don't like to work, and who have a jolly disposition, also those who ask for money and have designs tattooed on their hands, are very common."

"Oh, but I'm sure this is the same one," declared Tom. "He wants to stay in this neighborhood until he locates his confederates. That's why he's hanging around. Now I have an idea that the deserted mansion, where Eradicate used to work, and which once housed General Harkness and his family, is the rendezvous of this gang of thieves."

"You are taking a great deal for granted, Tom."

"I don't think so, dad. I've got to assume something, and maybe I'm wrong, but I don't think so. At any rate, I'm going to try, if you'll let me."

"What do you mean to do?"

"I want to go to that deserted mansion and see what I can find. If I locate the thieves, well—"

"You may run into danger."

"Then you admit I may be on the right track, dad?"

"Not at all," and Mr. Swift smiled at the quick manner in which Tom turned the tables on him. "I admit there may be a band of tramps in that house. Very likely there is—almost any deserted place would be attractive to them. But they may not be the ones you seek. In fact, I hardly see how they can be. The men who stole my model and patent papers are wealthy. They would not be very likely to stay in deserted houses."

"Perhaps some of the scoundrels whom they hired might, and through them I can get on the track of the principals."

"Well, there is something in that," admitted Mr. Swift.

"Then may I go, dad?"

"I suppose so. We must leave nothing untried to get back the stolen model and papers. But I don't want you to run any risks. If you would only take some one with you. There's your chum, Ned Newton. Perhaps he would go."

"No, I'd rather work it alone, dad. I'll be careful. Besides, Ned could not get away from the bank. I may have to be gone a week, and he has no motor-cycle. I can manage all right."

Tom was off bright and early. He had carefully laid his plans, and had decided that he would not go direct to Pineford, which was the nearest village to the old Harkness mansion.

"If those fellows are in hiding they will probably keep watch on who comes to the village," thought Tom. "The arrival of some one on a motor-cycle will be sure to be reported to them, and they may skip out. I've got to come up from another direction, so I think I'll circle around, and reach the mansion from the stretch of woods on the north."

He had inquired from Eradicate as to the lay of the land, and had a good general idea of it. He knew there was a patch of woodland on one side of the mansion, while the other sides were open.

"I may not be able to ride through the woods," mused Tom, "but I'll take my machine as close as I can, and walk the rest of the way. Once I discover whether or not the gang is in the place, I'll know what to do."

To follow out the plan he had laid down for himself meant that Tom must take a roundabout way. It would necessitate being a whole day on the road, before he would be near the head of Lake Carlopa, where the Harkness house was located. The lake was a large one, and Tom had never been to the upper end.

When he was within a few miles of Pineford, Tom took a road that branched off and went around it. Stopping at night in a lonely farmhouse, he pushed on the next morning, hoping to get to the woods that night. But a puncture to one of the tires delayed him, and after that was repaired he discovered something wrong with his batteries. He had to go five miles out of his way to get new cells, and it was dusk when he came to the stretch of woods which he knew lay between him and the old mansion.

"I don't fancy starting in there at night," said Tom to himself. "Guess I'd better stay somewhere around here until morning, and then venture in. But the question is where to stay?"

The country was deserted, and for a mile or more he had seen no houses. He kept on for some distance farther, the dusk falling rapidly, and when he was about to turn back to retrace his way to the last farmhouse he had passed, he saw a slab shanty at the side of the road.

"That's better than nothing, provided they'll take me in for the night," murmured Tom. "I'm going to ask, anyhow."

He found the shanty to be inhabited by an old man who made a living burning charcoal. The place was not very attractive, but Tom did not mind that, and finding the charcoal-burner a kindly old fellow, soon made a bargain with him to remain all night.

Tom slept soundly, in spite of his strange surroundings, and after a simple breakfast in the morning inquired of the old man the best way of penetrating the forest.

"You'd best strike right along the old wood road," said the charcoal-burner. "That leads right to the lake, and I think will take you where you want to go. The old mansion is not far from the lake shore."

"Near the lake, eh?" mused Tom as he started off, after thanking the old fellow. "Now I wonder if I'd better try to get to it from the water or the land side?"

He found it impossible to ride fast on the old wood road, and when he judged he was so close to the lake that the noise of his motor-cycle might be heard, he shut off the power, and walked along, pushing it. It was hard traveling, and he felt weary, but he kept on, and about noon was rewarded by a sight of something glittering through the trees.

"That's the lake!" Tom exclaimed, half aloud. "I'm almost there."

A little later, having hidden his motor-cycle in a clump of bushes, he made his way through the underbrush and stood on the shore of Lake Carlopa. Cautiously Tom looked about him. It was getting well on in the afternoon, and the sun was striking across the broad sheet of water. Tom glanced up along the shore. Something amid a clump of trees caught his eyes. It was the chimney of a house. The young inventor walked a little distance along the lake shore. Suddenly he saw, looming up in the forest, a large building. It needed but a glance to show that it was falling into ruins, and had no signs of life about it. Nor, for that matter, was there any life in the forest around him, or on the lake that stretched out before him.

"I wonder if that can be the place?" whispered Tom, for, somehow, the silence of the place was getting on his nerves. "It must be it," he went on. "It's just as Rad described it."

He stood looking at it, the sun striking full on the mysterious mansion, hidden there amid the trees. Suddenly, as Tom looked, he heard the "put-put" of a motor-boat. He turned to one side, and saw, putting out from a little dock that he had not noticed before, a small craft. It contained one man, and no sooner had the young inventor caught a glimpse of him than he cried out:

"That's the man who jumped over our fence and escaped!"

Then, before the occupant of the boat could catch sight of him, Tom turned and fled back into the bushes, out of view.

CHAPTER XXIII

TOM IS PURSUED

Tom was so excited that he hardly knew what to do. His first thought was to keep out of sight of the man in the boat, for the young inventor did not want the criminals to suspect that he was on their trail. To that end he ran back until he knew he could not be seen from the lake. There he paused and peered through the bushes. He caught a glimpse of the man in the motor-boat. The craft was making fast time across the water.

"He didn't see me," murmured Tom. "Lucky I saw him first. Now what had I better do?"

It was a hard question to answer. If he only had some one with whom to consult he would have felt better, but he knew he had to rely on himself. Tom was a resourceful lad, and he had often before been obliged to depend on his wits. But this time very much was at stake, and a false move might ruin everything.

"This is certainly the house," went on Tom, "and that man in the boat is one of the fellows who helped rob me. Now the next thing to do is to find out if the others of the gang are in the old mansion, and, if they are, to see if dad's model and papers are there. Then the next thing to do will he to get our things away, and I fancy I'll have no easy job."

Well might Tom think this, for the men with whom he had to deal were desperate characters, who had already dared much to accomplish their ends, and who would do more before they would suffer defeat. Still, they under-estimated the pluck of the lad who was pitted against them.

"I might as well proceed on a certain plan, and have some system about this affair," reasoned the lad. "Dad is a great believer in system, so I'll lay out a plan and see how nearly I can follow it. Let's see—what is the first thing to do?"

Tom considered a moment, going over the whole situation in his mind. Then he went on, talking to himself alone there in the woods:

"It seems to me the first thing to do is to find out if the men are in the house. To do that I've got to get closer and look in through a window. Now, how to get closer?"

He considered that problem from all sides.

"It will hardly do to approach from the lake shore," he reasoned. "for if they have a motor-boat and a dock, there must be a path from the house to the water. If there is a path people are likely to walk up or down it at any minute. The man in the boat might come back unexpectedly and catch me. No, I can't risk approaching from the lake shore. I've got to work my way up to the house by going through the woods. That much is settled. Now to approach the house, and when I get within seeing distance I'll settle the next point. One thing at a time is a good rule, as dad used to say. Poor dad! I do hope I can get his model and papers back for him."

Tom, who had been sitting on a log under a bush, staring at the lake, arose. He was feeling rather weak and faint, and was at a loss to account for it, until he remembered that he had had no dinner.

"And I'm not likely to get any," he remarked. "I'm not going to eat until I see who's in that house. Maybe I won't then, and where supper is coming from I don't know. But this is too important to be considered in the same breath with a meal. Here goes."

Cautiously Tom made his way forward, taking care not to make too much disturbance in the bushes. He had been on hunting trips, and knew the value of silence in the woods. He had no paths to follow, but he had noted the position of the sun, and though that luminary was now sinking lower and lower in the west, he could see the gleam of it through the trees, and knew in which direction from it lay the deserted mansion.

Tom moved slowly, and stopped every now and then to listen. All the sounds he heard were those made by the creatures of the woods— birds, squirrels and rabbits. He went forward for half an hour, though in that time he did not cover much ground, and he was just beginning to think that the house must be near at hand when through a fringe of bushes he saw the old mansion. It stood in the midst of what had once been a fine park, but which was now overgrown with weeds and tangled briars. The paths that led to the house were almost out of sight, and the once beautiful home was partly in ruins.

"I guess I can sneak up there and take a look in one of the windows," thought the young inventor. He was about to advance, when he suddenly stopped. He heard some one or some thing coming around the corner of the mansion. A moment later a man came into view, and Tom easily recognized him as one of those who had been in the automobile. The heart of the young inventor beat so hard that he was afraid the man would hear it, and Tom crouched down in the bushes to keep out of sight. The man evidently did not suspect the presence of a stranger, for, though he cast sharp glances into the tangled undergrowth that fringed the house like a hedge, he did not seek to investigate further. He walked slowly on, making a circuit of the grounds. Tom remained hidden for several minutes, and was about to proceed again, when the man reappeared. Then Tom saw the reason for it.

"He's on guard!" the lad said to himself. "He's doing sentry duty. I can't approach the house when he's there."

For an instant Tom felt a bitter disappointment. He had hoped to be able to carry out his plan as he had mapped it. Now he would have to make a change.

"I'll have to wait until night," he thought. "Then I can sneak up and look in. The guard won't see me after dark. But it's going to be no fun to stay here, without anything to eat. Still, I've got to do it."

He remained where he was in the bushes. Several times, before the sun set, the man doing sentry duty made the circuit of the house, and Tom noted that occasionally he was gone for a long period. He reasoned that the man had gone into the mansion to confer with his confederates.

"If I only knew what was going on in there," thought Tom. "Maybe, after all, the men haven't got the model and papers here. Yet, if they haven't, why are they staying in the old house? I must get a look in and see what's going on. Lucky there are no shades to the windows. I wish it would get dark."

It seemed that the sun would never go down and give place to dusk, but finally Tom, crouching in his hiding place, saw the shadows grow longer and longer, and finally the twilight of the woods gave place to a density that was hard to penetrate. Tom waited some time to see if the guard kept up the circuit, but with the approach of night the man seemed to have gone into the house. Tom saw a light gleam out from the lonely mansion. It came from a window on the ground floor.

"There's my chance!" exclaimed the lad, and, crawling from his hiding place, he advanced cautiously toward it.

Tom went forward only a few feet at a time, pausing almost every other step to listen. He heard no sounds, and was reassured. Nearer and nearer he came to the old house. The gleam of the light fell upon his face, and fearful that some one might be looking from the window, he shifted his course, so as to come up from one side. Slowly, very slowly he advanced, until he was right under the window. Then he found that it was too high up to admit of his looking in. He felt about until he had a stone to stand on.

Softly he drew himself up inch by inch. He could hear the murmur of voices in the room. Now the top of his head was on a level with the sill. A few more inches and his eyes could take in the room and the occupants. He was scarcely breathing. Up, up he raised himself until he could look into the apartment, and the sight which met his eyes nearly caused him to lose his hold and topple backward. For grouped around a table in a big room were the three men whom he had seen in the automobile. But what attracted his attention more than the sight of the men was an object on the table. It was the stolen model! The men were inspecting it, and operating it, as he could see. One of the trio had a bundle of papers in his hand, and Tom was sure they were the ones stolen from him. But there could be no doubt about the model of the turbine motor. There it was in plain sight. He had tracked the thieves to their hiding place.

Then, as he watched, Tom saw one of the men produce from under the table a box, into which the model was placed. The papers were next put in, and a cover was nailed on. Then the men appeared to consult among themselves.

By their gestures Tom concluded that they were debating where to hide the box. One man pointed toward the lake, and another toward the forest. Tom was edging himself up farther, in order to see better, and, if possible, catch their words, when his foot slipped, and he made a slight noise. Instantly the men turned toward the window, but Tom had stooped down out of sight, just in time.

A moment later, however, he heard some one approaching through the woods behind him, and a voice called out:

"What are you doing? Get away from there!"

Rapid footsteps sounded, and Tom, in a panic, turned and fled, with an unknown pursuer after him.

CHAPTER XXIV

UNEXPECTED HELP

Tom rushed on through the woods. The lighted room into which he had been looking had temporarily blinded him when it came to plunging into the darkness again, and he could not see where he was going. He crashed full-tilt into a tree, and was thrown backward. Bruised and cut, he picked himself up and rushed off in another direction. Fortunately he struck into some sort of a path, probably one made by cows, and then, as his eyes recovered their faculties, he could dimly distinguish the trees on either side of him and avoid them.

His heart, that was beating fiercely, calmed down after his first fright, and when he had run on for several minutes he stopped.

"That—that must—have been—the—the man—from the boat," panted our hero, whispering to himself. "He came back and saw me. I wonder if he's after me yet?"

Tom listened. The only sound he could hear was the trill and chirp of the insects of the woods. The pursuit, which had lasted only a few minutes, was over. But it might be resumed at any moment. Tom was not safe yet, he thought, and he kept on.

"I wonder where I am? I wonder where my motor-cycle is? I wonder what I had better do?" he asked himself.

Three big questions, and no way of settling them; Tom pulled himself up sharply.

"I've got to think this thing out," he resumed. "They can't find me in these woods tonight, that's sure, unless they get dogs, and they're not likely to do that. So I'm safe that far. But that's about all that is in my favor. I won't dare to go back to the house, even if I could find it in this blackness, which is doubtful. It wouldn't be safe, for they'll be on guard now. It looks as though I was up against it. I'm afraid they may imagine the police are after them, and go away. If they do, and take the model and papers with them, I'll have an awful job to locate them again, and probably I won't be able to. That's the worst of it. Here I have everything right under my hands, and I can't do a thing. If I only had some one to help me; some one to leave on guard while I went for the police. I'm one against three—no, four, for the man in the boat is back. Let's see what can I do?"

Then a sudden plan came to him.

"The lake shore!" he exclaimed, half aloud. "I'll go down there and keep watch. If they escape they'll probably go in the boat, for they wouldn't venture through the woods at night. That's it. I'll watch on shore, and if they do leave in the boat—" He paused again, undecided. "Why, if they do," he finished, "I'll sing out, and make such a row that they'll think the whole countryside is after them. That may drive them back, or they may drop the box containing the papers and model, and cut for it. If they do I'll be all right. I don't care about capturing them, if I can get dad's model back."

He felt more like himself, now that he had mapped out another plan.

"The first thing to do is to locate the lake," reasoned Tom. "Let's see; I ran in a straight line away from the house—that is, as nearly straight as I could. Now if I turn around and go straight back, bearing off a little to the left, I ought to come to the water. I'll do it."

But it was not so easy as Tom imagined, and several times he found himself in the midst of almost impenetrable bushes. He kept on, however, and soon had the satisfaction of emerging from the woods out on the shore of the lake. Then, having gotten his bearings as well as he could in the darkness, he moved down until he was near the deserted house. The light was still showing from the window, and Tom judged by this that the men had not taken fright and fled.

"I suppose I could sneak down and set the motor-boat adrift," he argued. "That would prevent them leaving by way of the lake, anyhow. That's what I'll do! I'll cut off one means of escape. I'll set the boat adrift!"

Very cautiously he advanced toward where he had seen the small craft put out. He was on his guard, for he feared the men would be on the watch, but he reached the dock in safety, and was loosening the rope that tied the boat to the little wharf when another thought came to him.

"Why set this boat adrift?" he reasoned. "It is too good a boat to treat that way, and, besides, it will make a good place for me to spend the rest of the night. I've got to stay around here until morning, and then I'll see if I can't get help. I'll just appropriate this boat for my own use. They have dad's model, and I'll take their boat."

Softly he got into the craft, and with an oar which was kept in it to propel it in case the engine gave out, he poled it along the shore of the lake until he was some distance away from the dock.

That afternoon he had seen a secluded place along the shore, a spot where overhanging bushes made a good hiding place, and for this he headed the craft. A little later it was completely out of sight, and Tom stretched out on the cushioned seats, pulling a tarpaulin over him. There he prepared to spend the rest of the night.

"They can't get away except through the woods now, which I don't believe they'll do," he thought, "and this is better for me than staying out under a tree. I'm glad I thought of it."

The youth, naturally, did not pass a very comfortable night, though his bed was not a half bad one. He fell into uneasy dozes, only to arouse, thinking the men in the old mansion were trying to escape. Then he would sit up and listen, but he could hear nothing. It seemed as if morning would never come, but at length the stars began to fade, and the sky seemed overcast with a filmy, white veil. Tom sat up, rubbed his smarting eyes, and stretched his cramped limbs.

"Oh, for a hot cup of coffee!" he exclaimed. "But not for mine, until I land these chaps where they belong. Now the question is, how can I get help to capture them?"

His hunger was forgotten in this. He stepped from the boat to a secluded spot on the shore. The craft, he noted, was well hidden.

"I've got to go back to where I left my motor-cycle, jump on that, and ride for aid," he reasoned. "Maybe I can get the charcoal-burner to go for me, while I come back and stand guard. I guess that would be the best plan. I certainly ought to be on hand, for there is no telling when these fellows will skip out with the model, if they haven't gone already. I hate to leave, yet I've got to. It's the only way. I wish I'd done as dad suggested, and brought help. But it's too late for that. Well, I'm off."

Tom took a last look at the motor-boat, which was a fine one. He wished it was his. Then he struck through the woods. He had his bearings now, and was soon at the place where he had left his machine. It had not been disturbed. He caught a glimpse of the old mansion on his way out of the woods. There appeared to be no one stirring about it.

"I hope my birds haven't flown!" he exclaimed, and the thought gave him such uneasiness that he put it from him. Pushing his heavy machine ahead of him until he came to a good road, he mounted it, and was soon at the charcoal-burner's shack. There came no answer to his knock, and Tom pushed open the door. The old man was not in. Tom could not send him for help.

"My luck seems to be against me!" he murmured. "But I can get something to eat here, anyhow. I'm almost starved!"

He found the kitchen utensils, and made some coffee, also frying some bacon and eggs. Then, feeling much refreshed, and having left on the table some money to pay for the inroad he had made on the victuals, he started to go outside.

As our hero stepped to the door he was greeted by a savage growl that made him start in alarm.

"A dog!" he mused. "I didn't know there was one around."

He looked outside and there, to his dismay, saw a big, savage-appearing bulldog standing close to where he had left his motorcycle. The animal had been sniffing suspiciously at the machine.

"Good dog!" called Tom. "Come here!"

But the bulldog did not come. Instead the beast stood still, showed his teeth to Tom and growled in a low tone.

"Wonder if the owner can be near?" mused the young inventor. "That dog won't let me get my machine, I am afraid."

Tom spoke to the animal again and again the dog growled and showed his teeth. He next made a move as if to leap into the house, and Tom quickly stepped back and banged shut the door.

"Well, if this isn't the worst yet!" cried the youth to himself. "Here, just at the time I want to be off, I must be held up by such a brute as that outside. Wonder how long he'll keep me a prisoner?"

Tom went to a window and peered out. No person had appeared and the lad rightly surmised that the bulldog had come to the cottage alone. The beast appeared to be hungry, and this gave Tom a sudden idea.

"Maybe if I feed him, he'll forget that I am around and give me a chance to get away," he reasoned. "Guess I had better try that dodge on him."

Tom looked around the cottage and at last found the remains of a chicken dinner the owner had left behind. He picked up some of the bones and called the bulldog. The animal came up rather suspiciously. Tom threw him one bone, which he proceeded to crunch up vigorously.

"He's hungry right enough," mused Tom. "I guess he'd like to sample my leg. But he's not going to do it—not if I can help it."

At the back of the cottage was a little shed, the door to which stood open. Tom threw a bone near to the door of this shed and then managed to throw another bone inside the place. The bulldog found the first bone and then disappeared after the second.

"Now is my time, I guess," the young inventor told himself, and watching his chance, he ran from the cottage toward his motorcycle. He made no noise and quickly shoved the machine into the roadway. Just as he turned on the power the bulldog came out of the shed, barking furiously.

"You've missed it!" said Tom grimly as the machine started, and quickly the cottage and the bulldog were left behind. The road was rough for a short distance and he had to pay strict attention to what he was doing.

"I've got to ride to the nearest village," he said. "It's a long distance, and, in the meanwhile, the men may escape. But I can't do anything else. I dare not tackle them alone, and there is no telling when the charcoal-burner may come back. I've got to make speed, that's all."

Out on the main road the lad sent his machine ahead at a fast pace. He was fairly humming along when, suddenly, from around a curve in the highway he heard the "honk-honk" of an automobile horn. For an instant his heart failed him.

"I wonder if those are the thieves? Maybe they have left the house, and are in their auto!" he whispered as he slowed down his machine.

The automobile appeared to have halted. As Tom came nearer the turn he heard voices. At the sound of one he started. The voice exclaimed:

"Bless my spectacles! What's wrong now? I thought that when I got this automobile I would enjoy life, but it's as bad as my motor-cycle was for going wrong! Bless my very existence, but has anything happened?"

"Mr. Damon!" exclaimed Tom, for he recognized the eccentric individual of whom he had obtained the motor-cycle.

The next moment Tom was in sight of a big touring car, containing, not only Mr. Damon, whom Tom recognized at once, but three other gentlemen.

"Oh, Mr. Damon," cried Tom, "will you help me capture a gang of thieves? They are in a deserted mansion in the woods, and they have one of my father's patent models! Will you help me, Mr. Damon?"

"Why, bless my top-knots," exclaimed the odd gentleman. "If it isn't Tom Swift, the young inventor! Bless my very happiness! There's my motor-cycle, too! Help you? Why, of course we will. Bless my shoe-leather! Of course we'll help you!"

CHAPTER XXV

THE CAPTURE—GOOD-BY

Tom's story was soon told, and Mr. Damon quickly explained to his friends in the automobile how he had first made the acquaintance of the young inventor.

"But how does it happen that you are trusting yourself in a car like this?" asked Tom. "I thought you were done with gasolene machines, Mr. Damon."

"I thought so, too, Tom, but, bless my batteries, my doctor insisted that I must get out in the open air. I'm too stout to walk, and I can't run. The only solution was in an automobile, for I never would dream of a motor-cycle. I wonder that one of mine hasn't run away with you and killed you. But there! My automobile is nearly as bad. We went along very nicely yesterday, and now, just when I have a party of friends out, something goes wrong. Bless my liver! I do seem to have the worst luck!"

Tom lost no time in looking for the trouble. He found it in the ignition, and soon had it fixed. Then a sort of council of war was held.

"Do you think those scoundrels are there yet?" asked Mr. Damon.

"I hope so," answered Tom.

"So do I," went on the odd character. "Bless my soul, but I want a chance to pummel them. Come, gentlemen, let's be moving. Will you ride with us, Tom Swift, or on that dangerous motor-cycle?"

"I think I'll stick to my machine, Mr. Damon. I can easily keep up with you."

"Very well. Then we'll get along. We'll proceed until we get close to the old mansion, and then some of us will go down to the lake shore, and the rest of us will surround the house. We'll catch the villains red-handed, and I hope we bag that tramp among them."

"I hardly think he is there," said Tom.

In a short time the auto and the motor-cycle had carried the respective riders to the road through the woods. There the machines were left, and the party proceeded on foot. Tom had a revolver with him, and one member of Mr. Damon's party also had a small one, more to scare dogs than for any other purpose. Tom gave his weapon to one of the men, and cut a stout stick for himself, an example followed by those who had no firearms.

"A club for mine!" exclaimed Mr. Damon. "The less I have to

do with machinery the better I like it. Now, Tom Swift is just the other way around," he explained to his friends.

Cautiously they approached the house, and when within seeing distance of it they paused for a consultation. There seemed to be no one stirring about the old mansion, and Tom was fearful lest the men had left. But this could not be determined until they came closer. Two of Mr. Damon's friends elected to go down to the shore of the lake and prevent any escape in that direction, while the others, including Tom, were to approach from the wood side. When the two who were to form the water attacking party were ready, one of them was to fire his revolver as a signal. Then Tom, Mr. Damon and the others would rush in.

The young inventor, Mr. Damon, and his friend, whom he addressed as Mr. Benson, went as close to the house as they considered prudent. Then, screening themselves in the bushes, they waited. They conversed in whispers, Tom giving more details of his experience with the patent thieves.

Suddenly the silence of the woods was broken by some one advancing through the underbrush.

"Bless my gaiters, some one is coming!" exclaimed Mr. Damon in a hoarse whisper. "Can that be Munson or Dwight coming back?" He referred to his two friends who had gone to the lake.

"Or perhaps the fellows are escaping," suggested Mr. Benson. "Suppose we take a look."

At that moment the person approaching, whoever he was, began to sing. Tom started.

"I'll wager that's Happy Harry, the tramp!" he exclaimed. "I know his voice."

Cautiously Tom peered over the screen of bushes.

"Who is it?" asked Mr. Damon.

"It's Happy Harry!" said Tom. "We'll get them all, now. He's going up to the house."

They watched the tramp. All unconscious of the eyes of the men and boy in the bushes, he kept on. Presently the door of the house opened, and a man came out. Tom recognized him as Anson Morse—the person who had dropped the telegram.

"Say, Burke," called the man at the door, "have you taken the motor-boat?"

"Motor-boat? No," answered the tramp. "I just came here. I've had a hard time—nearly got caught in Swift's house the other night by that cub of a boy. Is the boat gone?"

"Yes. Appleson came back in it last night and saw some one looking in the window, but we thought it was only a farmer and chased him away. This morning the boat's gone. I thought maybe you had taken it for a joke."

"Not a bit of it! Something's wrong!" exclaimed Happy Harry. "We'd better light out. I think the police are after us. That young Swift is too sharp for my liking. We'd better skip. I don't believe that was a farmer who looked in the window. Tell the others, get the stuff, and we'd leave this locality."

"They're here still," whispered Tom. "That's good!"

"I wonder if Munson and Dwight are at the lake yet?" asked Mr. Damon. "They ought to be—"

At that instant a pistol shot rang out. The tramp, after a hasty glance around, started on the run for the house. The man in the doorway sprang out. Soon two others joined him.

"Who fired that shot?" cried Morse.

"Come on, Tom!" cried Mr. Damon, grabbing up his club and springing from the bushes. "Our friends have arrived!" The young inventor and Mr. Benson followed him.

No sooner had they come into the open space in front of the house than they were seen. At the same instant, from the rear, in the direction of the lake, came Mr. Munson and Mr. Dwight.

"We're caught!" cried Happy Harry.

He made a dash far the house, just as a man, carrying a box, rushed out.

"There it is! The model and papers are in that box!" cried Tom. "Don't let them get away with it!"

The criminals were taken by surprise. With leveled weapons the attacking party closed in on them. Mr. Damon raised his club threateningly.

"Surrender! Surrender!" he cried. "We have you! Bless my stars, but you're captured! Surrender!"

"It certainly looks so," admitted Anson Morse. "I guess they have us, boys."

The man with the box made a sudden dash toward the woods, but Tom was watching him. In an instant he sprang at him, and landed on the fellow's back. The two went down in a heap, and when Tom arose he had possession of the precious box.

"I have it! I have it!" he cried. "I've got dad's model back!"

The man who had had possession of the box quickly arose, and, before any one could stop him, darted into the bushes.

"After him! Catch him! Bless my hat-band, stop him!" shouted Mr. Damon.

Instinctively his friends turned to pursue the fugitive, forgetting, for the instant, the other criminals. The men were quick to take advantage of this, and in a moment had disappeared in the dense woods. Nor could any trace be found of the one with whom Tom had struggled.

"Pshaw! They got away from us!" cried Mr. Damon regretfully. "Let's see if we can't catch them. Come on, we'll organize a posse and run them down." He was eager for the chase, but his companions dissuaded him. Tom had what he wanted, and he knew that his father would prefer not to prosecute the men. The lad opened the box, and saw that the model and papers were safe.

"Let those fellows go," advised the young inventor, and Mr. Damon reluctantly agreed to this. "I guess we've seen the last of them," added the youth, but he and Mr. Swift had not, for the criminals made further trouble, which will be told of in the second volume of this series, to be called "Tom Swift and His Motor-Boat; or, The Rivals of Lake Carlopa." In that our hero will be met in adventures even more thrilling than those already related, and Andy Foger, who so nearly ran Tom down in the automobile, will have a part in them.

"Now," said Mr. Damon, after it had been ascertained that no one was injured, and that the box contained all of value that had been stolen, "I suppose you are anxious to get back home, Tom, aren't you? Will you let me take you in my car? Bless my spark plug, but I'd like to have you along in case of another accident!"

The lad politely declined, however, and, with the valuable model and papers safe on his motor-cycle, he started for Shopton. Arriving at the first village after leaving the woods, Tom telephoned the good news to his father, and that afternoon was safely at home, to the delight of Mr. Swift and Mrs. Baggert.

The inventor lost no time in fully protecting his invention by patents. As for the unprincipled men who made an effort to secure it, they had so covered up their tracks that there was no way of prosecuting them, nor could any action be held against Smeak & Katch, the unscrupulous lawyers.

"Well," remarked Mr. Swift to Tom, a few nights after the recovery of the model, "your motor-cycle certainly did us good service. Had it not been for it I might never have gotten back my invention."

"Yes, it did come in handy," agreed the young inventor. "There's that motor-boat, too. I wish I had it. I don't believe those fellows will ever come back for it. I turned it over to the county authorities, and they take charge of it for a while. I certainly had some queer adventures since I got this machine from Mr. Damon," concluded Tom. I think my readers will agree with him.

TOM SWIFT AND HIS MOTOR-BOAT

CHAPTER I

A MOTOR-BOAT AUCTION

"Where are you going, Tom?" asked Mr. Barton Swift of his son as the young man was slowly pushing his motor-cycle out of the yard toward the country road. "You look as though you had some object in view."

"So I have, dad. I'm going over to Lanton."

"To Lanton? What for?"

"I want to have a look at that motor-boat."

"Which boat is that, Tom? I don't recall your speaking about a boat over at Lanton. What do you want to look at it for?"

"It's the motor-boat those fellows had who tried to get away with your turbine model invention, dad. The one they used at the old General Harkness mansion, in the woods near the lake, and the same boat that fellow used when he got away from me the day I was chasing him here."

"Oh, yes, I remember now. But what is the boat doing over at Lanton?"

"That's where it belongs. It's the property of Mr. Bently Hastings. The thieves stole it from him, and when they ran away from the old mansion, the time Mr. Damon and I raided the place, they left the boat on the lake. I turned it over to the county authorities, and they found out it belonged to Mr. Hastings. He has it back now, but I understand it's somewhat damaged, and he wants to get rid of it. He's going to sell it at auction today, and I thought I'd go over and take a look at it. You see—"

"Yes, I see, Tom," exclaimed Mr. Swift with a laugh. "I see what you're aiming at. You want a motor-boat, and you're going all around Robin Hood's barn to get at it."

"No, dad, I only—"

"Oh, I know you, Tom, my lad!" interrupted the inventor, shaking his finger at his son, who seemed somewhat confused. "You have a nice rowing skiff and a sailboat, yet you are hankering for a motor-boat. Come now, own up. Aren't you?"

"Well, dad, a motor-boat certainly would go fine on Lake Carlopa. There's plenty of room to speed her, and I wonder there aren't more of them. I was going to see what Mr. Hastings' boat would sell for, but I didn't exactly think of buying it' Still—"

"But you wouldn't buy a damaged boat, would you?"

"It isn't much damaged," and in his eagerness the young

inventor (for Tom Swift had taken out several patents) stood his motor-cycle up against the fence and came closer to his father. "It's only slightly damaged," he went on. "I can easily fix it. I looked it all over before I gave it in charge of the authorities, and it's certainly a fine boat. It's worth nine hundred dollars—or it was when it was new."

"That's a good deal of money for a boat," and Mr. Swift looked serious, for though he was well off, he was inclined to be conservative.

"Oh, I shouldn't think of paying that much. In fact, dad, I really had no idea of bidding at the auction. I only thought I'd go over and get an idea of what the boat might sell for. Perhaps some day—"

Tom paused. Since his father had begun to question him some new plans had come into the lad's head. He looked at his parent and saw a smile beginning to work around the corners of Mr. Swift's lips. There was also a humorous look in the eyes of the older inventor. He understood boys fairly well, even if he only had one, and he knew Tom perfectly.

"Would you really like to make a bid on that boat Tom?" he asked.

"Would I, dad? Well—" The youth did not finish, but his father knew what he meant.

"I suppose a motor-boat would be a nice thing to have on Lake Carlopa," went on Mr. Swift musingly. "You and I could take frequent trips in it. It isn't like a motor-cycle, only useful for one. What do you suppose the boat will go for, Tom?"

"I hardly know. Not a high price, I believe, for motor-boats are so new on our lake that few persons will take a chance on them. But if Mr. Hastings is getting another, he will not be so particular about insisting on a high price for the old one. Then, too, the fact that it is damaged will help to keep the price down, though I know I can easily put it in good shape. I would like to make a bid, if you think it's all right."

Well, I guess you may, Tom, if you really want it. You have money of your own and a motor-boat is not a bad investment. What do you think ought to be the limit?"

"Would you consider a hundred and fifty dollars too high?"

Mr. Swift looked at Tom critically. He was plainly going over several matters in his mind, and not the least of them was the pluck his son had shown in getting back some valuable papers and a model from a gang of thieves. The lad certainly was entitled to some reward, and to allow him to get a boat might properly be part of it.

"I think you could safely go as high as two hundred dollars,

Tom," said Mr. Swift at length. "That would be my limit on a damaged boat for it might be better to pay a little more and get a new one. However, use your own judgment, but don't go over two hundred. So the thieves who made so much trouble for me stole that boat from Mr. Hastings, eh?"

"Yes, and they didn't take much care of it either. They damaged the engine, but the hull is in good shape. I'm ever so glad you'll let me bid on it. I'll start right off. The auction is at ten o'clock and I haven't more than time to get there."

"Now be careful how you bid. Don't raise your own figures, as I've sometimes seen women, and men too, do in their excitement. Somebody may go over your head; and if he does, let them. If you get the boat I'll be very glad on your account. But don't bring any of Anson Morse's gang back in it with you. I've seen enough of them."

"I'll not dad!" cried Tom as he trundled his motor-cycle out of the gate and into the country road that led to the village of Shopton, where he lived, and to Lanton, where the auction was to be held. The young inventor had not gone far before he turned back, leaving his machine standing on the side path.

"What's the matter?" asked his father, who had started toward one of several machine shops on the premises—shops where Mr. Swift and his son did inventive work.

"Guess I'd better get a blank check and some money," replied Tom as he entered the house. "I'll need to pay a deposit if I secure the boat."

"That's so. Well, good luck," and with his mind busy on a plan for a new kind of storage battery, the inventor went on to his workroom. Tom got some cash and his checkbook from a small safe he owned and was soon speeding over the road to Lanton, his motorcycle making quite a cloud of dust. While he is thus hurrying along to the auction I will tell you something about him.

Tom Swift, son of Barton Swift, lived with his father and a motherly housekeeper, Mrs. Baggert, in a large house on the outskirts of the town of Shopton, in New York State. Mr. Swift had acquired considerable wealth from his many inventions and patents, but he did not give up working out his ideas simply because he had plenty of money. Tom followed in the footsteps of his parent and had already taken out several patents.

Shortly before this story opens the youth had become possessed of a motor-cycle in a peculiar fashion. As told in the first volume of this series, entitled "Tom Swift and His Motor-cycle," Tom was riding to the town of Mansburg on an errand for his father one day when he was nearly run down by a motorcyclist. A little later the same motorcyclist, who was a Mr. Wakefield Damon, of Waterfield, collided with a tree near Tom's home and was severely cut and bruised, the machine being broken. Tom and his father cared for the injured rider, and Mr. Damon, who was an eccentric individual, was so disheartened by his attempts to ride the motor-cycle that he sold it to Tom for fifty dollars, though it had cost much more.

About the same time that Tom bought the motor-cycle a firm of rascally lawyers, Smeak & Katch by name, had, in conjunction with several men, made an attempt to get control of an invention of a turbine motor perfected by Mr. Swift. The men, who were Ferguson Appleson, Anson Morse, Wilson Featherton, alias Simpson, and Jake Burke, alias Happy Harry, who sometimes disguised himself as a tramp, tried several times to steal the model.

Their anxiety to get it was due to the fact that they had invested a large sum in a turbine motor invented by another man, but their motor would not work and they sought to steal Mr. Swift's. Tom was sent to Albany on his motor-cycle to deliver the model and some valuable papers to Mr. Crawford, of the law firm of Reid & Crawford, of Washington, attorneys for Mr. Swift. Mr. Crawford had an errand in Albany and had agreed to meet Tom there with the model.

But, on the way, Tom was attacked by the gang of unscrupulous men and the model was stolen. He was assaulted and carried far away in an automobile. In an attempt to capture the gang in a deserted mansion, in the woods on the shore of Lake Carlopa, Tom was aided by Mr. Damon, of whom he had purchased the motor-cycle. The men escaped, however, and nothing could be done to punish them.

Tom was thinking of the exciting scenes he had passed through about a month previous as he spun along the road leading to Lanton.

"I hope I don't meet Happy Harry or any of his gang today," mused the lad as he turned on a little more power to enable his machine to mount a hill. "I don't believe they'll attend the auction, though. It would be too risky for them."

As Tom swung along at a rapid pace he heard, behind him, the puffing of an automobile, with the muffler cut out. He turned and cast a hasty glance behind.

"I hope that ain't Andy Foger or any of his cronies," he said to himself. "He might try to run me down just for spite. He generally rushes along with the muffler open so as to attract attention and make folks think he has a racing car."

It was not Andy, however, as Tom saw a little later, as a man passed him in a big touring car. Andy Foger, as my readers will recollect, was a red-haired, squinty-eyed lad with plenty of money and not much else. He and his cronies, including Sam Snedecker, nearly ran Tom down one day, when the latter was on his bicycle, as told in the first volume of this series. Andy had been off on a tour with his chums during the time when Tom was having such strenuous adventures and had recently returned.

"If I can only get that boat," mused Tom as he swung back into the middle of the road after the auto had passed him, "I certainly will have lots of fun. I'll make a week's tour of Lake Carlopa and take dad and Ned Newton with me." Ned was Tom's most particular chum, but as young Newton was employed in the Shopton bank, the lad did not have much time for pleasure. Lake Carlopa was a large body of water, and it would take a moderately powered boat several days to make a complete circuit of the shore, so cut up into bays and inlets was it.

In about an hour Tom was at Lanton, and as he neared the home of Mr. Hastings, which was on the shore of the lake, he saw quite a throng going down toward the boathouse.

"There'll be some lively bidding," thought Tom as he got off his machine and pushed it ahead of him through the drive and down toward the river. I hope they don't go above two hundred dollars, though."

"Get out the way there!" called a sudden voice, and looking back, Tom saw that an automobile had crept up silently behind him. In it were Andy Foger and Sam Snedecker. "Why don't you get out the way?" petulantly demanded the red-haired lad.

"Because I don't choose to," replied Tom calmly, knowing that Andy would never dare to speed up his machine on the slope leading down to the lake.

"Go ahead, bump him!" the young inventor heard Sam whisper.

"You'd better try it, if you want to get the best trouncing you ever had!" cried Tom hotly.

"Hu! I s'pose you think you're going to bid on the boat?" sneered Andy.

"Is there any law against it?" asked Tom.

"Hu! Well, you'll not get it. I'm going to take that boat," retorted the squint-eyed bully. "Dad gave me the money to get it."

"All right," answered Tom non-committally. "Go ahead. It's a free country."

He stood his motor-cycle up against a tree and went toward a group of persons who were surrounding the auctioneer. The time had arrived to start the sale. As Tom edged in closer he brushed against a man who looked at him sharply. The lad was just wondering if he had ever seen the individual before, as there seemed to be something strangely familiar about him, when the man turned quickly away, as if afraid of being recognized.

"That's odd," thought Tom, but he had no further time for speculation, as the auctioneer was mounting on a soapbox and had begun to address the gathering.

CHAPTER II

SOME LIVELY BIDDING

"Attention, people!" cried the auctioneer. "Give me your attention for a few minutes, and we will proceed with the business in hand. As you all know, I am about to dispose of a fine motor-boat, the property of Mr. Bently Hastings. The reason for disposing of it at auction is known to most of you, but for the benefit of those who do not, I will briefly state them. The boat was stolen by a gang of thieves and recovered recently through the efforts of a young man, Thomas Swift, son of Barton Swift, our fellow-townsman, of Shopton." At that moment the auctioneer, Jacob Wood, caught sight of Tom in the press, and, looking directly at the lad, continued:

"I understand that young Mr. Swift is here today, and I hope he intends to bid on this boat. If he does, the bidding will be lively, for Tom Swift is a lively young man. I wish I could say that some of the men who stole the boat were here today."

The auctioneer paused and there were some murmurs from those in the throng as to why such a wish should be uttered. Tom felt some one moving near him, and, looking around, he saw the same man with whom he had come in contact before. The person seemed desirous of getting out on the edge of the crowd, and Tom felt a return of his vague suspicions. He looked closely at the fellow, but could trace no resemblance to any of the men who had so daringly stolen his father's model.

"The reason I wish they were here today," went on Mr. Wood, "is that the men did some slight damage to the boat, and if they were here today we would make them pay for it. However, the damage is slight and can easily be repaired. I mention that, as Mr. Hastings desired me to. Now we will proceed with the bidding, and I will say that an opportunity will first be given all to examine the boat. Perhaps Tom Swift will give us his opinion on the state it is in as we know he is well qualified to talk about machinery."

All eyes were turned on Tom, for many knew him.

"Humph! I guess I know as much about boats and motors as he does," sneered Andy Foger. "He isn't the only one in this crowd! Why didn't the auctioneer ask me?"

"Keep quiet," begged Sam Snedecker. "People are laughing at you, Andy."

"I don't care if they are," muttered the sandy haired youth. "Tom Swift needn't think he's everything."

"If you will come down to the dock," went on the auctioneer, "you can all see the boat, and I would be glad to have young Mr. Swift give us the benefit of his advice."

The throng trooped down to the lake, and, blushing somewhat, Tom told what was the matter with the motor and how it could be fixed. It was noticed that there was less enthusiasm over the matter than there had been, for certainly the engine, rusty and out of order as it was, did not present an attractive sight. Tom noted that the man, who had acted so strangely, did not come down to the dock.

"Guess he can't be much interested in the motor," decided Tom.

"Now then, if it's all the same to you folks, I'll proceed with the auction here," went on Mr. Wood. "You can all see the boat from here. It is, as you see, a regular family launch and will carry twelve persons comfortably. With a canopy fitted to it a person could cruise all about the lake and stay out over night, for you could sleep on the seat cushions. It is twenty-one feet in length and has a five-and-a-half-foot beam, the design being what is known as a compromise stern. The motor is a double-cylinder two-cycle one, of ten horsepower. It has a float-feed carburetor, mechanical oiler, and the ignition system is the jump-spark— the best for this style of motor. The boat will make ten miles an hour, with twelve in, and, of course, more than that with a lighter load. A good deal will depend on the way the motor is managed.

"Now, as you know, Mr. Hastings wishes to dispose of the boat partly because he does not wish to repair it and partly because he has a newer and larger one. The craft, which is named *Carlopa* by the way, cost originally nine hundred dollars. It could not be purchased new to day, in many places, for a thousand. Now what am I offered in its present condition? Will any one make an offer? Will you give me five hundred dollars?"

The auctioneer paused and looked critically at the throng. Several persons smiled. Tom looked worried. He had no idea that the price would start so high.

"Well, perhaps that is a bit stiff," went on Mr. Wood. "Shall we say four hundred dollars? Come now, I'm sure it's worth four hundred. Who'll start it at four hundred?"

No one would, and the auctioneer descended to three hundred, then to two and finally, as if impatient, he called out:

"Well, will any one start at fifty dollars?"

Instantly there were several cries of "I will!"

"I thought you would," went on the auctioneer. "Now we will get down to work. I'm offered fifty dollars for this twenty-one foot, ten horsepower family launch. Will any one make it sixty?"

"Sixty!" called out Andy Foger in a shrill voice. Several turned to look at him.

"I didn't know he was going to bid," thought Tom. "He may go above me. He's got plenty of money, and, while I have too, I'm not going to pay too much for a damaged boat."

"Sixty I'm bid, sixty—sixty!" cried Mr. Wood in a sing-song tone, "who'll make it seventy?"

"Sixty-five!" spoke a quiet voice at Tom's elbow, and he turned to see the mysterious man who had joined the crowd at the edge of the lake.

"Sixty-five from the gentleman in the white straw hat!" called Mr. Wood with a smile at his wit, for there were many men wearing white straw hats, the day being a warm one in June.

"Here, who's bidding above me?" exclaimed Andy, as if it was against the law.

"I guess you'll find a number going ahead of you, my young friend," remarked the auctioneer. "Will you have the goodness not to interrupt me, except when you want to bid?"

"Well, I offered sixty," said the squint-eyed bully, while his crony, Sam Snedecker, was vainly, pulling at his sleeve.

"I know you did, and this gentleman went above you. If you want to bid more you can do so. I'm offered sixty-five, sixty-five I'm offered for this boat. Will any one make it seventy-five?"

Mr. Wood looked at Tom, and our hero, thinking it was time for him to make a bid, offered seventy. "Seventy from Tom Swift!" cried the auctioneer. "There is a lad who knows a motor-boat from stem to stern, if those are the right words. I don't know much about boats except what I'm told, but Tom Swift does. Now, if he bids, you people ought to know that it's all right. I'm bid seventy—seventy I'm bid. Will any one make it eighty?"

"Eighty!" exclaimed Andy Foger after a whispered conference with Sam. "I know as much about boats as Tom Swift. I'll make it eighty."

"No side remarks. I'll do most of the talking. You just bid, young man," remarked Mr. Wood. "I have eighty bid for this boat— eighty dollars. Why, my friends, I can't understand this. I ought to have it up to three hundred dollars, at least. But I thank you all the same. We are coming on. I'm bid eighty—"

"Ninety!" exclaimed the quiet man at Tom's elbow. He was continually fingering his upper lip, as though he had a mustache there, but his face was clean-shaven. He looked around nervously as he spoke.

"Ninety!" called out the auctioneer.

"Ninety-five!" returned Tom. Andy Foger scowled at him, but the young inventor only smiled. It was evident that the bully did not relish being bid against. He and his crony whispered together again.

"One hundred!" called Andy, as if no one would dare go above that.

"I'm offered an even hundred," resumed Mr. Wood. "We are certainly coming on. A hundred I am bid, a hundred—a hundred—a hundred—"

"And five," said the strange man hastily, and he seemed to choke as he uttered the words.

"Oh, come now; we ought to have at least ten-dollar bids from now on," suggested Mr. Wood. "Won't you make it a hundred and ten?" The auctioneer looked directly at the man, who seemed to shrink back into the crowd. He shook his head, cast a sort of despairing look at the boat and hurried away.

"That's queer," murmured Tom. "I guess that was his limit, yet if he wanted the boat badly that wasn't a high price."

"Who's going ahead of me?" demanded Andy in loud tones.

"Keep quiet!" urged Sam. "We may get it yet."

"Yes, don't make so many remarks," counseled the auctioneer. "I'm bid a hundred and five. Will any one make it a hundred and twenty-five?"

Tom wondered why the man bad not remained to see if his bid was accepted, for no one raised it at once, but he hurried off and did not look back. Tom took a sudden resolve.

"A hundred and twenty-five!" he called out.

"That's what I like to hear," exclaimed Mr. Wood. "Now we are doing business. A hundred and twenty-five from Tom Swift. Will any one offer me fifty?"

Andy and Sam seemed to be having some dispute.

"Let's make him quit right now," suggested Andy in a hoarse whisper.

"You can't," declared Sam.

"Yes, I can. I'll go up to my limit right now."

"And some one will go above you—-maybe Tom will," was Sam's retort.

"I don't believe he can afford to," Andy came back with. "I'm going to call his bluffs. I believe he's only bidding to make others think he wants it. I don't believe he'll buy it."

Tom heard what was said, but did not reply. The auctioneer was calling monotonously: "I'm bid a hundred and twenty-five—twenty-five. Will any one make it fifty?"

"A hundred and fifty!" sang out Andy, and all eyes were directed toward him.

"Sixty!" said Tom quietly.

"Here, you—" began the red-haired lad. You—"

"That will do!" exclaimed the auctioneer sternly. "I am offered a hundred and sixty. Now who will give me an advance? I want to get the boat up to two hundred, and then the real bidding will begin."

Tom's heart sank. He hoped it would be some time before a two hundred dollar offer would be heard. As for Andy Foger, he was almost speechless with rage. He shook off the restraining arm of Sam, and, worming his way to the front of the throng, exclaimed:

"I'll give a hundred and seventy-five dollars for that boat!"

"Good!" cried the auctioneer. "That's the way to talk. I'm offered a hundred and seventy-five."

"Eighty," said Tom quietly, though his heart was beating fast.

"Well, of all—" began Andy, but Sam Snedecker dragged him back.

"You haven't got any more money," said the bully's crony. "Better stop now."

"I will not! I'm going home for more," declared Andy. "I must have that boat."

"It will be sold when you get back," said Sam.

"Haven't you got any money you can lend me?" inquired the squint-eyed one, scowling in Tom's direction.

"No, not a bit. There, some one raised Tom's bid."

At that moment a man in the crowd offered a hundred and eighty-one dollars.

"Small amounts thankfully received," said Mr. Wood with a laugh. Then the bidding became lively, a number making one-dollar advances.

The price got up to one hundred and ninety-five dollars and there it hung for several minutes, despite the eloquence of Mr. Wood, who tried by all his persuasive powers to get a substantial advance. But every one seemed afraid to bid. As for the young inventor, he was in a quandary. He could only offer five dollars more, and, if he bid it in a lump, some one might go to two hundred and five, and he would not get the boat. He wished he had secured permission from his father to go higher, yet he knew that as a fair proposition two hundred dollars was about all the motor-boat in its present condition was worth, at least to him. Then he made a sudden resolve. He thought he might as well have the suspense over.

"Two hundred dollars!" he called boldly.

"I'm offered two hundred!" repeated Mr. Wood. "That is something like it. Now who will raise that?"

There was a moment of silence. Then the auctioneer swung into an enthusiastic description of the boat. He begged for an advance, but none was made, though Tom's heart seemed in his throat, so afraid was he that he would not get the *Carlopa*.

"Two hundred—two hundred!" droned on Mr. Wood. "I am offered two hundred. Will any of you go any higher?" He paused a moment, and Tom's heart beat harder than ever. "If not," resumed the speaker, "I will declare the bidding closed. Are you all done? Once—twice—three times. Two hundred dollars. Going—going—gone!" He clapped his hands. "The boat is sold to Thomas Swift for two hundred dollars. If he'll step up I'll take his money."

There was a laugh as Tom, blushingly, advanced. He passed Andy Foger, who had worked his way over near him.

"You got the boat," sneered the bully, "and I s'pose you think you got ahead of me."

"Keep quiet!" begged Sam.

"I won't!" exclaimed Andy. "He outbid me just out of spite, and I'll get even with him. You see if I don't!"

Tom looked Andy Foger straight in the eyes, but did not answer, and the red-haired youth turned aside, followed by his crony, and started toward his automobile.

"I congratulate you on your bargain," said Mr. Wood as Tom proceeded to make out a check. He gave little thought to the threat Andy Foger had made, but the time was coming when he was to remember it well.

CHAPTER III

A TIMELY WARNING

"Well, are you satisfied with your bargain, Tom?" asked Mr. Wood when the formalities about transferring the ownership of the motor-boat had been completed.

"Oh, yes, I calculated to pay just what I did."

"I'm glad you're satisfied, for Mr. Hastings told me to be sure the purchaser was satisfied. Here he comes now. I guess he wasn't at the auction."

An elderly gentleman was approaching Mr. Wood and Tom. Most of the throng was dispersing, but the young inventor noticed that Andy Foger and Sam Snedecker stood to one side, regarding him closely.

"So you got my boat," remarked the former owner of the craft. "I hope you will be able to fix it up."

"Oh, I think I shall," answered the new owner of the *Carlopa*. "If I can't, father will help me."

"Yes, you have an advantage there. Are you going to keep the same name?" and Mr. Hastings seemed quite interested in what answer the lad would make.

"I think not," replied Tom. "It's a good name, but I want something that tells more what a fast boat it is, for I'm going to make some changes that will increase the speed."

"That's a good idea. Call it the Swift."

"Folks would say I was stuck up if I did that," retorted the youth quickly. "I think I shall call it the *Arrow*. That's a good, short name, and—"

"It's certainly speedy," interrupted Mr. Hastings. "Well now, since you're not going to use the name *Carlopa*, would you mind if I took it for my new boat? I have a fancy for it."

"Not in the least," said Tom. "Don't you want the letters from each side of the bow to put on your new craft?"

"It's very kind of you to offer them, and, since you will have no need for them, I'll be glad to take them off."

"Come down to my boat," invited Tom, using the word "my" with a proper pride, "and I'll take off the brass letters. I have a screw driver in my motor-cycle tool bag."

As the former and present owners of the *Arrow* (which is the name by which I shall hereafter designate Tom's motor-boat) walked down toward the dock where it was moored the young inventor gave a startled cry.

"What's the matter?" asked Mr. Hastings.

"That man! See him at my motor-boat?" cried Tom. He pointed to the craft in the lake. A man was in the cockpit and seemed to be doing something to the forward bulkhead, which closed off the compartment holding the gasoline tank.

"Who is he?" asked Mr. Hastings, while Tom started on a run toward the boat.

"I don't know. Some man who bid on the boat at the auction, but who didn't go high enough," answered the lad. As he neared the craft the man sprang out, ran along the lakeshore for a short distance and then disappeared amid the bushes which bordered the estate of Mr. Hastings. Tom hurriedly entered the *Arrow*.

"Did he do any damage?" asked Mr. Hastings.

"I guess he didn't have time," responded Tom. "But he was tampering with the lock on the door of the forward compartment. What's in there?"

"Nothing but the gasoline tank. I keep the bulkhead sliding door locked on general principles. I can't imagine what the fellow would want to open it for. There's nothing of value in there. Perhaps he isn't right in his head. Was he a tramp?"

"No, he was well dressed but he seemed very nervous during the auction, as if he was disappointed not to have secured the boat. Yet what could he want in that compartment? Have you the key to the lock, Mr. Hastings?"

"Yes, it belongs to you now, Mr. Swift," and the former owner handed it to Tom, who quickly unlocked the compartment. He slid back the door and peered within, but all he saw was the big galvanized tank.

"Nothing in there he could want," commented the former owner of the craft.

"No," agreed Tom in a low voice. "I don't see what he wanted to open the door for." But the time was to come, and not far off, when Tom was to discover quite a mystery connected with the forward compartment of his boat, and the solution of it was fated to bring him into no little danger.

"It certainly is odd," went on Mr. Hastings when, after Tom had secured the screw driver from his motor-cycle tool bag, he aided the lad in removing the letters from the bow of the boat "Are you sure you don't know the man?"

"No, I never saw him before. At first I thought his voice sounded like one of the members of the Happy Harry gang, but when I looked squarely at him I could not see a bit of resemblance.

Besides, that gang would not venture again into this neighborhood."

"No, I imagine not. Perhaps he was only a curious, meddlesome person. I have frequently been bothered by such individuals. They want to see all the working parts of an automobile or motor-boat, and they don't care what damage they do by investigating."

Tom did not reply, but he was pretty certain that the man in question had more of an object than mere curiosity in tampering with the boat. However, he could discover no solution just then, and he proceeded with the work of taking off the letters.

"What are you going to do with your boat, now that you have it?" asked Mr. Hastings. "Can you run it down to your dock in the condition in which it is now?"

"No, I shall have to go back home, get some tools and fix up the motor. It will take half a day, at least. I will come back this afternoon and, have the boat at my house by night. That is if I may leave it at your dock here."

"Certainly, as long as you like."

The young inventor had many things to think about as he rode toward home, and though he was somewhat puzzled over the actions of the stranger, he forgot about that in anticipating the pleasure he would have when the motor-boat was in running order.

"I'll take dad off on a cruise about the lake," he decided. "He needs a rest, for he's been working hard and worrying over the theft of the turbine motor model. I'll take Ned Newton for some rides, too, and he can bring his camera along and get a lot of pictures. Oh, I'll have some jolly sport this summer!"

Tom was riding swiftly along a quiet country road and was approaching a steep hill, which he could not see until he was close to it, owing to a sharp turn.

As he was about to swing around it and coast swiftly down the steep declivity he was startled by hearing a voice calling to him from the bushes at the side of the road.

"Hold on, dar I Hold on, Mistah Swift!" cried a colored man, suddenly popping into view. "Doan't go down dat hill."

"Why, it's Eradicate Sampson!" exclaimed Tom, quickly shutting off the power and applying the brakes. "What's the matter, Rad? Why shouldn't I go down that hill?"

"Beca'se, Mistah Swift, dere's a pow'ful monstrous tree trunk right across de road at a place whar yo' cain't see it till yo' gits right on top ob it. Ef yo' done hit dat ar tree on yo' lickity-split machine, yo' suah would land in kingdom come. Doan't go down dat hill!"

Tom leaped off his machine and approached the colored man.

Eradicate Sampson did odd jobs in the neighborhood of Shopton, and more than once Tom had done him favors in repairing his lawn mower or his wood-sawing machine. In turn Eradicate had given Tom a valuable clue as to the hiding place of the model thieves.

"How'd the log get across the road, Rad?" asked Tom.

"I dunno, Mistah Swift. I see it when I come along wid mah mule, Boomerang, an' I tried t' git it outer de way, but I couldn't. Den I left Boomerang an' mah wagon at de foot ob de hill an' I come up heah t' git a long pole t' pry de log outer de way. I didn't t'ink nobody would come along, case dis road ain't much trabeled."

"I took it for a short cut," said the lad. "Come on, let's take a look at the log."

Leaving his machine at the top of the slope, the young inventor accompanied the colored man down the hill. At the foot of it, well hidden from sight of any one who might come riding down, was a big log. It was all the way across the road.

"That never fell there," exclaimed Tom in some excitement. "That never rolled off a load of logs, even if there had been one along, which there wasn't. That log was put there!"

"Does yo' t'ink dat, Mistah Swift?" asked Eradicate, his eyes getting big.

"I certainly do, and, if you hadn't warned me, I might have been killed."

"Oh, I heard yo' lickity-split machine chug-chuggin' along when I were in de bushes, lookin' for a pryin' pole, an' I hurried out to warn yo. I knowed I could leave Boomerang safe, case he's asleep."

"I'm glad you did warn me," went on the youth solemnly. Then, as he went closer to the log, he uttered an exclamation.

"That has been dragged here by an automobile!" he cried. "It's been done on purpose to injure some one. Come on, Rad, let's see if we can't find out who did it."

Something on the ground caught Tom's eye. He stooped and picked up a nickle-plated wrench.

"This may come in handy as evidence," he murmured.

CHAPTER IV

TOM AND ANDY CLASH

Even a casual observer could have told that an auto had had some part in dragging the log to the place where it blockaded the road. In the dust were many marks of the big rubber tires and even the imprint of a rope, which had been used to tow the tree trunk.

"What fo' yo' t'ink any one put dat log dere?" asked the colored man as he followed Tom. Boomerang, the mule, so called because Eradicate said you never could tell what he was going to do, opened his eyes lazily and closed them again. "I don't know why, Rad, unless they wanted to wreck an automobile or a wagon. Maybe tramps did it for spite."

"Maybe some one done it to make yo' hab trouble, Mistah Swift."

"No, I hardly think so. I don't know of any one who would want to make trouble for me, and how would they know I was coming this way—"

Tom suddenly checked himself. The memory of the scene at the auction came back to him and he recalled what Andy Foger had said about "getting even."

"Which way did dat auto go?" resumed Eradicate.

"It came from down the road," answered Tom, not completing the sentence he had left unfinished. "They dragged the log up to the foot of the hill and left it. Then the auto went down this way." It was comparatively easy, for a lad of such sharp observation as was Tom, to trace the movements of the vehicle.

"Den if it's down heah, maybe we cotche 'm," suggested the colored man.

The young inventor did not answer at once. He was hurrying along, his eyes on the telltale marks. He had proceeded some distance from the place where the log was when he uttered a cry. At the same moment he hurried from the road toward a thick clump of bushes that were in the ditch alongside of the highway. Reaching them, he parted the leaves and called:

"Here's the auto, Rad!"

The colored man ran up, his eyes wider open than ever. There, hidden amid the bushes, was a large touring car.

"Whose am dat?" asked Eradicate.

Tom did not answer. He penetrated the underbrush, noting where the broken branches had been bent upright after the forced entrance of the car, the better to hide it. The young inventor was, seeking some clue to discover the owner of the machine. To this end he climbed up in the tonneau and was looking about when some one burst in through the screen of bushes and a voice cried: "Here, you get out of my car!"

"Oh, is it your car, Andy Foger?" asked Tom calmly as he recognized his squint-eyed rival. "I was just beginning to think it was. Allow me to return your wrench," and he held out the one he had picked up near the log. "The next time you drag trees across the road," went on the lad in the tonneau, facing the angry and dismayed Andy, "I'd advise you to post a notice at the top of the hill, so persons riding down will not be injured." "Notice—road—hill—logs!" stammered Andy, turning red under his freckles.

"That's what I said," replied Tom coolly.

"I—I didn't have anything to do with putting a log across any road," mumbled the bully. "I—I've been off toward the creek."

"Have you?" asked Tom with a peculiar smile.

"I thought you might have been looking for the wrench you dropped near the log. You should be more careful and so should Sam Snedecker, who's hiding outside the bushes," went on our hero, for he had caught sight of the form of Andy's crony. "I—I told him not to do it!" exclaimed Sam as he came from his hiding place.

"Shut up!" exclaimed Andy desperately.

"Oh, I think I know your secret," continued the young inventor. "You wanted to get even with me for outbidding you on the motor-boat. You watched which road I took, and then, in your auto, you came a shorter way, ahead of me. You hauled the log across the foot of the hill, hoping, I suppose, that my machine would be broken. But, let me tell you, it was a risky trick. Not only might I have been killed, but so would whoever else who happened to drive down the slope over the log, whether in a wagon or automobile. Fortunately Eradicate discovered it in time and warned me. I ought to have you arrested, but you're not worth it. A good thrashing is what such sneaks as you deserve!"

"You haven't got any evidence against us," sneered Andy confidently, his old bravado coming back.

"I have all I want," replied Tom. "You needn't worry. I'm not going to tell the police. But you've got to do one thing or I'll make you sorry you ever tried this trick. Eradicate will help me, to don't think you're going to escape."

"You get out of my automobile!" demanded Andy. "I'll have you arrested if you don't."

"I'll get out because I'm ready to, but not on account of your threats," retorted Mr. Swift's son. "Here's your wrench. Now I want you and Sam to start up this machine and haul that log out of the way."

"S'pose I won't do it?" snapped Andy.

"Then I'll cause your arrest, besides thrashing you into the bargain! You can take your choice of removing the log so travelers can pass or having a good hiding, you and Sam. Eradicate, you take Sam and I'll tackle Andy."

"Don't you dare touch me!" cried the bully, but there was a whine in his tones.

"You let me alone or I'll tell my father!" added Sam. "I—I didn't have nothin' to do with it, anyhow. I told Andy it would make trouble, but he made me help him."

"Say, what's the matter with you?" demanded Andy indignantly of his crony. "Do you want to—"

"I wish I'd never come with you," went on Sam, who was beginning to be frightened.

"Come now. Start up that machine and haul the log out of the way," demanded Tom again.

"I won't do it!" retorted the red-haired lad impudently.

"Yes, you will," insisted our hero, and he took a step toward the bully. They were out of the clump of bushes now and in the roadside ditch. "You let me alone," almost screamed Andy, and in his baffled rage he rushed at Tom, aiming a blow.

The young inventor quickly stepped to one side, and, as the bully passed him, Tom sent out a neat left-hander. Andy Foger went down in a heap on the grass.

CHAPTER V

A TEST OF SPEED

Whether Tom or Andy was the most surprised at the happening would be hard to say. The former had not meant to hit so hard and he certainly did not intend to knock the squint-eyed youth down. The latter's fall was due, as much as anything, to his senseless, rushing tactics and to the fact that he slipped on the green grass. The bully was up in a moment, however, but he knew better than to try conclusions with Tom again. Instead he stood out of reach and spluttered:

"You just wait, Tom Swift! You just wait!"

"Well, I'm waiting," responded the other calmly.

"I'll get even with you," went on Andy. "You think you're smart because you got ahead of me, but I'll get square!"

"Look here!" burst out the young inventor determinedly, taking a step toward his antagonist, at which Andy quickly retreated, "I don't want any more of that talk from you, Andy Foger. That's twice you've made threats against me today. You put that log across the road, and if you try anything like it for your second attempt I'll make you wish you hadn't. That applies to you, too, Sam," he added, glancing at the other lad.

"I—I ain't gone' to do nothin'," declared Sam.

"I told Andy not to put that tree—"

"Keep still, can't you!" shouted the bully. "Come on. We'll get even with him, that's all," he muttered as he went back into the bushes where the auto was. Andy cranked up and he and his crony getting into the car were about to start off.

"Hold on!" cried Tom. "You'll take that log from across the road or I'll have you arrested for obstructing traffic, and that's a serious offense."

"I'm goin' to take it away!" growled Andy. "Give a fellow a show can't you?"

He cast an ugly look at Tom, but the latter only smiled. It was no easy task for Sam and Andy to pull the log out of the way, as they could hardly lift it to slip the rope under. But they finally managed it, and, by the power of the car, hauled it to one side. Then they speed off.

"I 'clar t' gracious, dem young fellers am most as mean an' contrary as mah mule Boomerang am sometimes," observed Eradicate. "Only Boomerang ain't quite so mean as dat."

"I should hope not, Rad," observed Tom. "I'm ever so much obliged for your warning. I guess I'll be getting, home now. Come around next week; we have some work for you."

"'Deed an' I will," replied the colored man. "I'll come around an' eradicate all de dirt on yo' place, Mistah Swift. Yais, sah, I's Eradicate by name, and dat's my perfession—eradicatin' dirt. Much obleeged, I'll call around. Giddap, Boomerang!"

The mule lazily flicked his ears, but did not stir, and Tom, knowing the process of arousing the animal would take some time, hurried up the hill to where he had left his motor-cycle. Eradicate was still engaged on the task of trying to arouse his steed to a sense of its duty when the young inventor flashed by on his way home.

"So now you own a broken motor-boat," observed Mr. Swift when Tom had related the circumstances of the auction. "Well, now you have it, what are you going to do with it?"

"Fix it, first of all," replied his son. "It needs considerable tinkering up, but nothing but what I can do, if you'll help me."

"Of course I will. Do you think you can get any speed out of it?"

"Well, I'm not so anxious for speed. I wart a good, comfortable boat, and the *Arrow* will be that. I've named it, you see. I'm going back to Lanton this afternoon, take some tools along, and repair it so I can run the boat over to here. Then I'll get at it and fix it up. I've got a plan for you, dad."

"What is it?" asked the inventor, his rather tired face lighting up with interest.

"I'm going to take you on a vacation trip."

"A vacation trip?"

"Yes, you need a rest. You've been working, too hard over that gyroscope invention."

"Yes, Tom, I think I have," admitted Mr. Swift. "But I am very much interested in it, and I think I can get it to work. If I do it will make a great difference in the control of aeroplanes. It will make them more stable able to fly in almost any wind. But I certainly have puzzled my brains over some features of it. However, I don't quite see what you mean."

"You need a rest, dad," said Mr. Swift's son kindly. "I want you to forget all about patents, invention, machinery and even the gyroscope for a week or two. When I get my motor-boat in shape I'm going to take you and Ned Newton up the lake for a cruise. We can camp out, or, if we had to, we could sleep in the boat. I'm going to put a canopy on it and arrange some bunks. It will do you good and perhaps new ideas for your gyroscope may come to you after a rest."

"Perhaps they will, Tom. I am certainly tired enough to need a vacation. It's very kind of you to think of me in connection with your boat. But if you're going to get it this afternoon you'd better start if you expect to get back by night. I think Mrs. Baggert has dinner ready."

After the meal Tom selected a number of tools from his, own particular machine shop and carried them down to the dock on the lake, where his two small boats were tied.

"Aren't you going back on your motor-cycle" asked his father. "No, Dad, I'm going to row over to Lanton, and, if I can get the *Arrow* fixed, I'll tow my rowboat back."

"Very well, then you won't be in any danger from Andy Foger. I must speak to his father about him."

"No, dad, don't," exclaimed the young inventor quickly. "I can fight my own battles with Andy. I don't fancy he will bother me again right away."

Tom found it more of a task than he had anticipated to get the motor in shape to run the *Arrow* back under her own power. The magneto was out of order and the batteries needed renewing, while the spark coil had short-circuited and took considerable time to adjust. But by using some new dry cells, which Mr. Hastings gave him, and cutting out the magneto, or small dynamo which produces the spark that exploded the gasoline in the cylinders, Tom soon had a fine, "fat" hot spark from the auxiliary ignition system. Then, adjusting the timer and throttle on the engine and seeing that the gasoline tank was filled, the lad started up his motor. Mr. Hastings helped him, but after a few turns of the flywheel there were no explosions. Finally, after the carburetor (which is the device where gasoline is mixed with air to produce an explosive mixture) had been adjusted, the motor started off as if it had intended to do so all the while and was only taking its time about it.

"The machine doesn't run as smooth as it ought to," commented Mr. Hastings. "No, it needs a thorough overhauling," agreed the owner of the *Arrow*. "I'll get at it tomorrow," and with that he swung out into the lake, towing his rowboat after him.

"A motor-boat of my own!" exulted Tom as he twirled the steering wheel and noted how readily the craft answered her helm. "This is great!"

He steered down the lake and then, turning around, went up it a mile or more before heading for his own dock, as he wanted to see how the engine behaved.

"With some changes and adjustments I can make this a speedy boat," thought Tom. "I'll get right at it. I shouldn't wonder if I could make a good showing against Mr. Hastings' new *Carlopa*, though his boat's got four cylinders and mine has but two."

The lad was proceeding leisurely along the lakeshore, near his home, with the motor throttled down to test it at low speed, when he heard some one shout. Looking toward the bank, Tom saw a man waving his hands.

"I wonder what he wants?" thought our hero as he put the wheel over to send his craft to shore. He heard a moment later, for the man on the bank cried:

"I say, my young friend, do you know anything about automobiles? Of course you do or you wouldn't be running a motor-boat. Bless my very existence, but I'm in trouble! My machine has stopped on a lonely road and I can't seem to get it started. I happened to hear your boat and I came here to hail you. Bless my coat-pockets but I am in trouble! Can you help me? Bless my soul and gizzard!"

"Mr. Damon" exclaimed Tom, shutting off the power, for he was now near shore. "Of course I'll help you, Mr. Damon," for the young inventor had recognized the eccentric man of whom he had purchased the motor-cycle and who had helped him in rounding up the thieves.

"Why, bless my shoe-laces, if it isn't Tom Swift!" exclaimed Mr. Damon, who seemed very fond of calling down blessings upon himself or upon articles of his dress or person.

"Yes, I'm here," admitted Tom with a laugh.

"And in a motor-boat, too! Bless my pocketbook, but did that run away with some one who sold it to you cheap?"

"No, not exactly," and the lad explained how he had come into possession of it. By this time he was ashore and had tied the *Arrow* to an overhanging tree. Then Tom proceeded to where Mr. Damon had left his stalled automobile. The eccentric man was wealthy and his physician had instructed him to ride about in the car for his health. Tom soon located the trouble. The carburetor had become clogged, and it was soon in working order again.

"Well, now that you have a boat, I don't suppose you will be riding about the country so much," commented Mr. Damon as he got into his car. "Bless my spark-plug! But if you ever get over to Waterfield, where I live, come and see me. It's handy to get to by water."

"I'll come some day," promised the lad.

"Bless my hat band, but I hope so," went on the eccentric individual as he prepared to start his car.

Tom completed the remainder of the trip to his house without incident and his father came down to the dock to see the motor-boat. He agreed with his son that it was a bargain and that it could easily be put in fine shape.

The youth spent all the next day and part of the following working on the craft. He overhauled the ignition system, which was the jump-spark style, cleaned the magneto and adjusted the gasoline and compression taps so that they fitted better. Then he readjusted the rudder lines, tightening them on the steering wheel, and looked over the piping from the gasoline tank.

The tank was in the forward compartment, and, upon inspecting this, the lad concluded to change the plan by which the big galvanized iron box was held in place. He took out the old wooden braces and set them closer together, putting in a few new ones.

"The tank will not vibrate so when I'm going at full speed," he explained to his father.

"Is that where the strange man was tampering with the lock the day of the auction?" asked Mr. Swift.

"Yes, but I don't see what he could want in this compartment, do you dad?"

The inventor got into the boat and looked carefully into the rather dark space where the tank fitted. He went over every inch of it, and, pointing to one of the thick wooden blocks that supported the tank, asked:

"Did you bore that hole in there, Tom?"

"No, it was there before I touched the braces. But it isn't a hole, or rather, someone bored it and stopped it up again. It doesn't weaken the brace any."

"No, I suppose not. I was just wondering weather that was one of the new blocks or an old one."

"Oh, an old one. I'm going to paint them, too, so in case the water leaks in or the gasoline leaks out the wood won't be affected. A gasoline tank should vibrate as little as possible, if you don't want it to leak. I guess I'll paint the whole interior of this compartment white, then I can see away into the far corners of it."

"I think that's a good idea," commented Mr. Swift.

It was four days after his purchase of the boat before Tom was ready to make a long trip in it. Up to that time he had gone on short spins not far from the dock, in order to test the engine adjustment. The lad found it was working very well, but he decided with a new kind of spark plugs for the two cylinders that he could get more speed out of it. Finally the forward compartment was painted and a general overhauling given the hull and Tom was ready to put, his boat to a good test.

"Come on, Ned," he said to his chum early one evening after

Mr. Swift had said he was too tired to go out on a trial run. "We'll see what the *Arrow* will do now."

From the time Tom started up the motor it was evident that the boat was going through the water at a rapid rate. For a mile or more the two lads speeded along, enjoying it hugely. Then Ned exclaimed:

"Something's coming behind us."

Tom turned his head and looked. Then he called out:

"It's Mr. Hastings in his new *Carlopa*. I wonder if he wants a race?"

"Guess he'd have it all his own way," suggested Ned.

"Oh, I don't know. I can get a little more speed out of my boat."

Tom waited until the former owner of the *Arrow* was up to him.

"Want a race?" asked Mr. Hastings good-naturedly.

"Sure!" agreed Tom, and he shoved the timer ahead to produce quicker explosions.

The *Arrow* seemed to leap forward and for a moment was ahead of the *Carlopa*, but with a motion of his hand to the spark lever Mr. Hastings also increased his speed. For a moment the two boats were on even terms and then the larger and newer one forged ahead. Tom had expected it', but he was a little disappointed.

"That's doing first rate," complimented Mr. Hastings as he passed them. "Better than I was ever able to make her do even when she was new, Tom."

This made the present owner of the *Arrow* feel somewhat consoled. He and Ned ran on for a few miles, the *Carlopa* in the meanwhile disappearing from view around a bend. Then Tom and his chum turned around and made for the Swift dock.

"She certainly is a dandy!" declared Ned. "I wish I had one like it."

"Oh, I intend that you shall have plenty of rides in this," went on his friend. "When you get your vacation, you and dad and I are going on a tour," and he explained his plan, which, it is needless to say, met with Ned's hearty approval.

Just before going to bed, some hours later, Tom decided to go down to the dock to make sure he had shut off the gasoline cock leading from the tank of his boat to the motor. It was a calm, early summer night, with a new moon giving a little light, and the lad went down to the lake in his slippers. As he neared the boathouse he heard a noise.

"Water rat," he murmured, "or maybe muskrats. I must set some traps."

As Tom entered the boathouse he started back in alarm, for a bright light flashed up, almost in his eyes.

"Who's here?" he cried, and at that moment someone sprang out of his motor-boat, scrambled into a rowing craft which the youth could dimly make out in front of the dock and began to pull away quickly.

"Hold on there!" cried the young inventor. "Who are you? What do you want? Come back here!"

The person in the coat returned no answer. With his heart doing beats over-time Tom lighted a lantern and made a hasty examination of the *Arrow*. It did not appear to have been harmed, but a glance showed that the door of the gasoline compartment had been unlocked and was open. Tom jumped down into his craft.

"Some one has been at that compartment again!" he murmured. "I wonder if it was the same man who acted so suspiciously at the auction? What can his object be, anyhow?"

The next moment he uttered an exclamation of startled surprise and picked up something from the bottom of the boat. It was a bunch of keys, with a tag attached, bearing the owner's name.

"Andy Foger!" murmured Tom. "So this is, how he was trying to get even! Maybe he started to put a hole in the tank or in my boat."

CHAPTER VI

TOWING SOME GIRLS

With a sense of anger mingled with an apprehension lest some harm should have been done to his craft, the owner of the *Arrow* went carefully over it. He could find nothing wrong. The engine was all right and all that appeared to have been accomplished by the unbidden visitor was the opening of the locked forward compartment. That this had been done by one of the many keys on Andy Foger's ring was evident.

"Now what could have been his object?" mused Tom. "I should think if he wanted to put a hole in the boat he would have done it amidships, where the water would have a better chance to come in, or perhaps he wanted to flood it with gasoline and—"

The idea of fire was in Tom's mind, and he did not finish his half-completed thought.

"That may have been it," he resumed after a hasty examination of the gasoline tank, to make sure there were no leaks in it. "To get even with me for outbidding him on the boat, Andy may have wanted to destroy the *Arrow*. Well, of all the mean tricks, that's about the limit! But wait until I see him. I've got evidence against him," and Tom looked at the key ring. "I could almost have him arrested for this."

Going outside the boathouse, Tom stood on the edge of the dock and peered into the darkness. He could hear the faint sound of someone rowing across the lake, but there was no light.

"He had one of those electric flash lanterns," decided Tom. "If I hadn't found his keys, I might have thought it was Happy Harry instead of Andy."

The young inventor went back into the house after carefully locking the boat compartment and detaching from the engine an electrical device, without which the motor in the *Arrow* could not be started.

"That will prevent them from running away with my boat, anyhow," decided Tom. "And I'll tell Garret Jackson to keep a sharp watch tonight." Jackson was the engineer at Mr. Swift's workshop.

Tom told his father of the happening and Mr. Swift was properly indignant. He wanted to go at once to see Mr. Foger and complain of Andy's act, but Tom counseled waiting.

"I'll attend to Andy myself," said the young inventor. "He's getting desperate, I guess, or he wouldn't try to set the place on fire. But wait until I show him these keys."

Bright and early the next morning the owner of the motor-boat was down to the dock inspecting it. The engineer, who had been on watch part of the night, reported that there had been no disturbance, and Tom found everything all right. "I wonder if I'd better go over and accuse Andy now or wait until I see him and spring this evidence on him?" thought our hero. Then he decided it would be better to wait. He took the *Arrow* out after breakfast, his father going on a short spin with him.

"But I must go back now and work on my gyroscope invention," said Mr. Swift when about two hours had been spent on the lake. "I am making good progress with it."

"You need a vacation," decided Tom, "I'll be ready to take you and Ned in about two weeks. He will have two weeks off then and, we'll have some glorious times together."

That afternoon Tom put some new style spark plugs in the cylinders of his motor and found that he had considerably increased the revolutions of the engine, due to a better explosion being obtained. He also made some minor adjustments and the next day he went out alone for a long run.

Heading up the lake, Tom was soon in sight of a popular excursion resort that was frequently visited by church and Sunday-school organizations in the vicinity of Shopton. The lad saw a number of rowing craft and a small motor-boat circling around opposite the resort and remarked: "There must be a picnic at the grove today. Guess I'll run up and take a look."

The lad was soon in the midst of quite a flotilla of rowboats, most of them manned by pretty girls or in charge of boys who were giving sisters (their own or some other chap's) a trip on the water. Tom throttled his boat down to slow speed and looked with pleasure on the pretty scene. His boat attracted considerable attention, for motor craft were not numerous on Lake Carlopa.

As our hero passed a boat, containing three very pretty young ladies, Tom heard one of them exclaim:

"There he is now! That's Tom Swift."

Something in the tones of the voice attracted his attention. He turned and saw a brown-eyed girl smiling at him. She bowed and asked, blushing the while:

"Well, have you caught any more runaway horses lately?"

"Runaway horses—why—what? Oh, it's Miss Nestor!" exclaimed the lad, recognizing the young lady whose steed he had frightened one day when he was on his bicycle. As told in the first volume of this series, the horse had run away, being alarmed at the flashing of Tom's wheel, and Miss Mary Nestor, of Mansburg, was in grave danger.

"So you've given up the bicycle for the motor-boat," went on the young lady.

"Yes," replied Tom with a smile, shutting off the power, "and I haven't had a chance to save any girls since I've had it."

The two boats had drifted close together, and Miss Nestor introduced her two companions to Tom.

"Don't you want to come in and take a ride?" he asked.

"Is it safe?" asked Jennie Haddon, one of the trio.

"Of course it is, Jennie, or he wouldn't be out in it," said Miss Nestor hastily. "Come on, let's get in. I'm just dying for a motor-boat ride."

"What will we do with our boat?" asked Katie Carson.

"Oh, I can tow that," replied the youth. "Get right in and I'll take you all around the lake."

"Not too far," stipulated the girl who had figured in the runaway. "We must be back for lunch, which will be served in about an hour. Our church and Sunday-school are having a picnic."

"Maybe Mr. Swift will come and have some lunch with us," suggested Miss Carson, blushing prettily.

"Nothing would give me greater pleasure," answered Tom, and then he laughed at his formal reply, the girls joining in.

"We'd be glad to have you," added Miss Haddon. "Oh!" she suddenly screamed, "the boat's tipping over!"

"Oh, no," Tom hastened to assure her, coming, to the side to help her in. "It just tilts a bit, with the weight of so many on one side. It couldn't capsize if it tried."

In another moment the three were in the roomy cockpit and Tom had made the empty rowboat fast to the stern. He was about to start up when from another boat, containing two little girls and two slightly larger boys, came a plaintive cry:

"Oh, mister, give us a ride!"

"Sure!" agreed Tom pleasantly. "Just fasten your boat to the other rowboat and I'll tow you."

One of the boys did this, and then, with three pretty girls as his companions in the *Arrow* and towing the two boats, Tom started off.

The girls were very much interested in the craft and asked all sorts of questions about how the engine operated. Tom explained as clearly as he could how the gasoline exploded in the cylinders, about the electric spark and about the propeller. Then, when he had finished, Miss Haddon remarked naively:

"Oh, Mr. Swift, you've explained it beautifully, and I'm sure if our teacher in school made things as clear as you have that I could get along fine. I understand all about it, except I don't see what makes the engine go."

"Oh," said Tom faintly, and he wondering what would be the best remark to make under the circumstances, when Miss Nestor created a diversion by looking at her watch and exclaiming:

"Oh, girls, it's lunch time! We must go ashore. Will you kindly put about, Mr. Swift—I hope that is the proper term—and—land us—is that right?" and she looked archly at Tom.

"That's perfectly right," he admitted with a laugh and a glance into the girl's brown eyes. "I'll put you ashore at once," and he headed for a small dock.

"And come yourself to take lunch with us, added Miss Haddon.

"I'm afraid I might be in the way," stammered Tom. "I—I have a pretty good appetite, and—"

"I suppose you think that girls on a picnic don't take much lunch," finished Miss Nestor. "But I assure you that we have plenty, and that you will be very welcome," she added warmly.

"Yes, and I'd like to have him explain over again how the engine works," went on Miss Haddon. "I am so interested."

Tom helped the girls out, receiving their thanks as well as those of the children in the second boat. But as he walked with the young ladies through the grove the young inventor registered a mental vow that he would steer clear of explaining again how a gasoline engine worked.

"Now come right over this way to our table," invited Miss Nestor. "I want you to meet papa and mamma."

Tom followed her. As he stepped from behind a clump of trees he saw, standing not far away, a figure that seemed strangely familiar. A moment later the figure turned and Tom saw Andy Foger confronting him. At the sight of our hero the bully turned red and walked quickly away, while Tom's fingers touched the ring of keys in his pocket.

CHAPTER VII

A BRUSH WITH ANDY

So unexpected was his encounter with Andy that the young inventor hardly knew how to act, especially since he was a guest of the young ladies. Tom did not want to do or say anything to embarrass them or make a scene, yet he did want to have a talk, and a very serious talk, with Andy Foger.

Miss Nestor must have noticed Tom's sudden start at his glimpse of Andy, for she asked: "Did you see some one you knew, Mr. Swift?"

"Yes," replied Tom, "I did—er—that is—" He paused in some confusion.

"Perhaps you'd like—-that is prefer—to go with them instead of taking lunch with girls who don't know anything about engines?" she persisted.

"Oh, no indeed," Tom hastened to assure her. "He—that is—the person I saw wouldn't care to have me lunch with him," and the youth smiled grimly.

"Would you like to bring him over to our table?" inquired Miss Carson. "We have plenty for him."

"No, I think that would hardly do," continued the lad, who tried not to smile at the picture of the red-haired and squint-eyed Andy Foger making one of a party with the girls. The young ladies fortunately had not noticed the bully, who was out of view by this time.

Tom was presented to Mr. and Mrs. Nestor, who told him how glad they were to meet the young man who had been instrumental in saving their daughter from injury, if not death. Tom was a bit embarrassed, but bore the praise as well as he could, and he was very glad when a diversion, in the shape of lunch, occurred.

After a meal on tables under the trees in the grove Tom took the girls and some of their friends out in his motor-boat again. They covered several miles around the lake before returning to the picnic ground.

As Tom was starting toward home in his boat, wondering what had become of Andy and trying to think of a reason why the bully should attend anything as "tame" as a church picnic, the object of his thoughts came strolling through the trees down to the shore of the lake. The moment he saw Tom the red-haired lad started back, but the young inventor, leaping out of his boat, called out:

"Hold on there, Andy Foger, I want to see you!" and there was menace in Tom's tone.

"But, I don't want to see you!" retorted the other sulkily. "I've got no use for you."

"No more have I for you," was Tom's quick reply. "But I want to return you these keys. You dropped them in my boat the other night when you tried to set it afire. If I ever catch you—"

"My keys! Your boat! On fire!" gasped Andy, so plainly astonished that Tom knew his surprise was genuine.

"Yes, your keys. You were a little, too quick for me or I'd have caught you at it. The next time you pick a lock don't leave your keys behind you," and he held out the jingling ring.

Andy Foger advanced slowly. He took the bunch of keys and looked at the tag.

"They are mine," he said slowly, as if there was some doubt about it.

"Of course they are," declared Tom. "I found them where you dropped them—in my boat."

"Do you mean over at the auction?"

"No, I mean down in my boathouse, where you sneaked in the other night and tried to do some damage.

"The other night!" cried Andy. "I never was near your boathouse any night and I never lost my keys there! I lost these the day of the auction, on Mr. Hastings' ground, and I've been looking for them ever since."

"Didn't you sneak in my boathouse the other night and try to do some mischief? Didn't you drop them then?"

"No, I didn't," retorted Andy earnestly. "I lost those keys at the auction, and I can prove it to you. Look, I advertised for them in the weekly Gazette."

The red-haired lad pulled a crumpled paper from his pocket and showed Tom an advertisement offering a reward of two dollars for a bunch of keys on a ring, supposed to have been lost at the auction on Mr. Hastings' grounds in Lanton. The finder was to return them to Andy Foger.

"Does that look as if I lost the keys in your boathouse?" demanded the bully sneeringly. "I wouldn't have advertised them that way if I' been trying to keep my visit quiet. Besides, I can prove that I was out of town several nights. I was over to an entertainment in Mansburg one night and I didn't get home until two o'clock in the morning, because my machine broke down. Ask Ned Newton. He saw me at the entertainment."

Andy's manner was so earnest that Tom could not help believing him. Then there was the evidence of the advertisement. Clearly the squint-eyed youth had not been the mysterious visitor to the boathouse and had not unlocked the forward compartment. But if it was not he, who could it have been and how did the keys get there? These were questions which racked Tom's brain.

"You can ask Ned Newton," repeated Andy. "He'll prove that I couldn't have been near your place, if you don't believe me."

"Oh, I believe you all right," answered Tom, for there could be no doubting Andy's manner, even though he and the young inventor were not on good terms. "But how did your keys get in my boat?"

"I don't know, unless you found them, kept them and dropped them there," was the insolent answer.

"You know better than that," exclaimed Tom.

"Well, I owe you a reward of two dollars for giving them back to me," continued the bully patronizingly. "Here it is," and he hauled out some bills.

"I don't want your money!" fired back Tom.

"But I'd like to know who it was that was in my boat."

"And I'd like to know who it was took my keys," and Andy stuffed the money back in his pocket. Tom did not answer. He was puzzling over a queer matter and he wanted to be alone and think. He turned aside from the red-haired lad and walked toward his motor-boat.

"I'll give you a surprise in a few days," Andy called after him, but Tom did not turn his head nor did he inquire what the surprise might be.

Mr. Swift was somewhat puzzled when his son related the outcome of the key incident. He agreed with Tom that some one might have found the ring and kept it, and that the same person might have been the one whom Tom had surprised in the boathouse.

"But it's idle to speculate on it," commented the inventor. "Andy might have induced some of his chums to act for him in harming your boat, and the key advertisement might have been only a ruse."

"I hardly think so," answered his son, shaking his head. "It strikes me as being very curious, and I'm going to see if I can't get at the bottom of it."

But a week or more passed and Tom had no clue. In the meanwhile he was working away at his motor-boat, installing several improvements.

One of these was a better pump, which circulated the water around the cylinders, and another was a new system of lubrication under forced feed.

"This ought to give me a little more speed," reasoned Tom, who was not yet satisfied with his craft. "Guess I'll take it out for a spin."

He was alone in the *Arrow*, taking a long course up the lake when, as he passed a wooded point that concealed from view a sort of bay, he heard the puffing of another motor-boat.

"Maybe that's Mr. Hastings," thought Tom. "If I raced with him now, I think the *Arrow* could give a better account of herself."

The young inventor looked at the boat as it came into view. It needed but a glance to show that it was not the *Carlopa*. Then, as it came nearer, Tom saw a familiar figure in it—a red-haired, squint-eyed chap.

"Andy Foger!" exclaimed Tom. "He's got a motor-boat! This is the surprise he spoke of."

The boat was rapidly approaching him, and he saw that it was painted a vivid red. Then he could make out the name on the bow, *Red Stread*. Andy was sending the craft toward him at a fast rate.

"You needn't think you're the only one on this lake who has a gasoline boat!" called Andy boastfully. "This is my new one and the fastest thing afloat around here. I can go all around you. Do you want to race?"

It was a "dare," and Tom never took such things when he could reasonably enter a contest. He swung his boat around so as to shoot alongside of Andy and answered:

"Yes, I'll race you. Where to?"

"Down opposite Kolb's dock and back to this point," was the answer. "I'll give you a start, as my engine has three cylinders. This is a racing boat."

"I don't need any start," declared Tom. "I'll race you on even terms. Go ahead!"

Both lads adjusted their timers to get more speed. The water began to curl away from the sharp prows, the motors exploded faster and faster. The race was on between the *Arrow* and the *Red Streak*.

CHAPTER VIII

OFF ON A TRIP

Glancing with critical eyes at the craft of his rival, Tom saw that Andy Foger had a very fine boat. The young inventor also realized that if he was to come anywhere near winning the race he would have to get the utmost speed out of his engine, for the new boat the bully had was designed primarily, for racing, while Tom's was an all-around pleasure craft, though capable of something in the speed line.

"I'll be giving you a tow in a few minutes, as soon as my engine gets warmed up!" sneered Andy.

"Maybe," said Tom, and then he crouched down to make as little resistance as possible to the wind. Andy, on the contrary, sat boldly upright at the auto steering wheel of his boat.

On rushed the two motor craft, their prows exactly even and the propellers tossing up a bulge in the water at their sterns. Rapidly acquiring speed after the two lads had adjusted the timers on their motors, the boats were racing side by side, seemingly on even terms.

The *Red Streak* had a very sharp prow, designed to cut through the water. It was of the type known as an automobile launch. That is, the engine was located forward, under a sort of hood, which had two hinged covers like a bat's wings. The steering-wheel shaft went through the forward bulkhead, slantingly, like the wheel of an auto, and was arranged with gasoline and sparking levers on the center post in a similar manner. At the right of the wheel was a reversing lever, by which the propeller blades could be set at neutral, or arranged so as to drive the boat backward. Altogether the *Red Streak* was a very fine boat and had cost considerably more than had Tom's, even when the latter was new. All these things the young owner of the *Arrow* thought of as he steered his craft over the course.

"I hardly think I can win," Tom remarked to himself in a whisper. "His boat is too speedy for this one. I have a chance, though, for his engine is new, and I don't believe he understands it as well as I do mine. Then, too, I am sure I have a better ignition system."

But if Tom had any immediate hopes of defeating Andy, they were doomed to disappointment, for about two minutes after the race started the *Red Streak* forged slowly ahead.

"Come on!" cried the red-haired lad. "I thought you wanted a race."

"I do," answered the young inventor. "We're a long way from the dock yet, and we've got to come back."

"You'll be out of it by the time I get to the dock," declared Andy.

Indeed it began to look so, for the auto boat was now a full length ahead of Tom's craft and there was open water between them. But our hero knew a thing or two about racing, though he had not long been a motor-boat owner. He adjusted the automatic oiler on the cylinders to give more lubrication, as he intended to get more speed out of his engine. Then he opened the gasoline cock a trifle more and set his timer forward a few notches to get an earlier spark. He was not going to use the maximum speed just yet, but he first wanted to see how the motor of the *Arrow* would behave under these conditions. To his delight he saw his boat slowly creeping up on Andy's. The latter, with a glance over his shoulder, saw it too, and he advanced his spark. His craft forged ahead, but the rate of increase was not equal to Tom's. "If I can keep up to him I suppose I ought to be glad," thought the young inventor, "for his boat is away ahead of mine in rating."

Through the water the sharp bows cut. There were only a few witnesses to the race, but those who were out in boats saw a pretty sight as the two speedy craft came on toward the dock, which was the turning point.

Andy's boat reached it first, and swung about in a wide circle for the return. Tom decided it was time to make his boat do its best, so he set the timer at the limit, and the spark, coming more quickly, increased the explosions.

Up shot the *Arrow* and, straightening out after the turn, Tom's craft crept along until it lapped the stern of the *Red Streak*. Andy looked back in dismay. Then he tried to get more speed out of his engine. He did cause the screw to revolve a little faster, and Tom noted that he was again being left behind. Then one of those things, which may happen at any time to a gasoline motor, happened to Andy's. It began to miss explosions. At first it was only occasionally, then the misses became more frequent.

The owner of the *Red Streak* with one hand on the steering wheel, tried with the other to adjust the motor to get rid of the trouble, but he only made it worse. Andy's boat began to fall back and Tom's to creep up. Frantically Andy worked the gasoline and sparking levers, but without avail. At last one cylinder went completely out of service.

The two boats were now on even terms and were racing along side by side toward the wooded, point, which marked the finish.

"I'll beat you yet!" exclaimed Andy fiercely.

"Better hurry up!" retorted Tom.

But the young inventor was not to have it all his own way. With a freakishness equal to that with which it had ceased to explode the dead cylinder came to life again, and the *Red Streak* shot ahead. Once more Andy's boat had the lead of a length and the finish of the race was close at hand. The squint-eyed lad turned and shouted: "I told you I'd beat you! Want a tow now?"

It began to look as though Tom would need it, but he still had something in reserve. One of the improvements he had put in the *Arrow* was a new auxiliary ignition system. This he now decided to use.

With a quick motion Tom threw over the switch that put it into operation. A hotter, "fatter" spark was at once produced, and adjusting his gasoline cock so that a little more of the fluid would be drawn in, making a "richer" mixture, the owner of the *Arrow* saw the craft shoot forward as if, like some weary runner, new life had been infused.

In vain did Andy frantically try to get more speed out of his motor. He cut out the muffler, and the explosions sounded loudly over the lake. But it was no use. A minute later the *Arrow*, which had slowly forged ahead, crossed the bows of the *Red Streak* opposite the finishing point, and Tom had won the race.

"Well, was that fair?" our hero called to Andy, who had quickly shut off some of his power as he saw his rival's daring trick. "Did I beat you fair?"

"You wouldn't have beaten me if my engine hadn't gone back on me," grumbled Andy, chagrin showing on his face. "Wait until my motor runs smoother and I'll give you a big handicap and beat you. My boat's faster than yours. It ought to be. It cost fifteen hundred dollars and it's a racer."

"I guess it doesn't like racing," commented Tom as he swung the prow of his craft down the lake toward his home. But he knew there was some truth in what Andy had said. The *Red Streak* was a more speedy boat, and, with proper handling, could have beaten the *Arrow*. That was where Tom's superior knowledge came in useful. "Just you wait, I'll beat you yet," called Andy, after the young inventor, but the latter made no answer. He was satisfied.

Mr. Swift was much interested that night in his son's account of the race.

"I had no idea yours was such a speedy boat," he said.

"Well, it wasn't originally," admitted Tom, "but the improvements I put on it made it so. But, dad, when are we going on our tour? You look more worn out than I've seen you in some time, not excepting when the turbine model was stolen. Are you worrying over your gyroscope invention?"

"Somewhat, Tom. I can't seem to hit on just what I want. It's a difficult problem."

"Then I tell you what let's do, dad. Let's drop everything in the inventive line and go off on a vacation. I'll take you up the lake in my boat and you can spend a week at the Lakeview Hotel at Sandport. It will do you good."

"What will you do, Tom?"

"Oh, Ned Newton and I will cruise about and we'll take you along any time you want to go. We're going to camp out nights or sleep in the boat if it rains. I've ordered a canopy with side curtains. Ned and I don't care for the hotel life in the summer. Will you go?"

Mr. Swift considered a moment. He did need a rest, for he had been working hard and his brain was weary with thinking of many problems. His son's program sounded very attractive.

"I think I will accept," said the inventor with a smile. "When can you start, Tom?"

"In about four days. Ned Newton, will get his vacation then and I'll have the canopy on. I'll start to work at it tomorrow. Then we'll go on a trip."

Sandport was a summer resort at the extreme southern end of Lake Carlopa, and Mr. Swift at once wrote to the Lakeview Hotel there to engage a room for himself. In the meanwhile Tom began to put the canopy on his boat and arrange for the trip, which would take nearly a whole day. Ned Newton was delighted with the prospect of a camping tour and helped Tom to get ready. They took a small tent and plenty of supplies, with some food. They did not need to carry many rations, as the shores of the lake were lined with towns and villages where food could be procured.

Finally all was ready for the trip and the night before the start Ned Newton stayed at Tom's house so as to be in readiness for going off early in the morning. The day was all that could be desired, Tom noted, as he and his chum hurried down to the dock before breakfast to put their blankets in the boat. As the young inventor entered the craft he uttered an exclamation.

"What's the matter?" asked Ned.

"I was sure I locked the sliding door of that forward compartment," was the reply. "Now it's open." He looked inside the space occupied by the gasoline tank and cried out: "One of the braces is gone! There's been some one at my boat in the night and they tried to damage her."

"Much harm done?" asked Ned anxiously.

"No, none at all, to speak of," replied Tom. "I can easily put a new block under the tank. In fact, I don't really need all I have. But why should any one take one out, and who did it? That's what I want to know."

The two lads looked carefully about the dock and boat for a sign of the missing block or any clues that might show who had been tampering with the *Arrow*, but they could find nothing.

"Maybe the block fell out," suggested Ned.

"It couldn't," replied Tom. "It was one of the new ones I put in myself and it was nailed fast. You can see where it's been pried loose. I can't, understand it," and Tom thought rapidly of several mysterious occurrences of late in which the strange man at the auction and the person he had surprised one night in the boathouse had a part.

"Well, it needn't delay our trip," resumed the young inventor. "Maybe there's a hoodoo around here, and it will do us good to get away a few days. Come on, we'll have breakfast, get dad and start."

A little later the *Arrow* was puffing away up the lake in the direction of Sandport.

CHAPTER IX

MR. SWIFT IS ALARMED

"Don't you feel better already, dad?" asked Tom that noon as they stopped under a leaning, overhanging tree for lunch on the shore of the lake. "I'll leave it to Ned if you don't look more contented and less worried."

"I believe he does," agreed the other lad. "Well, I must say I certainly have enjoyed the outing so far," admitted the inventor with a smile. "And I haven't been bothering about my gyroscope. I think I'll take another sandwich, Tom, and a few more olives."

"That's the way to talk!" cried the son. "Your appetite is improving, too. If Mrs. Baggert could see you she'd say so."

"Oh, yes, Mrs. Baggert. I do hope she and Garret will look after the house and shops well," said Mr. Swift, and the old, worried look came like a shadow over his face.

"Now don't be thinking of that, dad," advised Tom, "Of course everything will be all right. Do you think some of those model thieves will return and try to get some of your other inventions?"

"I don't know, Tom. Those men were unscrupulous scoundrels, and you can never tell what they might do to revenge themselves on us for defeating their plans."

"Well, I guess Garret and Mrs. Baggert will look out for them," remarked his son. "Don't worry."

"Yes, it's bad for the digestion," added Ned. "If you don't mind, Tom, I'll have some more coffee and another sandwich myself."

"Nothing the matter with your appetite, either," commented the young inventor as he passed the coffee pot and the plate.

They were soon on their way again, the *Arrow* making good time up the lake. Tom was at the engine, making several minor adjustments to it, while Ned steered. Mr. Swift reclined on one of the cushioned seats under the shade of the canopy. The young owner of the *Arrow* looked over the stretch of water from time to time for a possible sight of Andy Foger, but the *Red Streak* was not to be seen. The Lakeview Hotel was reached late that afternoon and the boat was tied up to the dock, while Tom and Ned accompanied Mr. Swift to see him comfortably established in his room.

"Won't you stay to supper with me?" invited the inventor to his son and the latter's chum. "Or do you want to start right in on camp life?"

"I guess we'll stay to supper and remain at the hotel tonight," decided Tom. "We got here a little later than I expected, and Ned and I hardly have time to go very far and establish a temporary camp. We'll live a life of luxurious ease tonight and begin to be 'wanderlusters' and get back to nature tomorrow."

In the morning Tom and his chum, full of enthusiasm for the pleasures before them, started off, promising to come back to the hotel in a few days to see how Mr. Swift felt. The trip had already done the man good and his face wore a brighter look.

Tom and Ned, in the speedy *Arrow*, cruised along the lake-shores all that morning. At noon they, went ashore, made a temporary camp and arranged to spend the night there in the tent. After this was erected they got out their fishing tackle and passed the afternoon at that sport, having such good luck that they provided their own supper without having to depend on canned stuff.

They lived this life for three days, making a new camp each night, being favored with good weather, so that they did not have to sleep in the boat to keep dry. On the afternoon of the third day Tom, with a critical glance at the sky, remarked:

"I shouldn't be surprised if it rained tomorrow, Ned."

"Me either. It does look sort of hazy, and the wind is in a bad quarter."

"Then what do you say to heading for the hotel? I fancy dad will be glad to see us." "That suits me. We can start camp life again after the storm passes."

They started for Sandport that afternoon. When within about two miles of the hotel dock Tom saw, just ahead of them, a small motor-boat. Ned observed it too and called out:

"S'pose that's Andy looking for another race?"

"No, the boat's too small for his. We'll put over that way and see who it is."

The other craft did not appear to be moving very rapidly and the *Arrow* was soon overhauling it. As the two chums came nearer they could hear the puffing of the motor. Tom listened with critical ears.

"That machine isn't working right," he remarked to his chum.

At that moment there sounded a loud explosion from the other boat and at the same time there came over the water a shrill cry of alarm. "That's a girl in that boat!" exclaimed Ned. "Maybe she's hurt."

"No, the motor only backfired," observed Tom. "But we'll go over and see if we can help her. Perhaps she doesn't understand it. Girls don't know much about machinery."

A little later the *Arrow* shot up alongside the other craft, which had come to a stop. The two lads could see a girl bending over the motor, twirling the flywheel and trying to get it started. "Can I help you?" asked Tom, shutting off the power from his craft.

The young lady glanced up. Her face was red and she seemed ill at ease. At the sight of the young inventor she uttered an exclamation of relief.

"Why, Mr. Swift!" she cried. "Oh, I'm in such trouble. I can't make the machine work, and I'm afraid it's broken; it exploded."

"Miss Nestor!" blurted out Tom, more surprised evidently to see his acquaintance of the runaway again than she was at beholding him. "I didn't know you ran a motor-boat," he added. "I don't," said she simply and helplessly. "That's the trouble, it won't run."

"How comes it that you are up here?" went on Tom.

"I am stopping with friends, who have a cottage near the Lakeview Hotel. They have a motor-boat and I got Dick Blythe—he's the owner of this—to show me how to run it. I thought I knew, and I started out a little while ago. At first it went beautifully, but a few minutes ago it blew up, or—or something dreadful happened."

"Nothing very dreadful, I guess," Tom assured her. "I think I can fix it." He got into the other boat and soon saw what the trouble was. The carburetor had gotten out of adjustment and the gasoline was not feeding properly. The young inventor soon had it in order, and, testing the motor, found that it worked perfectly.

"Oh, I can't thank you enough," cried Miss Nestor with a flash from her brown eyes that made Tom's heart beat double time. "I was afraid I had damaged the boat, and I knew Dick, who is a sort of second cousin of mine, would never forgive me."

"There's no harm done," Tom assured her. "But you had better keep near us on your way back, that is, if you are going back."

"Oh, indeed I am. I was frightened when I found I'd come so far away from shore, and then, when that explosion took place—well, you can imagine how I felt. Indeed I will keep near you. Are you stopping near here? If you are, I wish you'd come and see me, you and Mr. Newton" she added, for Tom had introduced his chum.

"I'll be very glad to," answered our hero, and he told how he happened to be in the neighborhood. "I'll give you a few lessons in managing a boat, if you like," he added.

"Oh, will you? That will be lovely! I won't tell Dick about it, and I'll surprise him some day by showing him how well I can run his boat."

"Good idea," commented Tom.

He started the motor for Miss Nestor, having stopped it after his first test, and then, with the *Dor*, which was the name of the small boat Miss Nestor was in, following the larger *Arrow*, the run back to the hotel was made. The young lady turned off near the Lakeview dock to go to the cottage where she was stopping and the lads tied up at the hotel boathouse.

"Yes, we are in for a storm," remarked Tom as he and his chum walked up toward the hotel. "I wonder how dad is? I hope the outing is doing him good."

"There he comes now," observed Ned, and, looking up, Tom saw his father approaching. The young inventor was at once struck by the expression on his parent's face. Mr. Swift looked worried and Tom anxiously hastened forward to meet him.

"What's the matter dad?" he asked as cheerfully as he could. "Have you been figuring over that gyroscope problem again, against my express orders?" and he laughed a little.

"No, Tom, it's not the gyroscope that's worrying me."

"What is it then?"

"Those scoundrels are around again, Tom!" and Mr. Swift looked apprehensively about him.

"You mean the men who stole the turbine model?"

"Yes. I was walking in the woods near the hotel yesterday and I saw Anson Morse. He did not see me, for I turned aside as quickly as I had a glimpse of him. He was talking to another man."

"What sort of a man?"

"Well, an ordinary enough individual, but I noticed that he had tattooed on the little finger of his left hand a blue ring."

"Happy Harry, the tramp!" exclaimed Tom. "What can he and Morse be doing here?"

"I don't know, Tom, but I'm worried. I wish I was back home. I'm afraid something may happen to some of my inventions. I want to go back to Shopton, Tom."

"Nonsense, dad. Don't worry just because you saw some of your former enemies. Everything is all right at home. Mrs. Baggert and Garret Jackson will look after things. But, if you like, I, can find out for you how matters are."

"How, Tom?"

"By taking a run down there in my motor-boat. I can do it tomorrow and get back by night, if I start early. Then you will not worry."

"All right, Tom; I wish you would. Come up to my room and we will talk it over. I'd rather leave you go than telephone, as I don't like to talk of my business over the wire if I can avoid it."

CHAPTER X

A CRY FOR HELP

"Now, dad, tell me all about it," requested Tom when he and Ned were in Mr. Swift's apartment at the hotel, safe from the rain that was falling. "How did you happen to see Anson Morse and Happy Harry?" My old readers will doubtless remember that the latter was the disguised tramp who was so vindictive toward Tom, while Morse was the man who endeavored to sneak in Mr. Swift's shop and steal a valuable invention.

"Well, Tom," proceeded the inventor, "there isn't much to tell. I was out walking in the woods yesterday, and when I was behind a clump of bushes I heard voices. I looked out and there I saw the two men."

"At first I thought they were trailing me, but I saw that they had not seen me, and I didn't see how they could know I was in the neighborhood. So I quietly made my way back to the hotel."

"Could you hear what they were saying?"

"Not all, but they seemed angry over something. The man with the blue ring on his finger asked the other man whether Murdock had been heard from."

"Who is Murdock?"

"I don't know, unless he is another member of the gang or unless that is an assumed name."

"It may be that. What else did you hear?"

"The man we know as Morse replied that he hadn't heard from him, but that he suspected Murdock was playing a double game. Then the tramp—Happy Harry—asked this question: 'Have you any clue to the sparkler?' And Morse answered: 'No, but I think Murdock has hid it somewhere and is trying to get away with it without giving us our share.' Then the two men walked away, and I came back to the hotel," finished Mr. Swift.

"Sparkler," murmured Tom. "I wonder what that can be?"

"That's a slang word for diamonds," suggested Ned.

"So it is. In that case, dad, I think we have nothing to worry about. Those fellows must be going to commit a diamond robbery or perhaps it has already taken place."

The inventor seemed relieved at this theory of his son. His face brightened and he said: "If they are going to commit a robbery, Tom, we ought to notify the police."

"But if they said that 'Murdock,' whoever he is, had the sparkler and was trying to get away with it without giving them their share, wouldn't that indicate that the robbery had already taken place?" asked Ned.

"That's so," agreed Tom. "But it won't do any harm to tell the hotel detective that suspicious characters are around, no matter if the has been committed. Then he can be on the lookout. But I don't think we have anything to worry about, dad. Still, if you like, I'll take a run down to the house to see that everything is all right, though I'm sure it will be found that we have nothing to be alarmed over."

"Well, I will be more relieved if you do," said the inventor, "However, suppose we have a good supper now and you boys can stay at the hotel tonight. Then you and Ned can start off early in the morning."

"All right," agreed Tom, but there was a thoughtful look on his face and he appeared to be planning something that needed careful attention to details.

After supper that night Tom took his chum to one side and asked: "Would you mind very much if you didn't make the trip to Shopton with me?"

"No, Tom, of course not, if it will help you any. Do you want me to stay here?"

"I think it will be a good plan. I don't like to leave dad alone if those scoundrels are around. Of course he's able to look after himself, but sometimes he gets absent minded from thinking too much about his inventions."

"Of course I'll stay here at the hotel. This is just as good a vacation as I could wish."

"Oh, I don't mean all the while. Just a day or so—until I come back. I may be here again by tomorrow night and find that my father is needlessly alarmed. Then something may have happened at home and I would be delayed. If I should be, I'd feel better to know that you were here."

"Then I'll stay, and if I see any of those men—"

"You'd better steer clear of them," advised Tom quickly. "They are dangerous customers."

"All right. Then I'll go over and give Miss Nestor lessons on how to run a motor-boat," was the smiling response. "I fancy, with what she and I know, we can make out pretty well."

"Hold on there!" cried Tom gaily. "No trespassing, you know."

"Oh, I'll just say I'm your agent," promised Ned with a grin. "You can't object to that."

"No, I s'pose not. Well, do the best you can. She is certainly a nice girl."

"Yes, but you do seem to turn up at most opportune times. Luck is certainly with you where she is concerned. First you save her in a runaway—"

"After I start the runaway," interrupted Tom.

"Then you take her for a ride in your motor-boat, and, lastly, you come to her relief when she is stalled in the middle of the lake. Oh you certainly are a lucky dog!"

"Never mind, I'm giving you a show. Now let's get to bed early, as I want to get a good start."

Tom awoke to find a nasty, drizzling rainstorm in progress, and the lake was almost hidden from view by a swirling fog. Still he was not to be daunted from his trip to Shopton by the weather, and, after a substantial breakfast, he bade his father and Ned good-by and started off in the *Arrow*.

The canopy he had provided was an efficient protection against the rain, a celluloid window in the forward hanging curtains affording him a view so that he could steer.

Through the mist puffed the boat, the motor being throttled down to medium speed, for Tom was not as familiar with the lake as he would like to have been, and he did not want to run aground or into another craft.

He was thinking over what his father had told him about the presence of the men and vainly wondering what might be their reference to the "sparkler." His thoughts also dwelt on the curious removal of the bracing block from under the gasoline tank of his boat.

"I shouldn't be surprised but what Andy Foger did that," he mused. "Some day he and I will have a grand fight, and then maybe he'll let me alone. Well, I've got other things to think about now. The hotel detective can keep a lookout for the men around the hotel, after the, warning I gave him, and I'll see that all is right at home."

The fog lifted somewhat and Tom put on more speed. As he was steering the boat along near shore he heard, off to the woods at his right, the report of a gun. It came so suddenly that he jumped involuntarily. A moment later there sounded, plainly through the damp air, a cry for help.

"Some one's hurt—shot" cried the youth aloud.

He turned the boat in toward the bank. As he shut off the power from the motor he heard the cry again:

"Help! Help! Help!"

"I must go ashore!" he exclaimed. "Probably some one is badly wounded by a gun."

He paused for a moment as the fear came to him that it might be some of the patent thieves. Then, dismissing that idea as the *Arrow*'s prow touched the gravel, Tom sprang out, drew the boat up a little way, fastened the rope to a tree and hurried off into the dripping woods in the direction of the voice that was calling for aid.

CHAPTER XI

A QUICK RUN

"Where are you?" cried Tom. "Are you hurt? Where are you?"

Uttering these words after he had hurried into the woods a short distance, the young inventor paused for an answer. At first he could hear nothing but the drip of water from the branches of the trees; then, as he listened intently, he became aware of a groan not far away.

"Where are you?" cried the lad again. "I've come to help you. Where are you?"

He had lost what little fear he had had at first, that it might be one of the unscrupulous gang, and came to the conclusion that he might safely offer to help.

Once more the groan sounded and it was followed by a faint voice speaking:

"Here I am, under the big oak tree. Oh, whoever you are, help me quickly! I'm bleeding to death!"

With the sound of the voice to guide him, Tom swung around. The appeal had come from the left and, looking in that direction, he saw, through the mist, a large oak tree. Leaping over the underbrush toward it he caught sight of the wounded man at its foot. Beside him lay a gun and there was a wound in the man's right arm.

"Who shot you?" cried Tom, hurrying to the side of the man. "Was it some of those patent thieves?" Then, realizing that a stranger would know nothing of the men who had stolen the model, Tom prepared to change the form of his question. But, before he had an opportunity to do this, the man, whose eyes were closed, opened them, and, as he got a better sight of his face, Tom uttered a cry.

"Why, it's Mr. Duncan!" exclaimed the lad. He had recognized the rich hunter, whom he had first met in the woods that spring shortly after Happy Harry, the tramp, had disabled Tom's motorcycle. "Mr. Duncan," the young inventor repeated, "how did you get shot?"

"Is that you, Tom Swift?" asked the gunner. "Help me, please. I must stop this bleeding in my arm. I'll tell you about it afterward. Wind something around it tight—your handkerchief will do."

The man sighed weakly and his eyes closed again. The lad saw the blood spurting from an ugly wound.

"I must make a tourniquet," the youth exclaimed. "That will

check the bleeding until I can get him to a doctor."

With Tom to think was to act. He took out his knife and cut off Mr. Duncan's sleeves below the injury, slashing through coat and shirts. Then he saw that part of a charge of shot had torn away some of the large muscular development of the upper arm. The hunter seemed to have fainted and the youth worked quickly. Tying his handkerchief above the wound and inserting a small stone under the cloth, so that the pebble would press on the main artery, Tom put a stick in the handkerchief and began to twist it. This had the effect of tightening the linen around the arm, and in a few seconds the lad was glad to see that the blood had stopped spurting out with every beat of the heart. Giving the tourniquet a few more twists to completely stop the flow of blood, Tom fastened the stick-lever in place by a bit of string.

"That's—that's better," murmured Mr. Duncan. "Now if you can go for a doctor—" He had to pause for breath.

"I'll not leave you here alone while I go for a doctor," declared Tom. "I have my motor-boat on the lake. Do you think I could get you down to it and take you home?"

"Perhaps—maybe. I'll be stronger in a moment, now that the bleeding has stopped. But not—not home—frighten my wife. Take me to the sanitarium if you can—sanitarium up the lake, a few miles from here."

The unfortunate man, who had tried to sit upright, had to lean back against the tree again. Tom understood what he meant in spite of the broken sentences. Mr. Duncan did not want to be taken home in the condition he was then in, for fear of alarming his wife. He wanted to be taken to the sanitarium, and Tom knew where this was, a well-known resort for the treatment of various diseases and surgical cases. It was about five miles away and on the opposite shore of the lake.

"Water—a drink!" murmured Mr. Duncan.

Seeing that his patient would be all right, for a few minutes at least, Tom hurried to his motor-boat, got a cup and, filling it with water from a jug he carried, he hastened with it to the hunter. The fluid revived the man wonderfully and now that the bleeding had almost completely stopped, Mr. Duncan was much stronger.

"Do you think you can get to the boat, if I help you?" asked Tom.

"Yes, I believe so. To think of meeting you again, and under such circumstances! It is providential."

"Did someone shoot you?" inquired Tom, who could not get out of his head the notion of the men who had once assaulted him.

"No, I shot myself," answered Mr. Duncan as he got to his feet with Tom's help. "I was out with my gun, practicing just as I was that day when I met you in the woods. I stooped down to crawl under a bush and the weapon went off, the muzzle being close against my arm. I can't understand how it happened. I fell down and called for help. Then I guess I must have fainted, but I came to when I heard you talking to me. I shouldn't have come out today as it is so wet, but I had some new shot shells I wished to try in order to test them before the hunting season. But if I can get to the sanitarium, I will be well taken care of. I know one of the doctors there."

With Tom leading him and acting as a sort of support, the journey to the motor-boat was slowly made. Making as comfortable a bed as possible out of the seat cushions, Tom assisted Mr. Duncan to it, and then starting the engine he sent his boat out from shore at half speed, as the fog was still thick and he did not want to run upon a rock.

"Do you know where the sanitarium is?" asked the wounded hunter.

"About," answered Tom a little doubtfully, "but I'm afraid it's going to be hard to locate it in this fog."

"There's a compass in my coat pocket," said Mr. Duncan. "Take it out and I'll tell you how to steer. You ought to carry a compass if you're going to be a sailor."

Tom was beginning to think so himself and wondered that he had not thought of it before. He found the one the hunter had, and placing it on the seat near him, he carefully listened to the wounded man's directions. Tom easily comprehended and soon had the boat headed in the proper direction. After that it was comparatively easy to keep on the right course, even in the fog.

But there was another danger, however, and this was that he might run into another boat. True, there were not many on Lake Carlopa, but there were some, and one of the few motor-boats might be out in spite of the bad weather.

"Guess I'll not run at full speed," decided Tom. "I wouldn't like to crash into the *Red Streak*. We'd both sink."

So he did not run his motor at the limit and sat at the steering-wheel, peering ahead into the fog for the first sight of another craft.

He turned to look at Mr. Duncan and was alarmed at the pallor of his face. The man's eyes were closed and he was breathing in a peculiar manner.

"Mr. Duncan," cried Tom, "are you worse?"

There was no answer. Leaving the helm for a moment, Tom bent over the injured hunter. A glance showed him what had happened. The tourniquet had slipped and the wound was bleeding again. Tom quickly shut off the motor, so that he might give his whole attention to the work of tightening the handkerchief. But something seemed to be wrong. No matter how tightly he twisted the stick the blood did not stop flowing. The lad was frightened. In a short time the man would bleed to death.

"I've got to get him to the sanitarium in record time!" exclaimed Tom. "Fog or no fog, I've got to run at full speed! I've got to chance it!"

Making the bandage as tight as he could and fastening it in place, the young inventor sprang to the motor and set it in motion. Then he went to the wheel. In a few minutes the *Arrow* was speeding through the water as it had never done before, except when it had raced the *Red Streak*. "If I hit anything—good-by!" thought Tom grimly. His hands were tense on the rim of the steering-wheel and he was ready in an instant to reverse the motor as he sat there straining his eyes to see through the curtain of mist that hung over the lake. Now and then he glanced at the compass, to keep on the right course, and from time to time he looked at Mr. Duncan. The hunter was still unconscious.

How Tom accomplished that trip he hardly remembered afterward. Through the fog he shot, expecting any moment to crash into some other boat. He did pass a rowing craft in which sat a lone fisherman. The lad was upon him in an instant, but a turn of the wheel sent the *Arrow* safely past, and the startled fisherman, whose frail craft was set to rocking violently by the swell from the motor-boat, sent an objecting cry through the fog after Tom. But the youth did not reply. On and on he raced, getting the last atom of power from his motor.

He feared Mr. Duncan would be dead when he arrived, but when he saw the dock of the sanitarium looming up out of the mist and shut off the power to slowly run up to it, he placed his hand on the wounded man's heart and found it still beating.

"He's alive, anyhow," thought the youth, and then his craft bumped up against the bulkhead and a man in the boathouse on the dock was sent on the run for a physician.

Mr. Duncan was quickly taken up to the sanitarium on a stretcher and Tom followed.

"You must have made a record run," observed one of the physicians a little while afterward, when Tom was telling of his trip while waiting in the office to hear the report on the hunter's condition.

"I guess I did," muttered the young inventor "only I didn't think so at the time. It seemed as if we were only crawling along."

CHAPTER XII

SUSPICIOUS CHARACTERS

Under the skill of the physicians at the lake sanitarium Mr. Duncan's wound was quickly attended to and the bleeding, which Tom had partly checked, was completely stopped. Some medicines having been administered, the hunter regained a little of his strength, and, about an hour after he had been brought to the resort, he was able to see Tom, who, at his request, was admitted to his room. The young inventor found Mr. Duncan propped up in bed, with his injured arm bandaged.

"Is the injury a bad one?" asked Tom, entering softly.

"Not as bad as I feared," replied the hunter, while a trained nurse placed a chair for the lad at the bedside. "If it had not been for you, though, I'm afraid to think of what might have happened."

"I am glad I chanced to be going past when you called," replied the lad.

"Well, you can imagine how thankful I am," resumed Mr. Duncan. "I'll thank you more properly at another time. I hope I didn't delay you on your trip."

"It's not of much consequence," responded the youth. "I was only going to see that everything was all right at our house," and he explained about his father being at the hotel and mentioned his worriment. "I will go on now unless I can do something more for you," resumed Tom. "I will probably stay at our house all night tonight instead of trying to get back to Sandport."

"I'd like to send word to my wife about what has happened," said the hunter. "If it would not be too much out of your way, I'd appreciate it if you could stop at my home in Waterford and tell her, so she will not be alarmed at my absence."

"I'll do it," replied our hero. "There is no special need of my hurrying. I have brought your gun and compass up from the boat. They are down in the office."

"Will you do me a favor?" asked Mr. Duncan quickly.

"Of course."

"Then please accept that gun and compass with my compliments. They are both of excellent make, and I don't think I shall use that gun this season. My wife would be superstitious about it. As for the compass, you'll need one in this fog, and I can recommend mine as being accurate."

"Oh, I couldn't think of taking them," expostulated Tom, but his eyes sparkled in anticipation, for he had been wishing for a gun such as Mr. Duncan owned. He also needed a compass.

"If you don't take them I shall feel very much offended," the hunter said, "and the nurse here will tell you that sick persons ought to be humored. Hadn't they?" and he appealed to the pretty young woman, who was smiling at Tom.

"That's perfectly true," she said, showing her white, even teeth. "I think, Mr. Swift, I shall have to order you to take them."

"All right," agreed Tom, "only it's too much for what I did."

"It isn't half enough," remarked Mr. Duncan solemnly. "Just explain matters to my wife, if you will, and tell her the doctor says I can be out in about a week. But I'm not going hunting or practicing shots again."

A little later Tom, with the compass before him to guide him on his course through the fog, was speeding his boat toward Waterford. Now and then he glanced at the fine shotgun which he had so unexpectedly acquired.

"This will come in dandy this fall!" he exclaimed. "I'll go hunting quail and partridge as well as wild ducks. This compass is just what I need, too."

Mrs. Duncan was at first very much alarmed when Tom started to tell her of the accident, but she soon calmed down as the lad went more into details and stated how comparatively out of danger her husband now was. The hunter's wife insisted that Tom remain to dinner, and as he had made up his mind he would have to devote two days instead of one to the trip to his house, he consented.

The fog lifted that afternoon, and Tom, rejoicing in the sunlight, which drove away the storm clouds, speeded up the *Arrow* until she was skimming over the lake like a shaft from a bow.

"This is something like," he exclaimed. "I'll soon be at home, find everything all right and telephone to dad. Then I'll sleep in my own room and start back in the morning."

When Tom was within a few miles of his own boathouse he heard behind him the "put-put" of a motor craft. Turning, he saw the *Red Streak* fairly flying along at some distance from him.

"Andy certainly is getting the speed out of her now," he remarked. "He'd beat me if we were racing, but the trouble with his boat and engine is that he can't always depend on it. I guess he doesn't understand how to run it. I wonder if he'll offer to race now?"

But the red-haired owner of the auto boat evidently did not intend to offer Tom a race. The *Red Streak* went on down the lake, passing the *Arrow* about half a mile away. Then the young inventor saw that Andy had two other lads in the boat with him.

"Sam Snedecker and Pete Bailey, I guess," he murmured. "Well, they're a trio pretty much alike. The farther off they are the better I like it."

Tom once more gave his attention to his own boat. He was going at a fair speed, but not the limit, and he counted on reaching home in about a half hour. Suddenly, when he was just congratulating himself on the smooth-running qualities of his motor, which had not missed an explosion, the machinery stopped.

"Hello!" exclaimed the young inventor in some alarm. "What's up now?"

He quickly shut off the gasoline and went back to the motor. Now there are so many things that may happen to a gasoline engine that it would be difficult to name them all offhand, and Tom, who had not had very much experience, was at a loss to find what had stopped his machinery. He tried the spark and found that by touching the wire to the top of the cylinder, when the proper connection was, made, that he had a hot, "fat one." The compression seemed all right and the supply pipe from the gasoline tank was in perfect order. Still the motor would not go. No explosion resulted when he turned the flywheel over, not even when he primed the cylinder by putting a little gasoline in through the cocks on the cylinder heads.

"That's funny," he remarked to himself as he rested from his labors and contemplated the "dead" motor. "First time it has gone back on me." The boat was drifting down the lake, and, at the sound of another motor craft approaching, Tom looked up. He saw the *Red Streak*, containing Andy Foger and his cronies. They had observed the young inventor's plight.

"Want a tow?" sneered Andy.

"What'll you take for your second-hand boat that won't run?" asked Pete Bailey.

"Better get out of the way or you might be run down," added Sam Snedecker.

Tom was too angry and chagrined to reply, and the *Red Streak* swept on.

"I'll make her go, if it takes all night!" declared Tom energetically. Once more he tried to start the motor. It coughed and sighed, as if in protest, but would not explode. Then Tom cried: "The spark plug! That's where the trouble is, I'll wager. Why didn't I think of it before?"

It was the work of but a minute to unscrew the spark plugs from the tops of the cylinders. He found that both had such accumulations of carbon on them that no spark could ever have reached the mixture of gasoline and air.

"I'll put new ones in," he decided, for he carried a few spare plugs for emergencies. Inside of five minutes, with the new plugs in place, the motor was running better than before.

"Now for home!" cried Tom, "and if I meet Andy Foger I'll race him this time."

But the *Red Streak* was not in sight, and, a little later, Tom had run the *Arrow* into the boathouse, locked the door and was on his way up to the mansion.

"I suppose Mrs. Baggert and Garret will be surprised to see me," he remarked. "Maybe they'll think we don't trust them, by coming back in this fashion to see that everything is safe. But then, I suppose, dad is naturally nervous about some of his valuable machinery and inventions. I think I'll find everything all right, though."

As Tom went up the main path and swung off to a side one, which was a short cut to the house, he saw in the dusk, for it was now early evening, a movement in the bushes that lined the walk.

"Hello, Garret!" exclaimed the lad, taking it for granted it was the engineer employed by Mr. Swift.

There was no reply, and Tom, with a sudden suspicion, sprang toward the bushes. The shrubbery was more violently agitated and, as the lad reached the screen of foliage, he saw a man spring up from the ground and take to his heels.

"Here! Who are you? What do you want?" yelled Tom.

Hardly had he spoken when from behind a big apple tree another man sprung. It was light enough so that the lad could see his face, and a glimpse of it caused him to cry out:

"Happy Harry, the tramp!"

Before he could call again the two men had disappeared.

CHAPTER XIII

TOM IN DANGER

"Garret! Garret Jackson!" cried Tom as he struggled through the hedge of bushes and ran after the men. "Where are you, Garret? Come on and help me chase these men!"

But there came no answer to Tom's hail. He could not hear the sound of the retreating footsteps of the men now and concluded that they had made their escape. Still he would not give up, but dashed on, slipping and stumbling, now and then colliding with a tree.

"What can they be doing here?" thought Tom in great anxiety. "Are they after some more of dad's inventions because they didn't get his turbine motor?"

"Hello! Who's there? Who are you?" called a voice suddenly.

"Oh, Garret! Where have you been?" asked the young inventor, recognizing the tones of his father's keeper. "I've been calling you. Some of those scoundrels are around again!"

"Why if it isn't Tom!" ejaculated the engineer. "However in the world did you get here? I thought you were at Sandport."

"I'll explain later, Garret. Just now I want to catch those men, if I can."

"Which men?"

"Happy Harry and another one. I saw them hiding down by the orchard path. Come on, they're right ahead of us."

But though they hunted as well as they were able to in the fast-gathering darkness, there was no trace of the intruders. They had to give up, and Tom, after going to the boathouse to see that the *Arrow* was all right, returned to the house, where he told the engineer and housekeeper what had brought him back and how he had surprised the two men.

"Is everything all right, Garret?" he concluded. "Dad is nervous and frightened. I must telephone him at the hotel tonight and let him know, for I promised to come back. I can't, though, until tomorrow."

"Everything is all right as far as I know," answered Jackson. "I've kept a careful watch and the burglar alarm has been in working order. Mrs. Baggert and I haven't been disturbed a single night since you went away. It's curious that the men should be here the very night you come back. Maybe they followed you."

"I hardly think so, for they didn't know I was coming."

"You can't tell what those fellows know," commented the engineer. "But, anyhow, I don't suppose they could have gotten here from Sandport as soon as you did."

"Oh, yes they could, in their automobile," declared Tom. "But I don't believe they knew I was coming. They knew we were away, however, and thought it would be a good time to steal something, I guess. Are you sure nothing has been taken?"

"Perfectly sure, but you and I will take a look around the shop."

They made a hasty examination, but found nothing disturbed and no signs that anyone had tried to break in.

"I think I'll telephone dad that everything is all right," decided Tom. "It is as far as his inventions are concerned, and if I tell about seeing the men it will only worry him. I can explain that part better when I see him. But when I go back, Garret, you will have to be on your guard, since those men are in the neighborhood."

"I will, Tom. Don't worry."

Mr. Swift was soon informed by his son over the telephone that nothing in the shops had been disturbed, and the inventor received the news with evident satisfaction. He requested Tom to come back to the hotel in the morning, in order that the three of them might go for a ride about the lake in the afternoon, and Tom decided to make an early start.

The night passed without incident, though Tom, who kept the gun Mr. Duncan had given him in readiness for use, got up several times, thinking he heard suspicious noises. After an early breakfast, and having once more cautioned the engineer and housekeeper to be on their guard, Tom started back in the *Arrow*. As it would not be much out of his way, the young inventor decided to cut across the lake and stop at the sanitarium, that he might inquire about Mr. Duncan. He thought he could speed the *Arrow* up sufficiently to make up for any time he might lose, and, with this in mind, he headed out toward the middle of Lake Carlopa. The engine was working splendidly with the new spark plugs, and Tom was wondering if there was any possible method of getting more revolutions out of the motor. He had about come to the conclusion that a new propeller might answer his purpose when he heard the noise of an approaching boat. He looked up quickly and exclaimed:

"Andy Foger again, and Pete and Sam are with him. It's a wonder he wouldn't go off on a trip instead of cruising around so near home. Guess he's afraid he'll get stuck."

Idly Tom watched the *Red Streak*. It was cutting through the water at a fast rate, throwing up curling foam on either side of the sharp bow. "He seems to be heading this way," mused Tom. "Well,

I'm not going to race with him today."

Nearer and nearer came the speedy craft, straight for the *Arrow*. The young inventor shifted his helm in order to get out of Andy's course, but to his surprise he saw that the red haired lad changed the direction of his own boat.

"Guess he wants to see how close he can come to me," thought our hero. "Maybe he wants to show how fast he's going."

The *Red Streak* was now so close that the features of the occupants could easily be distinguished. There were grins on the faces of Andy and his cronies.

"Get out of the way or we'll run you down!" cried the bully. "We've got the right of way."

"Don't you try anything like that!" shouted Tom in some alarm, not that he was afraid of Andy, but the *Red Streak* was getting dangerously near, and he knew Andy was not a skillful helmsman. The autoboat was now headed directly at the *Arrow* and coming on speedily. Andy was bending over the wheel and Tom had begun to turn his, in order to get well out of the way of the insolent, squint-eyed lad and his friends.

Suddenly Andy uttered a cry and leaped up.

"Look out! Look out!" he yelled. "My steering gear has broken! I can't change my course. Look out!"

The *Red Streak* was bearing right down on Tom's boat.

"Shut off your power! Reverse!" shouted Tom.

Andy seemed confused and did not know what to do. Sam Snedecker sprang to the side of his crony, but he knew even less about a motor-boat. It looked as if Tom would be run down, and he was in great danger.

But the young inventor did not lose his head. He put his wheel hard over and then, leaping to his motor, sent it full speed forward. Not a moment too soon had he acted, for an instant later the other boat shot past the stern of the *Arrow*, hitting it a severe but glancing blow. Tom's boat quivered from end to end and he quickly shut off the power. By this time Andy had succeeded in slowing down his craft. The young inventor hastily looked over the side of the *Arrow*. One of the rudder fastenings had been torn loose.

"What do you mean by running me down?" shouted Tom angrily.

"I—I didn't do it on purpose," returned Andy contritely. "I was seeing how near I could come to you when my steering gear broke. I hope I haven't damaged you."

"My rudder's broken," went on Tom "and I've got to put back to repair it. I ought to have you arrested for this!"

"I'll pay for the damage," replied Andy, and he was so frightened that he was white, in spite of his tan and freckles.

"That won't do me any good now," retorted Tom. "It will delay me a couple of hours. If you try any tricks like that again, I'll complain to the authorities and you won't be allowed to run a boat on this lake."

Andy knew that his rival was in the right and did not reply. The bully and his cronies busied themselves over the broken steering gear, and the young inventor, finding that he could make a shift to get back to his boathouse, turned his craft around and headed for there, in order to repair the damage.

CHAPTER XIV

THE *ARROW* DISAPPEARS

Paying no heed to the occupants of the bully's boat, who, by reason of their daring, had been responsible for his accident that might have resulted seriously, Tom was soon at his dock. He had it conveniently arranged for hoisting craft out of the water to repair them, and in a few minutes the stern of the *Arrow* was elevated so that he could get at the rudder.

"Well, it's not as bad as I thought," he remarked when, with critical eye, he had noted the damage done. "I can fix it in about an hour if Garret helps me."

Going up to the house to get some tools and to tell the engineer that he had returned, Tom looked out over the lake and saw Andy's boat moving slowly off.

"They've got her fixed up in some kind of shape," he murmured. "It's a shame for a chump like Andy to have a good boat like that. He'll spoil it in one season. He's getting altogether too reckless. First thing he knows, he and I will have a clash and I'll pay back some of the old scores."

Mr. Jackson was much surprised to see the young inventor home again so soon, as was also Mrs. Baggert. Tom explained what had happened, and he and the engineer went to work repairing the damage done by the *Red Streak*. As the owner of the *Arrow* had anticipated, the work did not take long, and, shortly before dinner time, the boat was ready to resume the interrupted trip to Sandport.

"Better stay and have lunch," urged Mrs. Baggert. "You can hardly get to the hotel by night, anyhow, and maybe it would be better not to start until tomorrow."

"No, I must get back tonight or dad would be worried," declared Tom. "I've been gone longer now than I calculated on. But I will have dinner here, and, if necessary, I can do the last half of the trip after dark. I know the way now and I have a compass and a good searchlight."

The *Arrow* was let down into the water again and tied outside the boathouse ready for a quick start. The dinner Mrs. Baggert provided was so good that Tom lingered over it longer than he meant to, and he asked for a second apple dumpling with hard sauce on. So it was with a very comfortable feeling indeed and with an almost forgiving spirit toward Andy Foger that our hero started down the path to the lake.

"Now for a quick run to Sandport," he said aloud. "I hope I shan't see any more of those men and that dad hasn't been bothered by them. His suspicions about the house weren't altogether unfounded, for I did see the tramp and some one else sneaking around, but I don't believe they'll come back now."

Tom swung around the path that led to the dock. As he came in sight of the water, he stared as if he could not believe what he saw, or, rather, what he did not see. For there was no craft tied to the string-piece, where he had fastened his motor-boat. He looked again, rubbed his eyes to make sure and then cried out:

"The *Arrow* is gone!"

There was no doubt of it. The craft was not at the dock. Breaking into a run, Tom hastened to the boathouse. The *Arrow* was not in there, and a look across the lake showed only a few row-boats in sight.

"That's mighty funny," mused the youth. "I wonder—"

He paused suddenly in his thoughts.

"Maybe Garret took it out to try and see that it worked all right," he said hopefully. "He knows how to run a boat. Maybe he wanted to see how the rudder behaved and is out in it now. He got through dinner before I did. But I should have thought he'd have said something to me if he was going out in it."

This was the one weak point in Tom's theory, and he felt it at once.

"I'll see if Garret is in his shop," he went on as he turned back toward the house.

The first person he met as he headed for the group of small structures where Mr. Swift's inventive work was carried on was Garret Jackson, the engineer.

"I—I thought you were out in my boat!" stammered Tom.

"Your boat! Why would I be out in your boat?" and Mr. Jackson removed his pipe from his mouth and stared at the young inventor.

"Because it's gone!"

"Gone!" repeated the engineer, and then Tom told him. The two hurried down to the dock, but the addition of another pair of eyes was of no assistance in locating the *Arrow*. The trim little motor craft was nowhere to be seen.

"I can't understand it," said Tom helplessly. "I wasn't gone more than an hour at dinner, and yet—"

"It doesn't take long to steal a motor-boat," commented the engineer.

"But I think I would have heard them start it," went on the lad. "Maybe it drifted off, though I'm sure I tied it securely."

"No, there's not much likelihood of that. There's no wind today and no currents in the lake. But it could easily have been towed off by some one in a rowboat and then you would not have heard the motor start."

"That's so," agreed the youth. "That's probably how they did it. They sneaked up here in a rowboat and towed the *Arrow* off. I'm sure of it."

"And I'll wager I know who did it," exclaimed Mr. Jackson energetically.

"Who?" demanded Tom quickly.

"Those men who were sneaking around—Happy Harry and his gang. They stole the boat once and they'd do it again. Those men took your boat, Tom."

The young inventor shook his head.

"No," he answered, "I don't believe they did."

"Why not?"

"Well, because they wouldn't dare come back here when they knew we're on the lookout for them. It would be too risky."

"Oh, those fellows don't care for risk," was the opinion of Mr. Jackson. "Take my word for it, they have your boat. They have been keeping watch, and as soon as they saw the dock unprotected they sneaked up and stole the *Arrow*."

"I don't think so," repeated Mr. Swift's son.

"Who do you think took it then?"

"Andy Foger!" was the quick response. "I believe he and his cronies did it to annoy me. They have been trying to get even with me-or at least Andy has—for outbidding him on this boat. He's tried several times, but he hasn't succeeded—until now. I'm sure Andy Foger has my boat," and Tom, with a grim tightening of his lips, swung around as though to start in instant pursuit.

"Where are you going?" asked Mr. Jackson.

"To find Andy and his cronies. When I locate them I'll make them tell me where my boat is."

"Hadn't you better send some word to your father? You can hardly get to Sandport now, and he'll be worried about you."

"That's so, I will. I'll telephone dad that the boat—no, I'll not do that either, for he'd only worry and maybe get sick. I'll just tell him I've had a little accident, that Andy ran into me and that I can't come back to the hotel for a day or two. Maybe I'll be lucky to find my boat in that time. But dad won't worry then, and, when I see him, I can explain. That's what I'll do," and Tom was soon talking to Mr. Swift by telephone.

The inventor was very sorry his son could not come back to

rejoin him and Ned, but there was no help for it, and, with as cheerful voice as he could assume, the lad promised to start for Sandport at the earliest opportunity.

"Now to find Andy and my boat!" Tom exclaimed as he hung up the telephone receiver.

CHAPTER XV

A DISMAYING STATEMENT

Trouble is sometimes good in a way; it makes a person re-sourceful. Tom Swift had had his share of annoyances of late, but they had served a purpose. He had learned to think clearly and quickly. Now, when he found his boat stolen, he at once began to map out a plan of action.

"What will you do first?" asked Mr. Jackson as he saw his employer's son hesitating.

"First I'm going to Andy Foger's house," declared the young inventor. "If he's home I'm going to tell him what I think of him. If he's not, I'm going to find him."

"Why don't you take your sailboat and run down to his dock?" suggested the engineer. "It isn't as quick as your motor-boat, but it's better than walking."

"So it is," exclaimed the lad. "I will use my catboat. I had for-gotten all about it of late. I'm glad you spoke."

He was soon sailing down the lake in the direction of the boat-house on the waterfront of Mr. Foger's property. It needed but a glance around the dock to show him that the *Red Streak* was not there, but Tom recollected the accident to the steering gear and thought perhaps Andy had taken his boat to some wharf where there was a repair shop and there left it to return home himself. But inquiry of Mrs. Foger, who was as nice a woman as her son was a mean lad, gave Tom the information that his enemy was not at home.

"He telephoned to me that his boat was damaged," said Mrs. Foger gently, "and that he had taken it to get fixed. Then, he said, he and some friends were going on a little cruise and might not be back tonight."

"Did he say where he was going?" asked our hero, who did not tell Andy's mother why he wanted to see her son.

"No, and I'm worried about him. Sometimes I think Andy is too—well, too impetuous, and I'm afraid he will get into trouble."

Tom, in spite of his trouble, could hardly forbear smiling. Andy's mother was totally unaware of the mean traits of her son and thought him a very fine chap. Tom was not going to undeceive her.

"I'm afraid something will happen to him," she went on. "Do you think there is any danger being out on the lake in a motor-boat, Mr. Swift? I understand you have one."

"Yes, I have one," answered Tom. He was going to say he had once had one, but thought better of it. "No, there is very little danger this time of year," he added.

"I am very glad to hear you say so," went on Mrs. Foger with a sigh. "I shall feel more at ease when Andy is away now. When he returns home, I shall tell him you called upon him and he will return your visit. I am glad to see that the custom of paying calls has not died out among the present generation. It is a pleasant habit, and I am glad to have my son conform to it. He shall return your kind visit."

"Oh, no, it's of no consequence," replied Tom quickly, thinking grimly that his visit was far from a friendly one. "There is no need to tell your son I was here. I will probably see him in a day or two.

"Oh, but I shall tell him," insisted Mrs. Foger with a kind smile. "I'm sure he will appreciate your call."

There was much doubt concerning this in the mind of the young inventor, but he did not express it and soon took his leave. Up and down the lake for the rest of the day he cruised, looking in vain for a sight of Andy Foger in the *Red Streak*, but the racing boat appeared to be well hidden.

"If I only could find where they've taken mine," mused Tom. "Hang it all, this is rotten luck!" and for the first time he began to feel discouraged.

"Maybe you'd better notify the police," suggested Mr. Jackson when Tom returned to the Swift house that night. "They might help locate it."

"I think I can do as well as the police," answered the youth. "If the boat is anywhere it's on the lake, and the police have no craft in which to make a search."

"That's so," agreed the engineer. "I wish I could help you, but I don't believe it would be wise for me to leave the house, especially since those men have been about lately."

"No, you must stay here," was Tom's opinion. "I'll take another day or two to search. By this time Andy and his gang will return, I'm sure, and I can tackle them."

"Suppose they don't?"

"Well, then I'll make a tour of the lake in my sailboat and I'll run up to Sandport and tell dad, for he will wonder what's keeping me. I'll know better next time than to leave my boat at the dock without taking out the connection at the spark coil, so no one can start the motor. I should have done that at first, but you always think of those things afterward."

The lad began his search again the next morning and cruised

about in little bays and gulfs looking for a sight of the *Red Streak* or the *Arrow*, but he saw neither, and a call at Andy's house showed that the red-haired youth had not returned. Mrs. Foger was quite nervous over her son's continued absence, but Mr. Foger thought it was all right.

Another day passed without any results and the young inventor was getting so nervous, partly with worrying over the loss of his boat and partly on his father's account, that he did not know what to do.

"I can't stand it any longer," he announced to Mrs. Baggert the night of the third day, after a telephone message had been received from Mr. Swift. The inventor wanted to know why his son did not return to the hotel to join him and Ned. "Well, what will you do?" asked the housekeeper.

"If I don't find my boat tomorrow, I'll sail to Sandport, bring home dad and Ned and we three will go all over the lake. My boat must be on it somewhere, but Lake Carlopa is so cut up that it could easily be hidden."

"It's queer that the Foger boy doesn't come home. That makes it look as if he was guilty."

"Oh, I'm sure he took it all right," returned Tom. "All I want is to see him. It certainly is queer that he stays away as long as he does. Sam Snedecker and Pete Bailey are with him, too. But they'll have to return some time."

Tom dreamed that night of finding his boat and that it was a wreck. He awoke, glad to find that the latter part was not true, but wishing that some of his night vision might come to pass during the day.

He started out right after breakfast, and, as usual, headed for the Foger home. He almost disliked to ask Mrs. Foger if her son had yet returned, for Andy's mother was so polite and so anxious to know whether any danger threatened that Tom hardly knew how to answer her. But he was saved that embarrassment on this occasion, for as he was going up the walk from the lake to the residence he met the gardener and from him learned that Andy had not yet come back.

"But his mother had a message from him, I did hear," went on the man. "He's on his way. It seems he had some trouble."

"Trouble. What kind of trouble?" asked Tom.

"I don't rightly know, sir, but," and here the gardener winked his eye, "Master Andy isn't particular what kind of trouble he gets into."

"That's right," agreed our hero, and as he went down again to where he had left his boat he thought: "Nor what kind of trouble he gets other people into. I wish I had hold of him for about five minutes!"

The sailboat swung slowly from the dock and heeled over to the gentle breeze. Hardly knowing what to do, Tom headed for the middle of the lake. He was discouraged and tired of making plans only to have them fail.

As he looked across the stretch of water he saw a boat coming toward him. He shaded his eyes with his hand to see better, and then, with a pair of marine glasses, took an observation. He uttered an exclamation.

"That's the *Red Streak* as sure as I'm alive!" he cried. "But what's the matter with her? They're rowing!"

The lad headed his boat toward the approaching one. There was no doubt about it. It was Andy Foger's craft, but it was not speeding forward under the power of the motor. Slowly and laborious the occupants were pulling it along, and as it was not meant to be rowed, progress was very slow.

"They've had a breakdown," thought Tom. "Serves 'em right! Now wait till I tackle 'em and find out where my boat is. I've a good notion to have Andy Foger arrested!"

The sailing craft swiftly approached the motor-boat. Tom could see the three occupants looking at him, apprehensively as well as curiously, he thought.

"Guess they didn't think I'd keep after 'em," mused the young inventor, and a little later he was beside the *Red Streak*.

"Well," cried Tom angrily, "it's about time you came back!"

"We've had a breakdown," remarked Andy, and he seemed quite humiliated. He was beginning to find out that he didn't know as much about a motor-boat as he thought he did.

"I've been waiting for you," went on Tom.

"Waiting for us? What for?" asked Sam Snedecker.

"What for? As if you didn't know!" blurted out the owner of the *Arrow*. "I want my boat, Andy Foger, the one you stole from me and hid! Tell me where it is at once or I'll have you arrested!"

"Your boat!" repeated the bully, and there was no mistaking the surprise in his tones.

"Yes, my boat! Don't try to bluff me like that."

"I'm not trying to bluff you. We've been away, three days and just got back."

"Yes, I know you have. You took my boat with you, too."

"Are you crazy?" demanded Pete Bailey.

"No, but you fellows must have been to think you could take my boat and me not know it," and Tom, filled with wrath, grasped the gunwale of the *Red Streak* as if he feared it would suddenly shoot away.

"Look here!" burst out Andy, and he spoke sincerely, "we didn't touch your boat. Did we, fellows?"

"No!" exclaimed Sam and Pete at once, and they were very much in earnest.

"We didn't even know it was stolen, did we?" went on Andy.

"No," agreed his chums. Tom looked unconvinced.

"We haven't taken your boat and we can prove it," continued the bully. "I know you and I have had quarrels, but I'm telling you the truth, Tom Swift. I never touched your boat."

There was no mistaking the sincerity of Andy. He was not a skilful deceiver, and Tom, looking into his squint-eyes, which were opened unusually wide, could not but help believing the fellow.

"We haven't seen it since the day we had the collision," added Andy, and his chums confirmed this statement.

"We went off on a little cruise," continued the red-haired bully, "and broke down several times. We had bad luck. Just as we were nearing home something went wrong with the engine again. I never saw such a poor motor. But we never took your boat, Tom Swift, and we can prove it."

Tom was in despair. He had been so sure that Andy was the thief, that to believe otherwise was difficult. Yet he felt that he must. He looked at the disabled motor of the *Red Streak* and viewed it with the interested and expert eye of a machinist, no matter if the owner of it was his enemy. Then suddenly a brilliant idea came into Tom's head.

CHAPTER XVI

STILL ON THE SEARCH

"You seem to have lots of trouble with your boat, Andy," said Tom after a few moments of rather embarrassed silence.

"I do," admitted the owner of the *Red Streak*. "I've had bad luck ever since I got it, but usually I've been able to fix it by looking in the book. This time I can't find out what the trouble is, nor can any of the fellows. It stopped when we were out in the middle of the lake and we had to row. I'm sick of motor boating."

"Suppose I fix it for you?" went on Tom.

"If you do, I'll pay you well."

"I wouldn't do it for pay—not the kind you mean," continued the young inventor.

"What do you mean then?" and Andy's face, that had lighted up, became glum again.

"Well, if I fix your boat for you, will you let me run it a little while?"

"You mean show me how to run it?"

"No, I mean take it myself. Look here, Andy, my boat's been stolen, and I thought you took it to get even with me. You say you didn't—"

"And I didn't touch it," interposed the squint-eyed lad quickly.

"All right, I believe you. But somebody stole it, and I think I know who."

"Who?" asked Sam Snedecker.

"Well, you wouldn't know if I told you, but I suspect some men with whom I had trouble before," and Tom referred to Happy Harry and his gang. "I think they have my boat on this lake, and I'd like to get another speedy craft to cruise about it and make a further search. How about it, Andy? If I fix your boat, will you let me take it to look for my boat?"

"Sure thing!" agreed the bully quickly, and his voice for once was friendly toward Tom. "Fix the engine so it will run, and you can use the *Red Streak* as long as you like."

"Oh, I probably wouldn't want it very long. I could cover the lake in about three days, and I hope by that time I could locate the thieves. Is it a bargain?"

"Sure," agreed Andy again, and Tom got into the motor-boat to look at the engine. He found that it would require some time to adjust it properly and that it would be necessary to take the motor apart.

"I think I'd better tow you to my dock," the young inventor said to Andy. "I can use some tools from the shop then, and by tonight I'll have the *Red Streak* in running order."

The breeze was in the right quarter, fortunately, and with the motor-boat dragging behind, the *Arrow*'s owner put the nose of the sailing craft toward his home dock.

When Tom reached his house he found that Mrs. Baggert had received another telephone message from Mr. Swift, inquiring why his son had not returned to Sandport.

"He says if you don't come back by tomorrow," repeated the housekeeper, "that he'll come home by train. He's getting anxious, I believe."

"Shouldn't wonder," admitted Tom. "But I want him to stay there. The change will do him good. I'll soon have my boat back, now that I can go about the lake swiftly, and then I'll join him. I'll tell him to be patient."

Tom talked with his father at some length, assuring him that everything was well at the Shopton house and promising to soon be with him. Then the young inventor began work on the motor of the *Red Streak*. He found it quite a job and had to call on Mr. Jackson to help him, for one of the pistons had to be repaired and a number of adjustments made to the cylinders.

But that night the motor was fully mended and placed back in the boat. It was in better shape than it had been since Andy had purchased the craft.

"There," remarked Tom, "now I'm ready to hunt for those scoundrels. Will you leave your boat at my dock tonight, Andy?"

"Yes, so you can start out early in the morning. I'm not going."

"Why not?" demanded Tom quickly.

"Well—er—you see I've had enough of motoring for a while," explained Andy. "Besides, I don't believe my mother would like me to go out on a chase after thieves. If we had to shoot I might hit one of them, and—"

"Oh, I see," answered Tom. "But I don't like to take your boat alone. Besides, I don't fancy there will be much shooting. I know I'm not going to take a gun. In fact, the one Mr. Duncan gave me is in the boat. All I want is to get the *Arrow* back."

"That's all right," went on Andy. "You take my boat and use it as long as you like. I'll rest up a few days. When you find your boat you can bring mine back."

Tom understood. He was just as glad not to have Andy accompany him in the chase, as he and the red-haired lad had never been good friends and probably never would be. So it would cause some embarrassment to be together in a boat all day. Then again Tom knew he could manage the *Red Streak* better alone, but, of course, he did not want to mention this when he asked for the loan of the craft. Andy's own suggestion, however, had solved the difficulty. Tom had an idea that Andy felt a little timid about going in pursuit of the thieves, but naturally it would not do to mention this, for the squint-eyed lad considered himself quite a fighter.

Early the next morning, alone in the *Red Streak*, Tom continued the search for his stolen boat. He started out from his home dock and mapped out a course that would take him well around the lake.

"I s'pose I could take a run to Sandport now," mused the youth as he shot in and out of the little bays, keeping watch for the *Arrow*. "But if I do dad will have to be told all about it, and, he'll worry. Then, too, he might want to accompany me, and I think I can manage this better alone, for the *Red Streak* will run faster with only one in. I ought to wind up this search in two days, if my boat is still on the lake. And if those scoundrels have sunk her I'll make them pay for it."

On shot the speedy motor-boat, in and out along the winding shoreline, with the lad in the bow at the steering-wheel peering with eager eyes into every nook and corner where his craft might be hidden.

CHAPTER XVII

"THERE SHE IS!"

Anticipating that he would be some time on his search, the young inventor had gone prepared for it. He had a supply of provisions and he had told Mrs. Baggert he might not be back that night. But he did not intend to sleep aboard the *Red Streak*, which, being a racing boat, was not large enough to afford much room for passengers. Tom had planned, therefore, to put up at some hotel near the lake in case his hunt should last beyond one night.

That it would do this was almost certain, for all that morning he searched unavailingly for the *Arrow*. A distant mill whistle sounding over Lake Carlopa told him it was noon.

"Dinner time," he announced to himself. "Guess I'll run up along shore in the shade and eat."

Selecting a place where the trees overhung the water, forming a quiet, cool nook, Tom sent the boat in there, and, tying it to a leaning tree, he began his simple meal. Various thoughts filled his mind, but chief among them was the desire to overtake the thieves who had his boat. That it was Happy Harry's gang he was positive.

The lad nearly finished eating and was considering what direction he might best search in next when he heard, running along a road that bordered the lake, an automobile.

"Wonder who that is?" mused Tom. "It won't do any harm to take a look, for it might be some of those thieves again. They probably still have their auto or Happy Harry couldn't have gotten from Sandport to Shopton so quickly."

The young inventor slipped ashore from the motor-boat, taking care to make no noise. Stealing silently along toward the road, he peered through the underbrush for a sight of the machine, which seemed to be going slowly. But before the youth had a glimpse of it he was made aware who the occupant was by hearing someone exclaim:

"Bless my shoe laces if this cantankerous contraption isn't going wrong again! I wonder if it's going to have a fit here in this lonely place. It acts just as if it was. Bless my very existence! Hold on now. Be nice! Be nice!"

"Mr. Damon!" exclaimed Tom, and, without knowing it, he had spoken aloud.

"Hold on there! Hold on! Who's calling me in this forsaken locality? Bless my shirt studs! But who is it?" and the eccentric man who had sold Tom the motor-cycle looked intently at the bushes.

"Here I am, Mr. Damon," answered the lad, stepping out into the road. "I knew it was you as soon as I saw you."

"Bless my liver, but that's very true! I suppose you heard my unfortunate automobile puffing along. I declare I don't know what ails it. I got it on the advice of my physician, who said I must get out in the air, but, bless my gears, it's the auto who needs a doctor more than I do! It's continually out of order. Something is going to happen right away. I can tell by the way it's behaving."

Mr. Damon had thrown out the clutch, but the engine was still running, though in a jerky, uncertain fashion, which indicated to the trained ear of the young inventor that something was wrong.

"Perhaps I can fix it for you as I did before," ventured Tom.

"Bless my eyebrows! Perhaps you can," cried the eccentric man hopefully. "You always seem to turn up at the right moment. How do you manage it?"

"I don't know. I remember the time you turned up just when I wanted you to help me capture Happy Harry and his gang, and now, by, a strange coincidence, I'm after them again."

"You don't say so! My good gracious! Bless my hatband! But that's odd. There!" he ejaculated suddenly as the automobile engine stopped with a choking sigh, "I knew something was going to happen."

"Let me take a look," proposed the lad, and he was soon busy peering into the interior of the machine. At first he could not find the trouble, but being a persistent youth, Tom went at it systematically and located it in two places. The clutch was not rightly adjusted and the carburetor float feed needed fixing. The young inventor was not long in making the slight repairs and then he assured Mr. Damon that his automobile would run properly.

"Bless my very existence, but what a thing it is to have a head for mechanics!" exclaimed the odd man gratefully. "Now it would bother me to adjust a nutmeg grater if it got out of order, but I dare say you could fix it in no time."

"Yes," answered Tom, "I could and so could you, for there's nothing about it to fix. But you can go ahead now if you wish."

"Thank you. It just shows how ignorant I am of machinery. I presume something will go wrong in another mile or two. But may I ask what you are doing here? I presume you are in your motor-boat, sailing about for pleasure. And didn't I understand you to say you were after those chaps again? Bless my watch charm, but I was so interested in my machine that I didn't think to ask you."

"Yes, I am after those thieves again."

"In your motor-boat, I presume. Well, I hope you catch them. What have they stolen now?"

"My motor-boat. That's why I'm after them, but I had to borrow a craft to chase them with."

"Bless my soul! You don't tell me! How did it happen?"

Thereupon the lad related as much of the story as was necessary to put Mr. Damon in possession of the facts and he ended up with:

"I don't suppose you have seen anything of the men in my boat, have you?"

Mr. Damon seemed strangely excited. He had entered his auto, but as the lad's story progressed the odd gentleman had descended. When Tom finished he exclaimed:

"Don't say a word now—not a word. I want to think, and that is a process, which, for me, requires a little time. Don't speak a word now. Bless my left hand, but I think I can help you!"

He frowned, stamped first one foot, then the other, looked up at the sky, as if seeking inspiration there, and then down at the ground, as if that would help him to think. Then he clapped his hands smartly together and cried out:

"Bless my shoe buttons!"

"Have you seen them?" asked Tom eagerly.

"Was your boat one with a red arrow painted on the bow?" asked Mr. Damon in turn.

"It was!" and the lad was now almost as excited as was his friend.

"Then I've seen it and, what's more, this morning! Bless my spark plug, I've seen it!"

"Tell me about it!" pleaded the young inventor, and Mr. Damon, calming himself after an effort, resumed:

"I was out for an early spin in my auto," he said, "and was traveling along a road that bordered the lake, about fifteen miles above here. I heard a motor-boat puffing along near shore, and, looking through the trees, I saw one containing three men. It had a red arrow on the bow, and that's why I noticed it, because I recalled that your boat was named the DART."

"*Arrow*," corrected Tom.

"The *Arrow*. Oh, yes, I knew it was something like that. Well of course at the time I didn't think that it was your boat, but I associated it in my mind with yours. Do you catch my meaning?"

Tom did and said so, wishing Mr. Damon would hurry and get to the point. But the eccentric character had to do things in his own way.

"Exactly," he resumed. "Well, I didn't think that was your boat, but, at the same time, I watched the men out of curiosity, and I was struck with their behavior. They seemed to be quarreling, and, from what I could hear, two of them seemed to be remonstrating with the third one for having taken some sort of a piece of wood from the forward compartment. I believe that is the proper term."

"Yes!" Tom almost shouted. "But where did they go? What became of them? What was the man doing to the forward compartment—where the gasoline tank is?"

"Exactly. I was trying to think what was kept there. That's it, the gasoline tank. Well, the boat kept on up the lake, and I don't know what became of the men. But about that piece of wood. It seems that one of the men removed a block, from under the tank and the others objected. That's why they were quarreling."

"That's very strange," exclaimed the lad. "There must be some mystery about my boat that I don't understand. But that will keep until I get the boat itself. Good-by, Mr. Damon. I must be off."

"Where to?"

"Up the lake after those thieves. I must lose no time," and Tom started to go back to where he had left the *Red Streak*.

"Hold on!" cried Mr. Damon. "I have something to propose, Tom. Two heads are better than one, even if one doesn't know how to adjust a nutmeg grate. Suppose I come along with you? I can point out the direction the men took, at any rate."

"I'll be very glad to have you," answered the lad, who felt that he might need help if there were three of the thieves in his craft. "But what will you do with your automobile?"

"I'll just run it down the road a way to where a friend of mine has a stable. I'll leave it in there and join you. Will you let me come? Bless my eye glasses, but I'd like to help catch those scoundrels!"

"I'll be very glad to have you. Go ahead, put the auto in the barn and I'll wait for you."

"I have a better plan than that," replied Mr. Damon. "Run your boat down to that point," and he indicated one about a mile up the lake. "I'll be there waiting for you, and we'll lose no time. I can cover the ground faster in my auto than you can in your boat."

Tom saw the advantage of this and was soon under way, while he heard on shore the puffing of his friend's car. On the trip to the point Tom puzzled over the strange actions of the man in taking one of the braces from under the gasoline tank.

"I'll wager he did it before," thought the lad. "It must be the same person who was tampering with the lock of the forward compartment the day I bought the boat. But why—that's the question—why?"

He could find no answer to this, puzzle over it as he did, and he gave it up. His whole desire now was to get on the trail of the thieves, and he had strong hopes, after the clue Mr. Damon had given him. The latter was waiting for him on the point, and so nimble was the owner of the auto, in spite of his size, that Tom was not delayed more than the fraction of a minute ere he was under way again, speeding up the lake.

"Now keep well in toward shore," advised Mr. Damon. "Those fellows don't want to be observed any more than they can help, and they'll sneak along the bank, They were headed in that direction," and he pointed it out. "Now I hope you won't think I'm in the way. Besides, you know, if you get your boat back, you'll want some one to help steer it, while you run this one. I can do that, at all events, bless my very existence!"

"I am very glad of your help," replied the lad, but he did not take his eyes from the water before him, and he was looking for a sight of his boat with the men in it.

For three hours or more Tom and Mr. Damon cruised in and out along the shore of the lake, going farther and farther up the body of water. Tom was beginning to think that he would reach Sandport without catching sight of the thieves, and he was wondering if, after all, he might not better stop off and see his father when, above the puffing of the motor in the *Red Streak*, he heard the put-put of another boat.

"Listen!" cried Mr. Damon, who had heard it at the same time.

Tom nodded.

"They're just ahead of us," whispered his companion.

"If it's them," was the lad's reply.

"Speed up and we'll soon see," suggested Mr. Damon, and Tom shoved the timer over. The *Red Streak* forged ahead. The sound of the other boat came more plainly now. It was beyond a little point of land. The young inventor steered out to get around it and leaned eagerly forward to catch the first glimpse of the unseen craft. Would it prove to be the *Arrow*?

The put-put became louder now. Mr. Damon was standing up, as if that would, in some mysterious way, help. Then suddenly the other boat came into view. Tom saw it in an instant and knew it for the *Arrow*.

"There she is!" he cried.

CHAPTER XVIII

THE PURSUIT

For an instant after Tom's exultant cry the men in the boat ahead were not aware that they were being pursued. Then, as the explosions from the motor of the *Red Streak* sounded over the water, they turned to see who was coming up behind them. There was no mistaking the attitude of the young inventor and his companion. They were leaning eagerly forward, as if they could reach out and grasp the criminals who were fleeing before them.

"Put on all the speed you can, Tom!" begged Mr. Damon. "We'll catch the scoundrels now. Speed up the motor! Oh, if I only had my automobile now. Bless my crank shaft, but one can go so much faster on land than on water."

The lad did not reply, but thought, with grim humor, that running an automobile over Lake Carlopa would be no small feat. Mr. Damon, however, knew what he was saying.

"We'll catch them! We'll nab 'em!" he cried. "Speed her up, Tom."

The youth was doing his best with the motor of the *Red Streak*. He was not as well acquainted with it as he was with the one in his boat, but he knew, even better than Andy Foger, how to make it do efficient work. It was a foregone conclusion that the *Red Streak*, if rightly handled, could beat the *Arrow*, but there were several points in favor of the thieves. The motor of Tom's boat was in perfect order, and even an amateur, with some knowledge of a boat, could make it do nearly its best. On the other hand, the *Red Streak*'s machinery needed "nursing." Again, the thieves had a good start, and that counted for much. But Tom counted on two other points. One was that Happy Harry and his gang would probably know little about the fine points of a motor. They had shown this in letting the motor of the boat they had first stolen get out of order, and Tom knew the ins and outs of a gasoline engine to perfection. So the chase was not so hopeless as it seemed.

"Do you think you can catch them?" asked Mr. Damon anxiously.

"I'm going to make a big try," answered his companion.

"They're heading out into the middle of the lake!" cried the eccentric man.

"If they do, I can cut them off!" murmured Tom as he put the wheel over.

But whoever was steering the *Arrow* knew better than to send it on a course that would enable the pursuing boat to cut across and shorten the distance to it. After sending the stolen craft far enough out from shore to clear points of land that jutted out into the lake, the leading boat was sent straight ahead.

"A stern chase and a long chase!" murmured Mr. Damon. "Bless my rudder, but those fellows are not going to give up easily."

"I guess not," murmured Tom. "Will you steer for a while, Mr. Damon?"

"Of course I will. If I could get out and pull the boat after me, to make it go faster, I would. But as I always lose my breath when I run, perhaps it's just as well that I stay in here." Tom thought so too, but his attention was soon given to the engine. He adjusted the timer to get if possible a little more speed out of the boat he had borrowed from Andy, and he paid particular attention to the oiling system.

"We're going a bit faster!" called Mr. Damon' encouragingly, "or else they're slacking up."

Tom peered ahead to see if this was so. It was hard to judge whether he was overhauling the *Arrow*, as it was a stern chase, and that is always difficult to judge. But a glimpse along shore showed him that they were slipping through the water at a faster speed.

"They're up to something!" suddenly exclaimed Mr. Damon a moment later. "I believe they're going to fire on us, Tom. They are pointing something this way."

The lad stood up and gazed earnestly at his boat, which seemed to be slipping away from him so fast. One of the occupants was in the stern, aiming some glittering object at those in the *Red Streak*. For a moment Tom thought it might be a gun. Then, as the man turned, he saw what it was.

"A pair of marine glasses," cried the lad. "They're trying to make out who we are."

"I guess they know well enough," rejoined Mr. Damon. "Can't you go any faster, Tom?"

"I'm afraid not. But we'll land them, sooner or later. They can't go very far in this direction without running ashore and we'll have them. They're cutting across the lake now."

"They may escape us if it gets dark. Probably that's what they're working for. They want to keep ahead of us until nightfall."

The young inventor thought of this too, but there was little he could do. The motor was running at top speed. It could be made to go faster, Tom knew, with another ignition system, but that was out of the question now.

The man with the glasses had resumed his seat, and the efforts of the trio seemed concentrated on the motor of the *Arrow*. They, too, wished to go faster. But they had not skill enough to accomplish it, and in about ten minutes, when Tom took another long and careful look to ascertain if possible whether or not he was over-hauling the thieves, he was delighted to see that the distance between the boats had lessened.

"We're catching them! We're creeping up on them!" cried Mr. Damon. "Keep it up, Tom." There was nothing to do, however, save wait. The boat ahead had shifted her course somewhat and was now turning in toward the shore, for the lake was narrow at this point, and abandoning their evident intention of keeping straight up the lake, the thieves seemed now bent on something else.

"I believe they're going to run ashore and get out!" cried Mr. Damon.

"If they do, it's just what I want," declared the lad. "I don't care for the men. I want my boat back!"

The occupants of the *Arrow* were looking to the rear again, and one—Happy Harry, Tom thought—shook his fist.

"Ah, wait until I get hold of you!" cried Mr. Damon, following his example. "I'll make you wish you'd behaved yourselves, you scoundrels! Bless my overcoat! Catch them if you can, Tom."

There was now no doubt of the intention of the fleeing ones. The shore was looming up ahead and straight for it was headed the *Arrow*. Tom sent Andy's boat in the same direction. He was rapidly overhauling the escaping ones now, for they had slowed down the motor. Three minutes later the foremost boat grated on the beach of the lake. The men leaped out, one of them pausing an instant in the bow.

"Here, don't you damage my boat!" cried Tom involuntarily, for the man seemed to be hammering something.

The fellow leaped over the side, holding something in his hand.

"There they go! Catch them!" yelled Mr. Damon.

"Let them go!" answered the lad as the men ran toward the wood. "I want my boat. I'm afraid they've damaged her. One of them tore something from the bow."

At the same instant the two companions of the fellow who had paused in the forward part of the *Arrow* saw that he had something in his hand. With yells of rage they dashed at him, but he, shaking his fist at them, plunged into the bushes and could be heard breaking his way through, while his companions were in pursuit.

"They've quarreled among themselves," commented Mr. Damon as high and angry voices could be heard from the woods. "There's some mystery here, Tom."

"I don't doubt it, but my first concern is for my boat. I want to see if they have damaged her."

Tom had run so closely in shore with the *Red Streak* that he had to reverse to avoid damaging the craft against the bank. In a mass of foam he stopped her in time, and then springing ashore, he hurried to his motor-boat.

CHAPTER XIX

A QUIET CRUISE

"Have they done any damage?" asked Mr. Damon as he stood in the bow of the *Red Streak*.

Tom did not answer for a moment. His trained eye was looking over the engine.

"They yanked out the high tension wire instead of stopping the motor with the switch," he answered at length, and then, when he had taken a look into the compartment where the gasoline tank was, he added: "And they've ripped out two more of the braces I put in. Why in the world they did that I can't imagine."

"That's evidently what one man had that the others wanted," was Mr. Damon's opinion.

"Probably," agreed Tom. "But what could he or they want with wooden braces?"

That was a puzzler for Mr. Damon, but he answered:

"Perhaps they wanted to damage your boat and those two men were mad because the other got ahead of them."

"Taking out the braces wouldn't do much damage. I can easily put others in. All it would do would be to cause the tank to sag down and maybe cause a leak in the pipe. But that would be a queer thing to do. No, I think there's some mystery that I haven't gotten to the bottom of yet. But I'm going to."

"Good!" exclaimed Mr. Damon. "I'll help you. But can you run your boat back home?"

"Not without fixing it a bit. I must brace up that tank and put in a new high-tension wire from the spark coil. I can do it here, but I'd rather take it to the shop. Besides, with two boats to run back, for I must return Andy's to him, I don't see how I can do it very well unless you operate one, Mr. Damon."

"Excuse me, but I can't do it. Bless my slippers, but I would be sure to run on a rock! The best plan will be for you to tow your boat and I'll ride in it and steer. I can do that much, anyhow. You can ride in the *Red Streak*."

Tom agreed that this would be a good plan. So, after temporarily bracing up the tank in the *Arrow*, it was shoved out into the lake and attached to Andy's craft.

"But aren't you going to make a search for those men?" asked Mr. Damon when Tom was ready to start back.

"No, I think it would be useless. They are well away by this time, and I don't fancy chasing them through the woods, especially as night is coming on. Besides, I won't leave these boats."

"No doubt you are right, but I would like to see them punished, and I am curious enough to wish to know what object that scoundrel could have in ripping out the blocks that served as a brace for the tank."

"I feel the same way myself," commented the lad, "especially since this is the second time that's happened. But we'll have to wait, I guess."

A little later the start back was made, Mr. Damon steering the *Arrow* skillfully enough so that it did not drag on the leading boat, in which Tom rode. His course took him not far from the lake sanitarium, where Mr. Duncan, the hunter, had been brought, and desiring to know how the wounded man was getting on, the youth proposed that they make a halt, explaining to Mr. Damon his reason.

"Yes, and while you're about it you'd better telephone your father that you will join him tomorrow," suggested the other. "I know what it is to fret and worry. You can fix your boat up in time to go to Sandport tomorrow, can't you?"

"Yes, I'm glad you reminded me of it. I'll telephone from the sanitarium, if they'll let me."

Mr. Duncan was not at the institution, Tom was told, his injury having healed sufficiently to allow of his being removed to his home. The youth readily secured permission to use the telephone, and was soon in communication with Mr. Swift. While not telling him all the occurrences that had delayed him, Tom gave his father and Ned Newton enough information to explain his absence. Then the trip to Shopton was resumed in the two boats.

"What are you going to do about your automobile?" asked Tom as they neared the point where the machine had been left.

"Never mind about that," replied Mr. Damon. "It will do it good to have a night's vacation. I will go on to your house with you, and perhaps I can get a train back to my friend's home, so that I can claim my car."

"Won't you stay all night with me?" invited the young inventor. "I'd be glad to have you."

Mr. Damon agreed, and, Tom putting more speed on the *Red Streak*, was soon opposite his own dock. The *Arrow* was run in the boathouse and the owner hastily told Mrs. Baggert and the engineer what had occurred. Then he took Andy's boat to Mr. Foger's dock and warmly thanked the red-haired lad for the use of his craft.

"Did you find your boat?" asked Andy eagerly. "How did the

Red Streak run?"

"I got my boat and yours runs fine," explained Tom.

"Good! I'll race you again some day," declared Andy.

Mr. Damon enjoyed his visit at our hero's house, for Mrs. Baggert cooked one of her best suppers for him. Tom and the engineer spent the evening repairing the motor-boat, Mr. Damon looking on and exclaiming "Bless my shoe leather" or some other part of his dress or anatomy at every stage of the work. The engineer wanted to know all about the men and their doings, but he could supply no reason for their queer actions regarding the braces under the gasoline tank.

In the morning Tom once more prepared for an early start for Sandport, and Mr. Damon, reconsidering his plans, rode as far with him as the place where the automobile had been left. There he took leave of the young inventor, promising to call on Mr. Swift in the near future.

"I hope you arrive at the hotel where your father is without any more accidents," remarked the automobilist. "Bless my very existence, but you seem to have the most remarkable series of adventures I ever heard of!"

"They are rather odd," admitted Tom. "I don't know that I particularly care for them, either. But, now that I have my boat back, I guess everything will be all right."

But Tom could not look ahead. He was destined to have still more exciting times, as presently will be related.

Without further incident he arrived at the Lakeview Hotel in Sandport that evening and found his father and Ned very glad to see him. Of course he had to explain everything then, and, with his son safely in his sight, Mr. Swift was not so nervous over the recital as he would have been had Tom not been present.

"Now for some nice, quiet trips," remarked the lad when he had finished his account. "I feel as if I had cheated you out of part of your vacation, Ned, staying away as long as I did."

"Well, of course we missed you," answered his chum. "But your father and I had a good time."

"Yes, and I invented a new attachment for a kitchen boiler," added Mr. Swift. "I had a chance for it when I passed through the hotel kitchen one day, for I wanted to see what kind of a range they used."

"I guess there's no stopping you from inventing," replied his son with a laugh and a hopeless shake of the head. "But don't let it happen again when you go away to rest."

"Oh, I only just thought of it," said Mr. Swift. "I haven't worked the details out yet."

Then he wanted to know about everything at home and he seemed particularly anxious lest the Happy Harry gang do some damage.

"I don't believe they will," Tom assured him. "Garret and Mrs. Baggert will be on guard."

The next few days were pleasant ones for Tom, his father and Ned Newton. They cruised about the lake, went fishing and camped in the woods. Even Mr. Swift spent one night in the tent and said he liked it very much. For a week the three led an ideal existence, going about as they pleased, Ned taking a number of photographs with his new camera. The *Arrow* proved herself a fine boat, and Tom and Ned, when Mr. Swift did not accompany them, explored the seldom visited parts of Lake Carlopa.

The three had been out one day and were discussing the necessity of returning home soon when Ned spoke.

"I shall hate to give up this life and go to slaving in the bank again," he complained. "I wish I was an inventor."

"Oh, we inventors don't have such an easy time," said Mr. Swift. "You never know when trouble is coming," and he little imagined how near the truth he was.

A little later they were at the hotel dock. When Tom had tied up his boat the three walked up the path to the broad veranda that faced the lake. A boy in uniform met them.

"Some one has just called you on the telephone, Mr. Swift," he reported.

"Some one wants me? Who is it?"

"I think he said his name is Jackson, sir, Garret Jackson, and he says the message is very important."

"Tom, something has happened at home!" exclaimed the inventor as he hurried up the steps. "I'm afraid there's bad news."

Unable to still the fear in his heart, Tom followed his father.

CHAPTER XX

NEWS OF A ROBBERY

With a hand that trembled so he could scarcely hold the receiver of the telephone, Mr. Swift placed it to his ear.

"Hello! Hello!" he cried into the transmitter. "Yes, this is Mr. Swift—yes, Garret. What is it?"

Then came a series of clicks, which Tom and Ned listened to. The inventor spoke again.

"What's that? The same men? Broke in early this evening? Oh, that's too bad! Of course, I'll come at once."

There followed more meaningless clicks, which Tom wished he could translate. His father hung up the receiver, turned to him and exclaimed:

"I've been robbed again!"

"Robbed again! How, dad?"

"By that same rascally gang, Garret thinks. This evening, when he and Mrs. Baggert were in the house the burglar alarm went off. The indicator showed that the electrical shop had been entered, and the engineer hurried there. He saw a light inside and the shadows of persons on the windows. Before he could reach the shop, however, the thieves heard him coming and escaped. Oh, Tom, I should never have come away!"

"But did they take anything, dad? Perhaps Garret frightened them away before they had a chance to steal any of your things. Did you ask him that?"

"I didn't need to. He said he made a hasty exanimation before he called me up, and he is sure a number of my electrical inventions are missing. Some of them are devices I never have had patented, and if I lose them I will have no recovery."

"But just what ones are they? Perhaps we can send out a police alarm tonight."

"Garret couldn't tell that," answered Mr. Swift as he paced to and fro in the hotel office. "He doesn't know all the tools and machinery I had in there. But it is certain that some of my most valuable things have been taken."

"Never mind. Don't worry, dad," and Tom tried to speak soothingly, for he saw that his father was much excited. "We may be able to get them back. How does Garret know the same men who stole the turbine model broke in the shop this evening?"

"He saw them. One was Happy Harry, he is positive. The others he did not know, but he recognized the tramp from our description of him."

"Then we must tell the police at once."

"Yes, Tom, I wish you would telephone. I'll give you a description of the things. No, I can't do that either, for I don't know what was stolen. I must go home at once to find out. It's a good thing the motor-boat is here. Come, let's start at once. What is my bill here?" and the inventor turned to the hotel proprietor, who had come into the office. "I have suffered a severe loss and must leave at once."

"I am very sorry, sir. I'll have it ready for you in a few minutes."

"All right. Tom, is your boat ready for a quick trip?"

"Yes, dad, but I don't like to make it at night with three in. Of course it might be perfectly safe, but there's a risk, and I don't like to take it."

"Don't worry about the risk on my account, Tom. I'm not afraid. I must get home and see of what I have been robbed."

The young inventor was in a quandary. He wanted to do as his father requested and to aid him all he could, yet he knew that an all-night trip in the boat down the lake would be dangerous, not only from the chance of running on an unknown shore or into a hidden rock, but because Mr. Swift was not physically fitted to stand the journey.

"Come, Tom," exclaimed the aged inventor impatiently, "we must start at once!"

"Won't morning do as well, dad?"

"No, I must start now. I could not sleep worrying over what has happened. We will start—"

At that instant there came a low, rumbling peal of thunder. Mr. Swift started and peered from a window. There came a flash of lightning and another vibrant report from the storm-charged clouds.

"There is your bill, Mr. Swift," remarked the proprietor, coming up, "but I would not advise you to start tonight. There is a bad storm in the west, and it will reach here in a few minutes. Storms on Lake Carlopa, especially at this open and exposed end, are not to be despised, I assure you."

"But I must get home!" insisted Tom's father.

The lace curtain over the window blew almost straight out with a sudden breeze, and a flash of lightning so bright that it reflected even in the room where the incandescent electrics were glowing made several others jump. Then came a mighty crash, and with that the flood-gates of the storm were opened, and the rain came down in torrents. Tom actually breathed a sigh of relief. The problem was solved for him. It would be impossible to start tonight, and he was glad of it, much as he wanted to get on the trail of the thieves.

There was a scurrying on the part of the hotel attendants to close the windows, and the guests who had been enjoying the air out on the porches came running in. With a rush, a roar and a muttering, as peal after peal of thunder sounded, the deluge continued.

"It's a good thing we didn't start," observed Ned.

"I should say so," agreed Tom. "But we'll get off the first thing in the morning, dad."

Mr. Swift did not reply, but his nervous pacing to and fro in the hotel office showed how anxious he was to be at home again. There was no help for it, however, and, after a time, finding that to think of reaching his house that night was out of the question, the inventor calmed down somewhat,

The storm continued nearly all night, as Tom could bear witness, for he did not sleep well, nor did his father. And when he came down to breakfast in the morning Mr. Swift plainly showed the effects of the bad news. His face was haggard and drawn and his eyes smarted and burned from lack of sleep.

"Well, Tom, we must start early," he said nervously. "I am glad it has cleared off. Is the boat all ready?"

"Yes, and it's a good thing it was under shelter last night or we'd have to bail it out now, and that would delay us."

An hour later they were under way, having telephoned to the engineer at the Swift home that they were coming. Garret Jackson reported over the wire that he had notified the Shopton police of the robbery, but that little could be done until the inventor arrived to give a description of the stolen articles.

"And that will do little good, I fear," remarked Tom. "Those fellows have evidently been planning this for some time and will cover their tracks well. I'd like to catch them, not only to recover your things, dad, but to find out the mystery of my boat and why the man took the tank braces."

CHAPTER XXI

THE BALLOON ON FIRE

Down Lake Carlopa speeded the *Arrow*, those on board watching the banks slip past as the motor-boat rapidly cut through the water.

"What time do you think we ought to reach home, Tom?" asked Mr. Swift.

"Oh, about four o'clock, if we don't stop for lunch."

"Then we'll not stop," decided the inventor. "We'll eat what we have on board. I suppose you have some rations?" and he smiled, the first time since hearing the bad news.

"Oh, yes, Ned and I didn't eat everything on our camping trips," and Tom was glad to note that the fine weather which followed the storm was having a good effect on his father.

"We certainly had a good time," remarked Ned. "I don't know when I've enjoyed a vacation so."

"It's too bad it had to be cut short by this robbery," commented Mr. Swift.

"Oh, well, my time would be up in a few days more," went on the young bank employee. "It's just as well to start back now."

Tom took the shortest route he knew, keeping in as close to shore as he dared, for now he was as anxious to get home as was his father. On and on speeded the *Arrow*, yet fast as it was, it seemed slow to Mr. Swift, who, like all nervous persons, always wanted to go wherever he desired to go instantly.

Tom headed his boat around a little point of land, and was urging the engine to the top notch of speed, for now he was on a clear course, with no danger from shoals or hidden rocks, when he saw, darting out from shore, a tiny craft which somehow seemed familiar to him. He recognized a peculiar put-putter of the motor.

"That's the *Dot*," he remarked in a low voice to Ned, "Miss Nestor's cousin's boat."

"Is she in it now?" asked Ned.

"Yes," answered Tom quickly.

"You've got good eyesight," remarked Ned dryly, "to tell a girl at that distance. It looks to me like a boy."

"No, it's Mary—I mean Miss Nestor," the youth quickly corrected himself, and a close observer would have noticed that he blushed a bit under his coat of tan.

Ned laughed, Tom blushed still more, and Mr. Swift, who was

in a stern seat, glanced up quickly.

"It looks as if that boat wanted to hail us," the inventor remarked.

Tom was thinking the same thing, for, though he had changed his course slightly since sighting the *Dot*, the little craft was put over so as to meet him. Wondering what Miss Nestor could want, but being only too willing to have a chat with her, the young inventor shifted his helm. In a short time the two craft were within hailing distance.

"How do you do?" called Miss Nestor, as she slowed down her motor. "Don't you think I'm improving, Mr. Swift?"

"What's that? I—er—I beg your pardon, but I didn't catch that," exclaimed the aged inventor quickly, coming out of a sort of day-dream. "I beg your pardon." He thought she had addressed him.

Miss Nestor blushed and looked questioningly at Tom.

"My father," he explained as he introduced his parent. Ned needed none, having met Miss Nestor before. "Indeed you have improved very much," went on our hero. "You seem able to manage the boat all alone."

"Yes, I'm doing pretty well. Dick lets me take the *Dot* whenever I want to, and I thought I'd come out for a little trial run this morning. I'm getting ready for the races. I suppose you are going to enter them?" and she steered her boat alongside Tom's, who throttled down his powerful motor so as not to pass his friend.

"Races? I hadn't heard of them," he replied.

"Oh, indeed there are to be fine ones under the auspices of the Lanton Motor Club. Mr. Hastings, of whom you bought that boat, is going to enter his new *Carlopa*, and Dick has entered the *Dot*, in the baby class of course. But I'm going to run it, and that's why I'm practicing."

"I hope you win," remarked Tom. "I hadn't heard of the races, but I think I'll enter. I'm glad you told me. Do you want to race now?" and he laughed as he looked into the brown eyes of Mary Nestor.

"No, indeed, unless you give me a start of several miles."

They kept together for some little time longer, and then, as Tom knew his father would be restless at the slow speed, he told Miss Nestor the need of haste, and, advancing his timer, he soon left the *Dot* behind. The girl called a laughing good-by and urged him not to forget the races, which were to take place in about two weeks.

"I suppose Andy Foger will enter his boat," commented Ned.

"Naturally," agreed Tom. "It's a racer, and he'll probably think it can beat anything on the lake. But if he doesn't manage his motor differently, it won't."

The distance from Sandport to Shopton had been more than half covered at noon, when the travelers ate a lunch in the boat. Mr. Swift was looking anxiously ahead to catch the first glimpse of his dock and Tom was adjusting the machinery as finely as he dared to get out of it the maximum speed.

Ned Newton, who happened to be gazing aloft, wondering at the perfect beauty of the blue sky after the storm, uttered a sudden exclamation. Then he arose and pointed at some object in the air.

"Look!" he cried, "A balloon! It must have gone up from some fair."

Tom and his father looked upward. High in the air, almost over their heads, was an immense balloon. It was of the hot-air variety, such as performers use in which to make ascensions from fair grounds and circuses, and below it dangled a trapeze, upon which could be observed a man, only he looked more like a doll than a human being.

"I shouldn't like to be as high as that," remarked Ned.

"I would," answered Tom as he slowed down the engine the better to watch the balloon. "I'd like to go up in an airship, and I intend to some day."

"I believe he's going to jump!" suddenly exclaimed Ned after a few minutes. "He's going to do something, anyhow."

"Probably come down in a parachute," said Tom. "They generally do that."

"No! No!" cried Ned. "He isn't going to jump. Something has happened! The balloon is on fire! He'll be burned to death!"

Horror stricken, they all gazed aloft. From the mouth of the balloon there shot a tongue of fire, and it was followed by a cloud of black smoke. The big bag was getting smaller and seemed to be descending, while the man on the trapeze was hanging downward by his hands to get as far as possible away from the terrible heat.

CHAPTER XXII

THE RESCUE

"Jump! Jump!" cried Mr. Swift, leaping to his feet and motioning to the man on the trapeze of the balloon. But it is doubtful whether or not the performer heard him. Certainly he could not see the frantic motions of the inventor. "Why doesn't he jump?" Mr. Swift went on piteously to the two lads. "He'll surely be burned to death if he hangs on there!"

"It's too far to leap!" exclaimed Tom. "He's a good way up in the air, though it looks like only a short distance. He would be killed if he dropped now."

"He ought to have a parachute," added Ned. "Most of those men do when they go up in a balloon. Why doesn't he come down in that? I wonder how the balloon took fire?"

"Maybe he hasn't a parachute," suggested Tom, while he slowed down the motor-boat still more so as to remain very nearly under the blazing balloon.

"Yes, he has!" cried Ned. "See, it's hanging to one side of the big bag. He ought to cut loose. He could save himself then. Why doesn't he?"

The balloon was slowly twisting about, gradually settling to the surface of the lake, but all the while the flames were becoming fiercer and the black clouds of smoke increased in size.

"There, see the parachute!" went on Ned.

The twisting of the bag had brought into view the parachute or big, umbrella-shaped bag, which would have enabled the man to safely drop to the surface of the lake. Without it he would have hit the water with such force that he would have been killed as surely as if he had struck the solid earth. But the boys and Mr. Swift also saw something else, and this was that the balloon was on fire on the same side where the parachute was suspended.

"Look! Look!" shouted Tom, bringing his boat to a stop. "That's why he can't jump! He can't reach the parachute!"

By this time the balloon had settled so low that the actions of the man could be plainly seen. That he was in great agony of fear, as well as in great pain from the terrific heat over his head was evident. He shifted about on the trapeze bar, now hanging by one hand, so as to bring his body a little farther below the blazing end of the bag, then, when one arm tired, he would hang by the other. If the balloon would only come down more quickly it would get to within such a short distance of the water that the man could safely make the drop. But the immense canvas bag was settling so slowly, for it was still very buoyant, that considerable time must elapse before it would be near enough to the water to make it safe for the unfortunate man to let go the trapeze.

"Oh, if we could only do something!" cried Tom. "We have to remain here helpless and watch him burn to death. It's awful!"

The three in the boat continued to gaze upward. They could see the man making frantic efforts to reach his parachute from time to time. Once, as a little current of air blew the flames and smoke to one side, he thought he had a chance. Up on the trapeze bar he pulled himself and then edged along it in an endeavor to grasp the ring of the parachute. Once he almost had hold of that and also the cord, which ran to a knife blade. This cord, being pulled, would sever the rope that bound it to the balloon, and he would be comparatively safe, so he might drop to the lake. But, just as he was about to grasp the ring and cord the smoke came swirling down on him and the hungry flames seemed to put out their fiery tongues to devour him. He had to slide back and once more hung by his hands.

"I thought he was saved then," whispered Tom, and even the whisper sounded loud in the silence.

Several men came running along the shore of the lake now. They saw the occupants in the *Arrow* and cried out:

"Why don't you save him? Go to his rescue!"

"What can we do?" asked Ned quietly of his two friends, but he did not trouble to answer the men on shore, who probably did not know what they were saying.

The motor-boat had drifted from a spot under the unfortunate balloonist, and at a word from his father the young inventor started the engine and steered the craft back directly under the blazing bag again.

"If he does drop, perhaps we may be able to pick him up," said Mr. Swift. "I wish we could save him!"

A cry from Ned startled Tom and his father, and their eyes, that had momentarily been directed away from the burning bag high in the air, were again turned toward it.

"The balloon is falling apart!" exclaimed Ned. "It's all up with him now!"

Indeed it did seem so, for pieces of the burning canvas, blazing and smoking, were falling in a shower from the part of the bag already consumed, and the fiery particles were fairly raining down on the man. But he still had his wits about him, though his perilous position was enough to make any one lose his mind, and he swung from side to side on the bar, shifting skillfully with his hands and dodging the larger particles of blazing canvas. When some small sparks fell on his clothing he beat them out with one hand, while with the other he clung to the trapeze.

There was scarcely any wind or the man's plight might have been more bearable, for the current of air would have carried the smoke and fire to one side. As it was, most of the smoke and flames went straight up, save now and then, when a draught created by the heat would swirl the black clouds down on the performer, hiding him from sight for a second or two. A breeze would have carried the sparks away instead of letting them fall on him.

Nearer and nearer to the surface of the lake sank the balloon. By this time the crowd on the bank had increased and there were excited opinions as to what was best to do. But the trouble was that little could be done. If the man could hold out until he got near enough to the water to let go he might yet be saved, but this would not be for some time at the present rate the balloon was falling. The performer realized this, and, as the fire was getting hotter, he made another desperate attempt to reach the parachute. It was unavailing and he had to drop back, hanging below the slender bar.

Suddenly there came a puff of wind, fanning the faces of those in the motor-boat, and they looked intently to observe if there was any current as high as was the balloonist. They saw the big bag sway to one side and the flames broke out more fiercely as they caught the draught. The balloon moved slowly down the lake.

"Keep after it, Tom!" urged his father. "We may be able to save him!"

The lad increased the speed of his engine and Ned, who was at the wheel, gave it a little twist. Then, with a suddenness that was startling, the blazing canvas airship began to settle swiftly toward the water. It had lost much of its buoyancy.

"Now he can jump! He's near enough to the water now!" cried Tom.

But a new danger arose. True, the balloon was rapidly approaching the surface of the lake and in a few seconds more would be within such a short distance that a leap would not be fatal. But the burning bag was coming straight down and scarcely would the man be in the water ere the fiery canvas mass would be on top of him.

In such an event he would either be burned to death or so held down that drowning must quickly follow.

"If there was only wind enough to carry the balloon beyond him after he jumped he could do it safely!" cried Ned.

Tom said nothing. He was measuring, with, his eye, the distance the balloon had yet to go and also the distance away the motor-boat was from where it would probably land.

"He can do it!" exclaimed the young inventor.

"How?" asked his father.

For answer Tom caught up a newspaper he had purchased at the hotel that morning. Rolling it quickly into a cone, so that it formed a rough megaphone, he put the smaller end to his mouth, and, pointing the larger opening at the balloonist, he called out:

"Drop into the lake! We'll pick you up before the bag falls on you! Jump! Let go now!"

The balloonist heard and understood. So did Ned and Mr. Swift. Tom's quick wit had found a way to save the man.

Faster and faster the blazing bag settled toward the surface of the water. It was now merely a mushroom-shaped piece of burning and smoking canvas, yet it was supporting the man almost as a parachute would have done.

With one look upward to the burning mass above him and a glance downward to the lake, the aeronaut let go his hold. Like a shot he came down, holding his body rigid and straight as a stick, for he knew how to fall into water, did that balloonist.

Tom Swift was ready for him. No sooner had the lad called his directions through the megaphone than the young inventor had speeded up his engine to the top notch.

"Steer so as to pick him up!" Tom cried to Ned, who was at the wheel. "Pass by him on a curve, and, as soon as I grab him, put the wheel over so as to get out from under the balloon."

It was a risky thing to do, but our hero had it all planned out. He made a loop of the boat's painter, and, hurrying to the bow, leaned over as far as he could, holding the rope in readiness. His idea was to have the balloonist grab the strands and be pulled out of danger by the speedy motor-boat, for the blazing canvas would cover such an extent of water that the man could not have swum out of the danger zone in time.

Down shot the balloonist and down more slowly settled the collapsed bag, yet not so slowly that there was any time to spare. It needed only a few seconds to drop over the performer, to burn and smother him.

Into the water splashed the man, disappearing from sight as when a stick is dropped in, point first. Ned was alert and steered the boat to the side in which the man's face was, for he concluded that the aeronaut would strike out in that direction when he came up. The *Arrow* was now directly under the blazing balloon and cries of fear from the watchers on shore urged upon Tom and his companions the danger of their position. But they had to take some risk to rescue the man.

"There he is!" cried Mr. Swift, who was on the watch, leaning over the side of the boat. Tom and Ned saw him at the same instant. Ned shifted his wheel and the young inventor bent over, holding out the rope for the man to grasp. He saw it and struck out toward the *Arrow*. But there was no need for him to go far. An instant more and the speeding motor-boat shot past him. He grabbed the rope and Tom, aided by Mr. Swift, began to lift him out of the water.

"Quick! To one side, Ned!" yelled Tom, for the heat of the descending mass of burning canvas struck him like a furnace blast.

Ned needed no urging. With a swirl of the screw the *Arrow* shot herself out of the way, carrying the aeronaut with her. A moment later the burning balloon, or what there was left of it, settled down into the lake, hissing angrily as the fire was quenched by the water and completely covering the spot where, but a few seconds before, the man had been swimming. He had been saved in the nick of time.

CHAPTER XXIII

PLANS FOR AN AIRSHIP

"Slow her down, Ned!" cried Tom, for the *Arrow* was shooting so swiftly through the water that the young inventor found it impossible to pull up the balloonist. Ned hurried back to the motor, and, when the boat's way had been checked, it was an easy matter to pull the dripping and almost exhausted man into the craft.

"Are you much hurt?" asked Mr. Swift anxiously, for Tom was too much out of breath with his exertion to ask any questions. For that matter the man was in almost as bad a plight. He was breathing heavily, as one who had run a long race.

"I—I guess I'm all right," he panted. "Only burned a little on my hands. That—that was a close call!"

The boat swung around and headed for shore, on which was quite a throng of persons. Some of them had cheered when they saw the plucky rescue.

"I'm afraid we can't save your balloon," gasped Tom as he looked at the place where the canvas was still floating and burning.

"No matter. It wasn't worth much. That's the last time I'll ever go up in a hot-air balloon," said the man with more energy than he had before exhibited. "I'm done with 'em. I've had my lesson. Hereafter an aeroplane or a gas balloon for me. I only did this to oblige the fair committee. I'll not do it again."

The man spoke in short, crisp sentences, as though he was in too much of a hurry to waste his words.

"Let it sink," he went on. "It's no good. Glad to see the last of it."

Almost as he spoke, with a final hiss and a cloud of steam that mingled with the black smoke, the remains of the big bag sunk beneath the surface of the lake.

"We must get you ashore at once and to a doctor," said Mr. Swift. "You must be badly burned."

"Not much. Only my hands, where some burning pieces of canvas fell on' em. If I had a little oil to put on I'd be all right."

"I can fix you up better than that," put in Tom. "I have some Vaseline."

"Good! Just the thing. Pass it over," and the man, though he spoke shortly, seemed grateful for the offer. "My name's Sharp," he went on, "John Sharp, of no place in particular, for I travel all over. I'm a professional balloonist. Ha! That's the stuff!"

This last was in reference to a bottle of Vaseline, which Tom produced. Mr. Sharp spread some over the backs of his hands and went on:

"That's better. Much obliged. I can't begin to thank you for what you did for me—saved my life. I thought it was all up with me—would have been but for you. Mustn't mind my manner—it's a way I have—have to talk quick when you're balloonin'—no time—but I'm grateful all the same. Who might you people be?"

Tom told him their names and Mr. Swift asked the aeronaut if he was sure he didn't need the services of a physician.

"No doctor for me," answered the balloonist. "I've been in lots of tight places, but this was the worst squeeze. If you'll put me ashore, I guess I can manage now."

"But you're all wet," objected Tom. "Where will you go? You need some other clothes," for the man wore a suit of tights and spangles.

"Oh, I'm used to this," went on the performer. "I frequently have to fall in the water. I always carry a little money with me so as to get back to the place where I started from. By the way, where am I?"

"Opposite Daleton," answered Tom. "Where did you go up from?"

"Pratonia. Big fair there. I was one of the features."

"Then you're about fifteen miles away," commented Mr. Swift. "You can hardly get back before night. Must you go there?"

"Left my clothes there. Also a valuable gas balloon. No more hot-air ones for me. Guess I'd better go back," and the aeronaut continued to speak in his quick, jerky sentences.

"We'd be very glad to have you come with us, Mr. Sharp," went on the inventor. "We are not far from Shopton, and if you would like to remain over night I'm sure we would make you comfortable. You can proceed to Pratonia in the morning."

"Thanks. Might not be a bad idea," said Mr. Sharp. "I'm obliged to you. I've got to go there to collect my money, though I suppose they won't give it all to me."

"Why not?" demanded Ned.

"Didn't drop from my parachute. Couldn't. Fire was one reason—couldn't reach the parachute, and if I could have, guess it wouldn't have been safe. Parachute probably was burned too. But I'm done with hot-air balloons though I guess I said that before."

The boys were much interested in the somewhat odd performer, and, on his part, he seemed to take quite a notion to Tom, who told him of several things that he had invented. "Well," remarked Mr. Swift after a while, during which the boat had been moving slowly down the lake, "if we are not to go ashore for a doctor for you, Mr. Sharp, suppose we put on more speed and get to my home? I'm anxious about a robbery that occurred there," and he related some facts in the case.

"Speed her up!" exclaimed Mr. Sharp. "Wish I could help you catch the scoundrels, but afraid I can't—hands too sore," and he looked at his burns. Then he told how he had made the ascension from the Pratonia fair grounds and how, when he was high in the air, he had discovered that the balloon was on fire. He described his sensations and told how he thought his time had surely come. Sparks from the hot air used to inflate it probably caused the blaze, he said.

"I've made a number of trips," he concluded, "hot air and gas bags, but this was the worst ever. It got on my nerves for a few minutes," he added coolly.

"I should think it would," agreed Tom as he speeded up the motor and sent the *Arrow* on her homeward way.

The boys and Mr. Swift were much interested in the experiences of the balloonist and asked him many questions, which he answered modestly. Several hours passed and late that afternoon the party approached Shopton.

"Here we are!" exclaimed Mr. Swift, relief in his tones. "Now to see of what I have been robbed and to get the police after the scoundrels!"

When the boat was nearing the dock Mr. Sharp, who had been silent for some time, suddenly turned to Tom and asked:

"Ever invent an airship?"

"No," replied the lad, somewhat surprised. "I never did."

"I have," went on the balloonist. "That is, I've invented part of it. I'm stuck over some details. Maybe you and I'll finish it some day. How about it?"

"Maybe," assented Tom, who was occupied just then in making a good landing. "I am interested in airships, but I never thought I could build one."

"Easiest thing in the world," went on Mr. Sharp, as if it was an everyday matter. "You and I will get busy as soon as we clear up this robbery." He talked as though he had been a friend of the family for some time, for he had a genial, taking manner.

A little later Mr. Swift was excitedly questioning Garret Jackson concerning the robbery and making an examination of the electrical shop to discover what was missing.

"They've taken some parts of my gyroscope!" he exclaimed, "and some valuable tools and papers, as well as some unfinished work that will be difficult to replace."

"Much of a loss?" asked Mr. Sharp with a business-like air.

"Well, not so large as regards money," answered the inventor, "but they took things I can never replace, and I will miss them very much if I cannot get them back."

"Then we'll get them back!" snapped the balloonist, as if that was all there was to it.

The police were called up on the telephone and the facts given to them, as well as a description of the stolen things. They promised to do what they could, but, in the light of past experiences, Tom and his father did not think this would be much. There was little more that could be done that evening. Ned Newton went to his home, and, after Mr. Swift had insisted in calling in his physician to look after Mr. Sharp's burns the balloonist was given a room next to Tom's. Then the Swift household settled down.

"Well," remarked Tom to his father, as he got ready for bed, "this sure has been an exciting day."

"And my loss is a serious one," added the inventor somewhat sadly.

"Don't worry, dad," begged his son. "I'll do my best to recover those things for you."

Several days passed, but there was no clue to the thieves. That they were the same ones who had stolen the turbine model there was little doubt, but they seemed to have covered their tracks well. The police were at a loss, and, though Tom and Mr. Sharp cruised about the lake, they could get no trace of the men. The balloonist had sent to Pratonia for his clothing and other baggage and was now installed in the Swift home, where he was invited to stay a week or two.

One night when he was looking over some papers he had taken from his trunk the balloonist came over to where Tom was making a drawing of a new machine he was planning and said:

"Like to see my idea for an airship? Different from some. It's a dirigible balloon with an aeroplane front and rear to steer and balance it in big winds. It would be a winner, only for one thing. Maybe you can help me."

"Maybe I can," agreed Tom, who was at once interested.

"We ought to be able to do something. Look at our names—Swift and Sharp—quick and penetrating—a good firm to build airships," and he laughed genially. "Shall we do it?"

"I'm willing," agreed Tom, and the balloonist spread his plans out on the table, he and the young inventor soon being deep in a discussion of them.

CHAPTER XXIV

THE MYSTERY SOLVED

From then on, for several days, the young inventor and his new friend lived in an atmosphere of airships. They talked them from morning until night, and even Mr. Swift, much as he was exercised over his loss, took part in the discussions.

In the meanwhile efforts had not ceased to locate the robbers and recover the stolen goods, but so far without success.

One afternoon, about two weeks after the thrilling rescue of John Sharp, Tom said to the balloonist:

"Wouldn't you like to come for a ride in the motor-boat? Maybe it will help us to solve the puzzle of the airship. We'll take a trip across and up the opposite shore."

"Good idea," commented Mr. Sharp. "Fine day for a sail. Come on. Blow the cobwebs from our brains."

Mr. Swift declined an invitation to accompany them, as he said he would stay home and try to straighten out his affairs, which were somewhat muddled by the robbery.

Out over the blue waters of Lake Carlopa shot the *Arrow*. It was making only moderate speed, as Tom was in no hurry, and he knew his engine would last longer if not forced too frequently. They glided along, crossed the lake and were proceeding up the opposite shore when, as they turned out from a little bay and rounded a point of land, Mr. Sharp exclaimed:

"Look out, Tom, there's rowboat just ahead!"

"Oh, I'll pass well to one side of that," answered the young inventor, looking at the craft. As he did so, noting that there were four men in it, one of the occupants caught a glimpse of the *Arrow*. No sooner had he done so than he spoke to his companions, and they all turned to stare at Tom. At first the lad could scarcely believe his eyes, but as he looked more intently he uttered a cry.

"There they are!"

"Who?" inquired Mr. Sharp.

"Those men—the thieves! We must catch them!"

Tom had spoken loudly, but even though the men in the row-boat did hear what he said, they would have realized without that that they were about to be pursued, for there was no mistaking the attitude of our hero.

Two of the thieves were at the oars, and, with one accord, they at once increased their speed. The boat swung about sharply and was headed for the shore, which they seemed to have come from only a short time previous, as the craft was not far out in the lake.

"No, you don't!" cried Tom. "I see your game! You want to get to the woods, where you'll have a better chance to escape! If this isn't great luck, coming upon them this way!"

It was the work of but a moment to speed up the engine and head the *Arrow* for the rowboat. The men were pulling frantically, but they had no chance.

"Get between them and the shore!" cried Mr. Sharp. "You can head them off then." This was good advice and Tom followed it. The men, among whom the lad could recognize Happy Harry and Anson Morse, were all excited. Two of them stood up, as though to jump overboard, but their companions called to them to stop.

"If we only had a gun now, not to shoot at them but to intimidate them," murmured the balloonist, "maybe they'd stop."

"Here's one," answered Tom, pointing to the seat locker, where he kept the shotgun Mr. Duncan had given him. In a moment Mr. Sharp had it out.

"Surrender!" he cried, pointing the weapon at the men in the small boat.

"Don't shoot! Don't fire on us! We'll give up!" cried Happy Harry, and the two with the oars ceased pulling.

"Don't take any chances," urged Mr. Sharp in a low voice. "Keep between them and the shore. I'll cover them." Tom was steering from an auxiliary side wheel near the motor, and soon the *Arrow* had cut off the retreat of the men. They could not land and to row across the lake meant speedy capture.

"Well, what do you want of us?" growled Morse. "What right have you got to interfere with us in this fashion?"

"The best of right," answered Tom. "You'll find out when you're landed in jail."

"You can't arrest us," sneered Happy Harry. "You're not an officer and you haven't any warrant."

Tom hadn't thought of that, and his chagrin showed in his face. Happy Harry was quick to see it.

"You'd better let us go," he threatened "We can have you arrested for bothering us. You haven't any right to stop us, Tom Swift."

"Maybe he hasn't, but I have!" exclaimed John Sharp suddenly.

"You! Who are you?" demanded Featherton, alias Simpson, the man who had run the automobile that carried Tom away.

"Me. I'm a special deputy sheriff for this county," answered the balloonist simply. "Here's my badge," and, throwing back his coat, he displayed it. "You see I got the appointment in order to have some authority in the crowds that gather to watch me go up," he explained to Tom, who plainly showed his astonishment. "I found it very useful to be able to threaten arrest, but in this case I'll do more than threaten. You are my prisoners," he went on to the men in the boat, and he handled the shotgun as if he knew how to use it. "I'll take you into custody on complaint of Mr. Swift for robbery. Now will you go quietly or are you going to make a fuss?" and Mr. Sharp shut his jaw grimly.

"Well, seeing as how you have the drop on us, I guess we'll have to do as you say," admitted Happy Harry, alias Jim Burke. "But you can't prove anything against us. We haven't any of Mr. Swift's property."

"Well, you know where it is then," retorted Tom quickly.

Under the restraining influence of the gun the men made no resistance. While Mr. Sharp covered them, Tom towed their boat toward shore. Then, while the young inventor held the gun, the balloonist tied the hands and feet of the thieves in a most scientific manner, for what he did not know about ropes and knots was not worth putting into a book.

"Now, I guess they'll stay quiet for a while," remarked Mr. Sharp as he surveyed the crestfallen criminals. "I'll remain on guard here, Tom, while you go notify the nearest constable and we'll take them to jail. We bagged the whole lot as neatly as could be desired."

"No, you didn't get all of us!" exclaimed Happy Harry, and there was a savage anger in his tones.

"Keep quiet!" urged Morse.

"No, I'll not keep quiet! It's a shame that we have to take our medicine while that trimmer, Tod Boreck, goes free. He ought to have been with us, and he would be, only he's trying to get away with that sparkler!"

"Keep quiet," again urged Morse.

Tom was all attention. He had caught the word "sparkler," and he at once associated it with the occasion he had heard the men use it before. He felt that he was on the track of solving the mystery connected with his boat.

He looked at the men. They were the same four who had been involved in the former theft—Appleson, Featherton, Morse and Burke. Were there five of them? He recalled the man who had been caught tampering with his boat—the man who had tried to bid on the *Arrow* at the auction. Where was he?

"Boreck didn't get what he was after," resumed Happy Harry, "and I'm going to spoil his game for him. Say, kid," he went on to

Tom, "look in the front part of your boat—where the gasoline tank is."

Tom felt his heart beating fast. At last he felt that he would solve the puzzle. He opened the forward compartment. To his disappointment it seemed as usual. Morse and the others were making a vain effort to silence Happy Harry.

"I don't see anything here," said Tom.

"No, because it's hidden in one of those blocks of wood you use for a brace," continued the man. "Which one it is, Boreck didn't know, so he pulled out two or three, only to be fooled each time. You must have shifted them, kid, from the way they were when we had the boat."

"I did," answered the young inventor, recollecting how he had taken out some of the braces and inserted new ones, then painted the interior of the compartment. "What is in the braces, anyhow?"

"The sparkler—a big diamond—in a hollow place in the wood, kid!" exclaimed Happy Harry, blurting out the words. "I'm not going to let Tod Boreck get away with it while we stay in jail."

"Take out all the braces that haven't been moved and have a look," suggested Mr. Sharp. Tom only had to remove two, those farthest back, for all the others had, at one time or another, been changed or taken away by the thief.

One of the blocks did not seem to have anything unusual about it, but at the sight of the other Tom could not repress a cry. It was the one that seemed to have had a hole bored in it and then plugged up again. He remembered his father noticing it on the occasion of overhauling the boat.

"The sparkler's in there," said the tramp as he saw the brace. "Boreck was after it several times, but he never pulled out the right one."

With his knife Tom dug out the putty that covered the round hole in the block. No sooner had he done so than there rolled out into his hand a white object. It was something done up in tissue paper, and as he removed the wrapper, there was a flash in the sunlight and a large, beautiful diamond was revealed. The mystery had been solved.

CHAPTER XXV

WINNING A RACE

"Where did this diamond come from?" demanded Mr. Sharp of the quartette of criminals.

"That's for us to know and you to find out," sneered Happy Harry. "I don't care as long as that trimmer Boreck didn't get it. He tried to do us out of our share."

"Well, I guess the police will make you tell," went on the balloonist. "Go for the constable, Tom."

Leaving his friend to guard the ugly men, who for a time at least were beyond the possibility of doing harm, Tom hurried off through the woods to the nearest village. There he found an officer and the gang was soon lodged in jail. The diamond was turned over to the authorities, who said they would soon locate the owner.

Nor were they long in doing it, for it appeared the gem was part of a large jewel robbery that had taken place some time before in a distant city. The Happy Harry gang, as the men came to be called, were implicated in it, though they got only a small share of the plunder. Search was made for Tod Boreck and he was captured about a week after his companions. Seeing that their game was up, the men made a partial confession, telling where Mr. Swift's goods had been secreted, and the inventor's valuable tools, papers and machinery were recovered, no damage having been done to them.

It developed that after the diamond theft, and when the gang still had possession of Mr. Hastings' boat, Boreck, sometimes called Murdock by his cronies, unknown to them, had secreted the jewel in one of the braces under the gasoline tank. He expected to get it out secretly, but the capture of the gang and the sale of the boat prevented this. Then he tried to buy the craft to take out the diamond, but Tom overbid him. It was Boreck who found Andy's bunch of keys and used one to open the compartment lock when Tom surprised him. The man did manage to remove some of the blocks, thinking he had the one with the diamond in it, but the fact of Tom changing them, and painting the compartment deceived him. The gang hoped to get some valuables from Mr. Swift's shops, and, to a certain extent, succeeded after hanging around for several nights and following him to Sandport, but Tom eventually proved too much for them. Even stealing the *Arrow*, which was taken to aid the gang in robbing Mr. Swift, did not succeed, and Boreck's plan then to get possession of the diamond fell through.

It was thought that the gang would get long terms in prison, but one night, during a violent storm, they escaped from the local jail and that was the last seen of them for some time.

A few days after the capture as Tom was in the boathouse making some minor repairs to the motor he heard a voice calling:

"Mistah Swift, am yo' about?"

"Hello, Rad, is that you?" he inquired, recognizing the voice of the colored owner of the mule Boomerang.

"Yais, sa, dat's me. I got a lettah fo' yo'. I were passin' de post-office an' de clerk asted me to brung it to yo' case as how it's marked 'hurry,' an' he said he hadn't seen yo' today."

"That's right. I've been so busy I haven't had time to go for the mail," and Tom took the letter, giving Eradicate ten cents for his trouble.

"Ha, that's good!" exclaimed Tom as he read it.

"Hab some one done gone an' left yo' a fortune, Mistah Swift?" asked the negro.

"No, but it's almost as good. It's an invitation to take part in the motor-boat races next week. I'd forgotten all about them. I must get ready."

"Good land! Dat's all de risin' generation t'inks about now," observed Eradicate, "racin' an' goin' fast. Mah ole mule Boomerang am good enough fo' me," and, shaking his head in a woeful manner, Eradicate went on his way.

Tom told Mr. Sharp and his father of the proposed races of the Lanton Motor-boat Club, and, as it was required that two persons be in a craft the size of the *Arrow*, the young inventor arranged for the balloonist to accompany him. Our hero spent the next few days in tuning up his motor and in getting the *Arrow* ready for the contest.

The races took place on that side of Lake Carlopa near where Mr. Hastings lived, and he was one of the officials of the club. There were several classes, graded according to the horsepower of the motors, and Tom found himself in a class with Andy Foger.

"Here's where I beat you," boasted the red-haired youth exultantly, though his manner toward Tom was more temperate than usual. Andy had learned a lesson.

"Well, if you can beat me I'll give you credit for it," answered Tom.

The first race was for high-powered craft, and in this Mr. Hastings' new *Carlopa* won. Then came the trial of the small boats, and Tom was pleased to note that Miss Nestor was on hand in the tiny *Dot*.

"Good luck!" he called to her as he was adjusting his timer, for his turn would come soon. "Remember what I told you about the spark," for he had given her a few lessons.

"If I win it will be due to you," she called brightly.

She did win, coming in ahead of several confident lads who had better boats. But Miss Nestor handled the *Dot* to perfection and crossed the line a boat's length ahead of her nearest competitor.

"Fine!" cried Tom, and then came the warning gun that told him to get ready for his trial.

This was a five-mile race and had several entrants. The affair was a handicap one and Tom had no reason to complain of the rating allowed him.

"Crack!" went the starting pistol and away went Tom and one or two others who had the same allowance as did he. A little later the others started and finally the last class, including Andy Foger. The *Red Streak* shot ahead and was soon in the lead, for Andy and Sam had learned better how to handle their craft. Tom and Mr. Sharp were worried, but they stuck grimly to the race and when the turning stake was reached Tom's motor had so warmed up and was running so well that he crept up on Andy. A mile from the final mark Andy and Tom were on even terms, and though the red-haired lad tried to shake off his rival he could not. Andy's ignition system failed him several times and he changed from batteries to magneto and back again in the hope of getting a little more speed out of the motor.

But it was not to be. A half-mile away from the finish Tom, who had fallen behind a little, crept up on even terms. Then he slowly forged ahead, and, a hundred rods from the stake, the young inventor knew that the race was his. He clinched it a few minutes later, crossing the line amid a burst of cheers. The *Arrow* had beaten several boats out of her own class and Tom was very proud and happy.

"My, but we certainly did scoot along some!" cried Mr. Sharp. "But that's nothing to how we'll go when we build our airship, eh, Tom?" and he looked at the flushed face of the lad.

"No, indeed," agreed the young inventor. "But I don't know that we'll take part in any races in it. We'll build it, however, as soon as we can solve that one difficulty."

They did solve it, as will be told in the next book of this series, to be called "Tom Swift and His Airship; or, The Stirring Cruise of the *Red Cloud*." They had some remarkable adventures in the wonderful craft, and solved the mystery of a great bank robbery.

This ended the contests of the motor-boats and the little fleet crowded up to the floats and docks, where the prizes were to be awarded. Tom received a handsome silver cup and Miss Nestor a gold bracelet.

"Now I want all the contestants, winners and losers, to come up to my house and have lunch," invited Mr. Hastings.

As Tom and the balloonist strolled up the walk to the handsome house Andy Foger passed them.

"You wouldn't have beaten me if my spark coil hadn't gone back on me," he said, somewhat sneeringly.

"Maybe," admitted Tom, and just then he caught sight of Mary Nestor. "May I take you in to lunch?" he asked.

"Yes," she said, "because you helped me to win," and she blushed prettily. And then they all sat down to the tables set out on the lawn, while Tom looked so often at Mary Nestor that Mr. Sharp said afterward it was a wonder he found time to eat. But Tom didn't care. He was happy.

TOM SWIFT
AND HIS AIRSHIP

CHAPTER 1

AN EXPLOSION

"Are you all ready, Tom?"

"All ready, Mr. Sharp," replied a young man, who was stationed near some complicated apparatus, while the questioner, a dark man, with a nervous manner, leaned over a large tank.

"I'm going to turn on the gas now," went on the man. "Look out for yourself. I'm not sure what may happen."

"Neither am I, but I'm ready for it. If it does explode it can't do much damage."

"Oh, I hope it doesn't explode. We've had so much trouble with the airship, I trust nothing goes wrong now."

"Well, turn, on the gas, Mr. Sharp," advised Tom Swift. "I'll watch the pressure gauge, and, if it goes too high, I'll warn you, and you can shut it off."

The man nodded, and, with a small wrench in his hand, went to one end of the tank. The youth, looking anxiously at him, turned his gaze now and then toward a gauge, somewhat like those on steam boilers, which gauge was attached to an aluminum, cigar-shaped affair, about five feet long.

Presently there was a hissing sound in the small frame building where the two were conducting an experiment which meant much to them. The hissing grew louder.

"Be ready to jump," advised Mr. Sharp.

"I will," answered the lad. "But the pressure is going up very slowly. Maybe you'd better turn on more gas."

"I will. Here she goes! Look out now. You can't tell what is going to happen."

With a sudden hiss, as the powerful gas, under pressure, passed from the tank, through the pipes, and into the aluminum container, the hand on the gauge swept past figure after figure on the dial.

"Shut it off!" cried Tom quickly. "It's coming too fast! Shut her off!"

The man sprang to obey the command, and, with nervous fingers, sought to fit the wrench over the nipple of the controlling valve. Then his face seemed to turn white with fear.

"I can't move it!" Mr. Sharp yelled. "It's jammed! I can't shut off the gas! Run! Look out! She'll explode!"

Tom Swift, the young inventor, whose acquaintance some of you have previously made, gave one look at the gauge, and seeing that the pressure was steadily mounting, endeavored to reach, and open, a stop-cock, that he might relieve the strain. One trial showed him that the valve there had jammed too, and catching up a roll of blue prints the lad made a dash for the door of the shop. He was not a second behind his companion, and hardly had they passed out of the structure before there was a loud explosion which shook the building, and shattered all the windows in it.

Pieces of wood, bits of metal, and a cloud of sawdust and shavings flew out of the door after the man and the youth, and this was followed by a cloud of yellowish smoke.

"Are you hurt, Tom?" cried Mr. Sharp, as he swung around to look back at the place where the hazardous experiment had been conducted.

"Not a bit! How about you?"

"I'm all right. But it was touch and go! Good thing you had the gauge on or we'd never have known when to run. Well, we've made another failure of it," and the man spoke somewhat bitterly.

"Never mind, Mr. Sharp," went on Tom Swift. "I think it will be the last mistake. I see what the trouble is now; and know how to remedy it. Come on back, and we'll try it again; that is if the tank hasn't blown up."

"No, I guess that's all right. It was the aluminum container that went up, and that's so light it didn't do much damage. But we'd better wait until some of those fumes escape. They're not healthy to breathe."

The cloud of yellowish smoke was slowly rolling away, and the man and lad were approaching the shop, which, in spite of the explosion that had taken place in it, was still intact, when an aged man, coming from a handsome house not far off, called out, "Tom, is anyone hurt?"

"No, dad. We're all right."

"What happened?"

"Well, we had another explosion. We can't seem to get the right mixture of the gas, but I think we've had the last of our bad luck. We're going to try it again. Up to now the gas has been too strong, the tank too weak, or else our valve control is bad."

"Oh dear, Mr. Swift! Do tell them to be careful!" a woman's voice chimed in. "I'm sure something dreadful will happen! This is about the tenth time something has blown up around here, and-"

"It's only the ninth, Mrs. Baggert," interrupted Tom, somewhat indignantly.

"Well, goodness me! Isn't nine almost as bad as ten? There I was, just putting my bread in the oven," went on Mrs. Baggert, the housekeeper, "and I was so startled that I dropped it, and now the dough is all over the kitchen floor. I never saw such a mess."

"I'm sorry," answered the youth, trying not to laugh. "We'll see that it doesn't happen again."

"Yes; that's what you always say," rejoined the motherly-looking woman, who looked after the interests of Mr. Swift's home.

"Well, we mean it this time," retorted the lad. "We see where our mistake was; don't we. Mr. Sharp?"

"I think so," replied the other seriously.

"Come on back, and we'll see what damage was done," proposed Tom. "Maybe we can rig up another container, mix some fresh gas, and make the final experiment this afternoon."

"Now do be careful," cautioned Mr. Swift, the aged inventor, once more. "I'm afraid you two have set too hard a task for yourselves this time."

"No we haven't, dad," answered his son. "You'll see us yet skimming along above the clouds."

"Humph! If you go above the clouds I shan't be very likely to see you. But go slowly, now. Don't blow the place up again."

Mr. Swift went into the house, followed by Mrs. Baggert, who was loudly bewailing the fate of her bread. Tom and Mr. Sharp started toward the shop where they had been working. It was one of several buildings, built for experimental purposes and patent work by Mr. Swift, near his home.

"It didn't do so very much damage," observed Tom, as he peered in through a window, void of all the panes of glass. "We can start right in."

"Hold on! Wait! Don't try it now!" exclaimed Mr. Sharp, who talked in short, snappy sentences, which, however, said all he meant. "The fumes of that gas aren't good to breathe. Wait, until they have blown away. It won't be long. It's safer."

He began to cough, choking from the pungent odor, and Tom felt an unpleasant tickling sensation in his throat.

"Take a walk around," advised Mr. Sharp. "I'll be looking over the blue prints. Let's have 'em."

Tom handed over the roll he had grabbed up when he ran from the shop, just before the explosion took place, and, while his companion spread them out on his knee, as he sat on an upturned barrel, the lad walked toward the rear of the large yard. It was enclosed by a high board fence, with a locked gate, but Tom, undoing the fastenings, stepped out into a broad, green meadow at the rear of his father's property. As he did so he saw three boys running toward him.

"Hello!" exclaimed our hero. "There are Andy Foger, Sam Snedecker and Pete Bailey. I wonder what they're heading this way for?"

On the trio came, increasing their pace as they caught sight of Tom. Andy Foger, a red-haired and squint-eyed lad, a sort of town bully, with a rich and indulgent father, was the first to reach the young inventor.

"How-how many are killed?" panted Andy.

"Shall we go for doctors?" asked Sam.

"Can we see the place?" blurted out Pete, and he had to sit down on the grass, he was so winded.

"Killed? Doctors?" repeated Tom, clearly much puzzled. "What are you fellows driving at, anyhow?"

"Wasn't there a lot of people killed in the explosion we heard?" demanded Andy, in eager tones.

"Not a one," replied Tom.

"There was an explosion!" exclaimed Pete. "We heard it, and you can't fool us!"

"And we saw the smoke," added Snedecker.

"Yes, there was a small explosion," admitted Tom, with a smile, "but no one was killed; or even hurt. We don't have such things happen in our shops."

"Nobody killed?" repeated Andy questioningly, and the disappointment was evident in his tones.

"Nobody hurt?" added Sam, his crony, and he, too, showed his chagrin.

"All our run for nothing," continued Pete, another crony, in disgust.

"What happened?" demanded the red-haired lad, as if he had a right to know. "We were walking along the lake road, and we heard an awful racket. If the police come out here, you'll have to tell what it was, Tom Swift." He spoke defiantly.

"I've no objection to telling you or the police," replied Tom. "There was an explosion. My friend, Mr. Sharp, the balloonist, and I were conducting an experiment with a new kind of gas, and it was too strong, that's all. An aluminum container blew up, but no particular damage was done. I hope you're satisfied."

"Humph! What you making, anyhow?" demanded Andy, and again he spoke as if he had a right to know.

"I don't know that it's any of your business," Tom came back at him sharply, "but, as everyone will soon know, I may as well tell you. We're building an airship."

"An airship?" exclaimed Sam and Pete in one breath.

"An airship?" queried Andy, and there was a sneer in his voice. "Well, I don't think you can do it, Tom Swift! You'll never build an airship; even if you have a balloonist to help you!"

"I won't, eh?" and Tom was a trifle nettled at the sneering manner of his rival.

"No, you won't! It takes a smarter fellow than you are to build an airship that will sail. I believe I could beat you at it myself."

"Oh, you think you could?" asked Tom, and this time he had mastered his emotions. He was not going to let Andy Foger make him angry. "Maybe you can beat me at racing, too?" he went on. "If you think so, bring out your Red Streak and I'll try the Arrow against her. I beat you twice, and I can do it again!"

This unexpected taunt disconcerted Andy. It was the truth, for, more than once had Tom, in his motor-boat, proved more than a match for the squint-eyed bully and his cronies.

"Go back at him, Andy," advised Sam, ire low voice. "Don't take any of his guff!"

"I don't intend to," spluttered Andy. "Maybe you did beat me in the races, because my motor wasn't working right," he conceded, "but you can't do it again. Anyhow, that's got nothing to do with an airship. I'll bet you can't make one!"

"I don't bet," replied Tom calmly, "but if you wait a few weeks you'll see me in an airship, and then, if you want to race the Red Streak against that, I'll accommodate you. Or, if you want to enter into a competition to build a dirigible balloon or an aeroplane I'm willing."

"Huh! Think you're smart, don't you? Just because you helped save that balloonist from being killed when his balloon caught fire," went on Andy, for want of something better to say. "But you'll never build an airship!"

"Of course he won't!" added Sam and Pete, bound to side with their crony, to whom they were indebted for many automobile and motor-boat rides.

"Just wait," advised Tom, with a tantalizing smile. "Meanwhile, if you want to try the Red Streak against the Arrow, I'm willing. I have an hour or so to spare."

"Aw, keep still!" muttered Andy, much discomfited, for the defeat of his speedy boat, by a much smaller and less powerful one, was a sore point with him. "You just wait, that's all. I'll get even with you!"

"Look here!" cried Tom, suddenly. "You always say that whenever I get the best of you. I'm sick of hearing it. I consider that a threat, and I don't like it. If you don't look out, Andy Foger, you'll have trouble with me, and at no very distant date!"

Tom, with flashing eyes, and clenched fists, took a step forward. Andy shrank back.

"Don't be afraid of him," advised Sam. "We'll stand by you, Andy."

"I ain't afraid," muttered the red-haired lad, but it was noticed that he shuffled off. " You just wait, I'll fix you," he added to Tom. The bully was plainly in a rage.

The young inventor was about to reply, and, possibly would have made a more substantial rejoinder to Andy than mere words, when the gate opened, and Mr. Sharp stepped out.

"The fumes have all cleared away, Tom," he said. "We can go in the shop, now."

Without further notice of Andy Foger, Tom Swift turned aside, and followed the aeronaut into the enclosed yard.

CHAPTER 2

NED SEES MYSTERIOUS MEN

"Who were those fellows?" asked the balloonist, of his companion.

"Oh, some chaps who think we'll never build our airship, Mr. Sharp. Andy Foger, and his crowd."

"Well, we'll show them whether we will or not," rejoined the man. "I've just thought of one point where we made a mistake. Your father suggested it to me. We need a needle valve in the gas tank. Then we can control the flow of vapor better."

"Of course!" cried Tom. "Why didn't I think of that? Let's try it." And the pair hurried into the machine shop, eager to make another test, which they hoped would be more successful.

The young inventor, for Tom Swift was entitled to that title, having patented several machines, lived with his father, Barton Swift, on the outskirts of the small town of Shopton, in New York State. Mr. Swift was quite wealthy, having amassed a considerable fortune from several of his patents, as he was also an inventor. Tom's mother had been dead since he was a small child, and Mrs. Baggert kept house for the widower and his son. There was also, in their household, an aged engineer, named Garret Jackson, who attended to the engine and boilers that operated machinery and apparatus in several small shops that surrounded the Swift homestead; for Mr. Swift did most of his work at home.

As related in the first volume of this series, entitled "Tom Swift and His Motor-Cycle," the lad had passed through some strenuous adventures. A syndicate of rich men, disappointed in a turbine motor they had acquired from a certain inventor, hired a gang of scoundrels to get possession of a turbine Mr. Swift had invented. Just before they made the attempt, however, Tom became possessed of a motor-cycle. It had belonged to a wealthy man, Mr. Wakefield Damon, of Waterford, near Lake Carlopa, which body of water adjoined the town of Shopton; but Mr. Damon had two accidents with the machine, and sold it to Tom cheap. Tom was riding his motorcycle to Albany, to deliver his father's model of the turbine motor to a lawyer, in order to get a patent on it, when he was attacked by the gang of bad men. These included Ferguson Appleson, Anson Morse, Wilson Featherton, alias Simpson, Jake Burke, alias Happy Harry, who sometimes masqueraded as a tramp, and Tod Boreck, alias Murdock. These men knocked Tom unconscious, stole the valuable model and some papers, and carried the youth away in their automobile.

Later the young inventor, following a clue given him by Eradicate Sampson, an aged colored man, who, with his mule, Boomerang, went about the country doing odd jobs, got on the trail of the thieves in a deserted mansion in the woods at the upper end of the lake. Our hero, with the aid of Mr. Damon, and some friends of the latter, raided the old house, but the men escaped.

In the second book of the series, called "Tom Swift and His Motor-Boat," there was related the doings of the lad, his father and his chum, Ned Newton, on Lake Carlopa. Tom bought at auction, a motor-boat the thieves had stolen and damaged, and, fixing it up, made a speedy craft of it so speedy, in fact that it beat the racing-boat Red Streak-owned by Andy Foger. But Tom did more than race in his boat. He took his father on a tour for his health, and, during Mr. Swift's absence from home, the gang of bad men stole some of the inventor's machinery. Tom set out after them in his motor boat, but the scoundrels even managed to steal that, hoping to get possession of a peculiar and mysterious treasure in it, and Tom had considerable trouble.

Among other things he did when he had his craft, was to aid a Miss Mary Nestor, who, in her cousin's small boat, the Dot, was having trouble with the engine, and you shall hear more of Miss Nestor presently, for she and Tom became quite friendly. Events so shaped themselves that Andy Foger was glad to loan Tom the Red Streak in which to search for the stolen Arrow, and it was in the later craft that Tom, his father and Ned Newton had a most thrilling adventure.

They were on their way down the lake when, in the air overhead they saw a balloon on fire, with a man clinging to the trapeze. They managed to save the fellow's life, after a strenuous endeavor. The balloonist, John Sharp, was destined to play quite a part in Tom's life.

Mr. Sharp was more than an aeronaut-he was the inventor of an airship—that is, he had plans drawn for the more important parts, but he had struck a "snag of clouds," as he expressed it, and could not make the machine work. His falling in with Mr. Swift and his son seemed providential, for Tom and his father were at once interested in the project for navigating the upper air. They began a study of Mr. Sharp's plans, and the balloonist was now in a fair way to have the difficulty solved.

His airship was, primarily an aeroplane, but with a sustaining aluminum container, shaped like a cigar, and filled with a secret gas, made partly of hydrogen, being very light and powerful. It was testing the effect of this gas on a small model of the aluminum container that the explosion, told of in the first chapter, occurred. In fact it was only one of several explosions, but, as Tom said, all the while they were eliminating certain difficulties, until now the airship seemed almost a finished thing. But a few more details remained to be worked out, and Mr. Swift and his son felt that they could master these.

So it was with a feeling of no little elation, that the young inventor followed Mr. Sharp into the shop. The balloonist, it may be explained, had been invited to live with the Swifts pending the completion of the airship.

"Do you think we'll get on the right track if we put the needle valve in?" asked Tom, as he noted with satisfaction that the damage from the explosion was not great.

"I'm sure we will," answered the aeronaut. "Now let's make another model container, and try the gas again."

They set to work, with Mr. Swift helping them occasionally, and Garret Jackson, the engineer, lending a hand whenever he was needed. All that afternoon work on the airship progressed. The joint inventors of it wanted to be sure that the sustaining gas bag, or aluminum container, would do its work properly, as this would hold them in the air, and prevent accidents, in case of a stoppage of the engine or propellers.

The aeroplane part of the airship was all but finished, and the motor, a powerful machine, of new design, built by Mr. Swift, was ready to be installed.

All that afternoon Tom, his father and Mr. Sharp labored in the shop. As it grew dusk there sounded from the house the ringing of a bell.

"Supper time," remarked Tom, laying aside a wrench. "I wish Mrs. Baggert would wait about an hour. I'd have this valve nearly done, then."

But the housekeeper was evidently not going to wait, for her voice supplemented the bell.

"Supper! Sup-per!" she called. "Come now, Mr. Swift; Tom, Mr. Sharp! I can't wait any longer! The meat and potatoes will be spoiled!"

"I s'pose we'd better go in," remarked Mr. Sharp, with something of a sigh. "We can finish tomorrow."

The shop, where certain parts of the airship were being made, was doubly locked, and Jackson, the engineer, who was also a sort of watchman, was bidden to keep good guard, for the fear of the gang of unscrupulous men, who had escaped from jail during a great storm, was still in the minds of Mr. Swift and his son.

"And give an occasional look in the shed, where the aeroplane is," advised Mr. Sharp. "It wouldn't take much to damage that, now."

"I'll pay particular attention to it," promised the engineer. "Don't worry, Mr. Sharp."

After supper the three gathered around the table on which were spread out sheets of paper, covered with intricate figures and calculations, which Mr. Swift and the balloonist went over with care. Tom was examining some blue prints, which gave a sectional view of the proposed ship, and was making some measurements when the bell rang, and Mrs. Baggert ushered in Ned Newton, the most particular chum of the young inventor.

"Hello, Ned!" exclaimed Tom. "I was wondering what had become of you. Haven't seen you in a dog's age."

"That's right," admitted Ned. "We've been working late nights at the bank. Getting ready for the regular visit of the examiner, who usually comes along about this time. Well, how are things going; and how is the airship?" for, of course, Ned had heard of that.

"Oh, pretty good. Had another explosion today, I s'pose you heard."

"No, I hadn't."

"I thought everyone in town had, for Andy Foger and his two cronies were on hand, and they usually tell all they know."

"Oh, Andy Foger! He makes me sick! He was scooting up the street in his auto just as I was coming in, `honking-honking' his horn to beat the band! You'd think no one ever had an auto but him. He certainly was going fast."

"Wait until I get in our airship," predicted Tom. "Then I'll show you what speed is!"

"Do you really think it will go fast?"

"Of course it will! Fast enough to catch Anson Morse and his crowd of scoundrels if we could get on their track."

"Why, I thought they were in jail," replied Ned, in some surprise. "Weren't they arrested after they stole your boat?"

"Yes, and put in jail, but they managed to get out, and now they're free to make trouble for us again."

"Are you sure they're out of jail?" asked Ned, and Tom noted that his chum's face wore an odd look.

"Sure? Of course I am. But why do you ask?"

Ned did not answer for a moment. He glanced at Tom's father, and the young inventor understood. Mr. Swift was getting rather along in age, and his long years of brain work had made him nervous. He had a great fear of Morse and his gang, for they had made much trouble for him in the past. Tom appreciated his chum's hesitancy, and guessed that Ned had something to say that he did not want Mr. Swift to hear.

"Come on up to my room, Ned. I've got something I want to show you," exclaimed Tom, after a pause.

The two lads left the room, Tom glancing apprehensively at his father. But Mr. Swift was so engrossed, together with the aeronaut, in making some calculations regarding wind pressure, that it is doubtful if either of the men were aware that the boys had gone.

"Now what is it, Ned?" demanded our hero, when they were safe in his apartment. "Something's up. I can tell by your manner. What is it?"

"Maybe it's nothing at all," went on his chum. "If I had known, though that those men had gotten out of jail, I would have paid more attention to what I saw tonight, as I was leaving the bank to come here."

"What did you see?" demanded Tom, and his manner, which had been calm, became somewhat excited.

"Well, you know I've been helping the payingteller straighten up his books," went on the young bank employee, "and when I came out tonight, after working for several hours, I was glad enough to hurry away from the 'slave-den,' as I call it. I almost ran up the street, not looking where I was going, when, just as I turned the corner, I bumped into a man."

"Nothing suspicious or wonderful in that," commented Tom. "I've often run into people."

"Wait," advised Ned. "To save myself from falling I grabbed the man's arm. He did the same to me, and there we stood, for a moment, right under a gas lamp. I looked down at his hands, and I saw that on the little finger of the left one there was tattooed a blue ring, and-"

"Happy Harry-the tramp!" exclaimed Tom, now much excited. "That's where he wears a tattooed ring!"

"That's what I thought you had told me," resumed Ned, "but I didn't pay any attention to it at the time, as I had no idea that the men were out of jail."

"Well, what else happened?" inquired Tom

"Not much more. I apologized to the man, and he to me, and we let go of each other."

"Are you sure about the ring on his finger?"

"Positive. His hand was right in the light. But wait, that isn't all.

I hurried on, not thinking much about it, when, I saw another man step out of the dark shadows of Peterby's grocery, just beyond the bank. The man must have mistaken me for some one else, for he spoke to me."

"What did he say?"

"He asked me a question. It was: `Is there any chance tonight?' "

"What did you tell him?"

"Well, I was so surprised that I didn't know what to say, and, before I could get my wits together the man had seen his mistake and hurried on. He joined the man I had collided with, and the two skipped off in the darkness. But not before a third man had come across the street, from in front of the bank, and hurried off with them."

"Well?" asked Tom, as his chum paused.

"I don't know what to think," resumed Ned. "These men were certainly acting suspiciously, and, now that you tell me the Anson Morse gang is not locked up-well, it makes me feel that these must be some of their crowd."

"Of course they are!" declared Tom positively. "That blue ring proves it!"

"I wouldn't go so far as to say that," declared Ned. "The man certainly had a blue ring tattooed on his finger-the same finger where you say Happy Harry had his. But what would the men be doing in this neighborhood? They certainly have had a lesson not to meddle with any of your things."

"No, I don't believe they are after any of dad's inventions this time. But I tell you what I do believe."

"What?"

"Those men are planning to rob the Shopton Bank, Ned! And I advise you to notify the officers. That Morse gang is one of the worst in the country," and Tom, much excited, began to pace the room, while Ned, who had not dreamed of such an outcome to his narrative, looked startled.

CHAPTER 3

WHITEWASHED

"Let's tell your father, Tom," suggested Ned, after a pause. "He'll know what to do."

"No, I'd rather not," answered the young inventor quickly. "Dad has had trouble enough with these fellows, and I don't want him to worry any more. Besides, he is working on a new invention, and if I tell him about the Happy Harry gang it will take his attention from it."

"What invention is he planning now?"

"I don't know, but it's something important by the way he keeps at it. He hardly spares time to help Mr. Sharp and me on the airship. No, we'll keep this news from dad."

"Then I'll inform the bank officials, as you suggest. If the place was robbed they might blame me; if they found out I had seen the men a failed to tell them."

"Well, that gang would only be too glad to have the blame fall on some one else."

Tom little knew how near the truth he had come in his chance expression, or how soon he himself was to fall under suspicion in connection with this same band of bad men.

"I'll telephone to the president on my way home," decided Ned, "and he can notify the watchman at the bank. But do you really expect to have your airship in shape to fly soon?"

"Oh, yes. Now that we have found out our mistake about the gas, the rest will be easy."

"I think I'd like to take a trip in one myself, if it didn't go too high," ventured Ned.

"I'll remember that, when we have ours completed," promised his chum, "and I'll take you for a spin."

The boys talked for perhaps an hour longer, mostly about the airship, for it was the latest mechanical affair in which Tom was interested, and, naturally, foremost in his thoughts. Then Ned went home first, however, telephoning from Tom's house to the bank president about having seen the suspicious men. That official thanked his young employee, and said he would take all necessary precautions. The telephone message was not sent until Mr. Swift was out of hearing, as Tom was determined that his father should have no unnecessary worry about the unscrupulous men. As it was, the news that the gang was out of jail had caused the aged inventor some alarm.

It was not without some anxiety that Tom arose the next morning, fearing he would hear news that the bank had been broken into, but no such alarming report circulated in Shopton. In fact having made some inquiries that day of Ned, he learned that no trace had been seen of the mysterious men. The police had been on the lookout, but they had seen nothing of them.

"Maybe, after all, they weren't the same ones," suggested Ned, when he paid Tom another visit the next night.

"Well, of course it's possible that they weren't," admitted the young inventor. "I'd be very glad to think so. Even if they were, your encounter with them may have scared them off; and that would be a good thing."

The next two weeks were busy ones for Tom and Mr. Sharp. Aided occasionally by Mr. Swift, and with Garret Jackson, the engineer, to lend a hand whenever needed, the aeronaut and the owner of the speedy Arrow made considerable progress on their airship.

"What is your father so busy over?" asked Mr. Sharp one day, when the new aluminum gas holder was about completed.

"I don't know," answered Tom, with a somewhat puzzled air. "He doesn't seem to want to talk about it, even to me. He says it will revolutionize travel along a certain line, but whether he is working on an airship that will rival ours, or a new automobile, I can't make out. He'll tell us in good time. But when do you think we will finish the-well, I don't know what to call it-I mean our aeroplane?"

"Oh, in about a month now. That's so, though, we haven't a name for it. But we'll christen it after it's completed. Now if you'll tighten up some of those bolts I'll get the gas generating apparatus in readiness for another test."

A short description of the new airship may not be out of place now. It was built after plans Mr. Sharp had shown to Tom and his father soon after the thrilling rescue of the aeronaut from the blazing balloon over Lake Carlopa. The general idea of the airship was that of the familiar aeroplane, but in addition to the sustaining surfaces of the planes, there was an aluminum, cigar-shaped tank, holding a new and very powerful gas, which would serve to keep the ship afloat even when not in motion.

Two sets of planes, one above the other, were used, bringing the airship into the biplane class. There were also two large propellers, one in front and the other at the rear. These were carefully made, of different layers of wood "built up" as they are called, to make them stronger. They were eight feet in diameter, and driven by a twenty-cylinder, air-cooled, motor, whirled around at the rate of fifteen hundred revolutions a minute. When operated at full speed the airship was capable of making eighty miies an hour, against a moderate wind.

But if the use of the peculiarly-shaped planes and the gas container, with the secret but powerful vapor in it were something new in airship construction, so was the car in which the operator and travelers were to live during a voyage. It was a complete living room, with the engine and other apparatus, including that for generating the gas, in a separate compartment, and the whole was the combined work of Tom and Mr. Sharp. There were accommodations for five persons, with sleeping berths, a small galley or kitchen, where food could be prepared, and several easy chairs where the travelers could rest in comfort while skimming along high in the air, as fast as the fastest railroad train.

There was room enough to carry stores for a voyage of a week or more, and enough gas could be manufactured aboard the ship, in addition to that taken in the aluminum case before starting, to sustain the ship for two weeks. The engine, steering apparatus, and the gas machine were within easy reach and control of the pilot, who was to be stationed in a small room in the "bow" of the ship. An electric stove served to warm the interior of the car, and also provided means for cooking the food.

The airship could be launched either by starting it along the ground, on rubber-tired wheels, as is done in the case of the ordinary aeroplane, or it could be lifted by the gas, just as is done with a balloon. In short there were many novel features about the ship.

The gas test, which took place a few days later, showed that the young inventor and Mr. Sharp had made no mistake this time. No explosion followed, the needle valve controlling the powerful vapor perfectly.

"Well," remarked Mr. Sharp, one afternoon, "I think we shall put the ship together next week, Tom, and have a trial flight. We shall need a few more aluminum bolts, though, and if you don't mind you might jump on your motor-cycle and run to Mansburg for them. Merton's machine shop ought to have some."

Mansburg was the nearest large city to Shopton, and Merton was a machinist who frequently did work for Mr. Swift.

"All right," agreed Tom. "I'll start now. How many will you need?"

"Oh, a couple of dozen."

Tom started off, wheeling his cycle from the shed where it was kept. As he passed the building where the big frame of the airship, with the planes and aluminum bag had been assembled, he looked in.

"We'll soon be flying through the clouds on your back," he remarked, speaking to the apparatus as if it could understand. "I guess we'll smash some records, too, if that engine works as well when it's installed as it does now."

Tom had purchased the bolts, and was on his way back with them, when, as he passed through one of the outlying streets of Mansburg, something went wrong with his motor-cycle. He got off to adjust it, finding that it was only a trifling matter, which he soon put right, when he was aware of a man standing, observing him. Without looking up at the man's face, the young inventor was unpleasantly aware of a sharp scrutiny. He could hardly explain it, but it seemed as if the man had evil intentions toward him, and it was not altogether unexpected on Tom's part, when, looking up, he saw staring at him, Anson Morse, the leader of the gang of men who had caused such trouble for him.

"Oh, it's you; is it?" asked Morse, an ugly scowl on his face. "I thought I recognized you." He moved nearer to Tom, who straightened up, and stood leaning on his wheel.

"Yes; it's me," admitted the lad.

"I've been looking for you," went on Morse. "I'm not done with you yet, nor your father, either."

"Aren't you?" asked Tom, trying to speak coolly, though his heart was beating rather faster than usual. Morse had spoken in a threatening manner, and, as the youth looked up and down the street he saw that it was deserted; nor were there any houses near.

"No, I'm not," snapped the man. "You got me and my friends in a lot of trouble, and-"

"You didn't get half what you deserved!" burst out Tom, indignant at the thought of what he and his father had suffered at the hands of the gang. "You ought to be in jail now, instead of out; and if I could see a policeman, I'd have you arrested for threatening me! That's against the law!"

"Huh! I s'pose you think you know lots about the law," sneered Morse. "Well, I tell you one thing, if you make any further trouble for me, I'll—"

"I'll make all the trouble I can!" cried Tom, and he boldly faced the angry man. "I'm not afraid of you!"

"You'd better be!" and Morse spoke in a vindictive manner. "We'll get even with you yet, Tom Swift. In fact I've a good notion now to give you a good thrashing for what you've done."

Before Tom was aware of the man's intention, Morse had stepped quickly into the street, where the lad stood beside his wheel, and grasped him by the shoulder. He gave Tom a vicious shake.

"Take your hand off me!" cried Tom, who was hampered by having to hold up his heavy machine.

"I will when I've given you what I owe you!" retorted the scoundrel. "I'm going to have satisfaction now if I never-"

At that instant there came from down the street the sound of a rattling and bumping. Tom looked up quickly, and saw approaching a rattletrap of a wagon. drawn by a big, loose-jointed mule, the large ears of which were flapping to and fro. The animal was advancing rapidly, in response to blows and words from the colored driver, and, before the uplifted fist of Morse could fall on Tom's head, the outfit was opposite them.

"Hold on dar, mistah! Hold on!" cried the colored man in the wagon. "What are yo' doin' to mah friend, Mistah Swift?"

"None of your business!" snapped Morse. "You drive on and let me manage this affair if you don't want trouble! Who are you anyhow?"

"Why doan't yo' know me?" asked the colored man, at whom Tom looked gratefully. "I's Eradicate Sampson, an' dish yeah am mah mule, Boomerang. Whoa, Boomerang! I reckon yo' an' I better take a hand in dish yeah argument."

"Not unless you want trouble!" cried Morse.

"I doan't mind trouble, not in de leastest," answered Eradicate cheerfully. "Me an' Boomerang has had lots of trouble. We's used to it. No, Mistah Man, you'd better let go ob mah friend, Mistah Swift, if yo' doan't want trouble yo' ownse'f."

"Drive on, and mind your business!" cried Morse, now unreasoningly angry. "This is my affair," and he gave Tom a shake.

Our hero was not going to submit tamely, however. He had one hand free, and raised to strike Morse, but the latter, letting go his hold on the lad's shoulder, grasped with that hand, the fist which the young inventor had raised. Then, with his other hand, the scoundrel was about to hit Tom.

"Break away four him, Mistah Swift!" directed the colored man. "Yo' can fight him, den!"

"I guess he'll have his own troubles doing that," sneered Morse.

"Not ef I help him," answered Eradicate promptly, as he climbed back off the seat, into the body of his ramshackle vehicle.

"Don't you interfere with me!" stormed the man.

An instant later Tom broke away from his tormentor, and laid his motor-cycle on the ground, in order to have both hands free for the attack he felt would follow.

"Ha! You think you're going to escape, do you?" cried Morse, as he started toward Tom, his eyes blazing. "I'll show you who you're dealing with!"

"Yes, an' I reckon I'll show yo' suffin yo' ain't lookin' fer!" suddenly cried Eradicate.

With a quick motion he picked up a pail of white-wash from his wagon, and, with sure aim, emptied the contents of the bucket over Morse, who was rushing at Tom. The white fluid spread over the man from head to foot, enveloping him as in a white shroud, and his advance was instantly checked.

"Dar! I reckon dat's de quickest white-washin' job I done in some time!" chuckled Eradicate, as he grasped his long handled brush, and clambered down from the wagon, ready for a renewal of the hostilities on the part of Morse. "De bestest white-washin' job I done in some time; yais, sah!"

CHAPTER 4

A TRIAL TRIP

There was no fear that Anson Morse would return to the attack. Blinded by the whitewash which ran in his eyes, but which, being slaked, did not burn him, he grouped blindly about, pawing the air with his outstretched hands.

"You wait! You wait! You'll suffer for this!" he spluttered, as soon as he could free his mouth from the trickling fluid. Then, wiping it from his face, with his hands, as best he could, he shook his fist at Tom. "I'll pay you and that black rascal back!" he cried. "You wait!"

"I hopes yo' pays me soon," answered Eradicate, "'case as how dat whitewash was wuff twenty-five cents, an' I got t' go git mo' to finish doin' a chicken coop I'm wurkin' on. Whoa, oar Boomerang. Dere ain't goin' t' be no mo' trouble I reckon."

Morse did not reply. He had been most unexpectedly repulsed, and, with the white-wash dripping from his garments, he turned and fairly ran toward a strip of woodland that bordered the highway at that place.

Tom approached the colored man, and held out a welcoming hand.

"I don't know what I'd done if you hadn't come along, Rad," the lad said. "That fellow was desperate, and this was a lonely spot to be attacked. Your whitewash came in mighty handy."

"Yais, sah, Mistah Swift, dat's what it done. I knowed I could use it on him, ef he got too obstreperous, an' dat's what he done. But I were goin' to fight him wif mah bresh, ef he'd made any more trouble."

"Oh, I fancy we have seen the last of him for some time," said Tom, but he looked worried. It was evident that the Happy Harry gang was still hanging around the neighborhood of Shopton, and the fact that Morse was bold enough to attack our hero in broad day-light argued that he felt little fear of the authorities.

"Ef yo' wants t' catch him, Mistah Swift," went on Eradicate, "yo' kin trace him by de whitewash what drops offen him," and he pointed to a trail of white drops which showed the path Morse had taken.

"No, the less I have to do with him the better I like it," answered the lad. "But I can't thank you enough, Rad. You have helped me out of difficulties several times now. You put me on the trail of the men in the deserted mansion, you warned me of the log Andy Foger placed across the road, and now you have saved me from Morse."

"Oh, dat's nuffin, Mistah Swift. Yo' has suah done lots fo' me. 'Sides, mah mule, Boomerang, am entitled t' de most credit dish yeah time. I were comin' down de street, on mah way t' a whitewashin' job, when I seen yo', an yo' lickitysplit machine," for so Eradicate designated a motorcycle. "I knowed it were yo', an' I didn't laik de looks ob dat man. Den I see he had hold ob you, an' I t'ought he were a burglar. So I yelled t' Boomerang t' hurry up. Now, mostly, when I wants Boomerang t' hurry, he goes slow, an' when I wants him t' go slow, he runs away. But dish yeah time he knowed he were comin' t' help yo', an' he certainly did leg it, dat's what he done! He run laik he were goin' home t' a stable full ob oats, an' dat's how I got heah so quick. Den I t'ought ob de whitewash, an' I jest. used it."

"It was the most effective weapon you could have used," said Tom, gratefully.

"Deed no, Mistah Swift, I didn't hab no weapon," spoke Eradicate earnestly. "I ain't eben got mah razor, 'case I left it home. I didn't hab no weapon at all. I jest used de whitewash, laik yo' seen me."

"That's what I meant," answered Tom, trying not to laugh at the simple negro's misunderstanding. "I'm ever so much obliged to you, just the same, and here's a half dollar to pay for the whitewash."

"Oh, no, Mistah Swift, I doan't want t' take it. I kin make mo' whitewash."

But Tom insisted, and picked up his machine to sprint for home. Eradicate started to tell over again, how he urged Boomerang on, but the lad had no time to listen.

"But I didn't hab no weapon, Mistah Swift, no indeedy, none at all, not even mah razor," repeated Eradicate. "Only de pail ob whitewash. That is, lessen yo' calls mah bresh a weapon."

"Well, it's a sort of one," admitted Tom, with a laugh as he started his machine. "Come around next week, Rad. We have some dirt eradicating for you to attend to."

"Deed an' I will, Mistah Swift. Eradicate is mah name, an' I eradicates de dirt. But dat man such did look odd, wif dat pail ob whitewash all ober him. He suah did look most extraordinarily. Gidap, Boomerang. See if yo' can break some mo' speed records now."

But the mule appeared to be satisfied with what he had done, and, as he rode off, Tom looked back to see the colored man laboring to get the sleepy, animal started.

The lad did not tell his father of the adventure with Morse, but he related the occurrence to Mr. Sharp.

"I'd like to get hold of that scoundrel, and the others in the gang!" exclaimed the balloonist. "I'd take him up in the airship, and drop him down into the lake. He's a bad man. So are the others. Wonder what they -want around here?"

"That's what's puzzling me," admitted Tom. "I hope dad doesn't hear about them or he will be sure to worry; and maybe it will interfere with his new ideas."

"He hasn't told you yet what he's engaged in inventing; has he?"

"No, and I don't like to ask him. He said the other day, though, that it would rival our airship, but in a different way."

"I wonder what be meant?"

"It's hard to say. But I don't believe he can invent anything that will go ahead of our craft, even if he is my own father, and the best one in the world," said Tom, half jokingly. "Well, I got the bolts, now let's get to work. I'm anxious for a trial trip."

"No more than I am. I want to see if my ideas will work out in practice as well as they do in theory."

For a week or more Tom and Mr. Sharp labored on the airship, with Mr. Jackson to help them. The motor, with its twenty cylinders, was installed, and the big aluminum holder fastened to the frame of the planes. The rudders, one to control the elevation and depression of the craft, and the other to direct its flight to the right or left, were attached, and the steering wheel, as well as the levers regulating the motor were put in place.

"About all that remains to be done now," said the aeronaut one night, as he and Tom stood in the big shed, looking at their creation, "is to fit up the car, and paint the machine."

"Can't we make a trial trip before we fit up the car ready for a long flight?" asked the young inventor.

"Yes, but I wouldn't like to go out without painting the ship. Some parts of it might rust if we get into the moist, cloudy, upper regions."

"Then let's paint it tomorrow, and, as soon as it's dry we'll have a test."

"All right. I'll mix the paint the first thing in the morning."

It took two days to paint the machine, for much care had to be used, and, when it was finished Tom looked admiringly up at it.

"We ought to name it," suggested Mr. Sharp, as he removed a bit of paint from the end of the nose.

"To be sure," agreed Tom. "And hold on, I have the very name for it—*Red Cloud!*"

"*Red Cloud?*" questioned Mr. Sharp.

"Yes!" exclaimed Tom, with enthusiasm. "It's painted red-at least the big, aluminum gas container is-and we hope to go above the clouds in it. Why not *Red Cloud?*"

"That's what it shall be!" conceded the balloonist. "If I had a bottle of malted milk, or something like that, I'd christen it."

"We ought to have a young lady to do that part," suggested Tom. "They always have young ladies to name ships."

"Were you thinking of any particular young lady?" asked Mr. Sharp softly, and Tom blushed; as he replied

"Oh no-of course that is-well—Oh, hang it, christen it yourself, and let me alone," he finished.

"Well, in the absence of Miss Mary Nestor, who, I think, would be the best one for the ceremony," said Mr. Sharp, with a twinkle in his eyes, "I christen thee *Red Cloud*," and with that he sprinkled some water on the pointed nose of the red aluminum gas bag, for the aeronaut and Tom were on a high staging, on a level with the upper part of the airship.

"*Red Cloud* it is!" cried Tom, enthusiastically. "Now, tomorrow we'll see what it can do."

The day of the test proved all that could be desired in the way of weather. The fact that an airship was being constructed in the Swift shops had been kept as secret as possible, but of course many in Shopton knew of it, for Andy Foger had spread the tidings.

"I hope we won't have a crowd around to see us go up," said Tom, as he and Mr. Sharp went to the shed to get the *Red Cloud* in readiness for the trial. "I shouldn't want to have them laugh at us, if we fail to rise."

"Don't worry. We'll go up all right," declared Mr. Sharp. "The only thing I'm at all worried about is our speed. I want to go fast, but we may not be able to until our motor gets 'tuned-up'. But we'll rise."

The gas machine had already been started, and the vapor was hissing inside the big aluminum holder. It was decided to try to go up under the lifting power of the gas, and not use the aeroplane feature for sending aloft the ship, as there was hardly room, around the shops, for a good start.

When enough of the vapor had been generated to make the airship buoyant, the big doors of the shed were opened, and Tom and Mr. Sharp, with the aid of Garret and Mr. Swift, shoved it slowly out.

"There it is! There she comes!" cried several vices outside the high fence that surrounded the Swift property. "They're going up!"

"Andy Foger is in that bunch," remarked Tom with a grim smile. "I hope we don't fail."

"We won't. Don't worry," advised Mr. Sharp.

The shouts outside the fence increased. It was evident that quite a crowd of boys, as well as men, had collected, though it was early in the morning. Somehow, news of the test had leaked out.

The ship continued to get lighter and lighter as more gas was generated. It was held down by ropes, fastened to stakes driven in the ground. Mr. Sharp entered the big car that was suspended, below the aeroplanes.

"Come on, Tom," the aeronaut called. "We're almost ready to fly. Will you come too, Mr. Swift, and Garret?"

"Some other time," promised the aged inventor. "It looks as though you were going to succeed, though. I'll wait, however, until after the test before I venture."

"How about you, Garret?" asked Tom of the engineer, as the young inventor climbed into the car.

"The ground is good enough for me," was the answer, with a smile. "Broken bones don't mend so easily when you're past sixty-five."

"But we're not going to fall!" declared Mr. Sharp. "All ready, Tom. Cast off! Here we go!"

The restraining ropes were quickly cast aside. Slowly at first, and then with a rush, as though feeling more and more sure of herself, the *Red Cloud* arose in the air like a gigantic bird of scarlet plumage. Up and up it went, higher than the house, higher than the big shed where it had been built, higher, higher, higher!

"There she is!" cried the shrill voices of the boys in the meadow, and the hoarser tones of the men mingled with them.

"Hurrah!" called Tom softly to the balloonist. "We're off!" and he waved his hand to his father and Garret.

"I told you so," spoke Mr. Sharp confidently. "I'm going to start the propellers in a minute."

"Oh, dear me, goodness sakes alive!" cried Mrs. Baggert, the housekeeper, running from the house and wringing her hands. "I'm sure they'll fall!"

She looked up apprehensively, but Tom only waved his hand to her, and threw her a kiss. Clearly he had no fears, though it was the first time he had ever been in an airship. Mr. Sharp was as calm and collected as an ocean captain making his hundredth trip across the Atlantic.

"Throw on the main switch," he called to our hero, and Tom,

moving to amidships in the car, did as directed. Mr. Sharp pulled several levers, adjusted some valves, and then, with a rattle and bang, the huge, twenty-cylinder motor started.

Waiting a moment to see that it was running smoothly, Mr. Sharp grasped the steering wheel. Then, with a quick motion he threw the two propellers in gear. They began to whirl around rapidly.

"Here we go!" cried Tom, and, sure enough, the *Red Cloud*, now five hundred feet in the air, shot forward, like a boat on the water, only with such a smooth, gliding, easy motion, that it seemed like being borne along on a cloud.

"She works! She works!" cried the balloonist. "Now to try our elevation rudder," and, as the *Red Cloud* gathered speed, he tilted the small planes which sent the craft up or down, according to the manner in which they were tilted. The next instant the airship was pointed at an angle toward the clouds, and shooting along at swift speed, while, from below came the admiring cheers of the crowd of boys and men.

CHAPTER 5

COLLIDING WITH A TOWER

"She seems to work," observed Tom, looking from where he was stationed near some electrical switches, toward Mr. Sharp.

"Of course she does," replied the aeronaut. "I knew it would, but I wasn't so sure that it would scoot along in this fashion. We're making pretty good speed, but we'll do better when the motor gets to running smoother."

"How high up are we?" asked Tom.

The balloonist glanced at several gauges near the steering wheel.

"A little short of three thousand feet," he answered. "Do you want to go higher?"

"No-no-I-I guess not," was Tom's answer. He halted over the works, and his breath came in gasps.

"Don't get alarmed," called Mr. Sharp quickly, noting that his companion was in distress because of the high altitude. "That always happens to persons who go into a thin air for the first time; just as if you had climbed a high mountain. Breathe as slowly as you can, and swallow frequently. That will relieve the pressure on your ear drums. I'll send the ship lower."

Tom did as he was advised, and the aeronaut, deflecting the rudder, sent the *Red Cloud* on a downward slant. Tom at once felt relieved, both because the action of swallowing equalized the pressure on the ear drums, and because the airship was soon in a more dense atmosphere, more like that of the earth.

"How are you now?" asked the man of the lad, as the craft was again on an even keel.

"All right," replied Tom, briskly. "I didn't know what ailed me at first."

"I was troubled the same way when I first went up in a balloon," commented Mr. Sharp. "We'll run along for a few miles, at an elevation of about five hundred feet, and then we'll go to within a hundred feet of the earth, and see how the *Red Cloud* behaves under different conditions. Take a look below and see what you think of it."

Tom looked low, through one of several plate glass windows in the floor of the car. He gave a gasp of astonishment.

"Why! We're right over Lake Carlopa!" he gasped.

"Of course," admitted Mr. Sharp with a laugh. "And I'm glad to say that we're better off than when I was last in the air over this same body of water," and he could scarcely repress a shudder as he thought of his perilous position in the blazing balloon, as related in detail in "Tom Swift and His Motor-Boat."

The lake was spread out below the navigators of the air like some mirror of silver in a setting of green fields. Tom could see a winding river, that flowed into the lake, and he noted towns, villages, and even distant cities, interspersed here and there with broad farms or patches of woodlands, like a bird's-eye view of a stretch of country.

"This is great!" he exclaimed, with enthusiasm. "I wouldn't miss this for the world!"

"Oh, you haven't begun to see things yet," replied Mr. Sharp. "Wait until we take a long trip, which we'll do soon, as this ship is behaving much better than I dared to hope. Well, we're five hundred feet high now, and I'll run along at that elevation for a while."

Objects on the earth became more distinct now, and Tom could observe excited throngs running along and pointing upward. They were several miles from Shopton, and the machinery was running smoothly; the motor, with its many cylinders purring like a big cat.

"We could have lunch, if we'd brought along anything to eat," observed Tom.

"Yes," assented his companion. "But I think we'll go back now. Your father may be anxious. Just come here, Tom, and I'll show you how to steer. I'm going down a short distance."

He depressed the rudder, and the *Red Cloud* shot earthward. Then, as the airship was turned about, the young inventor was allowed to try his hand at managing it. He said, afterward, that it was like guiding a fleecy cloud.

"Point her straight for Shopton,". counseled Mr. Sharp, when he had explained the various wheels and levers to the lad.

"Straight she is," answered the lad, imitating a sailor's reply. "Oh, but this is great! It beats even my motor-boat!"

"It goes considerably faster, at all events," remarked Mr. Sharp. "Keep her steady now, while I take a look at the engine. I want to be sure it doesn't run hot."

He went aft, where all the machinery in the car was located, and Tom was left alone in the small pilot house. He felt a thrill as he looked down at the earth beneath him, and saw the crowds of wonder-gazers pointing at the great, red airship flying high over their heads. Rapidly the open fields slipped along, giving place to a large city.

"Rocksmond," murmured Tom, as he noted it. "We're about

fifty miles from home, but we'll soon be back in the shed at this rate. We certainly are slipping along. A hundred and fifty feet elevation," he went on, as he looked at a gauge. I wonder if I'll ever get used to going several miles up in the air?"

He shifted the rudder a bit, to go to the left. The *Red Cloud* obeyed promptly, but, the next instant something snapped. Tom, with a startled air, looked around. He could see nothing wrong, but a moment later, the airship dipped suddenly toward the earth. Then it seemed to increase its forward speed, and, a few seconds later, was rushing straight at a tall, ornamental tower that rose from one corner of a large building.

"Mr. Sharp! Mr. Sharp!" cried the lad. "Something has happened! We're heading for that tower!"

"Steer to one side!" called the balloonist.

Tom tried, but found that the helm had become jammed. The horizontal rudder would not work, and the craft was rushing nearer and nearer, every minute, to the pile of brick and mortar.

"We're going to have a collision!" shouted Tom. "Better shut off the power!"

The two propellers were whirling around so swiftly that they looked like blurs of light. Mr. Sharp came rushing forward, and Tom relinquished the steering wheel to him. In vain did the aeronaut try to change the course of the airship. Then, with a shout to Tom to disconnect the electric switch, the man turned off the power from the motor.

But it was too late. Straight at the tower rushed the *Red Cloud*, and, a moment later had hit it a glancing blow, smashing the forward propeller, and breaking off both blades. The nose of the aluminum gas container knocked off a few bricks from the tower, and then, the ship losing way, slowly settled to the flat roof of the building.

"We're smashed!" cried Tom, with something like despair in his voice.

"That's nothing! Don't worry! It might be worse! Not the first time I've had an accident. It's only one propeller, and I can easily make another," said Mr. Sharp, in his quick, jerky sentences. He had allowed some of the gas to escape from the container, making the ship less buoyant, so that it remained on the roof.

The aeronaut and Tom looked from the windows of the car, to note if any further damage had been done. They were just congratulating themselves that the rudder marked the extent, when, from a scuttle in the roof there came a procession of young ladies, led by an elderly matron, wearing spectacles and having a very determined, bristling air.

"Well, I must say, this is a very unceremonious proceeding!" exclaimed the spectacled woman. "Pray, gentlemen, to what are we indebted for this honor?"

"It was an accident, ma'am," replied Mr. Sharp, removing his hat, and bowing. A mere accident!"

"Humph! I suppose it was an accident that the tower of this building was damaged, if not absolutely loosened at the foundations. You will have to pay the damages!" Then turning, and seeing about two score of young ladies behind her on the flat roof, each young lady eying with astonishment, not unmixed with admiration, the airship, the elderly one added: "Pupils! To your rooms at once! How dare you leave without permission?"

"Oh, Miss Perkman!" exclaimed a voice, at the sound of which Tom started. "Mayn't we see the airship? It will be useful in our natural philosophy study!"

Tom looked at the young lady who had spoken. "Mary Nestor!" he exclaimed.

"Tom-I mean Mr. Swift!" she rejoined. "How in the world did you get here?"

"I was going to ask you the same question," retorted the lad. "We flew here."

"Young ladies! Silence!" cried Miss Perkman, who was evidently the principal of the school. "The idea of any one of you daring to speak to these-these persons-without my permission, and without an introduction! I shall make them pay heavily for damaging my seminary," she added, as she strode toward Mr. Sharp, who, by this time, was out of the car. "To your rooms at once!" Miss Perkman ordered again, but not a young lady moved. The airship was too much of an attraction for them.

CHAPTER 6

GETTING OFF THE ROOF

For a few minutes Mr. Sharp was so engrossed with looking underneath the craft, to ascertain in what condition the various planes and braces were, that he paid little attention to the old maid school principal, after his first greeting. But Miss Perkman was not a person to be ignored.

"I want pay for the damage to the tower of my school," she went on. "I could also demand damages for trespassing on my roof, but I will refrain in this case. Young ladies, will you go to your rooms?" she demanded.

"Oh, please, let us stay," pleaded Mary Nestor, beside whom Tom now stood. "Perhaps Professor Swift will lecture on clouds and air currents and-and such things as that," the girl went on slyly, smiling at the somewhat embarrassed lad.

"Ahem! If there is a professor present, perhaps it might be a good idea to absorb some knowledge," admitted the old maid, and, unconsciously, she smoothed her hair, and settled her gold spectacles straighter on her nose. "Professor, I will delay collecting damages on behalf of the Rocksmond Young Ladies Seminary, while you deliver a lecture on air currents," she went on, addressing herself to Mr. Sharp.

"Oh, I'm not a professor," he said quickly. "I'm a professional balloonist, parachute jumper. Give exhibitions at county fairs. Leap for life, and all that sort of thing. I guess you mean my friend. He's smart enough for a professor. Invented a lot of things. How much is the damage?"

"No professor?" cried Miss Perkman indignantly. "Why I understood from Miss Nestor that she called some one professor."

"I was referring to my friend, Mr. Swift," said Mary. "His father's a professor, anyhow, isn't he, Tom? I mean Mr. Swift!"

"I believe he has a degree, but he never uses it," was the lad's answer.

"Ha! Then I have been deceived! There is no professor present!" and the old maid drew herself up as though desirous of punishing some one. "Young ladies, for the last time, I order you to your rooms," and, with a dramatic gesture she pointed to the scuttle through which the procession had come.

"Say something, Tom—I mean Mr. Swift," appealed Mary Nestor, in a whisper, to our hero. "Can't you give some sort of a lecture?

The girls are just crazy to hear about the airship, and this ogress won't let us. Say something!"

"I-I don't know what to say," stammered Tom.

But he was saved the necessity for just then several women, evidently other teachers, came out on the roof.

"Oh, an airship!" exclaimed one. "How lovely! We thought it was an earthquake, and we were afraid to come up for quite a while. But an airship! I've always wanted to see one, and now I have an opportunity. It will be just the thing for my physical geography and natural history class. Young ladies, attention, and I will explain certain things to you."

"Miss Delafield, do you understand enough about an airship to lecture on one?" asked Miss Perkman smartly.

"Enough so that my class may benefit," answered the other teacher, who was quite pretty.

"Ahem! That is sufficient, and a different matter," conceded Miss Perkman. "Young ladies, give your undivided attention to Miss Delafield, and I trust you will profit by what she tells you. Meanwhile I wish to have some conversation concerning damages with the persons who so unceremoniously visited us. It is a shame that the pupils of the Rocksmond Seminary should be disturbed at their studies. Sir, I wish to talk with you," and the principal pointed a long, straight finger at Mr. Sharp.

"Young ladies, attention!" called Miss Delafield. "You will observe the large red body at the top, that is-"

"I'd rather have you explain it," whispered Mary Nestor to Tom. "Come on, slip around to the other side. May I bring a few of my friends with me? I can't bear Miss Delafield. She thinks she knows everything. She won't see us if we slip around."

"I shall be delighted," replied Tom, "only I fear I may have to help Mr. Sharp out of this trouble."

"Don't worry about me, Tom," said the balloonist, who overheard him. "Let me do the explaining. I'm an old hand at it. Been in trouble before. Many a time I've had to pay damages for coming down in a farmer's corn field. I'll attend to the lady principal, and you can explain things to the young ones," and, with a wink, the jolly aeronaut stepped over to where Miss Perkman, in spite of her prejudice against the airship, was observing it curiously.

Glad to have the chance to talk to his young lady friend, Tom slipped to the opposite side of the car with her and a few of her intimate friends, to whom she slyly beckoned. There Tom told how the *Red Cloud* came to be built, and of his first trip in the air, while, on the opposite side, Miss Delafield lectured to the entire school on aeronautics, as she thought she knew them.

Mr. Sharp evidently did know how to "explain" matters to the irate principal, for, in a short while, she was smiling. By this time Tom had about finished his little lecture, and Miss Delafield was at the end of hers. The entire school of girls was grouped about the *Red Cloud*, curiously examining it, but Mary Nestor and her friends probably learned more than any of the others. Tom was informed that his friend had been attending the school in Rocksmond since the fall term opened.

"I little thought, when I found we were going to smash into that tower, that you were below there, studying," said the lad to the girl.

"I'm afraid I wasn't doing much studying," she confessed. "I had just a glimpse of the airship through the window, and I was wondering who was in it, when the crash came. Miss Perkman, who is nothing if not brave, at once started for the roof, and we girls all followed her. However, are you going to get the ship down?"

"I'm afraid it is going to be quite a job," admitted Tom ruefully. "Something went wrong with the machinery, or this never would have happened. As soon as Mr. Sharp has settled with your principal we'll see what we can do."

"I guess he's settled now," observed Miss Nestor. "Here he comes."

The aeronaut and Miss Perkman were approaching together, and the old maid did not seem half so angry as she had been.

"You see," Mr. Sharp was saying, "it will be a good advertisement for your school. Think of having the distinction of having harbored the powerful airship, *Red Cloud*, on your roof."

"I never thought of it in that light," admitted the principal. "Perhaps you are right. I shall put it in my next catalog."

"And, as for damages to the tower, we will pay you fifty dollars," continued the balloonist. "Do you agree to that, Mr. Swift?" he asked Tom. "I think your father, the professor, would call that fair."

"Oh, as long as this airship is partly the property of a professor, perhaps I should only take thirty-five dollars," put in Miss Perkman. "I am a great admirer of professors-I mean in a strictly educational sense," she went on, as she detected a tendency on the part of some of the young ladies to giggle.

"No, fifty dollars will be about right," went on Mr. Sharp, pulling out a well-filled wallet. "I will pay you now."

"And if you will wait I will give you a receipt," continued the principal, evidently as much appeased at the mention of a professor's title, as she was by the money.

"We're getting off cheap," the balloonist whispered to Tom, as the head of the seminary started down the scuttle to the class-rooms below.

"Maybe it's easier getting out of that difficulty than it will be to get off the roof," replied the lad.

"Don't worry. Leave that to me," the aeronaut said. It took considerable to ruffle Mr. Sharp. .

With a receipt in full for the damage to the tower, and expressing the hope that, some day, in the near future, Professor Swift would do the seminary the honor of lecturing to the young lady pupils, Miss Perkman bade Mr. Sharp and Tom good-by.

"Young ladies, to your rooms!" she commanded. "You have learned enough of airships, and there may be some danger getting this one off the roof."

"Wouldn't you like to stay and take a ride in it?" Tom asked Miss Nestor.

"Indeed I would," she answered daringly. "It's better than a motor-boat. May I?"

"Some day, when we get more expert in managing it," he replied, as he shook hands with her.

"Now for some hard work," went on the young inventor to Mr. Sharp, when the roof was cleared of the last of the teachers and pupils. But the windows that gave a view of the airship in its odd position on the roof were soon filled with eager faces, while in the streets below was a great crowd, offering all manner of suggestions.

"Oh, it's not going to be such a task," said Mr. Sharp. "First we will repair the rudder and the machinery, and then we'll generate some more gas, rise and fly home."

"But the broken propeller?" objected Tom.

"We can fly with one, as well as we can with two, but not so swiftly. Don't worry. We'll come out all right," and the balloonist assumed a confident air.

It was not so difficult a problem as Tom had imagined to put the machinery in order, a simple break having impaired the working of the rudder. Then the smashed propeller was unshipped and the gas machine started. With all the pupils watching from windows, and a crowd observing from the streets and surrounding country, for word of the happening had spread, Tom and his friend prepared to ascend.

They arose as well as they had done at the shed at home, and in a little while, were floating over the school. Tom fancied he could observe a certain hand waving to him, as he peered from the window of the car-a hand in one of the school casements, but where there were so many pretty girls doing the same thing, I hardly see how Tom could pick out any certain one, though he had extraordinarily good eyesight. However, the airship was now afloat and, starting the motor, Mr. Sharp found that even with one propeller the *Red Cloud* did fairly well, making good speed.

"Now for home, to repair everything, and we'll be ready for a longer trip," the aeronaut said to the young inventor, as they turned around, and headed off before the wind, while hundreds below them cheered.

"We ought to carry spare propellers if we're going to smash into school towers," remarked Tom. "I seem to be a sort of hoodoo."

"Nonsense! It wasn't your fault at all," commented Mr. Sharp warmly. "It would have happened to me had I been steering. But we will take an extra propeller along after this."

An hour later they arrived in front of the big shed and the *Red Cloud* was safely housed. Mr. Swift was just beginning to get anxious about his son and his friend, and was glad to welcome them back.

"Now for a big trip, in about a week!" exclaimed Mr. Sharp enthusiastically. "You'll come with us, won't you, Mr. Swift?"

The inventor slowly shook his head.

"Not on a trip," he said. "I may go for a trial spin with you, but I've got too important a matter under way to venture on a long trip," and he turned away without explaining what it was. But Tom and Mr. Sharp were soon to learn.

CHAPTER 7

ANDY TRIES A TRICK

Without loss of time the young inventor and the aeronaut began to repair the damage done to the *Red Cloud* by colliding with the tower. The most important part to reconstruct was the propeller, and Mr. Sharp decided to make two, instead of one, in order to have an extra one in case of future accidents.

Tom's task was to arrange the mechanism so that, hereafter, the rudder could not become jammed, and so prevent the airship from steering properly. This the lad accomplished by a simple but effective device which, when the balloonist saw it, caused him to compliment Tom.

"That's worth patenting," he declared. "I advise you to take out papers on that."

"It seems such a simple thing," answered the youth. "And I don't see much use of spending the money for a patent. Airships aren't likely to be so numerous that I could make anything off that patent."

"You take my advice," insisted Mr. Sharp. "Airships are going to be used more in the future than you have any idea of. You get that device patented."

Tom did so, and, not many years afterward he was glad that he had, as it brought him quite an income.

It required several days' work on the *Red Cloud* before it was in shape for another trial. During the hours when he was engaged in the big shed, helping Mr. Sharp, the young inventor spent many minutes calling to mind the memory of a certain fair face, and I think I need not mention any names to indicate whose face it was.

"She promised to go for a ride with me," mused the lad. "I hope she doesn't back out. But I'll want to learn more about managing the ship before I venture with her in it. It won't do to have any accidents then. There's Ned Newton, too. I must take him for a skim in the clouds. Guess I'll invite him over some afternoon, and give him a private view of the machine, when we get it in shape again."

About a week after the accident at the school Mr. Sharp remarked to Tom one afternoon

"If the weather is good tomorrow, we'll try another flight. Do you suppose your father will come along?"

"I don't know," answered the lad. "He seems much engrossed in something. It's unusual, too, for he most generally tells me what he is engaged upon. However, I guess he will say something about it when he gets ready."

"Well, if he doesn't feel just like coming, don't argue him. He might be nervous, and, while the ship is new, I don't want any nervous passengers aboard. I can't give them my attention and look after the running of the machinery."

"I was going to propose bringing a friend of mine over to see us make the trip tomorrow," went on the young inventor. "Ned Newton, you know him. He'd like a ride."

"Oh, I guess Ned's all right. Let him come along. We won't go very high tomorrow. After a trial rise by means of the gas, I'm going to lower the ship to the ground, and try for an elevation by means of the planes. Oh, yes, bring your friend along."

Ned Newton was delighted the next day to receive Tom's invitation, and, though a little dubious about trusting himself in an airship for the first time, finally consented to go with his chum. He got a half holiday from the bank, and, shortly after dinner went to Tom's house.

"Come on out in the shed and take a look at the *Red Cloud*," proposed the young inventor. "Mr. Sharp isn't quite ready to start yet, and I'll explain some things to you."

The big shed was deserted when the lads entered, and went to the loft where they were on a level with the big, red aluminum tank. Tom began with a description of the machinery, and Ned followed him with interest.

"Now we'll go down into the car or cabin," continued the young navigator of the air, "and I'll show you what we do when we're touring amid the clouds."

As they started to descend the flight of steps from the loft platform, a noise on the ground below attracted their attention.

"Guess that's Mr. Sharp coming," said Ned.

Tom leaned over and looked down. An instant later he grasped the arm of his chum, and motioned to him to keep silent.

"Take a look," whispered the young inventor.

"Andy Foger!" exclaimed Ned, peering over the railing.

"Yes, and Sam Snedecker and Pete Bailey are with him. They sneaked in when I left the door open. Wonder what they want?"

"Up to some mischief, I'll wager," commented Ned. "Hark! They're talking."

The two lads on the loft listened intently. Though the cronies on the ground below them did not speak loudly, their voices came plainly to the listeners.

"Let's poke a hole in their gas bag," proposed Sam. "That will make them think they're not so smart as they pretend."

"Naw, we can't do that," answered Andy.

"Why not?" declared Pete.

"Because the bag's away up in the top part of the shed, and I'm not going to climb up there."

"You're afraid," sneered Sam.

"I am not! I'll punch your face if you say that again! Besides the thing that holds the gas is made of aluminum, and we can't make a hole in it unless we take an axe, and that makes too much noise."

"We ought to play some sort of a trick on Tom Swift," proposed Pete. "He's too fresh!"

Tom shook his fist at the lads on the ground, but of course they did not see him.

"I have it!" came from Andy.

"What?" demanded his two cronies.

"We'll cut some of the guy wires from the planes and rudders. That will make the airship collapse. They'll think the wires broke from the strain. Take out your knives and saw away at the wires. Hurry, too, or they may catch us."

"You're caught now," whispered Ned to Tom. "Come on down, and give 'em a trouncing."

Tom hesitated. He looked quickly about the loft, and then a smile replaced the frown of righteous anger on his face.

"I have a better way," he said.

"What is it?"

"See that pile of dirt?" and he pointed to some refuse that had been swept up from the floor of the loft. Ned nodded. "It consists of a lot of shavings, sawdust and, what's more, a lot of soot and lampblack that we used in mixing some paint. We'll sweep the whole pile down on their heads, and make them wish they'd stayed away from this place."

"Good!" exclaimed Ned, chuckling. "Give me a broom. There's another one for you."

The two lads in the loft peered down. The red-headed, squint-eyed bully and his chums had their knives out, and were about to cut some of the important guy wires, when, at a signal from Tom, Ned, with a sweep of his broom, sent a big pile of the dirt, sawdust and lampblack down upon the heads of the conspirators. The young inventor did the same thing, and for an instant the lower part of the shed looked as if a dirtstorm had taken place there. The pile of refuse went straight down on the heads of the trio, and, as they were looking up, in order to see to cut the wires, they received considerable of it in their faces.

In an instant the white countenances of the lads were changed to black-as black as the burnt-cork performers in a minstrel show. Then came a series of howls.

"Wow! Who did that!"

"I'm blinded! The shed is falling down!"

"Run fellows, run!" screamed Andy. "There's been an explosion. We'll be killed!"

At that moment the big doors of the shed were thrown open, and Mr. Sharp came in. He started back in astonishment at the sight of the three grotesque figures, their faces black with the soot, and their clothes covered with sawdust and shavings, rushing wildly around.

"That will teach you to come meddling around here. Andy Roger!" cried Tom.

"I-I-you-you-Oh, wait-I-you-" spluttered the bully, almost speechless with rage. Sam and Pete were wildly trying to wipe the stuff from their faces, but only made matters worse. They were so startled that they did not know enough to run out of the opened doors.

"Wish we had some more stuff to put on 'em," remarked Ned, who was holding his sides that ached from laughter.

"I have it!" cried Tom, and he caught up a bucket of red paint, that had been used to give the airship its brilliant hue. Running to the end of the loft Tom stood for an instant over the trio of lads who were threatening and imploring by turns.

"Here's another souvenir of your visit," shouted the young inventor, as he dashed the bucket of red paint down on the conspirators. This completed the work of the dirt and soot, and a few seconds later, each face looking like a stage Indian's ready for the warpath, the trio dashed out. They shed shavings, sawdust and lampblack at every step, and from their clothes and hands and faces dripped the carmine paint.

"Better have your pictures taken!" cried Ned, peering from an upper window.

"Yes, and send us one," added Tom, joining his chum. Andy looked up at them. He dug a mass of red paint from his left ear, removed a mass of soot from his right cheek, and, shaking his fist, which was alternately striped red and black, cried out in a rage

"I'll get even with you yet, Tom Swift!"

"You only got what was coming to you," retorted the young inventor. "The next time you come sneaking around this airship, trying to damage it, you'll get worse, and I'll have you arrested. You've had your lesson, and don't forget it."

The red-haired bully, doubly red-haired now, had nothing more to say. There was nothing he could say, and, accompanied by his companions, he made a bee-line for the rear gate in the fence, and darted across the meadow. They were all sorry enough looking specimens, but solely through their own fault.

CHAPTER 8

WINNING A PRIZE

"Well, Tom, what happened?" asked Mr. Sharp, as he saw the trio running away. "Looks as if you had had an exciting time here."

"No, those fellows had all the excitement," declared Ned. "We had the fun." And the two lads proceeded to relate what had taken place.

"Tried to damage the airship, eh?" asked Mr. Sharp. "I wish I'd caught them at it; the scoundrels! But perhaps you handled them as well as I could have done."

"I guess so," assented Tom. "I must see if they did cut any of the wires."

But the young inventor and his chum had acted too quickly, and it was found that nothing, had been done to the *Red Cloud*.

A little later the airship was taken out of the shed, and made ready for a trip. The gas ascension was first used, and Ned and Mr. Swift were passengers with Tom and Mr. Sharp. The machine went about a thousand feet up in the air, and then was sent in various directions, to the no small delight of a large crowd that gathered in the meadow back of the Swift property; for it only required the sight of the airship looming its bulk above the fence and buildings, to attract a throng. It is safe to say this time, however, that Andy Foger and his cronies were not in the audience. They were probably too busy removing the soot and red paint.

Although it was the first time Mr. Swift had ever been in an airship, he evinced no great astonishment. In fact he seemed to be thinking deeply, and on some subject not connected with aeronautics. Tom noticed the abstraction of his father, and shook his head. Clearly the aged inventor was not his usual self.

As for Ned Newton his delight knew no bounds, At first he was a bit apprehensive as the big ship went higher and higher, and swung about, but he soon lost his fear, and enjoyed the experience as much as did Tom. The young inventor was busy helping Mr. Sharp manage the machinery, rudders-planes and motor.

A flight of several miles was made, and Tom was wishing they might pay another visit to the Rocksmond Seminary, but Mr. Sharp, after completing several evolutions, designed to test the steering qualities of the craft, put back home.

"We'll land in the meadow and try rising by the planes alone," he said. In this evolution it was deemed best for Mr. Swift and Ned to alight, as there was no telling just how the craft would behave. Tom's father was very willing to get out, but Ned would have remained in, only for the desire of his friend.

With the two propellers whirring at a tremendous speed, and all the gas out of the aluminum container, the *Red Cloud* shot forward, running over the level ground of the meadow, where a starting course had been laid out.

"Clear the track!" cried Mr. Sharp, as he saw the crowd closing up in front of him. The men, boys, several girls and women made a living lane. Through this shot the craft, and then, when sufficient momentum had been obtained, Tom, at a command from the aeronaut, pulled the lever of the elevation rudder. Up into the air shot the nose of the *Red Cloud* as the wind struck the slanting surface of the planes, and, a moment later it was sailing high above the heads of the throng.

"That's the stuff!" cried Mr. Sharp. "It works as well that way as it does with the gas!"

Higher and higher it went, and then, coming to a level keel, the craft was sent here and there, darting about like a bird, and going about in huge circles.

"Start the gas machine, and we'll come to rest in the air," said the balloonist, and Tom did so. As the powerful vapor filled the container the ship acquired a bouyancy, and there was no need of going at high speed in order to sustain it. The propellers were stopped, and the *Red Cloud* floated two thousand feet in the air, only a little distance below some fleecy, white masses from which she took her name. The demonstration was a great success. The gas was again allowed to escape, the propellers set in motion, and purely as an aeroplane, the ship was again sent forward. By means of the planes and rudders a perfect landing was made in the meadow, a short distance from where the start had been made. The crowd cheered the plucky youth and Mr. Sharp.

"Now I'm ready to go on a long trip any time you are, Tom," said the aeronaut that night.

"We'll fit up the car and get ready," agreed the `youth. "How about you, dad?"

"Me? Oh, well-er-that is, you see; well, I'll think about it," and Mr. Swift went to his own room, carrying with him a package of papers, containing intricate calculations.

Tom shook his head, but said nothing. He could not understand his father's conduct.

Work was started the next day on fitting up the car, or cabin, of the airship, so that several persons could live, eat and sleep in it for two weeks, if necessary. The third day after this task had been commenced the mail brought an unusual communication to Tom and Mr. Sharp. It was from an aero club of Blakeville, a city distant about a hundred miles, and stated that a competition for aeroplanes and dirigible balloons was to be held in the course of two weeks. The affair was designed to further interest in the sport, and also to demonstrate what progress had been made in the art of conquering the air. Prizes were to be given, and the inventors of the *Red Cloud*, the achievements of which the committee of arrangements had heard, were invited to compete.

"Shall we go in for it, Tom?" asked the balloonist.

"I'm willing if you are."

"Then let's do it. We'll see how our craft shows up alongside of others. I know something of this club. It is all right, but the carnival is likely to be a small one. Once I gave a balloon exhibition for them. The managers are all right. Well, we'll have a try at it. Won't do us any harm to win a prize. Then for a long trip!"

As it was not necessary to have the car, or cabin, completely fitted up in order to compete for the prize, work in that direction was suspended for the time being, and more attention was paid to the engine, the planes and rudders. Some changes were made and, a week later the *Red Cloud* departed for Blakeville. As the rules of the contest required three passengers, Ned Newton was taken along, Mr. Swift having arranged with the bank president so that the lad could have a few days off.

The *Red Cloud* arrived at the carnival grounds in the evening, having been delayed on the trip by a broken cog wheel, which was mended in mid-air. As the three navigators approached, they saw a small machine flying around the grounds.

"Look!" cried Ned excitedly. "What a small airship."

"That's a monoplane," declared Tom, who was getting to be quite an expert.

"Yes, the same kind that was used to cross the English Channel," interjected Mr. Sharp. "They're too uncertain for my purposes, though; they are all right under certain conditions."

Hardly had he spoken than a puff of wind caused the daring manipulator of the monoplane to swerve to one side. He had to make a quick descent-so rapid was it, in fact, that the tips of one of his planes was smashed.

"It'll take him a day to repair that," commented the aeronaut dryly.

The *Red Cloud* created a sensation as she slowly settled down in front of the big tent assigned to her. Tom's craft was easily the best one at the carnival, so far, though the managers said other machines were on the way.

The exhibition opened the next day, but no flights were to be attempted until the day following. Two more crafts arrived, a large triplane, and a dirigible balloon. There were many visitors to the ground, and Tom, Ned and Mr. Sharp were kept busy answering questions put by those who crowded into their tent. Toward the close of the day a fussy little Frenchman entered, and, making his way to where Tom stood, asked

"Air you ze ownair of zis machine?"

"One of them," replied the lad.

"Ha! Sacre! Zen I challenge you to a race. I have a monoplane zat is ze swiftest evaire! One thousand francs will I wager you, zat I can fly higher and farther zan you."

"Shall we take him up, Mr. Sharp?" asked Tom.

"We'll race with him, after we get through with the club entries." decided the aeronaut. "but not for money. It's against my principles, and I don't believe your father would like it. Racing for prizes is a different thing."

"Well, we will devote ze money to charity," conceded the Frenchman. This was a different matter, and one to which Mr. Sharp did not object, so it was arranged that a trial should take place after the regular affairs.

That night was spent in getting the *Red Cloud* in shape for the contests of the next day. She was "groomed" until every wire was taut and every cog, lever and valve working perfectly. Ned Newton helped all he could. So much has appeared in the newspapers of the races at Blakeville that I will not devote much space here to them. Suffice it to say that the *Red Cloud* easily distanced the big dirigible from which much was expected. It was a closer contest with the large triplane, but Tom's airship won, and was given the prize, a fine silver cup.

As the carnival was a small one, no other craft in a class with the *Red Cloud* had been entered, so Tom and Mr. Sharp had to be content with the one race they won. There were other contests among monoplanes and biplanes, and the little Frenchman won two races.

"Now for ze affaire wis ze monstaire balloon of ze rouge color!" he cried, as he alighted from his monoplane while an assistant filled the gasolene tank. "I will in circles go around you, up and down, zis side zen ze ozzer, and presto! I am back at ze starting place, before you have begun. Zen charity shall be ze richair!"

"All right, wait and see," said Tom, easily. But, though he showed much confidence he asked Mr. Sharp in private, just before the impromptu contest: "Do you think we can beat him?"

"Well," said the aeronaut, shrugging his shoulders, "you can't tell much about the air. His machine certainly goes very fast, but too much wind will be the undoing of him, while it will only help us. And I think," he added, "that we're going to get a breeze."

It was arranged that the *Red Cloud* would start from the ground, without the use of the gas, so as to make the machines more even. At the signal off they started, the motors making a great racket. The monoplane with the little Frenchman in the seat got up first.

"Ah, ha!" he cried gaily, "I leave you in ze rear! Catch me if you can!"

"Don't let him beat us," implored Ned.

"Can't you speed her up any more?" inquired Tom of Mr. Sharp.

The aeronaut nodded grimly, and turned more gasolene into the twenty-cylindered engine. Like a flash the *Red Cloud* darted forward. But the Frenchman also increased his speed and did, actually, at first, circle around the bigger machine, for his affair was much lighter. But when he tried to repeat that feat he found that he was being left behind.

"That's the stuff! We're winning!" yelled Tom, Ned joining in the shout.

Then came a puff of wind. The monoplane had to descend, for it was in danger of turning turtle. Still the navigator was not going to give up. He flew along at a lower level. Then Mr. Sharp opened up the *Red Cloud*'s engine at full speed, and it was the big machine which now sailed around the other.

"I protest! I protest!" cried the Frenchman, above the explosions of his motor. "Ze wind is too strong for me!"

Mr. Sharp said nothing, but, with a queer smile on his face he sent the airship down toward the earth. A moment later he was directly under the monoplane. Then, quickly rising, he fairly caught the Frenchman's machine on top of a square platform of the gas container, the bicycle wheels of the monoplane resting on the flat surface. And, so swiftly did the *Red Cloud* fly along that it carried the monoplane with it, to the chagrin of the French navigator.

"A trick! A trick!" he cried. "Eet is not fair!"

Then, dropping down, Mr. Sharp allowed the monoplane to proceed under its own power, while he raced on to the finish mark, winning, of course, by a large margin.

"Ha! A trick! I race you tomorrow and again tomorrow!" cried the beaten Frenchman as he alighted.

"No, thanks," answered Tom. "We've had enough. I guess

charity will be satisfied."

The little Frenchman was a good loser, and paid over the money, which was given to the Blakeville Hospital, the institution receiving it gladly.

At the request of the carnival committee, Mr. Sharp and Tom gave an exhibition of high and long flights the next day, and created no little astonishment by their daring feats.

"Well, I think we have reason to be proud of our ship," remarked Mr. Sharp that night. "We won the first contest we were ever in, and beat that speedy monoplane, which was no small thing to do, as they are very fast."

"But wait until we go on our trip," added Tom, as he looked at the cup they had won. He little realized what danger they were to meet with in the flight that was before them.

CHAPTER 9

THE RUNAWAY AUTO

Had the inventors of the *Red Cloud* desired, they could have made considerable money by giving further exhibitions at the Blakeville Aero Carnival, and at others which were to be held in the near future at adjoining cities. The fame of the new machine had spread, and there were many invitations to compete for prizes.

But Tom and Mr. Sharp wished to try their skill in a long flight, and at the close of the Blakeville exhibition they started for Shopton, arriving there without mishap, though Tom more than half hoped that they might happen to strike the tower of a certain school. I needn't specify where.

The first thing to be done was to complete the fitting-up of the car, or cabin. No berths had, as yet, been put in, and these were first installed after the *Red Cloud* was in her shed. Then an electrical heating and cooking apparatus was fitted in; some additional machinery, tanks for carrying water, and chemicals for making the gas, boxes of provisions, various measuring instruments and other supplies were put in the proper places, until the cabin was filled almost to its capacity. Of course particular attention had been paid to the ship proper, and every portion was gone over until Mr. Sharp was sure it was in shape for a long flight.

"Now the question is," he said to Tom one evening, "who shall we take with us? You and I will go, of course, but I'd like one more. I wonder if your father can't be induced to accompany us? He seemed to like the trial trip."

"I'll ask him tomorrow," said the lad. "He's very busy tonight. If he doesn't care about it, maybe Garret Jackson will go."

"I'm afraid not. He's too timid."

"I'd like to take Ned Newton, but he can't get any more time away from the bank. I guess we'll have to depend on dad."

But, to the surprise of Tom and Mr. Sharp, the aged inventor shook his head when the subject was broached to him next day.

"Why won't you go, dad?" asked his son.

"I'll tell you," replied Mr. Swift. "I was keeping it a secret until I had made some advance in what I am engaged upon. But I don't want to go because I am on the verge of perfecting a new apparatus for submarine boats. It will revolutionize travel under the water, and I don't want to leave home until I finish it. There is another point to be considered. The government has offered a prize for an under-water boat of a new type, and I wish to try for it."

"So that's what you've been working on, eh, dad?" asked his son.

"That's it, and, much as I should like to accompany you, I don't feel free to go. My mind would be distracted, and I need to concentrate myself on this invention. It will produce the most wonderful results, I'm sure. Besides, the government prize is no small one. It is fifty thousand dollars for a successful boat."

Mr. Swift told something more about his submarine, but, as I expect to treat of that in another book, I will not dwell on it here, as I know you are anxious to learn what happened on the trip of the *Red Cloud*.

"Well," remarked Mr. Sharp, somewhat dubiously, "I wonder who we can get to go? We need someone besides you and I, Tom."

"I s'pose I could get Eradicate Sampson, and his mule Boomerange," replied the lad with a smile. "Yet I don't know-"

At that instant there was a tremendous racket outside. The loud puffing of an automobile could be heard, but mingled with it was the crash of wood, and then the whole house seemed jarred and shaken.

"Is it an earthquake?" exclaimed Mr. Swift, springing to his feet, and rushing to the library windows.

"Something's happened!" cried Tom.

"Maybe an explosion of the airship gas!" yelled Mr. Sharp, making ready to run to the balloon shed. But there was no need. The crashing of wood ceased, and, above the puffing of an auto could be heard a voice exclaiming

"Bless my very existence! Bless my cats and dogs! Good gracious! But I never meant to do this!"

Tom, his father and Mr. Sharp rushed to the long, low windows that opened on the veranda. There, on the porch, which it had mounted by way of the steps, tearing away part of the railing, was a large touring car; and, sitting at the steering wheel, in a dazed sort of manner, was Mr. Wakefield Damon.

"Bless my shirt studs!" he went on feebly. "But I have done it now!"

"What's the matter?" cried Tom, hastening up to him. "What happened? Are you hurt?"

"Hurt? Not a bit of it! Bless my moonstone!

It's the most lucky escape I ever had! But I've damaged your porch, and I haven't done my machine any good. Do you see anything of another machine chasing me?"

Tom looked puzzled, but glanced up and down, the road. Far

down the highway could be discerned a cloud of dust, and, from the midst of it came a faint "chug-chug."

"Looks like an auto down there," he said.

"Thank goodness! Bless my trousers, but I've escaped 'em!" cried the eccentric man from whom Tom had purchased his motorcycle.

"Escaped who?" asked Mr. Swift.

"Those men. They were after me. But I may as well get out and explain. Dear me! However will I ever get my car off your porch?" and Mr. Damon seemed quite distressed.

"Never mind," answered Tom. "We can manage that. Tell us what happened."

"Exactly," replied Mr. Damon, growing calmer, "Bless my shoe buttons, but I had a fright, two of them, in fact.

"You see," he went on, "I was out partly on pleasure and partly on business. The pleasure consisted in riding in my auto, which my physician recommended for my health. The business consisted in bringing to the Shopton Bank a large amount of cash. Well, I deposited it all right, but, as I came out I saw some men hanging around. I didn't like their looks, and I saw them eyeing me rather sharply. I thought I had seen them before and, sure enough I had. Two of the men belonged to that Happy Harry gang. I".

Tom made a quick motion of a caution, pointing to his father, but it was not necessary, as Mr. Swift was absently-mindedly calculating an a piece of paper he had taken from his pocket, and had not heard what Mr. Damon said. The latter, however, knew what Tom meant, and went on.

"Well, I didn't like the looks of these men, and when I saw them sizing me up, evidently thinking I had drawn money out instead of putting it in, I decided to give them the slip. I got in my auto, but I was startled to see them get in their car. I headed for here, as I was coming to pay you a visit, anyhow, and the mysterious men kept after me. It became a regular race. I put on all the speed I could and headed for your house, Tom, for I thought you would help me. I went faster and faster, and so did they. They were almost up to me, and I was just thinking of slowing down to turn in here, when I lost control of my machine, and-well, I did turn in here, but not exactly as I intended. Bless my gaiters! I came in with rather more of a rush than I expected. It was awful-positively awful, I assure you. You've no idea how nervous I was. But I escaped those scoundrels, for they rushed on when they saw what I had done-smashed the porch railing".

"Probably they thought you'd smash them," observed Tom with

a laugh. "But why did they follow you?"

"Can't imagine! Haven't the least idea. Bless my spark-plug, but they might have imagined I had money. Anyhow I'm glad I escaped them!"

"It's lucky you weren't hurt," said Mr. Sharp.

"Oh, me? Bless my existence! I'm always having narrow escapes." Mr. Damon caught sight of the *Red Cloud* which was out in front of the big shed. "Bless my heart! What's that?" he added.

"Our new airship," answered Tom proudly. "We are just planning a long trip in it, but we can't find a third member of the party to go along."

"A third member!" exclaimed Mr. Damon. "Do you really mean it?"

"We do."

"Bless my shoe laces! Will you take me along?"

"Do you mean that?" asked Tom in turn, foreseeing a way out of their difficulties.

"I certainly do," answered the eccentric man. "I am much interested in airships, and I might as well die up in the clouds as any other way. Certainly I prefer it to being smashed up in an auto. Will you take me?"

"Of course!" cried Tom heartily, and Mr. Sharp nodded an assent. Then Tom drew Mr. Damon to one side. "We'll arrange the trip in a few minutes," the lad said. "Tell me more about those mysterious men, please."

CHAPTER 10

A BAG OF TOOLS

Wakefield Damon glanced at Mr. Swift. The inventor was oblivious to his surroundings, and was busy figuring away on some paper. He seemed even to have forgotten the presence of the eccentric autoist.

"I don't want father to hear about the men," went on Tom, in a low tone. "If he hears that Happy Harry and his confederates are in this vicinity, he'll worry, and that doesn't agree with him. But are you sure the men you saw are the same ones who stole the turbine model?"

"Very certain," replied Mr. Damon. "I had a good view of them as I came from the bank, and I was surprised to see them, until I remembered that they were out of jail."

"But why do you think they pursued you?"

"Bless my eyes! I can't say. Perhaps they weren't after me at all. I may have imagined it, but they certainly hurried off in their auto as soon as I left the bank, after leaving my money there. I'm glad I deposited it before I saw them. I was so nervous, as it was, that I couldn't steer straight. It's too bad, the way I've damaged your house."

"That doesn't matter. But how about the trip in the airship? I hope you meant it when you said you would go."

"Of course I did. I've never traveled in the air, but it can't be much worse than my experience with my motor-cycle and the auto. At least I can't run up any stoop, can I?" and Mr. Damon looked at Mr. Sharp.

"No," replied the aeronaut, as he scratched his head, "I guess you'll be safe on that score. But I hope you won't get nervous when we reach a great height."

"Oh, no. I'll just calm myself with the reflection that I can't die but once," and with this philosophical reflection Mr. Damon went back to look at the auto, which certainly looked odd, stuck up on the veranda.

"Well, you'd better make arrangements to go with us then," went on Tom. "Meanwhile I'll see to getting your car down. You'll want to send it home, I suppose?"

"No, not if you'll keep it for me. The fact is that all my folks are away, and will be for some time. I don't have to go home to notify them, and it's a good thing, as my wife is very nervous, and might object, if she heard about the airship. I'll just stay here, if you've no objection, until the *Red Cloud* sails, if sails is the proper term."

"'Sails' will do very well," answered Mr. Sharp. "But, Tom, let's see if you and I can't get that car down. Perhaps Mr. Damon would like to go in the house and talk to your father," for Mr. Swift had left the piazza.

The eccentric individual was glad enough not to be on hand when his car was eased down from the veranda and disappeared into the house. Tom and Mr. Sharp, with the aid of Garret Jackson, then released the auto from its position. They had to take down the rest of the broken railing, and their task was easy enough. The machine was stored in a disused shed, and Mr. Damon had no further concern until it was time to undertake the trip through the air.

"It will fool those men if I mysteriously disappear," he said, with a smile. "Bless my hat band, but they'll wonder what became of me. We'll just slip off in the *Red Cloud*, and they'll never be the wiser."

"I don't know about that," commented Tom. "I fancy they are keeping pretty close watch in this vicinity, and I don't like it. I'm afraid they are up to some mischief. I should think the bank authorities would have them locked upon suspicion. I think I'll telephone Ned about it."

He did so, and his chum, in turn, notified the bank watchman. But the next day it was reported that no sign of the men had been seen, and, later it was learned that an auto, answering the description of the one they were in, had been seen going south, many miles from Shopton.

The work of preparing the *Red Cloud* for the long trip was all but completed. It had been placed back in the shed while a few more adjustments were made to the machinery.

"Bless my eyelashes!" exclaimed Mr. Damon, a few days before the one set for the start, "but I haven't asked where we are bound for. Where are we going, anyhow, Mr. Sharp?"

"We're going to try and reach Atlanta, Georgia," replied the balloonist. "That will make a fairly long trip, and the winds at this season are favorable in that direction."

"That suits me all right," declared Mr. Damon. "I'm all ready and anxious to start."

It was decided to give the airship a few more trials around Shopton before setting out, to see how it behaved with the car heavier loaded than usual. With this in view a trip was made to Rocksmond, with Mr. Swift, Mr. Damon and Ned, in addition to Mr. Sharp and Tom, on board. Then, at Tom's somewhat blushing request, a stop was made near the Seminary, and, when the pupils came trooping out, the young inventor asked Miss Nestor if she didn't want to take a little flight. She consented, and with two pretty companions climbed rather hesitatingly into the car. No great height was attained, but the girls were fully satisfied and, after their first alarm really enjoyed the spin in the air, with Tom proudly presiding at the steering wheel, which Mr. Sharp relinquished to the lad, for he understood Tom's feelings.

Three days later all was in readiness for the trip to Atlanta. Mr. Swift was earnestly invited to undertake it, both Tom and Mr. Sharp urging him, but the veteran inventor said he must stay at home, and work on his submarine plans.

The evening before the start, when the aeronaut and Tom were giving a final inspection to the craft in the big shed, Mr. Sharp exclaimed "I declare Tom, I believe you'll have to take a run into town."

"What for?"

"Why to get that kit of special tools I ordered, which we might need to make repairs. There are some long-handled wrenches, some spare levers, and a couple of braces and bits. Harrison, the hardware dealer, ordered them for me from New York, and they were to be ready this afternoon, but I forgot them. Take an empty valise with you, and you can carry them on your motorcycle. I'm sorry to have forgotten it, but-"

"That's all right, Mr. Sharp, I'd just as soon go as not. It will make the time pass more quickly. I'll start right off."

An hour later, having received the tools, which made quite a bundle, the lad put them in the valise, and started back toward home. As he swung around the corner on which the bank was located-the same bank in which Ned Newton worked-one of the valves on the motor-cycle began to leak. Tom dismounted to adjust it, and had completed the work, being about to ride on, when down the street came Andy Foger and Sam Snedecker. They started at the sight of our hero.

"There he is now!" exclaimed Sam, as if he and the red-haired bully had been speaking of the young inventor.

"Let's lick him!" proposed Andy. "Now's our chance to get even for throwing that paint and soot on us."

Tom heard their words. He was not afraid of both the lads, for, though each one matched him in size and strength, Tom knew they were cowards.

"If you're looking for anything I guess I can accommodate you," he said, coolly.

"Come on, Andy," urged Sam. But, somehow Andy hung back.

Perhaps he didn't like the way Tom squared off. The young inventor had let down the rear brace of his motor-cycle, and was not obliged to hold it, so he had both hands free.

"We ought to lick him good and proper," growled the squint-eyed lad.

"Well, why don't you?" invited Tom.

He moved to one side, so as not to be hampered by his wheel. As he did so he knocked from the handle bars the valise of tools. They fell with a clatter and a thud to the pavement, and the satchel came open. It was under a gas lamp, and the glitter of the long-handled wrenches and other implements caught the eyes of Andy and his crony.

"Huh! If we fought you, maybe you'd use some of them on us," sneered Andy, glad of an excuse not to fight.

Tom quickly picked up his valise, shutting it, but he was aware of the close scrutiny of the two vindictive lads.

"I don't fight with such things," he said, somewhat annoyed, and he hung the tools back on the handle bars.

"What you doing around the bank at this hour?" asked Sam, as if to change the subject. "First thing you know the watchman will order you to move on. He might think you were a suspicious character."

"The same to you," retorted Tom, "but I'm going to ride on now, unless you want to have a further argument with me."

"You'd better be careful how you hang around a bank," added Andy. "The police are on the lookout here. There's been some mysterious men seen about."

Tom did not care to go into that, and, seeing that the two bullies had lost all desire to attack him, he put up the brace and mounted his wheel.

"Good-by," he called to Andy and Sam, as he rode off, the tools rattling and jingling in the valise, but it was a sarcastic farewell, and the two cronies did not reply.

"I hope I didn't damage any of the tools when I let them fall that time," mused the young inventor. "My, the way Sam and Andy stared at them it would make it seem as if I had a lot of weapons in the bag! They certainly took good note of them."

The time was to come, and very shortly, when Andy's and Sam's observation of the tools was to prove disastrous for our hero. As Tom turned the corner he looked back, and saw, still standing in front of the bank, the two cronies.

CHAPTER 11

THE *RED CLOUD* DEPARTS

"Well, dad, I wish you were going along with us," said Tom to his father next morning. "You don't know what you're going to miss. A fine trip of several hundred miles through the air, seeing strange sights, and experiencing new sensations."

"Yes, I wish you would reconsider your determination, and accompany us," added Mr. Damon. "I would enjoy your company."

"There's plenty of room. We can carry six persons with ease," said Mr. Sharp.

Mr. Swift shook his head, and smiled.

"I have too much work to do here at home," he replied. "Perhaps I may astonish you with something when you come back. I have nearly perfected my latest invention."

There was no combating such a resolution as this, and Tom and the others considered the decision of the aged inventor as final. The airship was ready for the start, and every one had arisen earlier than usual on this account. The bag of tools, for which Tom had gone to town, were put in their proper place, the last of the supplies were taken abroad, final tests were made of the various apparatus, the motor had been given a trial spin, disconnected from the propellers, and then the balloonist announced

"Well, Tom and Mr. Damon, you had better begin to think of starting. We've had breakfast here, but there's no telling where we will eat dinner."

"Bless my soul! Don't you talk that way!" exclaimed Mr. Damon. "You make me exceedingly nervous. Why shouldn't we know where we are going to eat dinner?"

"Oh, I meant we couldn't tell over just what part of the United States we would be when dinner time came," explained the aeronaut.

"Oh, that's different. Bless my pocket knife, but I thought you meant we might be dashed to pieces, and incapable of eating any dinner."

"Hardly," remarked Mr. Sharp. "The *Red Cloud* is not that kind of an airship, I hope. But get aboard, if you please."

Tom and Mr. Damon entered the car. It was resting on the ground, on the small wheels used to start the airship when the gas inflation method was not used. In this case, however, it had been decided to rise in the air by means of the powerful vapor, and not to use the wings and planes until another time. Consequently the ship was swaying slightly, and tugging at the restraining cables.

As Tom and Mr. Damon entered the cabin there drove into the Swift yard a dilapidated wagon, drawn by a bony mule, and it did not need the addition of a colored man's voice, calling: "Whoa, dar, Boomerang!" to tell Tom that his friend Eradicate Sampson was on hand. As for Eradicate, as soon as he saw the great airship, which he had never before beheld fully rigged, all ready for a flight, his eyes became big with wonder.

"Is dat yo' flyin' machine, Mistah Swift?" he asked.

"That's it, Rad," answered Tom. "Don't you want to come and take a ride with us?"

"Me? Good land a' massy! No indeedy, Mistah Swift," and the whitewasher, who had descended from his wagon, edged away, as if the airship might suddenly put out a pair of hands and grab him. "No indeedy I doant! I come t' do a little whitewashin' an' when I do dat I'se gwine on mah way. But dat's a pow'ful fine ship; it suah am!"

"Better come and try a flight, Rad," added Mr. Damon. "I'll look after you."

"No, sag, an' I doan't take it kind ob yo' all t' tempt me dat way, nuther," spoke Eradicate. But, when he saw that the craft was stationary, he ventured to approach closer. Gingerly he put out one hand and touched the framework of the wheels, just forward of the cabin. The negro grasped the timber, and lifted it slightly. To his astonishment the whole front of the airship tilted up, for it was about ready to fly, and a child might have lifted it, so buoyant was it. But Eradicate did not know this. Wonderingly he looked at the great bulk of the ship, looming above him, then he glanced at his arm. Once more, noting that the attention of his friends was elsewhere, he lifted the craft. Then he cried "Look yeah, Mistah Swift! Look yeah! No wonder day calls me Sampson. I done lifted dis monstrousness airship wif one hand, See, I kin do it! I kin do it!"

Once more he raised the *Red Cloud* slightly, and a delighted grin, not unmixed with a look of awe, spread over his honest countenance.

"I suppose you'll give up whitewashing and join a circus as a strong man, now," observed Mr. Sharp, with a wink at his companions.

"Days what I will!" announced Eradicate proudly. "I neber knowed I was dat strong, but ob course I allers knowed I had some muscle. Golly, I must hab growed strong ober night! Now, Boomerang, yo' suah has got t' look out fo' yo' sef. No mo' ob yo' cuttin' up capers, or I'll jest lift you up, an' sot yo' down on yo' back, I suah will," and the negro feeling of his biceps walked over to where the mule stood, with its eyes closed.

"I guess you can cast off, Tom," called Mr. Sharp, as he entered .the car, having seen that everything was all right. "We'll not go up very far at first, until Mr. Damon gets used to the thin air."

"Bless my soul, I believe I'm getting nervous," announced the eccentric man. "Bless my liver, but I hope nothing happens."

"Nothing will happen," Mr. Sharp assured him. "Just keep calm, when it feels as if the bottom was dropping out of everything and you'll soon get over it. Are you casting off those ropes, Tom? Is all clear?"

"All but the bow and stern lines."

"You attend to the bow line, and I'll go to the stern," and, going over to the gas generator, Mr. Sharp started it so as to force more vapor into the red aluminum container. This had the effect of rendering the airship more bouyant, and it tugged and strained harder than ever at the ropes.

"Good-by, Tom," called Mr. Swift, reaching up to shake hands with his son. "Drop me a line when you get a chance."

"Oh, Tom, do be careful," implored Mrs. Baggert, her kind face showing her anxiety. "May I kiss you good-by?"

"Of course," answered the young inventor, though the motherly housekeeper had not done this since he was a little chap. She had to stand on a soap box, which Eradicate brought in order to reach Tom's face, and, when she had kissed him she said:

"Oh, I'm so worried! I just know you'll be killed, risking your lives in that terrible airship!"

"Ha! Not a very cheerful view to take, madam," observed Mr. Damon. "Don't hold that view, I beg of you. Bless my eyelashes, but you'll see us coming home, covered with glory and star dust."

"I'm sure I hope so," answered Mrs. Baggert, laughing a little in spite of herself.

The last ropes were cast off. Good-bys were shouted as the airship shot into the air, and Mr. Sharp started the motor, to warm it up before the propellers were thrown into gear. The twenty cylinders began exploding with a terrific racket, as the muffler was open, and Tom, looking down, saw Boomerang awaken with a jump. The mule was so frightened that he started off on a dead run, swinging the rickety, old wagon along behind him.

Eradicate Sampson, who had been feeling his muscle since he discovered what he thought was his marvelous strength, saw what was happening.

"Whoa, dar, Boomerang!" he shouted. Then, as the tailboard of the wagon swung past him, he reached out and grabbed it. Perhaps he thought he could bring the runaway mule up standing, but, if he did, he was grievously disappointed. Boomerang pulled his master along the gravel walk, and kept running in spite of Eradicate's command to "whoa, dar!"

It might have gone hard with him, had not Garret Jackson, the engineer, running in front of Boomerang, caught the animal. Eradicate picked himself up, and gazed sadly at his arms. The navigators of the air could not hear what he said, but what he thought was evident to them.

Then, as Mr. Sharp deadened the explosions of the powerful motor. Tom, looking at a gauge, noted that their height was seven hundred feet. "High enough!" called Mr. Sharp, and it was time, for Mr. Damon, in spite of his resolution, was getting pale.

The gas was shut off, the propellers thrown into gear, and, with a rush the *Red Cloud* shot toward the south, passing over the Swift homestead, and high above the heads of the crowd that had gathered to witness the start. The eventful voyage of the air had begun.

CHAPTER 12

SOME STARTLING NEWS

"Well, there they go," remarked Mrs. Baggert to Mr. Swift, as she strained her eyes toward the sky, against the blue of which the airship was now only a large, black ball.

"Yes, and a fine start they made," replied the inventor. "I almost wish I had accompanied them, but I must not stop work on my submarine invention."

"I do hope nothing will happen to them," went on the housekeeper. "I declare, though, I feel just as if something was going to happen."

"Nervousness, pure nervousness," commented Mr. Swift. "Better take a little-er-I suppose catnip tea would be good."

"Catnip tea! The very idea!" exclaimed Mrs. Baggert. "That shows how much you know about nervousness, Mr. Swift," and she seemed a little indignant.

"Ha! Hum I Well, maybe catnip tea wouldn't be just the thing. But don't worry about Tom. I'm sure he can look after himself. As for Mr. Sharp he has made too many ascensions to run into any unnecessary danger."

"Nervous!" went on the housekeeper, who seemed to resent this state being applied to her. "I'm sure I'm not half as nervous as that Mr. Damon. He gives me the fidgets."

"Of course. Well, I must get back to my work," said the inventor. "Ah, are you hurt, Eradicate?" he went on, as the colored man came back, driving Boomerang, who had been stopped just before reaching the road.

"No, Mistah Swift, I ain't exactly damaged, but mah feelin's am suah hurted."

"How's that?"

"Well, I thought I had growed strong in de night, when I lifted dat airship, but when I went to stop mah mule I couldn't do it. He won't hab no respect fo' me now."

"Oh, I wouldn't let that worry me," commented Mr. Swift, and he explained to Eradicate how it was that he had so easily lifted the end of the bouyant ship, which weighed very little when filled with gas.

The colored man proceeded with his work of whitewashing, the inventor was in his library, puzzling over tables of intricate figures, and Mrs. Baggert was in the kitchen, sighing occasionally as she thought of Tom, whom she loved almost as a son, high in the air, when two men came up the walk, from the street, and knocked at the side door. Mrs. Baggert, who answered the summons, was somewhat surprised to see Chief of Police Simonson and Constable Higby.

"They probably came to see the airship start," she thought, "but they're too late."

"Ah, good morning, Mrs. Baggert," greeted the chief. "Is Mr. Swift and his son about this morning?"

"Mr. Swift is in his library, but Tom is gone."

"He'll be back though, won't he?" asked Constable Higby quickly—anxiously, Mrs. Baggert thought.

"Oh, yes," she replied. "He and—"

"Just take us to see Mr. Swift," interrupted the chief, with a look of caution at his aide. "We'll explain matters to him."

Wondering what could be the mission of the two officers, Mrs. Baggert led them to the library.

"It's queer," she thought, "that they don't ask something about the airship. I suppose that was what they came for. But maybe it's about the mysterious men who robbed Mr. Swift."

"Ah, gentlemen, what can I do for you?" asked the inventor, as he rose to greet the officials.

"Ahem, Mr. Swift. Ahem-er-that is-well, the fact is, Mr. Swift," stammered the chief, "we have come upon a very painful errand."

"What's that?" cried Tom's father. "I haven't been robbed again, have I?"

"There has been a robbery committed," spoke the constable quickly.

"But you are not the victim," interposed the chief.

"I'm glad of that," said Mr. Swift.

"Where is your son, Tom?" asked the head of the Shopton police force, sharply.

"What do you want with him?" inquired the inventor, struck by some strange tone in the other's voice.

"Mr. Swift," went on the chief, solemnly, "I said we came upon a very painful errand. It is painful, as I have known Tom since he was a little lad. But I must do my duty, no matter how painful it is. I have a warrant for the arrest of your son, Thomas Swift, and I have come to serve it. I need not tell you that it is your duty to give him up to us-the representatives of the law. I call upon you to produce your son."

Mr. Swift staggered to his feet.

"My son! You have come to arrest my son?" he stammered.

The chief nodded grimly.

"Upon what charge?" faltered the father.

"On a charge of breaking into the Shopton National Bank last night, and stealing from the vault seventy-five thousand dollars in currency!"

"Seventy-five thousand dollars! Tom accused of robbing the bank!" faltered Mr. Swift.

"That is the charge, and we've come to arrest him," broke in Constable Higby.

"Where is he?" added the chief.

"This charge is false! Absolutely false!" shouted the aged inventor.

"That may be," admitted the chief shaking his head. "But the charge has been made, and we hold the warrant. The courts will settle it. We must now arrest Tom. Where is he?"

"He isn't here!" cried Mr. Swift, and small blame to him if there was a note of triumph in his voice. "Tom sailed away not half an hour ago in the airship *Red Cloud!* You can't arrest him!"

"He's escaped!" shouted the constable. "I told you, chief, that he was a slippery customer, and that we'd better come before breakfast!"

"Dry up!" commanded the chief testily. "So he's foiled us, eh? Run away when he knew we were coming? I think that looks like guilt, Mr. Swift."

"Never!" cried the inventor. "Tom would never think of robbing the bank. Besides, he has all the money he wants. The charge is preposterous! I demand to be confronted with the proof."

"You shall be," answered Chief Simonson vindictively. "If you will come to the bank you can see the rifled vault, and hear the testimony of a witness who saw your son with burglar tools in his possession last night. We also have a warrant for Mr. Wakefield Damon. Do you know anything of him?"

"He has gone with my son in the airship."

"Ha! The two criminals with their booty have escaped together!" cried the chief. "But we'll nab them if we have to scour the whole country. Come on, Higby! Mr. Swift, if you'll accompany me to the bank, I think I can give you all the proof you want," and the officials, followed by the amazed and grief-stricken inventor, left the house.

CHAPTER 13

MR. DAMON IN DANGER

The sensations of the voyagers in the airship, who meanwhile, were flying along over the country surrounding Shopton, were not very different than when they had undertaken some trial flights. In fact Mr. Damon was a little disappointed after they had waved their farewells to Mr. Swift and Mrs. Baggert.

"I declare I'm not at all nervous," he remarked, as he sat in an easy chair in the enclosed car or cabin, and looked down at the earth through the plate-glass windows in the floor.

"I thought you'd be all right once we got started," commented Mr. Sharp. "Do you think you can stand going a trifle higher?"

"Try it,." suggested the eccentric man. "Bless my watch chain, but, as I said, I might as well die this way as any other. Hitting a cloud-bank is easier than trying to climb a tree on a motorcycle, eh, Tom?"

"Very much so, Mr. Damon," conceded the young inventor, with a laugh.

"Oh, we'll not attempt any cloud heights for a day or two," went on Mr. Sharp. "I want you, to gradually get used to the rarefied atmosphere, Mr. Damon. Tom and I are getting to be old hands at it. But, if you think you can stand it, I'll go up about a thousand feet higher."

"Make it two thousand, while you're at it," proposed the odd character. "Might as well take a long fall as a short one."

Accordingly, the elevation rudder was used to send the *Red Cloud* to a greater height while she was still skimming along like some great bird. Of course the desired elevation could have been obtained by forcing more gas from the machine into the big, red container overhead, but it was decided to be as sparing of this vapor as possible, since the voyagers did not want to descend to get more material, in case they used up what they had. It was just as easy to rise by properly working the rudders, when the ship was in motion, and that was the method now employed.

With the great propellers, fore and aft, making about a thousand revolutions a minute the craft slanted up toward the sky.

The ship was not being run at top speed as Mr. Sharp did not care to force it, and there was no need for haste. Long distance, rather than high speed was being aimed at on this first important flight.

Tom was at the steering wheel, and, with his I hand on the lever controlling the elevation rudder, kept watch of the face of Mr. Damon, occasionally noting what height the hand on the gauge registered. He fancied he saw the cheeks of his friend growing pale, and, when a height of thirty-five hundred feet was indicated, with a yank the young inventor put the airship on a level keel.

"Are you distressed, Mr. Damon?" he asked.

"Ye-yes, I-I have-some-some difficulty in breathing," was the answer.

Tom gave his friend the same advice the aeronaut had given the lad on his first trip, and the eccentric man soon felt better.

"Bless my buttons!" he ventured to explain. "But I feel as if I had lost several pounds of flesh, and I'm glad of it."

Mr. Sharp was busy with the motor, which needed some slight adjustments, and Tom was in sole charge of navigating the airship. He had lost the nervous feeling that first possessed him, and was becoming quite an expert at meeting various currents of wind encountered in the upper regions.

Below, the voyagers could see the earth spread out like a great map. They could not tell their exact location now, but by calculating their speed, which was about thirty miles an hour, Tom figured out that they were above the town of Centreford, near where he had been attacked once by the model thieves.

For several hours the airship kept on her way, maintaining a height of about a mile, for when it was found that Mr. Damon could accommodate himself to thirty-five hundred feet the elevation rudder was again shifted to send the craft upward.

By using glasses the travelers could see crowds on the earth watching their progress in the air, and, though airships, dirigible balloons and aeroplanes are getting fairly common now, the appearance of one as novel and as large as the *Red Cloud* could always be depended upon to attract attention.

"Well, what do you say to something to eat?" proposed Mr. Sharp, coming into the main cabin, from the motor compartment. "It's twelve o'clock, though we can't hear the factory whistles up, here."

"I'm ready, any time you are," called Tom, from the pilot house. "Shall I cook grub, Mr. Sharp?"

"No, you manage the ship, and I'll play cook. We'll not get a very elaborate meal this time, as I shall have to pay occasional visits to the motor, which isn't running just to suit me."

The electrical stove was set going, and some soup and beefsteak from among the stores, was put on the fire. In spite of the fact that the day was a warm one in October, it was quite cool in the cabin, until the stove took off the chill. The temperature of the upper regions was several degrees below that of the earth. At times the ship passed through little wisps of vapor-clouds in the making.

"Isn't this wonderful!" exclaimed Mr. Damon, as he sat in an easy chair, partaking of some of the food. "To think that I have lived to see the day when I can take my lunch a mile in the air, with a craft flying along like a bird. Bless my knife and fork but it certainly is wonderful."

Mr. Sharp relieved Tom at the wheel, while the young inventor ate, and then, with the airship heading southwest, the speed was increased a trifle, the balloonist desiring to see what the motor could accomplish under a heavy load.

A drop of several hundred feet was made about an hour later, and, as this made it warmer, Mr. Damon, who was a great lover of fresh air, decided to go out on the platform in front of the cabin. This platform, and a similar one at the rear, was railed about, to prevent accidents. A fine view could be had from them much better than through the floor windows of the car.

"Be careful of the propeller," advised Tom, as his friend went outside. "I don't believe you're tall enough to be hit by the blades, but don't take any chances of standing on your tiptoes."

"Bless my pocket handkerchief, indeed I'll not," came the answer. "But I think I shall wrap up my throat in the scarf I brought along. I am subject to neuralgia, and the breeze may bring on an attack of it."

Wrapping along, woolen scarf about his neck, the eccentric man ventured out on the open platform. About the middle of it, but sufficiently high to be above a person's head, was the forward propeller, whirring around at swift speed.

Tom, with his eye on the various gauges and the compass, was steering the airship. He glanced at Mr. Damon, who appeared to be enjoying the view from the platform. For an instant the eyes of the lad were taken from the form of his friend. He looked back suddenly, however, his attention attracted by a smothered cry. He was horrified by what he saw.

Mr. Damon was leaning far over the edge of the railing, with nothing between him and the earth a thousand feet below. He seemed to have lost his balance and had toppled forward, being doubled up on the iron pipe railing, his hands hanging limply over. Then, as Tom cried to Mr. Sharp to shut off the motor, the lad saw that, hanging to the blade of the propeller, and being whirled around in its revolutions, was a part of Mr. Damon's red scarf.

"Hurry! Hurry, Mr. Sharp!" yelled Tom, not daring to let go the steering wheel, for fear the ship would encounter a treacherous current and tilt. "Hurry to Mr. Damon!"

"What's the matter?" asked the balloonist.

"He's dead-or unconscious-hanging over the railing. He seems to be slipping! Hurry, or it will be too late!"

CHAPTER 14

ANDY GIVES THE CLUE

When Mr. Swift followed the chief of police and the constable to the town hall his mind was filled with many thoughts. All his plans for revolutionizing submarine travel, were, of course, forgotten, and he was only concerned with the charge that had been made against his son. It seemed incredible, yet the officers were not ones to perpetrate a joke. The chief and constable had driven from town in a carriage, and they now invited the inventor to ride back with them.

"Do you mean to tell me a warrant has actually been sworn out against my son, Chief?" asked the father, when they were near the town hall.

"That's just what I mean to say, Mr. Swift, and, I'm sorry, on your account, that I have to serve it."

"Hub! Don't look like you was goin' to serve it," remarked the constable. "He's skipped out."

"That's all right, Higby," went on the chief. "I'll catch em both. Even if they have escaped in an airship with their booty, I'll nab 'em. I'll have a general alarm out all over the country in less than an hour. They can't stay up in the air forever."

"A warrant for Tom-my son," murmured Mr. Swift, as if he could not believe it

"Yes, and for that Damon man, too," added the chief. "I want him as well as Tom, and I'll get 'em."

"Would you mind letting me see the warrants?" asked the inventor, and the official passed them over. The documents were made out in regular form, and the complaints had been sworn to by Isaac Pendergast, the bank president.

"I can't understand it," went on Tom's father. "Seventy-five thousand dollars. It's incredible! Why!" he suddenly exclaimed, "it can't be true. Just before he left, Mr. Damon-"

"Yes, what did he do?" asked the chief eagerly, thinking he might secure some valuable evidence.

"I guess I'll say nothing until I have seen the bank president," replied Mr. Swift, and the official was obviously disappointed.

The inventor found Mr. Pendergast, and some other bank officials in the town hall. The financiers were rather angry when they learned that the accused persons had not been caught, but the chief said he would soon have them in custody.

"In the meanwhile will you kindly explain, what this means?" asked Mr. Swift of the president.

"You may come and look at the looted vault, if you like, Mr. Swift," replied Mr. Pendergast. "It was a very thorough job, and will seriously cripple the bank."

There was no doubt that the vault had been forced open, for the locks and bars were bent and twisted as if by heavy tools. Mr. Swift made a careful examination, and was shown the money drawers that had been smashed.

"This was the work of experts," he declared.

"Exactly what we think," said the president. "Of course we don't believe your son was a professional bank robber, Mr. Swift. We have a theory that Mr. Damon did the real work, but that Tom helped him with the tools he had. There is no doubt about it."

"What right have you to accuse my son?" burst out the aged inventor. "Why have you any more cause to suspect him than any other lad in town? Why do you fix on him, and Mr. Damon? I demand to know."

"Mr. Damon's eccentric actions for a few days past, and his well-known oddity of character make him an object of suspicion," declared the president in judicial tones. "As for Tom, we have, I regret to say, even better evidence against him."

"But what is it? What? Who gave you any clues to point to my son?"

"Do you really wish to know?"

"I certainly do," was the sharp reply. Mr. Swift, the police and several bank officials were now in the president's office. The latter pressed an electric bell, and, when a messenger answered, he said

"Send young Foger here."

At the mention of this name, Mr. Swift started. He well knew the red-haired bully was an enemy of his son. Andy entered, walking rather proudly at the attention he attracted.

"This is Mr. Swift," said the president.

"Aw, I know him," blurted out Andy.

"You will please tell him what you told us," went on Mr. Pendergast.

"Well, I seen Tom Swift hanging around this bank with burglar tools in his possession last night, just before it was robbed," exclaimed the squint-eyed lad triumphantly.

"Hanging around the bank last night with burglar tools?" repeated Mr. Swift, in dazed tones.

"That's right," from Andy.

"How do you know they were burglar tools?"

"Because I saw 'em!" cried Andy. "He had 'em in a valise on his motor-cycle. He was standing at the corner, waiting for a chance to break into the bank, and when me and Sam Snedecker saw him, he pretended to be fixin' his machine. Then the bag of burglar tools fell off, the satchel came open, and I seen 'em! That's how I know."

"And you're sure they were burglar tools?" asked the chief, for he depended on Andy to be his most important witness.

"Sure I am. I seen a picture of burglar tools once, and the ones Tom had was just like 'em. Long-handled wrenches, brace an' bits, an' all. He tried to hide 'em, but me an' Sam was too quick for him. He wanted to lick me, too."

"No doubt you deserved it," murmured Mr. Swift. "But how do you know my son was waiting for a chance to break into the bank?"

"'Cause, wasn't it robbed right after he was hangin' around here with the burglar tools?" inquired Andy, as if that was unanswerable.

"What were you hanging around here for?" Mr. Swift demanded quickly.

"Me? Oh, well, me an' Sam Snedecker was out takin' a walk. That's all."

"You didn't want to rob the bank, did you?" went on the inventor, keenly.

"Of course not," roared the bully, indignantly. "I ain't got no burglar tools."

Andy told more along the same line, but his testimony of having seen Tom near the bank, with a bag of odd tools could not be shaken. In fact it was true, as far as it went, but, of course, the tools were only those for the airship; the same ones Mr. Sharp had sent the lad after. Sam Snedecker was called in after Andy, and told substantially the same story.

Mr. Swift could not understand it, for he knew nothing of Tom being sent for the tools, and had not heard any talk at home of the bag of implements ordered by the balloonist. Still, of course, he knew Tom had nothing to do with the robbery, and he knew his son had been at home all the night previous. Still this was rather negative evidence. But the inventor had one question yet to ask.

"You say you also suspect Mr. Damon of complicity in this affair?" he went on, to the chief of police.

"We sure do," replied Mr. Simonson.

"Then can you explain?" proceeded the inventor, "how it is that Mr. Damon has on deposit in this bank a large sum. Would he rob the bank where his own funds were?"

"We are prepared for that," declared the president. "It is true that Mr. Damon has about ten thousand dollars in our bank, but we believe he deposited it only as a blind, so as to cover up his tracks. It is a deep-laid scheme, and escaping in the airship is part of it. I am sorry, Mr. Swift, that I have to believe your son and his accomplice guilty, but I am obliged to. Chief, you had better send out a general alarm. The airship ought to be easy to trace."

"I'll telegraph at once," said the official.

"And you believe my son guilty, solely on the testimony of these two boys, who, as is well known, are his enemies?" asked Mr. Swift.

"The clue they gave us is certainly most important," said the president. "Andy came to us and told what he had seen, as soon as it became known that the bank had been robbed."

"And I'm going to get the reward for giving information of the robbers, too!" cried the bully.

"I'm going to have my share!" insisted Sam.

"Ah, then there is a reward offered?" inquired Mr. Swift.

"Five thousand dollars," answered Mr. Pendergast. "The directors, all of whom are present save Mr. Foger, Andy's father, met early this morning, and decided to offer that sum."

"And I'm going to get it," announced the redhaired lad again.

Mr. Swift was much downcast. There seemed to be nothing more to say, and, being a man unversed in the ways of the world, he did not know what to do. He returned hone. When Mrs. Baggert was made acquainted with the news, she waxed indignant.

"Our Tom a thief!" she cried. "Why don't they accuse me and Mr. Jackson and you? The idea! You ought to hire a lawyer, Mr. Swift, and prosecute those men for slander."

"Do you think it would be a good plan?"

"I certainly do. Why they have no evidence at all! What does that mean, sneaking Andy Foger amount to? Get a lawyer, and have Tom's interests looked after."

Mr. Swift, glad to have sane one share the responsibility with, felt somewhat better when a well-known Shopton attorney assured him that the evidence against Tom was of such a flimsy character that it would scarcely hold in a court of justice.

"But they have warrants for him and Mr. Damon," declared the inventor.

"Very true, but it is easy to swear out a warrant against any one. It's a different matter to prove a person guilty."

"But they can arrest my son."

"Yes—if they catch him. However, we can soon have him released on bail."

"It's disgraceful," said Mrs. Baggert.

"Not at all, my dear madam, not at all. Good and innocent persons have been arrested."

"They are going to send out a general alarm for my son," bewailed Mr. Swift.

"Yes, but I fancy it will be some time before they catch him and Mr. Damon, if the airship holds together. I can't think of a better way to keep out of the clutches of the police, and their silly charge," chuckled the lawyer. "Now don't worry, Mr. Swift. It will all come out right.

The inventor tried to believe so, but, though he knew his son was innocent, it was rather hard to see, within the next few days, big posters on all the vacant walls and fences, offering a reward of five thousand dollars for the arrest of Tom Swift and Wakefield Damon, who were charged with having flown away in an airship with seventyfive thousand dollars of the bank's money.

"I guess Tom Swift will wish he'd been more decent to me when I collect that money for his arrest," said Andy to his crony, Sam, the day the bills were posted.

"Yes, but I get my share, don't I?" asked Sam.

"Sure," answered the bully. "I wish they'd hurry up and arrest him."

Within the next few days the country was covered with posters telling of the robbery and the reward, and police officials in cities large and small, and in towns and villages, were notified by telegraph to arrest and capture, at any cost the occupants of a certain large, red airship.

Mr. Swift, on the advice of his lawyer, sent several telegrams to Tom, apprising him of what had happened. The telegraph company was asked to rush the telegrams to the first city when word came in that the *Red Cloud* had landed.

CHAPTER 15

FIRED UPON

Tom's excited call to the aeronaut, telling of the mishap to Mr. Damon, was answered immediately. Mr. Sharp jumped forward from the motor compartment, and, passing on his way the electric switch, he yanked it out, stopping the machinery, and the great propellers. Then he leaped out on the platform.

But something else happened. Just before the accident to the eccentric man, desiring to give a further test to the planes, the gas had been shut off, making the airship an aeroplane instead of a dirigible balloon. Consequently, as soon as the forward motion ceased the great ship began falling.

"We're sinking! We're sinking!" cried Tom, forgetting for a moment that he was not in his motor-boat.

"Slant your rudder up, and glide downward as slowly as you can!" directed Mr. Sharp. "I'll start the engine again as soon as I rescue him," for it was risky to venture out on the platform with the propeller whirring, as the dangling piece of scarf might whip around the balloonist and toss him off.

Mr. Sharp was soon at Mr. Damon's side. He saw that the man was unconscious, whether from fright or some injury could not then be determined. There was, however, no sign of a wound.

It was no easy task to carry, half dragging it, the heavy body of Mr. Damon off the platform, but the aeronaut was a muscular individual, and long hanging from a trapeze, at great heights, stood him in good stead.

He brought the unconscious man into the cabin, and then, quickly returning to the platform, he detached the piece of scarf from the propeller blade. Next he started the motor, and also turned on the gas tank, so that the airship, in a few minutes, could float in space without motion.

"You needn't steer now, Tom," said the balloonist. "Just give me a hand here."

"Is-is he dead?" inquired the lad, his voice faltering.

"No, his heart's beating. I can't understand what happened."

Mr. Sharp was something of a rough and ready surgeon and doctor, and a small box of medicines had been brought along in case of emergencies. With the *Red Cloud* now lazily floating in the air, for, once the falling motion had been checked by the engine, the motor had been stopped again, Mr. Sharp set about restoring Mr.

Damon to consciousness.

It was not long before the man opened his eyes. The color that had left his cheeks came back, and, after a drink of cold water he was able to sit up.

"Did I fall?" he asked. "Bless my very existence, but did I tumble off the airship?"

"No indeed," replied Tom, "though you came pretty near it. How do you feel? Were you hurt?"

"Oh, I'm all right now-just a trifle dizzy. But I thought sure I was a goner when I fell over the platform railing," and Mr. Damon could not repress a shudder. Mr. Sharp administered some more medicine and his patient was soon able to stand, and move about.

"How did it happen?" inquired the balloonist.

"I hardly know," answered Mr. Damon. "I was out on the platform, looking at the view, and thinking how much better my neuralgia was, with the scarf on. Suddenly the wind whipped loose one end of the scarf, and, before I knew it the cloth had caught on the propeller blade. I was blown, or drawn to one side, tossed against the railing, which I managed to grab, and then I lost my senses. It's a good thing I wasn't whirled around the propeller."

"It's a good thing you weren't tossed down to the earth," commented Tom, shivering as he thought of his friend's narrow escape.

"I became unconscious, partly because the wind was knocked from me as I hit the platform railing," went on Mr. Damon, "and partly from fright, I think. But I'm all right now, and I'm not going out on that platform again with a loose scarf on."

"I wouldn't go out at all again, if I were you, though, of course, I'm used to dizzy heights," spoke Mr. Sharp.

"Oh, I'm not so easily frightened," declared Mr. Damon. "If I'm going to be a balloonist, or an aeroplanist I've got to get used to certain things. I'm all right now," and the plucky man was, for the blow to his side did not amount to much. It was some time, however, before Tom got over the fright his friend had caused him.

They spent that night moving slowly south, and in the morning found they had covered about a hundred miles, not having run the ship to anything like its maximum speed. Breakfast was served above the clouds, for a change, Mr. Damon finding that he could stand the great height with comfort.

It was three days after the start, and the travelers were proceeding slowly along. They were totally unaware, of course, of the sensation which their leaving, conjointly with the bank robbery, had caused, not only in Shopton but in other places.

"We're over a good-sized city," announced Tom, on the noon of the third day. "Suppose we drop down, and leave some message? Dad will be anxious to hear from us."

"Good idea," commented Mr. Sharp. "Down it is. Shift the rudder."

Tom proceeded to do so, and, while Mr. Damon relieved him at the wheel the young inventor prepared a message to his father. It was placed in a weighted envelope, together with a sum of money, and the person picking it up was requested to send the letter as a telegram, retaining some money for his trouble.

As the ship got lower and lower over the city the usual crowds could be seen congregating in the streets, pointing and gazing upward.

"We're creating quite a stir," observed Tom.

"More than usual, it seems," added Mr. Sharp, peering down. "I declare, there seems to be a police parade under way."

"That's right," put in Mr. Damon, for, looking down, a squad of uniformed officers, some on horseback, could be seen hurrying along the main street, trying to keep pace with the airship, which was moving slowly.

"They're looking at us through telescopes," called Tom. "Guess they never saw a balloon down this way."

Nearer and nearer to the city dropped the *Red Cloud*. Tom was about to let go the weighted envelope, when, from the midst of the police came several puffs of white smoke. It was followed by vicious, zipping sounds about the cabin of the ship, the windows of which were open. Then came the reports of several rifles.

"They're firing at us!" yelled Tom.

"So they are!" cried Mr. Sharp. "They must be crazy! Can't they see that we're not a bird."

"Maybe they take us for a war balloon," suggested Mr. Damon.

Another volley was directed at the airship, and several bullets struck the big aluminum gas holder glancing blows.

"Here! Quit that!" yelled Tom, leaning out of the window. "Are you crazy? You'll damage us!"

"They can't hear you," called Mr. Sharp.

A third volley was fired, and this time several persons other than police officers seemed to be shooting at the airship. Revolvers as well as rifles were being used.

"We're got to get out of this!" shouted Mr. Sharp, as a bullet sang uncomfortably close to his head. "I can't imagine what's gotten into the people. Send her up, Tom!"

The lad quickly shifted the elevation rudder, and the *Red Cloud* sailed majestically aloft. The young inventor had not dropped his message, concluding that citizens who would fire on travelers of the air for no reason, would not be likely to accommodate them in the matter of sending messages.

The craft mounted rapidly upward, but before it was beyond rifle shot another volley was fired, one bullet sending some splinters flying from the wooden framework.

"Whew! That was a narrow escape!" exclaimed Mr. Sharp. "What in the world can those people be up to, anyhow?"

CHAPTER 16

OVER A FIERY FURNACE

Down below, the aeronauts could see the crowd, led by the police, scurrying to and fro. Many individuals beside the officers appeared to be holding weapons, and, from the puffs of smoke that spurted out, it was evident that more shots were being fired. But the bullets could do no harm, and the *Red Cloud*, under the force of the rapidly revolving propellers, was soon beyond the center of the city.

"Well, if that isn't the limit!" cried Tom. "They must have taken us for a German war balloon, about to drop explosives on them."

"Bless my liver!" ejaculated Mr. Damon, "I believe you're right. Eh, Mr. Sharp?"

The veteran balloonist took a careful look over the craft before replying. Then he spoke:

"It couldn't be that," and he shook his head, as if puzzled. "They would know no foreign airship would try any trick like that. Beside, if by some remote possibility they did imagine it, there would be soldiers shooting at us, instead of the police. As it was, the whole population seemed anxious to bring us down."

"And they nearly did," added Mr. Damon. "If they had shot a few holes in the gas bag where would we be?"

"Right in the air," answered the balloonist. "It would take several volleys of bullets to damage our aluminum container. It is in sections and when one, or even five compartments, for that matter, are pierced, there is enough gas in the others to sustain us. So they could not have damaged us much, even if they had shot a lot of holes in us. Even without the gas container we can keep afloat by constantly moving, for the planes will serve their purpose. Of course they could damage us, and maybe put some of our machinery out of business, and that would be a serious thing. But what puzzles me is why they fired at us at all."

"It couldn't be out of pure mischief; could it?" asked the young inventor.

"Hardly. If we were in a savage country I could understand the natives firing at some such object as this airship, but the people of that city must have known what our craft was. They probably have read something about it in the news papers, and to deliberately fire on us, with the chance of disabling us, seems worse than barbarous."

"Well, we won't give 'em another opportunity," commented

Mr. Damon.

"No, indeed, not this city, but who knows but what the example may spread? We may be fired at the next town we sail over."

"Then steer clear of the towns," advised Tom.

"Impossible. We must pass over some, but I'd like to solve this mystery."

The day passed without further incident, though they did not go low enough down over any city to drop any messages. It was decided that it would not be safe.

"We'll take a chance at night," suggested Tom, and that evening, approaching a good-sized town in the dusk, several of the weighted envelopes were dropped overboard. Doubtless persons walking along the street, who were startled by hearing something fall with a "thud" at their feet, were much startled to look up and see, dimly, a great, ghostly shape moving in the air. But there was no shooting, and, eventually, some of the messages reached Mr. Swift, in Shopton. But he could not answer them for the airship kept on the move.

The night was spent floating in the air, with the engine stopped, and the *Red Cloud* floating lazily this way and that as the gentle winds shifted, for it was calm. The "anchorage" if such it may be called, was above a sparsely settled part of the country, and if the lights of the airship were seen from below, the farmers doubtless took them for some new stars or, possibly, a comet.

"Now then for a fast, straight run!" cried Tom, after breakfast had been served, and the big motor, with its twenty cylinders, started. "We'll be able to make the turn today, and then make for home, won't we, Mr. Sharp?"

"Well, we could do it, Tom," was the answer, "but I like this mode of traveling so that I think I'll lengthen the voyage. Instead of turning at Atlanta, what do you say to making for Key West, and then starting back? That will be something of a trip. The *Red Cloud* is behaving much better than I hoped she would."

"I'm willing to go further if Mr. Damon is."

"Oh, bless my shoe strings, I'm game!" exclaimed the eccentric man. "I always did want to go to Key West, anyhow."

The craft was speeding along at a fast clip, and dinner that day was served about three miles in the air. Then, desiring to test the gliding abilities of the airship, it was sent down on a long slant, with the propellers stationary, the shifting planes and rudders alone guiding it.

As the craft fairly slid down out of the sky, like a sled on a bank of fleecy snow, Tom, who was peering ahead, with his hand on the steering wheel, cried out "I say! It looks as if we were going to run into a thunder storm!"

"How's that?" inquired Mr. Sharp, poking his head from the motor compartment.

"He says there's a big storm ahead," repeated Mr. Damon, "and I guess he's right. I see a big bank of dark clouds, and there is a roaring in the air."

Mr. Sharp, who had been making some adjustments to the motor went forward to take a look. The *Red Cloud* was swiftly gliding downward on a slant, straight toward a dark mass of vapor, that seemed to be rolling first one way, and then another, while as Mr. Damon had said, there was a low rumbling proceeding from it.

"That doesn't seem to be a thunder storm," spoke the balloonist, with a puzzled air.

They all regarded the dark mass of vapor intently for a few seconds. Tom had brought the airship to a more level keel, and it was now spinning along under its own momentum, like a flat piece of tin, scaled by some lead. But it was headed for the clouds, if such they were, though losing speed by degrees.

"I'll have to start the motor!" exclaimed Mr. Sharp. "We don't want to run into a storm, if we can help it, though I don't ever remember seeing a thunder disturbance like that."

"Whew! It's getting warm," suddenly announced the youth, and he let go of the steering wheel for a moment, while he took off his coat.

"That's what it is," agreed Mr. Damon, who also divested himself of his garments. "Bless my spark plug, but it's like a July day. No wonder there's a thunderstorm ahead."

Then Mr. Sharp uttered a cry. "That's no storm!" he fairly shouted. "It's a big forest fire! That's smoke we see! We must get out of this. Turn around Tom, while I start the engine. We must rise above it!"

He fairly leaped for the motor, and Tom and Mr. Damon could hear him turning the levers and wheels, ready to start. But before the explosions came something happened. There was a sound as of some great, siren whistle blowing, and then, with a howl of the on rushing air, the *Red Cloud*, the propellers of which hung motionless on their shafts, was fairly sucked forward toward the fire, as the current sucks a boat over a water fall.

"Start the motor! Start the motor, Mr. Sharp!" cried Tom.

"I'm trying to, but something seems to be the matter."

"We're being drawn right over the fire!" yelled Mr. Damon. "It's getting hotter every minute! Can't you do something?"

"You take the wheel," called the balloonist to Mr. Damon. "Steer around, just as if it was an auto when we start the engine. Tom, come here and give me a hand. The motor has jammed!"

The young inventor sprang to obey. Mr. Damon, his face showing some of the fear he felt, grasped the steering wheel. The airship was now about a quarter of a mile high, but instead of resting motionless in the air, sustained by the gas in the container, she was being pulled forward, right toward the heart of the mass of black vapor, which it could now be seen was streaked with bright tongues of flame.

"What's making us go ahead, if the motor isn't going?" asked Tom, as he bent over the machine, at which the aeronaut was laboring.

"Suction-draught from the fire!" explained Mr. Sharp. "Heated air rises and leaves a vacuum. The cold air rushes in. It's carrying us with it. We'll be right in the fire in a few minutes, if we can't get started with this motor! I don't see what ails it."

"Can't we steer to one side, as it is?"

"No. We're right in a powerful current of air, and steering won't do any good, until we have some motion of our own. Turn the gasolene lever on a little more, and see if you can get a spark."

Tom did so, but no explosion resulted. The twenty cylinders of the big engine remained mute. The airship, meanwhile, was gathering speed, sucked onward and downward as it was by the draught from the fire. The roaring was plainer now, and the crackling of the flames could be heard plainly. The heat, too, grew more, intense.

Frantically Tom and Mr. Sharp labored over the motor. With the perverseness usual to gas engines, it had refused to work at a critical moment.

"What shall I do?" cried Mr. Damon from his position in the pilot house. "We seem to be heading right for the midst of it?"

"Slant the elevation rudder," called Tom. "Send the ship up. It will be cooler the higher we go. Maybe we can float over it!"

"You'd better go out there," advised Mr. Sharp. "I'll keep at this motor. Go up as high as you can. Turn on more gas. That will elevate us, but maybe not quick enough. The gas doesn't generate well in great heat. I'm afraid we're in for it," he added grimly.

Tom sprang to relieve Mr. Damon. The heat was now intense. Nearer and nearer came the *Red Cloud* to the blazing forest, which seemed to cover several square miles. Great masses of smoke, with huge pieces of charred and blazing wood carried up by the great draught, circled around the ship. The *Red Cloud* was being pulled into the midst of the fire by the strong suction. Tom yanked over the elevation rudder, and the nose of the craft pointed upward. But it still moved downward, and, a moment later the travelers of the air felt as if they were over a fiery furnace.

CHAPTER 17

"WANTED FOR ROBBERY!"

Choking and gasping for breath, feeling as if they could not stand the intense heat more than a moment longer, the young inventor and his companions looked at each other. Death seemed ready to reach out and grasp them. The mass of heated air was so powerful that it swung and tossed the *Red Cloud* about as if it were a wisp of paper.

"We must do something!" cried Mr. Damon, beginning to take off his collar and vest. "I'm choking!"

"Lie down in the bottom of the car," suggested Mr. Sharp. "The smoke won't trouble you so much there."

The eccentric man, too startled, now, to use any of his "blessing" expressions, did so.

"Can't you start the motor?" asked Tom frantically, as he stuck to his post, with his hand on the steering wheel, the elevation lever jammed back as far as it would go.

"I've done my best," answered the balloonist, gasping as he swallowed some smoke. "I'm afraid—afraid it's all up with us. We should have steered clear of this from the first. My, how it roars!"

The crackling and snapping of the flames below them, as they fed on the dry wood, which no rain had wet for weeks, was like the rush of some great cataract. Up swirled the dark smoke-clouds, growing hotter and hotter all the while as the craft came nearer and nearer to the center of the conflagration.

"We must rise higher!" cried Tom. "It's our only chance. Turn on the gas machine full power, and fill the container. That will carry us up!"

"Yes, it's our only hope," muttered Mr. Sharp. "We must go up, but the trouble is the gas doesn't generate so fast when there's too much heat. We're bound to have to stay over this fiery pit for some time yet."

"We're going up a little!" spoke Tom hopefully, as he glanced at a gauge near him. "We're fifteen hundred feet now, and we were only twelve a while ago."

"Good! Keep the elevation rudder as it is, and I'll see what I can do with the gas," advised the balloonist. "It's our only hope," and he hurried into the engine room, which, like the other parts of the cabin, was now murky with choking vapor and soot.

Suddenly the elevation gauge showed that they were falling.

The airship was going down.

"What's the matter?" called Mr. Damon, from the cabin floor.

"I don't know," answered Tom, "unless the rudder has broken."

He peered through the haze. No, the big elevation rudder was still in place, but it seemed to have no effect on the shim

"It's a down draught!" cried Mr. Sharp. "We're being sucked down. It won't last but a few seconds. I've been in 'em before."

He seemed to have guessed rightly, for, the next instant the airship was shooting upward again, and relief came to the aeronauts, though it was not much, for the heat was almost unbearable, and they had taken off nearly all their clothing.

"Lighten ship!" sung out Mr. Sharp. "Toss over all the things you think we can spare, Tom. Some of the cases of provisions-we can get more-if we need 'em. We must rise, and the gas isn't generating fast enough!"

There was no need for the young inventor at the steering wheel now, for the craft simply could not be guided. It was swirled about, now this way, now that, by the currents of heated air. At times it would rise a considerable distance, only to be pulled down again, and, just before Tom began to toss overboard some boxes of food, it seemed that the end had come, for the craft went down so low that the upward leaping tongues of flame almost reached the lower frame.

"I'll help you," gasped Mr. Damon, and while he and Tom tossed from the cabin windows some of their stores, Mr. Sharp was frantically endeavoring to make the gas generate faster.

It was slow work, but with the lightening of the ship their situation improved. Slowly, so slowly that it seemed an age, the elevation pointer went higher and higher on the dial.

"Sixteen hundred feet!" sung out Tom, pausing for a look at the gauge. "That's the best yet!"

The heat was felt less, now, and every minute was improving their situation. Slowly the hand moved. The gas was being made in larger quantities now that the heat was less. Ten minutes more of agony, and their danger was over. They were still above the burning area, but sufficiently high so that only stray wisps of smoke enveloped them.

"Whew! But that was the worst ever!" cried Tom, as he sank exhausted on a bench, and wiped his perspiring face. "We sure were in a bad way!"

"I should say so," agreed Mr. Sharp. "And if we don't get a breeze we may have to stay here for some time."

"Why, can't you get that motor to work yet?" asked Mr. Damon.

"Bless my gaiters, but I'm all in, as the boys say."

"I'll have another try at the machine now," replied Mr. Sharp. "Probably it will work now, after we're out of danger without the aid of it."

His guess proved correct, for, in a few minutes, with the aid of Tom, the motor started, the propellers revolved, and the *Red Cloud* was sent swiftly out of the fire zone.

"Now we'd better take account of ourselves, our provisions, and the ship," said Mr. Sharp, when they had flown about twenty miles, and were much refreshed by the cooler atmosphere. "I don't believe the craft is damaged any, except some of the braces may be warped by the heat. As for the provisions, you threw over a lot; didn't you, Tom?"

"Well, I had to."

"Yes, I guess you did. Well, we'll make a landing."

"Do you think it will be safe?" asked Mr. Damon anxiously. "We might be fired upon again."

"Oh, there's no danger of that. But I'll take precautions. I don't want a big crowd around when we come down, so we'll pick out a secluded place and land just at dusk. Then in the morning we can look over the ship, and go to the nearest town to buy provisions. After that we can continue our journey, and we'll steer clear of forest fires after this."

"And people who shoot at us," added Mr. Damon.

"Yes. I wish I knew what that was done for," and once again came that puzzled look to the face of the balloonist.

The airship gently descended that evening in a large level field, a good landing being made. just before the descent Tom took an observation and located, about two miles from the spot they selected for an "anchorage," a good-sized village.

"We can get provisions there," he announced.

"Yes, but we must not let it be known what they are for," said Mr. Sharp, "or we'll have the whole population out here. I think this will be a good plan: Tom, you and Mr. Damon go into town and buy the things we need. I'll stay here with the airship, and look it all over. You can arrange to have the stuff carted out here in the morning, and left at a point say about a quarter of a mile away. Then we can carry it to the ship. In that way no one will discover us, and we'll not be bothered with curiosity-seekers."

This was voted a good idea, and, when the landing had been made, and a hasty examination showed that the ship had suffered no great damage from the passage over the fire, the young inventor and Mr. Damon started off.

They soon found a good road, leading to town, and tramped along it in the early evening. The few persons they met paid little attention to them, save to bow in a friendly fashion, and, occasionally wish them good evening.

"I wonder where we are?" asked Tom, as they hurried along.

"In some southern town, to judge by the voices of the people, and the number of colored individuals we've met," answered Mr. Damon.

"Let's ask," suggested Tom.

"No, if you do they'll know we're strangers, and they may ask a lot of questions."

"Oh, I guess if it's a small place they'll know we're strangers soon enough," commented Tom. "But when we get to the village itself we can read the name on the store windows."

A few minutes later found them in the midst of a typical southern town. It was Berneau, North Carolina, according to the signs, they saw.

"Here's a restaurant," called Tom, as they passed a neat-appearing one. "Let's go inside and get some supper before we buy our supplies."

"Good!" exclaimed Mr. Damon. "Bless my flapjacks, but I am beginning to feel hungry."

The eating place was a good one, and Tom's predictions about their being taken for strangers was verified, for, no sooner had they given their orders than the pretty, white girl, who waited on the table remarked

"Ah reckon yo' all are from th' no'th; aren't yo'?"She smiled, as she spoke, and Tom smiled back as he acknowledged it.

"Have you a paper-a newspaper I could look at?" he asked.

"Ah guess Ah can find one," went on the girl. "Ah reckon yo' all are from N' York. N' Yorkers are so desperant bent on readin' th' news." Her tones were almost like those of a colored person.

"Yes, we're from a part of New York," was Tom's reply.

When a newspaper was brought to him, after they had nearly finished their meal, the young inventor rapidly scanned the pages. Something on the front sheet, under a heading of big, black type caught his eye. He started as he read it:

WANTED FOR ROBBERY!
BANK LOOTERS ESCAPE IN RED AIRSHIP —
FIRED AT BUT DISAPPEAR

"Great Jehosophat!" exclaimed Tom, in a low voice. "What on earth can this mean?"

"What?" inquired Mr. Damon. "Has anything happened?"

"Happened? I should say there had," was the answer. "Why, we're accused of having robbed the Shopton Bank of seventy-five thousand dollars the night before we left, and to have taken it away in the *Red Cloud*. There's a general alarm out for us! Why this is awful!"

"It's preposterous!" burst out Mr. Damon. "I'll have my lawyers sue this paper. Bless my stocks and bonds, I!"

"Hush! Not so loud," cautioned Tom, for the pretty waitress was watching them curiously. "Here, read this, and then we'll decide what to do. But one thing is certain, we must go back to Shopton at once to clear ourselves of this accusation."

"Ha!" murmured Mr. Damon, as he read the article rapidly. "Now I know why they fired at us. They hoped to bring us down, capture us, and get the five thousand dollars reward!"

CHAPTER 18

BACK FOR VINDICATION

Tom glanced around the restaurant. There were few persons in it save himself and Mr. Damon. The pretty waitress was still regarding the two curiously.

"We ought to take that paper along with us, to show to Mr. Sharp," said Tom, in a low voice to his friend. "I haven't had time to take it all in myself, yet. Let's go. I've had enough to eat, haven't you?"

"Yes. My appetite is gone now."

As they arose, to pay their checks the girl advanced.

"Can you tell me where I can get a copy of this paper?" asked Tom, as he laid down a generous tip on the table, for the girl. Her eyes opened rather wide.

"Yo' all are fo'gettin' some of yo' money." she said, in her broad, southern tones. Tom thought her the prettiest girl he ever seen, excepting Mary Nestor.

"Oh, that's for you," replied the young inventor. "It's a tip. Aren't you in the habit of getting them down here?"

"Not very often. Thank yo' all. But what did yo' all ask about that paper?"

"I asked where I could get a copy of it. There is something in it that interests me."

"Yes, an' Ah reckon Ah knows what it is," exclaimed the girl. "It's about that airship with th' robbers in it!"

"How do you know?" inquired Tom quickly, and he tried to seem cool, though he felt the hot blood mounting to his cheeks.

"Oh, Ah saw yo' all readin' it. Everybody down heah is crazy about it. We all think th' ship is comin' down this way, 'cause it says th' robbers was intendin' to start south befo' they robbed th' bank. Ah wish Ah could collect thet five thousand dollars. If Ah could see that airship, I wouldn't work no mo' in this eatin' place. What do yo' all reckon thet airship looks like?" and the girl gazed intently at Tom and Mr. Damon.

"Why, bless my-" began the eccentric man, but Tom broke in hurriedly:

"Oh, I guess it looks like most any other airship," for he feared that if his companion used any of his odd expressions he might be recognized, since our hero had not had time to read the article in the paper through, and was not sure whether or not a description of himself, Mr. Damon and Mr. Sharp was given.

"Well, Ah suah wish I could collect thet reward," went on the girl. "Everybody is on th' lookout. Yo' all ain't see th' airship; have yo' all?"

"Where can we get a paper like this?" asked Tom, again, not wanting to answer such a leading question.

"Why, yo' all is suah welcome to that one," was the reply. "Ah guess Ah can affo'd to give it to yo' all, after th' generous way yo' all behaved to me. Take it, an' welcome. But are yo' all suah yo' are done eatin' ? Yo' all left lots."

"Oh, we had enough," replied Tom hurriedly. His sole aim now was to get away-to consult with Mr. Sharp, and he needed the paper to learn further details of the astonishing news. He and his friends accused of looting the bank, and taking away seventy-five thousand dollars in the airship! It was incredible! A reward of five thousand dollars offered for their capture! They might be arrested any minute, yet they could not go on without buying some provisions. What were they to do?

Once outside the restaurant, Mr. Damon and Tom walked swiftly on. They came to a corner where there was a street lamp, and there the young inventor paused to scan the paper again. It was the copy of a journal published in the nearby county seat, and contained quite a full account of the affair.

The story was told of how the bank had been broken into, the vault rifled and the money taken. The first clue, it said, was given by a youth named Andy Foger, who had seen a former acquaintance hanging around the bank with burglar tools. Tom recognized the description of himself as the "former acquaintance," but he could not understand the rest.

"Burglar tools? I wonder how Andy could say that?" he asked Mr. Damon.

"Wait until we get back, and we'll ask John Sharp," suggested his companion. "This is very strange. I am going to sue some one for spreading false reports about me! Bless my ledgers, why I have money on deposit in that bank! To think that I would rob it!"

"Poor dad!" murmured Tom. "This must be hard for him. But what about ordering food? Maybe if we buy any they will trail us, find the airship and capture it. I don't want to be arrested, even if I am innocent, and I certainly don't want the airship to fall into the hands of the police. They might damage it"

"We must go see Mr. Sharp," declared Mr. Damon, and back to where the *Red Cloud* was concealed they went.

To say that the balloonist was astonished is putting it mildly. He was even more excited than was Mr. Damon.

"Wait until I get hold of that Andy Foger!" he cried. "I'll make him sweat for this! I see he's already laid claim to the reward," he added, reading further along in the article. "He thinks he has put the police on our trail."

"So he seems to have done," added Tom. "The whole country has been notified to look out for us," the paper says. "We're likely to be fired upon whenever we pass over a city or a town."

"Then we'll have to avoid them," declared the balloonist.

"But we must go back," declared Tom.

"Of course. Back to be vindicated. We'll have to give up our trip. My, my! But this is a surprise!"

"I don't see what makes Andy say he saw me with burglar tools," commented Tom, with a puzzled air.

Mr. Sharp thought for a moment. Then he exclaimed "It was that bag of tools I sent you after-the long wrenches, the pliers, and the brace and bits. You "

"Of course!" cried Tom. "I remember now. The bag dropped and opened, and Andy and Sam saw the tools. But the idea of taking them for burglar tools!"

"Well, I suppose the burglars, whoever they were, did use tools similar to those to break open the vault," put in Mr. Damon. "Andy probably thought he was a smart lad to put the police on our track."

"I'll put him on the track, when I return," declared Mr. Sharp. "Well, now, what's to be done?"

"We've got to have food," suggested Tom.

"Yes, but I think we can manage that. I've been looking over the ship, as best I could in the dark. It seems to be all right. We can start early in the morning without anyone around here knowing we paid their town a visit. You and Mr. Damon go back to town, Tom, and order some stuff. Have the man leave it by the roadside early tomorrow morning. Tell him it's for some travelers, who will stop and pick it up. Pay him well, and tell him to keep quiet, as it's for a racing party. That's true enough. We're going to race home to vindicate our reputations. I think that will be all right."

"The man may get suspicious," said Mr. Damon.

"I hope not," answered the balloonist. "We've got to take a chance, anyhow."

The plan worked well, however, the store keeper promising to have the supplies on hand at the time and place mentioned. He winked as Tom asked him to keep quiet about it.

"Oh, I know yo' automobile fellers," he said with a laugh. "You want to get some grub on the fly, so you won't have to stop, an' can beat th' other fellow. I know you, fer I see them automobile goggles stickin' out of your pocket."

Tom and Mr. Damon each had a pair, to use when the wind was strong, but the young inventor had forgotten about his. They now served him a good turn, for they turned the thoughts of the store-keeper into a new channel. The lad let it go at that, and, paying for such things as he and Mr. Damon could not carry, left the store.

The aeronauts passed an uneasy night. They raised their ship high in the air, anchoring it by a rope fast to a big tree, and they turned on no lights, for they did not want to betray their position. They descended before it was yet daylight, and a little later hurried to the place where the provisions were left. They found their sup-plies safely on hand, and, carrying them into the airship, prepared to turn back to Shopton.

As the ship rose high in the air a crowd of negro laborers passing through a distant field, saw it. At once they raised a commo-tion, shouting and pointing to the wonderful sight.

"We're discovered!" cried Tom.

"No matter," answered Mr. Sharp. "We'll soon be out of sight, and we'll fly high the rest of this trip."

Tom looked down on the fast disappearing little hamlet, and he thought of the pretty girl in the restaurant.

CHAPTER 19

WRECKED

With her nose headed north, the *Red Cloud* swung along through the air. Those on board were thinking of many things, but chief among them was the unjust accusation that had been made against them, by an irresponsible boy-the red-haired Andy Foger. They read the account in the paper again, seeking to learn from it new things at each perusal.

"It's just a lot of circumstantial evidence that's what it is," said Tom. "I admit it might look suspicious to anyone who didn't know us, but Andy Foger has certainly done the most mischief by his conclusions. Burglar tools! The idea!"

"I think I shall sue the bank for damages," declared Mr. Damon. "They have injured my reputation by making this accusation against me. Anyhow, I'll certainly never do any more business with them, and I'll withdraw my ten thousand dollars deposit, as soon as we get back."

"Mr. Sharp doesn't seem to be accused of doing anything at all," remarked Tom, reading the article for perhaps the tenth time.

"Oh, I guess I'm a sort of general all-around bad man, who helped you burglars to escape with the booty," answered the balloonist, with a laugh. "I expect to be arrested along with you two."

"But must we be arrested?" inquired Tom anxiously. "I don't like that idea at all. We haven't done anything."

"This is my plan," went on Mr. Sharp. "We'll get back to Shopton as quickly as we can. We'll arrive at night, so no one will see us, and, leaving the airship in some secluded spot, we'll go to the police and explain matters. We can easily prove that we had nothing to do with the robbery. Why we were all home the night it happened! Mr. Swift, Mr. Jackson and Mrs. Baggert can testify to that."

"Yes," agreed Mr. Damon. "I guess they can. Bless my bank book, but that seems a good plan. We'll follow it."

Proceeding on the plan which they had decided was the best one, the *Red Cloud* was sent high into the air. So high up was it that, at tunes, a was above the clouds. Though this caused some little discomfort at first, especially to Mr. Damon, he soon became used to it, as did the others. And it had the advantage of concealing them from the persons below who might be on the lookout.

"For we don't want to be shot at again," explained Mr. Sharp. "It isn't altogether healthy, and not very safe. If we keep high up they can't see us; much less shoot at us. They'll take us for some big bird. Then, too, we can go faster."

"I suppose there will be another alarm sent out, from those negroes having sighted us," ventured Tom.

"Oh, yes, but those colored fellows were so excited they may describe us as having horns, hoofs and a tail, and their story may not be believed. I'm not worrying about them. My chief concern is to drive the *Red Cloud* for all she is worth. I want to explain some things back there in Shopton."

As if repenting of the way it had misbehaved over the forest fire, the airship was now swinging along at a rapid rate. Seated in the cabin the travelers would have really enjoyed the return trip had it not been for the accusation hanging over them. The weather was fine and clear, and as they skimmed along, now and then coming out from the clouds, they caught glimpses below them of the earth above which they were traveling. They had a general idea of their location, from knowing the town where the paper had given them such astounding news, and it was easy to calculate their rate of progress.

After running about a hundred miles or so, at high speed Mr. Sharp found it necessary to slow down the motor, as some of the new bearings were heating. Still this gave them no alarm, as they were making good time. They came to a stop that night, and calculated that by the next evening, or two at the latest, they would be back in Shopton. But they did not calculate on an accident.

One of the cylinders on the big motor cracked, as they started up next morning, and for some hours they had to hang in the air, suspended by the gas in the container, while Mr. Sharp and Tom took out the damaged part, and put in a spare one, the cylinders being cast separately. It was dusk when they finished, and too late to start up, so they remained about in the same place until the next day.

Morning dawned with a hot humidness, unusual at that time of the year, but partly accounted for by the fact that they were still within the influence of the southern climate. With a whizz the big propellers were set in motion, and, with Tom at the wheel, the ship being about three miles in the air, to which height it had risen after the repairs were made, the journey was recommenced.

"It's cooler up here than down below," remarked Tom, as he shifted the wheel and rudder a bit, in response to a gust of wind, that heeled the craft over.

"Yes, I think we're going to have a storm," remarked Mr. Sharp, eyeing the clouds with a professional air. "We may run ahead of it, or right into it. We'll go down a bit, toward night, when there's less danger of being shot."

So far, on their return trip, they had not been low enough, in the day time, to be in any danger from persons who hoped to earn the five thousand dollars reward.

The afternoon passed quickly, and it got dark early. There was a curious hum to the wind, and, hearing it, Mr. Sharp began to go about the ship, seeing that everything was fast and taut.

"We're going to have a blow," he remarked, "and a heavy one, too. We'll have to make everything snug, and be ready to go up or down, as the case calls for."

"Up or down?" inquired Mr. Damon.

"Yes. By rising we may escape the blow, or, by going below the strata of agitated air, we may escape it."

"How about rain?"

"Well, you can get above rain, but you can't get below it, with the law of gravitation working as it does at present. How's the gas generator, Tom?"

"Seems to be all right," replied the young inventor, who had relinquished the wheel to the balloonist.

They ate an early supper, and, hardly had the dishes been put away, when from the west, where there was a low-flying bank of clouds, there came a mutter of thunder. A little later there was a dull, red illumination amid the rolling masses of vapor.

"There's the storm, and she's heading right this way," commented Mr. Sharp.

"Can't you avoid it?" asked Mr. Damon, anxiously.

"I could, if I knew how high it was, but I guess we'll wait and see how it looks as we get closer."

The airship was flying on, and the storm, driven by a mighty wind, was rushing to meet it. Already there was a sighing, moaning sound in the wire and wooden braces of the *Red Cloud*.

Suddenly there came such a blast that it heeled the ship over on her side.

"Shift the equilibrium rudders!" shouted Mr. Sharp to Tom, turning the wheel and various levers over to the lad. "I'm going to get more speed out of the motor!"

Tom acted just in time, and, after bobbing about like a cork on the water, the ship was righted, and sent forging ahead, under the influence of the propellers worked at top speed. Nor was this any too much, for it needed all the power of the big engine to even partially overcome the force of the wind that was blowing right against the *Red Cloud*. Of course they might have turned and flown before it, but they wanted to go north, not south-they wanted to face their accusers.

Then, after the first fury of the blast had spent itself, there came a deluge of rain, following a dazzling glare of lightning and a bursting crash of thunder.

In spite of the gale buffeting her, the airship was making good progress. The skill of Tom and the balloonist was never shown to better advantage. All around them the storm raged, but through it the craft kept on her way. Nothing could be seen but pelting sheets of water and swirling mist, yet onward the ship was driven.

The thunder was deafening, and the lightning nearly blinded them, until the electrics were switched on, flooding the cabin with radiance. Inside the car they were snug and dry, though the pitching of the craft was like that of a big liner in the trough of the ocean waves.

"Will she weather it, do you think?" called Mr. Damon, in the ear of Mr. Sharp, shouting so as to be heard above the noise of the elements, and the hum of the motor.

The balloonist nodded.

"She's a good ship," he answered proudly.

Hardly had he spoken when there came a crash louder than any that had preceded, and the flash of rosy light that accompanied it seemed to set the whole heavens on fire. At the same time there was violent shock to the ship.

"We're hit! Struck by lightning!" yelled Tom.

"We're falling!" cried Mr. Damon an instant later.

Mr. Sharp looked at the elevation gauge. The hand was slowly swinging around. Down, down dropped the *Red Cloud*. She was being roughly treated by the storm.

"I'm afraid we're wrecked!" said the balloonist in a low voice, scarcely audible above the roar of the tempest. Following the great crash had come a comparatively light bombardment from the sky artillery.

"Use the gliding rudder, Tom," called Mr. Sharp, a moment later. "We may fall, but we'll land as easily as possible."

The wind, the rain, the lightning and thunder continued. Down, down sank the ship. Its fall was somewhat checked by the rudder Tom swung into place, and by setting the planes at a different angle. The motor had been stopped, and the propellers no longer revolved. In the confusion and darkness it was not safe to run ahead, with the danger of oolliding with unseen objects on the earth.

They tried to peer from the windows, but could see nothing. A moment later, as they stared at each other with fear in their eyes, there came a shock. The ship trembled from end to end.

"We've landed!" cried Tom, as he yanked back on the levers. The airship came to a stop.

"Now to see where we are," said Mr. Sharp grimly, "and how badly we are wrecked."

CHAPTER 20

TOM GETS A CLUE

Out of the cabin of the now stationary airship hurried the three travelers; out into the pelting rain, which was lashed into their faces by the strong wind. Tom was the first to emerge.

"We're on something solid!" he cried, stamping his feet. "A rock, I guess."

"Gracious, I hope we're not on a rock in the midst of a river!" exclaimed Mr. Damon. "Bless my soul, though! The water does seem to be running around my ankles."

"There's enough rain to make water run almost up to our necks," called Mr. Sharp, above the noise of the storm. "Tom, can you make out where we are?"

"Not exactly. Is the ship all right?"

"I can't see very well, but there appears to be a hole in the gas container. A big one, too, or we wouldn't have fallen so quickly."

The plight of the travelers of the air was anything but enviable. They were wet through, for it needed only a few minutes exposure to the pelting storm to bring this about. They could not tell, in the midst of the darkness, where they were, and they almost feared to move for fear they might be on top of some rock or precipice, over which they might tumble if they took a false step.

"Let's get back inside the ship," proposed Mr. Damon. "It's warm and dry there, at all events. Bless my umbrella, I don't know when I've been so wet!"

"I'm not going in until I find out where we are," declared Tom. "Wait a minute, and I'll go in and get an electric flash lantern. That will show us," for the lightning had ceased with the great crash that seemed to have wrecked the *Red Cloud*. The rain still kept up, however, and there was a distant muttering of thunder, while it was so black that had not the lights in the cabin of the airship been faintly glowing they could hardly have found the craft had they moved ten feet away from it.

Tom soon returned with the portable electric lamp, operated by dry batteries. He flashed it on the surface of where they were standing, and uttered an exclamation.

"We're on a roof!" he cried.

"A roof?" repeated Mr. Damon.

"Yes; the roof of some large building, and what you thought was a river is the rain water running off it. See!"

The young inventor held the light down so his companions could observe the surface of that upon which the airship rested. There was no doubt of it. They were on top of a large building.

"If we're on a roof we must be in the midst of a city," objected Mr. Damon. "But I can't see any lights around, and we would see them if we were in a city, you know."

"Maybe the storm put the lights out of business," suggested Mr. Sharp. "That often occurs."

"I know one way we can find out for certain," went on Tom.

"How?"

"Start up our search lamp, and play it all around. We can't make sure how large this roof is in the dark, and it's risky trying to trace the edges by walking around."

"Yes, and it would be risky to start our searchlight going," objected Mr. Sharp. "People would see it, and there'd be a crowd up here in less than no time, storm or no storm. No, we've got to keep dark until I can see what's the matter. We must leave here before daylight."

"Suppose we can't?" asked Mr. Damon. "The crowds will be sure to see us then, anyhow."

"I am pretty sure we can get away," was the opinion of the balloonist. "Even if our gas container is so damaged that it will not sustain us, we are still an aeroplane, and this roof being flat will make a good place to start from. No, we can leave as soon as this storm lets up a little."

"Then I'm going to have a look and find out what sort of a building this is," declared Tom, and, while Mr. Sharp began a survey, as well as he could in the dark, of the airship, the young inventor proceeded cautiously to ascertain the extent of the roof.

The rain was not coming down quite so hard now, and Tom found it easier to see. Mr. Damon, finding he could do nothing to help, went back into the cabin, blessing himself and his various possessions at the queer predicament in which they found themselves.

Flashing his light every few seconds, Tom walked on until he came to one edge of the roof. It was very large, as he could judge by the time it took him to traverse it. There was a low parapet at the edge. He peered over, and an expanse of dark wall met his eyes.

"Must have come to one side," he reasoned. "I want to get to the front. Then, maybe, I can see a sign that will tell me what I want to know."

The lad turned to the left, and, presently came to another parapet. It was higher, and ornamented with terra-cotta bricks. This, evidently, was the front. As Tom peered over the edge of the little raised ledge, there flashed out below him hundreds of electric lights. The city illuminating plant was being repaired. Then Tom saw flashing below him one of those large signs made of incandescent lights. It was in front of the building, and as soon as our hero saw the words he knew where the airship had landed. For what he read, as he leaned over, was this:

MIDDLEVILLE ARCADE

Tom gave a cry.

"What's the matter?" called Mr. Sharp.

"I've discovered something," answered Tom, hurrying up to his friend. "We're on top of the Middleville Arcade building."

"What does that mean?"

"It means that we're not so very far from home, and in the midst of a fairly large city. But it means more than that."

"What?" demanded the balloonist, struck by an air of excitement about the lad, for, as Tom stood in the subdued glow of the lights from one of the airship's cabin windows, all the others having been darkened as the storm slackened, his, eyes shone brightly.

"This is the building where Anson Morse, one of the gang that robbed dad, once had an office," went on Tom eagerly. "That was brought out at the trial. And it's the place where they used to do some of their conspiring. Maybe some of the crowd are here now laying low."

"Well, if they are, we don't want anything to do with that gang," said Mr. Sharp. "We can't arrest them. Besides I've found out that our ship is all right, after all. We can proceed as soon as we like. There is only a small leak in the gas container. It was the generator machine that was put out of business by the lightning, and I've repaired it."

"I want to see if I can get any trace of the rascals. Maybe I could learn something from the janitor of the Arcade about them. The janitor is probably here."

"But why do you want to get any information about that gang?"

"Because," answered Tom, and, as Mr. Damon at that moment started to come from the cabin of the airship, the lad leaped forward and whispered the remainder of the sentence into the ear of the balloonist.

"You don't mean it!" exclaimed Mr. Sharp, in a tense whisper. Tom nodded vigorously.

"But how can you enter the building?" asked the other. "You can't drop over the edge."

"Down the scuttle," answered Tom. "There must be one on the roof, for they have to come up here at times. We can force the lock, if necessary. I want to enter the building and see where Morse had his office."

"All right. Go ahead. I'll engage Mr. Damon here so he won't follow you. It will be great news for him. Go ahead."

Under pretense of wanting the help of the eccentric man in completing the repairs he had started, Mr. Sharp took Mr. Damon back into the cabin. Tom, getting a big screwdriver from an outside toolbox, approached the scuttle on the roof. He could see it looming up in the semidarkness, a sort of box, covering a stairway that led down into the building. The door was locked, but Tom forced it, and felt justified. A few minutes later, cautiously flashing his light, almost like a burglar he thought, he was prowling around the corridors of the office structure.

Was it deserted? That was what he wanted to know. He knew the office Morse had formerly occupied was two floors from the top. Tom descended the staircase, trying to think up some excuse to offer, in case he met the watchman or janitor. But he encountered no one. As he reached the floor where he knew Morse and his gang were wont to assemble, he paused and listened. At first he heard nothing, then, as the sound of the storm became less he fancied he heard the murmur of voices.

"Suppose it should be some of them?" whispered Tom.

He went forward, pausing at almost every other step to listen. The voices became louder. Tom was now nearly at the office, where Morse had once had his quarters. Now he could see it, and his heart gave a great thump as he noticed that the place was lighted. The lad could read the name on the door. "Industrial Development Company." That was the name of a fake concern headed by Morse. As our hero looked he saw the shadows of two men thrown on the ground glass.

"Some one's in there!" he whispered to himself. He could now hear the voices much plainer. They came from the room, but the lad could not distinguish them as belonging to any of the gang with whom he had come in contact, and who had escaped from jail.

The low murmur went on for several seconds.

The listener could make out no words. Suddenly the low, even mumble was broken. Some one cried out "There's got to be a divvy soon. There's no use letting Morse hold that whole seventy-five thousand any longer. I'm going to get what's coming to me, or-"

"Hush!" some one else cried. "Be quiet!"

"No, I won't! I want my share. I've waited long enough. If I don't get what's coming to me inside of a week, I'll go to Shagmon myself and make Morse whack up. I helped on the job, and I want my money!"

"Will you be quiet?" pleaded another, and, at that instant Tom heard some one's hand on the knob. The door opened a crack, letting out a pencil of light. The men were evidently coming out. The young inventor did not wait to hear more. He had a clue now, and, running on tiptoes, he made his way to the staircase and out of the scuttle on the roof.

CHAPTER 21

ON THE TRAIL

"What's the matter, Tom?" asked Mr. Sharp, as the lad came hurrying along the roof, having taken the precaution to fasten the scuttle door as well as he could. "You seem excited." "So would you, if you had heard what I did."

"What? You don't mean that some of the gang is down there?"

"Yes, and what's more I'm on the trail of the thieves who robbed the Shopton Bank of the seventy-five thousand dollars!"

"No! You don't mean it!"

"I certainly do."

"Then we'd better tell Mr. Damon. He's in the cabin."

"Of course I'll tell him. He's as much concerned as I am. He wants to be vindicated. Isn't it great luck, though?"

"But you haven't landed the men yet. Do you mean to say that the same gang-the Happy Harry crowd-robbed the bank?"

"I think so, from what I heard. But come inside and I'll tell you all about it."

"Suppose we start the ship first? It's ready to run. There wasn't as much the matter with it as I feared. The storm is over now, and we'll be safer up in the air than on this roof. Did you get all the information you could?"

"All I dared to. The men were coming out, so I had to run. They were quarreling, and when that happens among thieves-"

"Why honest men get their dues, everyone knows that proverb," interrupted Mr. Damon, again emerging from the cabin. "But bless my quotation marks, I should think you'd have something better to do than stand there talking proverbs."

"We have," replied Mr. Sharp quickly. "We're going to start the ship, arid then we have some news for you. Tom, you take the steering wheel, and I'll start the gas machine. We'll rise to some distance before starting the propellers, and then we won't create any excitement."

"But what news are you going to tell me?" asked Mr. Damon. "Bless my very existence, but you get me all excited, and then you won't gratify my curiosity."

"In a little while we will," responded Mr. Sharp. Lively now, Tom. Some one may see this airship on top of the building, as it's getting so much lighter now, after the storm."

The outburst of the elements was almost over and Tom taking

another look over the edge of the roof, could see persons moving about in the street below. The storm clouds were passing and a faint haze showed where a moon would soon make its appearance, thus disclosing the craft so oddly perched upon the roof. There was need of haste.

Fortunately the *Red Cloud* could be sent aloft without the use of the propellers, for the gas would serve to lift her. It had been found that lightning had struck the big, red aluminum container, but the shock had been a comparatively slight one, and, as the tank was insulated from the rest of the ship no danger resulted to the occupants. A rent was made in two or three of the gas compartments, but the others remained intact, and, when an increased pressure of the vapor was used the ship was almost as buoyant as before.

Into the cabin the three travelers hurried, dripping water at every step, for there was no time to change clothes. Then, with Tom and Mr. Sharp managing the machinery, the craft slowly rose. It was well that they had started for, when a few hundred feet above the roof, the moon suddenly shone from behind a bank of clouds and would most certainly have revealed their position to persons in the street. As it was several were attracted by the sight of some great object in the air. They called the attention of others to it, but, by the time glasses and telescopes had been brought to bear, the *Red Cloud* was far away.

"Dry clothes now, some hot drinks, and then Tom will tell us his secret," remarked Mr. Sharp, and, with the great ship swaying high above the city of Middleville Tom told what he had heard in the office building.

"They are the thieves who looted the bank, and caused us to be unjustly accused," he finished. "If we can capture them we'll get the reward, and turn a neat trick on Andy Foger and his cronies."

"But how can you capture them?" asked Mr. Damon. "You don't know where they are."

"Perhaps not where Morse and the men who have the money are. But I have a plan. It's this: We'll go to some quiet place, leave the airship, and then inform the authorities of our suspicions. They can come here and arrest the men who still seem to be hanging out in Morse's office. Then we can get on the trail of this Shagmon, who seems to be the person in authority this time, though I never heard of him before.

He seems to have the money, according to what one of the men in the office said, and he's the man we want."

"Shagmon!" exclaimed Mr. Damon. "Yes, Shagmon. The fellow I heard talking said he'd go to Shagmon and make Morse whack up. Shagmon may be the real head of the gang."

"Ha! I have it!" cried Mr. Damon suddenly. "I wonder I didn't think of it before. Shagmon is the headquarters, not the head of the gang!"

"What do you mean?" asked Tom, much excited.

"I mean that there's a town called Shagmon about fifty miles from here. That's what the fellow in the office meant. He is going to the town of Shagmon and make Morse whack up. That's where Morse is! That's where the gang is hiding! That's where the money is! Hurrah, Tom, we're on the trail!"

CHAPTER 22

THE SHERIFF ON BOARD

The announcement of Mr. Damon came as a great surprise to Tom and Mr. Sharp. They had supposed that the reference to Shagmon was to a person, and never dreamed that it was to a locality. But Mr. Damon's knowledge of geography stood them in good stead.

"Well, what's the first thing to do?" asked Tom, after a pause.

"The first thing would be to go to Shagmon, or close to it, I should say," remarked Mr. Sharp. "In what direction is it, Mr. Damon?"

"Northwest from where we were. It's a county seat, and that will suit our plans admirably, for we can call on the sheriff for help."

"That is if we locate the gang," put in Tom. "I fancy it will be no easy job, though. How are we going about it?"

"Let's first get to Shagmon," suggested the balloonist. "We'll select some quiet spot for a landing, and then talk matters over. We may stumble on the gang, just as you did, Tom, on the men in the office."

"No such good luck, I'm afraid."

"Well, I think we'll all be better for a little sleep," declared the eccentric man. "Bless my eyelids but I'm tired out."

As there was no necessity for standing watch, when the airship was so high up as to be almost invisible, they all turned in, and were soon sleeping soundly, though Tom had hard work at first to compose himself, for he was excited at the prospect of capturing the scoundrels, recovering the money for the bank, and clearing his good name, as well as those of his friends.

In the morning careful calculations were made to enable the travelers to tell when they had reached a point directly over the small city of Shagmon, and, with the skill of the veteran balloonist to aid them, this was accomplished. The airship was headed in the proper direction, and, about ten o'clock, having made out by using telescopes, that there was plenty of uninhabited land about the city, the craft was sent aloft again, out of a large crowd that had caught sight of it. For it was the intention of the travelers not to land until after dark, as they wanted to keep their arrival quiet. There were two reasons for this. One was that the whole country was eager to arrest them, to claim the reward offered by the bank, and they did not want this to happen. The other reason was that they wanted to go quietly into town, tell the sheriff their story, and enlist his aid.

All that day the *Red Cloud* consorted with the masses of fleecy vapor, several miles above the earth, a position being maintained, as nearly as could be judged by instruments, over a patch of woodland where Mr. Sharp had decided to land, as there were several large clearings in it. Back and forth above the clouds, out of sight, the airship drifted lazily to and fro; sometimes, when she got too far off her course, being brought back to the right spot by means of the propellers.

It was tedious waiting, but they felt it was the only thing to do. Mr. Sharp and Tom busied themselves making adjustments to several parts of apparatus that needed it. Nothing could be done toward repairing the hole in the aluminum container until a shop or shed was reached, but the ship really did not need these repairs to enable it to be used. Mr. Damon was fretful, and "blessed" so many things during the course of the day that there seemed to be nothing left. Dinner and supper took up some time, really good meals being served by Tom, who was temporarily acting as cook. Then they anxiously waited for darkness, when they could descend.

"I hope the moon isn't too bright," remarked Mr. Sharp, as he went carefully over the motor once more, for he did not want it to balk again. "If it shines too much it will discover us."

"But a little light would be a fine thing, and show us a good place to land," argued Tom.

Fortune seemed to favor the adventurers. There was a hazy light from the moon, which was covered by swiftly moving dark clouds, now and then, a most effective screen for the airship, as its great, moving shape, viewed from the earth, resembled nothing so much as one of the clouds.

They made a good landing in a little forest glade, the craft, under the skillful guidance of Mr. Sharp and Tom, coming down nicely.

"Now for a trip to town to notify the sheriff," said Mr. Sharp. "Tom, I think you had better go alone. You can explain matters, and Mr. Damon and I will remain here until you come back. I should say what you had best do, would be to get the sheriff to help you locate the gang of bank robbers. They're in this vicinity and he ought to be able, with his deputies, to find them."

"I'll ask him," replied Tom, as he set off.

It was rather a lonely walk into the city, from the woods where the airship had landed, but Tom did not mind it, and, reaching Shagmon, he inquired his way to the home of the sheriff, for it was long after office hours. He heard, as he walked along the streets, many persons discussing the appearance of the airship that morning, and he was glad they had planned to land after dark, for more than one citizen was regretting that he had not had a chance to get the five thousand dollars reward offered for the arrest of the passengers in the *Red Cloud*.

Tom found the sheriff, Mr. Durkin by name, a genial personage. At the mention of the airship the official grew somewhat excited.

"Are you one of the fellows that looted the bank?" he inquired, when Tom told him how he and his friends had arrived at Shagmon.

The young inventor denied the impeachment, and told his story. He ended up with a request for the sheriff's aid, at the same time asking if the officer knew where such a gang as the Happy Harry one might be in hiding.

"You've come just at the right time, young man," was the answer of Sheriff Durkin, when he was assured of the honesty of Tom's statements. "I've been on the point, for the last week, of raiding a camp of men, who have settled at a disused summer resort about ten miles from here. I think they're running a gambling game. But I haven't been able to get any evidence, and every time I sent out a posse some one warns the men, and we can find nothing wrong. I believe these men are the very ones you want. If we could only get to them without their suspecting it, I think I'd have them right."

"We can do that, Sheriff."

"How?"

"Go in our airship! You come with us, and we'll put you right over their camp, where you can drop down on their heads."

"Good land, I never rode in an automobile even, let alone an airship!" went on the officer. "I'd be scared out of my wits, and so would my deputies."

"Send the deputies on ahead," suggested Tom.

The sheriff hesitated. Then he slapped his thigh with his big hand.

"By golly! I'll go you!" he declared. "I'll try capturing criminals in an airship for the first, time in my life! Lead the way, young man!"

An hour later Sheriff Durkin was aboard the *Red Cloud*, and plans were being talked of for the capture of the bank robbers, or at least for raiding the camp where the men were supposed to be.

CHAPTER 23

ON TO THE CAMP

"Well, you sure have got a fine craft here," remarked Sheriff Durkin, as he looked over the airship after Tom and his friends had told of their voyage. "It will be quite up-to-date to raid a gang of bank robbers in a flying machine, but I guess it will be the only way we can catch those fellows. Now I'll go back to town, and the first thing in the morning I'll round-up my posse and start it off. The men can surround the camp, and lay quiet until we arrive in this ship. Then, when we descend on the heads of the scoundrels, right out of the sky, so to speak, my men can close in, and bag them all."

"That's a good plan," commented Mr. Sharp, "but are you sure these are the men we want? It's pretty vague, I think, but of course the clue Tom got is pretty slim; merely the name Shagmon."

"Well, this is Shagmon," went on the sheriff, "and, as I told your young friend, I've been trying for some time to bag the men at the summer camp. They number quite a few, and if they don't do anything worse, they run a gambling game there. I'm pretty sure, if the bank robbers are in this vicinity, they're in that camp. Of course all the men there may not have been engaged in looting the vault, and they may not all know of it, but it won't do any harm to round-up the whole bunch."

After a tour of the craft, and waiting to take a little refreshment with his new friends, the sheriff left, promising to come as early on the morrow as possible.

"Let's go to bed," suggested Mr. Sharp, after a bit. "We've got hard work ahead of us tomorrow."

They were up early, and, in the seclusion of the little glade in the woods, Tom and Mr. Sharp went over every part of the airship.

The sheriff arrived about nine o'clock, and announced that he had started off through the woods, to surround the camp, twenty-five men.

"They'll be there at noon," Mr. Durkin said, "and will close in when I give the signal, which will be two shots fired. I heard just before I came here that there are some new arrivals at the camp."

"Maybe those are the men I overheard talking in the office building," suggested Tom. "They probably came to get their share. Well, we must swoop down on them before they have time to distribute the money."

"That's what!" agreed the county official. Mr. Durkin was even more impressed by the airship in the daytime than he had been at night. He examined every part, and when the time came to start, he was almost as unconcerned as any of the three travelers who had covered many hundreds of miles in the air.

"This is certainly great!" cried the sheriff, as the airship rose swiftly under the influence of the powerful gas.

As the craft went higher and higher his enthusiasm grew. He was not the least afraid, but then Sheriff Durkin was accounted a nervy individual under all circumstances.

"Lay her a little off to the left," the officer advised Tom who was at the steering wheel. "The main camp is right over there. How long before we will reach it?"

"We can get there in about fifteen minutes, if we run at top speed," answered the lad, his hand on the switch that controlled the motor. "Shall we?"

"No use burning up the air. Besides, my men have hardly had time to surround the camp. It's in deep woods. If I were you I'd get right over it, and then rise up out of sight so they can't see you. Then, when it's noon you can go down, I'll fire the signal and the fun will commence-that is, fun for us, but not so much for those chaps, I fancy," and the sheriff smiled grimly.

The sheriff's plan was voted a good one, and, accordingly, the ship, after nearing a spot about over the camp, was sent a mile or two into the air, hovering as nearly as possible over one spot.

Shortly before twelve, the sheriff having seen to the weapons he brought with him, gave the signal to descend. Down shot the *Red Cloud* dropping swiftly when the gas was allowed to escape from the red container, and also urged toward the earth by the deflected rudder.

"Are you all ready?" cried the sheriff, looking at his watch.

"All ready," replied Mr. Sharp.

"Then here goes," went on the officer, drawing his revolver, and firing two shots in quick succession.

Two shots from the woods below answered him. Faster dropped the *Red Cloud* toward the camp of the criminals.

CHAPTER 24

THE RAID

"Look for a good place to land!" cried Mr. Sharp to Tom. "Any small, level place will do. Turn on the gas full power as soon as you feel the first contact, and then shut it off so as to hold her down. Then jump out and take a hand in the fight!"

"That's right," cried the sheriff. "Fight's the word! They're breaking from cover now," he added, as he looked over the side of the cabin, from one of the windows. "The rascals have taken the alarm!"

The airship was descending toward a little glade in the woods surrounding the old picnic ground. Men, mostly of the tramp sort, could be seen running to and fro.

"I hope my deputies close in promptly," murmured the sheriff. "There's a bigger bunch there than I counted on."

>From the appearance of the gang rushing about it seemed as if there were at least fifty of them. Some of the fellows caught sight of the airship, and, with yells, pointed upward.

Nearer and nearer to the earth settled the *Red Cloud*. The criminals in the camp were running wildly about. Several squads of them darted through the woods, only to come hurriedly back, where they called to their companions.

"Ha! My men are evidently on the job!" exclaimed the sheriff. "They are turning the rascals back!"

Some of the gang were so alarmed at the sight of the great airship settling down on their camp, that they could only stand and stare at it. Others were gathering sticks and stones, as if for resistance, and some could be seen to have weapons. Off to one side was a small hut, rather better than the rest of the tumbledown shacks in which the tramps lived. Tom noticed this, and saw several men gathered about it. One seemed familiar to the lad. He called the attention of Mr. Damon to the fellow.

"Do you know him?" asked Tom eagerly.

"Bless my very existence! If it isn't Anson Morse! One of the gang!" cried the eccentric man.

"That's what I thought," agreed Tom. "The bank robbers are here," he added, to the sheriff.

"If we only recover the money we'll be doing well," remarked Mr. Sharp.

Suddenly there came a shout from the fringe of woods surrounding the camp, and an instant later there burst from the bushes a number of men.

"My posse!" cried the sheriff. "We ought to be down now!"

The airship was a hundred feet above the ground, but Tom, opening wider the gas outlet, sent the craft more quickly down. Then, just as it touched the earth, he forced a mass of vapor into the container, making the ship buoyant so as to reduce the shock.

An instant later the ship was stationary.

Out leaped the sheriff.

"Give it to'em, men!" he shouted.

With a yell his men responded, and fired a volley in the air.

"Come on, Tom!" called Mr. Sharp. "We'll make for the hut where you saw Morse."

"I'll come too! I'll come too!" cried Mr. Damon, rushing along as fast as he could, a seltzer bottle in either hand.

Tom's chief interest was to reach the men he suspected were the bank robbers. The lad dashed through the woods toward the hut near which he had seen Morse. He and Mr. Sharp reached it about the same time. As they came in front of it out dashed Happy Harry, the tramp. He was followed by Morse and the man named Featherton. The latter carried a black valise.

"Hey! Drop that!" shouted Mr. Sharp.

"Drop nothing!" yelled the man.

"Go on! Go on!" urged Morse. "Take to the woods! We'll deal with these fellows!"

"Oh, you will, eh?" shouted Tom, and remembering his football days he made a dive between Morse and Happy Harry for the man with the bag, which he guessed contained the stolen money. The lad made a good tackle, and grabbed Featherton about the legs. He went down in a heap, with Tom on top. Our hero was feeling about for the valise, when he felt a stunning blow on the back of his head. He turned over quickly to see Morse in the act of delivering a second kick. Tom grew faint, and dimly saw the leader of the gang reach down for the valise.

This gave our hero sudden energy. He was not going to lose everything, when it was just within his grasp. Conquering, by a strong effort, his feeling of dizziness, he scrambled to his feet, and made a grab for Morse. The latter fended him off, but Tom came savagely back at him, all his fighting blood up. The effects of the cowardly blow were passing off.

The lad managed to get one hand on the handle of the bag.

"Let go!" cried Morse, and he dealt Tom a blow in the face. It staggered the youth, but he held on grimly, and raised his left hand

and arm as a guard. At the same time he endeavored to twist the valise loose from Morse's hold. The man raised his foot to kick Tom, but at that moment there was a curious hissing sound, and a stream of frothy liquid shot over the lad's head right into the face of the man, blinding him.

"Ha! Take that! And more of it!" shouted Mr. Damon, and a second stream of seltzer squirted into the face of Morse.

With a yell of rage he let go his hold of the satchel, and Tom staggered back with it. The lad saw Mr. Damon rushing toward the now disabled leader, playing both bottles of seltzer on him. Then, when all the liquid was gone the eccentric man began to beat Morse over the head and shoulders with the heavy bottles until the scoundrel begged for mercy.

Tom was congratulating himself on his success in getting the bag when Happy Harry, the tramp, rushed at him.

"I guess I'll take that!" he roared, and, wheeling Tom around, at the same time striking him full in the face, the ugly man made a grab for the valise.

His hand had hardly touched it before he went down like a log, the sound of a powerful blow causing Tom to look up. He saw Mr. Sharp standing over the prostrate tramp, who had been cleanly knocked out.

"Are you all right, Tom?" asked the balloonist.

"Yes-trifle dizzy, that's all-I've got the money!"

"Are you sure?"

Tom opened the valise. A glance was enough to show that it was stuffed with bills.

Happy Harry showed signs of coming to, and Mr. Sharp, with a few turns of a rope he had brought along, soon secured him. Morse was too exhausted to fight more, for the seltzer entering his mouth and nose, had deprived him of breath, and he fell an easy prisoner to Mr. Damon.

Morse was soon tied up. The other members of the Happy Harry gang had escaped.

Meanwhile the sheriff and his men were having a fight with the crowd of tramps, but as the posse was determined and the criminals mostly of the class known as "hobos," the battle was not a very severe one. Several of the sheriff's men were slightly injured, however, and a few of the tramps escaped.

"A most successful raid," commented the sheriff, when quiet was restored, and a number of prisoners were lined up, all tied securely. "Did you get the money?"

"Almost all of it," answered Tom, who, now that Morse and

Happy Harry were securely tied, had busied himself, with the aid of Mr. Sharp and Mr. Damon, in counting the bills. "Only about two thousand dollars are missing. I think the bank will be glad enough to charge that to profit and loss."

"I guess so," added the sheriff. "I'm certainly much obliged to you for the use of your airship. Otherwise the raid wouldn't have been so successful. Well, now we'll get the prisoners to jail."

It was necessary to hire rigs from nearby farmers to accomplish this. As for Morse and Happy Harry, they were placed in the airship, and, under guard of the sheriff and two deputies, were taken to the county seat. The criminals were too dazed over the rough treatment they had received, and over their sudden capture, to notice the fact of riding through the air to jail.

"Now for home!" cried Tom, when the prisoners had been disposed of. "Home to clear our names and take this money to the bank!"

"And receive the reward," added Mr. Sharp, with a smile. "Don't forget that!"

"Oh, yes, and I'll see that you get a share too, Mr. Durkin," went on Tom. "Only for your aid we never would have gotten these men and the money."

"Oh, I guess we're about even on that score," responded the official. "I'm glad to break up that gang."

The next morning Tom and his friends started for home in the *Red Cloud*.

They took with them evidence as to the guilt of the two men-Morse and Happy Harry. The men confessed that they and their pals had robbed the bank of Shopton, the night before Tom and his friends sailed on their trip. In fact that was the object for which the gang hung around Shopton. After securing their booty they had gone to the camp of the tramps at Shagmon, where they hid, hoping they would not be traced. But the words Tom had overheard had been their undoing. The men who arrived at the camp just before the raid were the same ones the young inventor heard talking in the office building. They had come to get their share of the loot, which Morse held, and with which he tried so desperately to get away. Tom's injuries were not serious and did not bother him after being treated by a physician.

CHAPTER 25

ANDY GETS HIS REWARD

Flying swiftly through the air the young inventor and his two companions were soon within sight of Shopton. As they approached the town from over the lake, and a patch of woods, they attracted no attention until they were near home, and the craft settled down easily in the yard of the Swift property.

That the aged inventor was glad to see his son back need not be said, and Mrs. Baggert's welcome was scarcely less warm than that of Mr. Swift. Mr. Sharp and Mr. Damon were also made to feel that their friends were glad to see them safe again.

"We must go at once and see Mr. Pendergast, the bank president," declared Mr. Swift. "We must take the money to him, and demand that he withdraw the offer of reward for your arrest."

"Yes," agreed Tom. "I guess the reward will go to some one besides Andy Foger."

There was considerable surprise on the part of the bank clerks when our hero, and his friends, walked in, carrying a heavy black bag. But they could only conjecture what was in the wind, for the party was immediately closeted with the president.

Mr. Pendergast was so startled that he hardly knew what to say when Tom, aided by Mr. Sharp, told his story. But the return of the money, with documents from Sheriff Durkin, certifying as to the arrest of Morse and Happy Harry, soon convinced him of the truth of the account.

"It's the most wonderful thing I ever heard," said the president.

"Well, what are you going to do about it?" asked Mr. Damon. "You have accused Tom and myself of being thieves, and-"

"I apologize-I apologize most humbly!" exclaimed Mr. Pendergast. "I also-"

"What about the reward?" went on Mr. Damon. "Bless my bank notes, I don't want any of it, for I have enough, but I think Tom and Mr. Sharp and the sheriff are entitled to it."

"Certainly," said the president, "certainly. It will be paid at once. I will call a meeting of the directors. In fact they are all in the bank now, save Mr. Foger, and I can reach him by telephone. If you will just rest yourselves in that room there I will summon you before the board, when it convenes, and be most happy to pay over the five thousand dollars reward. It is the most wonderful thing I ever heard of-most wonderful!"

In a room adjoining that of the president, Tom, his father and Mr. Damon waited for the directors to meet. Mr. Foger could be heard entering a little later.

"What's this I hear, Pendergast?" he cried, rubbing his hands. "The bank robbers captured, eh? Well, that's good news. Of course we'll pay the reward. I always knew my boy was a smart lad. Five thousand dollars will be a tidy sum for him. Of course his chum, Sam Snedecker is entitled to some, but not much. So they've caught Tom Swift and that rascally Damon, eh? I always knew he was a scoundrel! Putting money in here as a blind!"

Mr. Damon heard, and shook his fist.

"I'll make him suffer for that," he whispered.

"Tom Swift arrested, eh?" went on Mr. Foger. "I always knew he was a bad egg. Who caught them? Where are they?"

"In the next room," replied Mr. Pendergast, who loved a joke almost as well as did Tom. "They may come out now," added the president, opening the door, and sending Ned Newton in to summon Tom, Mr. Swift and Mr. Damon, who filed out before the board of directors.

"Gentlemen," began the president, "I have the pleasure of presenting to you Mr. Thomas Swift, Mr. Barton Swift and Mr. Wakefield Damon. I also have the honor to announce that Mr. Thomas Swift and Mr. Damon have been instrumental in capturing the burglars who recently robbed our bank, and I am happy to add that young Mr. Swift and Mr. Wakefeld Damon have, this morning, brought to me all but a small part of the money stolen from us. Which money they succeeded, after a desperate fight "

"A fight partly with seltzer bottles," interrupted Mr. Damon proudly. "Don't forget them."

"Partly with seltzer bottles," conceded the president with a smile. "After a fight they succeeded in getting the money back. Here it is, and I now suggest that we pay the reward we promised."

"What? Reward? Pay them? The money back? Isn't my son to receive the five thousand dollars for informing as to the identity of the thief—isn't he?" demanded Mr. Foger, almost suffocating from his astonishment at the unexpected announcement.

"Hardly," answered Mr. Pendergast dryly. "Your son's information happened to be very wrong. The tools he saw Tom have in the bag were airship tools, not burglar's. And the same gang that once robbed Mr. Swift robbed our, bank. Tom Swift captured them, and is entitled to the reward. It will be necessary for us directors to make up the sum, personally, and I, for one, am very glad to do so."

"So am I," came in a chorus from the others seated at the table.

"But-er-I understood that my son-" stammered Mr. Foger, who did not at all relish having to see his son lose the reward.

"It was all a mistake about your son," commented Mr. Pendergast. "Gentlemen, is it your desire that I write out a check for young Mr. Swift?"

They all voted in the affirmative, even Mr. Foger being obliged to do so, much against his wishes. He was a very much chagrined man, when the directors' meeting broke up. Word was sent at once, by telegraph, to all the cities where reward posters had been displayed, recalling the offer, and stating that Tom Swift and Mr. Damon were cleared. Mr. Sharp had never been really accused.

"Well, let's go home," suggested Tom when he had the five-thousand—dollar check in his pocket.

"I want another ride in the *Red Cloud* as soon as it's repaired."

"So do I!" declared Mr. Damon.

The eccentric man and Mr. Swift walked on ahead, and Tom strolled down toward the dock, for he thought he would take a short trip in his motor-boat.

He was near the lake, not having met many persons, when he saw a figure running up from the water. He knew who it was in an instant Andy Foger. As for the bully, at the sight of Tom he hesitated, than came boldly on. Evidently he had not heard of our hero's arrival.

"Ha!" exclaimed the red-haired lad, "I've been looking for you. The police want you, Tom Swift."

"Oh, do they?" asked the young inventor gently.

"Yes; for robbery. I'm going to get the reward, too. You thought you were smart, but I saw those burglar tools in your valise. I sent the police after you. So you've come back, eh? I'm going to tell Chief Simonson. You wait."

"Yes," answered Tom, "I'll wait. So the police want me, do they?"

"That's what they do," snarled Andy. "I told you I'd get even with you, and I've done it."

"Well," burst out Tom, unable to longer contain himself, as he thought of all he had suffered at the hands of the red-haired bully, "I said I'd get even with you, but I haven't done it yet. I'm going to now. Take off your coat, Andy. You and I are going to have a little argument."

"Don't you dare lay a finger on me!" blustered the squint-eyed one.

Tom peeled off his coat. Andy, who saw that he could not escape, rushed forward, and dealt the young inventor a blow on the chest. That was all Tom wanted, and the next instant he went at Andy hammer and tongs. The bully tried to fight, but he had no chance with his antagonist, who was righteously angry, and who made every blow tell. It was a sorry-looking Andy Foger who begged for mercy a little later.

Tom had no desire to administer more than a deserved reward to the bully, but perhaps he did add a little for interest. At any rate Andy thought so.

"You just wait!" he cried, as he limped off. "I'll make you sorry for this."

"Oh, don't go to any trouble on my account," said Tom gently, as he put on his coat. But Andy did go to considerable trouble to be revenged on the young inventor, and whether be succeeded or not you may learn by reading the fourth book of this series, to be called "Tom Swift and His Submarine Boat; or, Under the Ocean for Sunken Treasure," in which I shall relate the particulars of a voyage that was marvelous in the extreme.

Tom reached home in a very pleasant frame of mind that afternoon. Things had turned out much better than he thought they would. A few weeks later the two bank robbers, who were found guilty, were sentenced to long terms, but their companions were not captured. Tom sent Sheriff Durkin a share of the reward, and the lad invested his own share in bank stock, after giving some to Mr. Sharp. Mr. Damon refused to accept any. As for Mr. Swift, once he saw matters straightened out, and his son safe, he resumed his work on his prize submarine boat, his son helping him.

As for Tom, he alternated his spare time between trips in the airship and his motor-boat, and frequently a certain young lady from the Rocksmond Seminary was his companion. I think you know her name by this time. Now, for a while, we will take leave of Tom Swift and his friends, trusting to meet them again.

TOM SWIFT AND HIS SUBMARINE BOAT

CHAPTER ONE

NEWS OF A TREASURE WRECK

There was a rushing, whizzing, throbbing noise in the air. A great body, like that of some immense bird, sailed along, casting a grotesque shadow on the ground below. An elderly man, who was seated on the porch of a large house, started to his feet in alarm.

"Gracious goodness! What was that, Mrs. Baggert?" he called to a motherly-looking woman who stood in the doorway. "What happened?"

"Nothing much, Mr. Swift," was the calm reply "I think that was Tom and Mr. Sharp in their airship, that's all. I didn't see it, but the noise sounded like that of the *Red Cloud*."

"Of course! To be sure!" exclaimed Mr. Barton Swift, the well-known inventor, as he started down the path in order to get a good view of the air, unobstructed by the trees. "Yes, there they are," he added. "That's the airship, but I didn't expect them back so soon. They must have made good time from Shopton. I wonder if anything can be the matter that they hurried so?"

He gazed aloft toward where a queerly-shaped machine was circling about nearly five hundred feet in the air, for the craft, after Swooping down close to the house, had ascended and was now hovering just above the line of breakers that marked the New Jersey seacoast, where Mr. Swift had taken up a temporary residence.

"Don't begin worrying, Mr. Swift," advised Mrs. Baggert, the housekeeper. "You've got too much to do, if you get that new boat done, to worry."

"That's so. I must not worry. But I wish Tom and Mr. Sharp would land, for I want to talk to them."

As if the occupants of the airship had heard the words of the aged inventor, they headed their craft toward earth. The combined aeroplane and dirigible balloon, a most wonderful traveler of the air, swung around, and then, with the deflection rudders slanted downward, came on with a rush. When near the landing place, just at the side of the house, the motor was stopped, and the gas, with a hissing noise, rushed into the red aluminum container. This immediately made the ship more buoyant and it landed almost as gently as a feather.

No sooner had the wheels which formed the lower part of the craft touched the ground than there leaped from the cabin of the *Red Cloud* a young man.

"Well, dad!" he exclaimed. "Here we are again, safe and sound. Made a record, too. Touched ninety miles an hour at times—didn't we, Mr. Sharp?"

"That's what," agreed a tall, thin, dark-complexioned man, who followed Tom Swift more leisurely in his exit from the cabin. Mr. Sharp, a veteran aeronaut, stopped to fasten guy ropes from the airship to strong stakes driven into the ground.

"And we'd have done better, only we struck a hard wind against us about two miles up in the air, which delayed us," went on Tom. "Did you hear us coming, dad?"

"Yes, and it startled him," put in Mrs. Baggert. "I guess he wasn't expecting you."

"Oh, well, I shouldn't have been so alarmed, only I was thinking deeply about a certain change I am going to make in the submarine, Tom. I was day-dreaming, I think, when your ship whizzed through the air. But tell me, did you find everything all right at Shopton? No signs of any of those scoundrels of the Happy Harry gang having been around?" and Mr. Swift looked anxiously at his son.

"Not a sign, dad," replied Tom quickly. "Everything was all right. We brought the things you wanted. They're in the airship. Oh, but it was a fine trip. I'd like to take another right out to sea."

"Not now, Tom," said his father. "I want you to help me. And I need Mr. Sharp's help, too. Get the things out of the car, and we'll go to the shop."

"First I think we'd better put the airship away," advised Mr. Sharp. "I don't just like the looks of the weather, and, besides, if we leave the ship exposed we'll be sure to have a crowd around sooner or later, and we don't want that."

"No, indeed," remarked the aged inventor hastily. "I don't want people prying around the submarine shed. By all means put the airship away, and then come into the shop."

In spite of its great size the aeroplane was easily wheeled along by Tom and Mr. Sharp, for the gas in the container made it so buoyant that it barely touched the earth. A little more of the powerful vapor and the *Red Cloud* would have risen by itself. In a few minutes the wonderful craft, of which my readers have been told in detail in a previous volume, was safely housed in a large tent, which was securely fastened.

Mr. Sharp and Tom, carrying some bundles which they had taken from the car, or cabin, of the craft, went toward a large shed, which adjoined the house that Mr. Swift had hired for the season at the seashore. They found the lad's father standing before a great shape, which loomed up dimly in the semi-darkness of the building. It was like an immense cylinder, pointed at either end, and here and there were openings, covered with thick glass, like immense, bulging eyes. From the number of tools and machinery all about the place, and from the appearance of the great cylinder itself, it was easy to see that it was only partly completed.

"Well, how goes it, dad?" asked the youth, as he deposited his bundle on a bench. "Do you think you can make it work?"

"I think so, Tom. The positive and negative plates are giving me considerable trouble, though. But I guess we can solve the problem. Did you bring me the galvanometer?"

"Yes, and all the other things," and the young inventor proceeded to take the articles from the bundles he carried.

Mr. Swift looked them over carefully, while Tom walked about examining the submarine, for such was the queer craft that was contained in the shed. He noted that some progress had been made on it since he had left the seacoast several days before to make a trip to Shopton, in New York State, where the Swift home was located, after some tools and apparatus that his father wanted to obtain from his workshop there.

"You and Mr. Jackson have put on several new plates," observed the lad after a pause.

"Yes," admitted his father. "Garret and I weren't idle, were we, Garret?" and he nodded to the aged engineer, who had been in his employ for many years.

"No; and I guess we'll soon have her in the water, Tom, now that you and Mr. Sharp are here to help us," replied Garret Jackson.

"We ought to have Mr. Damon here to bless the submarine and his liver and collar buttons a few times," put in Mr. Sharp, who brought in another bundle. He referred to an eccentric individual Who had recently made an airship voyage with himself and Tom, Mr. Damon's peculiarity being to use continually such expressions as: "Bless my soul! Bless my liver!"

"Well, I'll be glad when we can make a trial trip," went on Tom. "I've traveled pretty fast on land with my motor-cycle, and we certainly have hummed through the air. Now I want to see how it feels to scoot along under water."

"Well, if everything goes well we'll be in position to make a trial trip inside of a month," remarked the aged inventor. "Look here, Mr. Sharp, I made a change in the steering gear, which I'd like you and Tom to consider."

The three walked around to the rear of the odd-looking structure, if an object shaped like a cigar can be said to have a front and rear, and the inventor, his son, and the aeronaut were soon deep in a discussion of the technicalities connected with under-water navigation.

A little later they went into the house, in response to a summons from the supper bell, vigorously rung by Mrs. Baggert. She was not fond of waiting with meals, and even the most serious problem of mechanics was, in her estimation, as nothing compared with having the soup get cold, or the possibility of not having the meat done to a turn.

The meal was interspersed with remarks about the recent air-ship flight of Tom and Mr. Sharp, and discussions about the new submarine. This talk went on even after the table was cleared off and the three had adjourned to the sitting-room. There Mr. Swift brought out pencil and paper, and soon he and Mr. Sharp were engrossed in calculating the pressure per square inch of sea water at a depth of three miles.

"Do you intend to go as deep as that?" asked Tom, looking up from a paper he was reading.

"Possibly," replied his father; and his son resumed his perusal of the sheet.

"Now," went on the inventor to the aeronaut, "I have another plan. In addition to the positive and negative plates which will form our motive power, I am going to install forward and aft propellers, to use in case of accident."

"I say, dad! Did you see this?" suddenly exclaimed Tom, getting up from his chair, and holding his finger on a certain place in the page of the paper.

"Did I see what?" asked Mr. Swift.

"Why, this account of the sinking of the treasure ship."

"Treasure ship? No. Where?"

"Listen," went on Tom. "I'll read it: 'Further advices from Montevideo, Uruguay, South America, state that all hope has been given up of recovering the steamship Boldero, which foundered and went down off that coast in the recent gale. Not only has all hope been abandoned of raising the vessel, but it is feared that no part of the three hundred thousand dollars in gold bullion which she carried will ever be recovered. Expert divers who were taken to the scene of the wreck state that the depth of water, and the many currents existing there, due to a submerged shoal, preclude any possibility of getting at the hull. The bullion, it is believed, was to have been used to further the interests of a certain revolutionary faction, but it seems likely that they will have to look elsewhere for the sinews of war. Besides the bullion the ship also carried several cases of rifles, it is stated, and other valuable cargo. The crew and what few passengers the Boldero carried were, contrary to the first reports, all saved by taking to the boats. It appears that some of the ship's plates were sprung by the stress in which she labored in a storm, and she filled and sank gradually.' There! what do you think of that, dad?" cried Tom as he finished.

"What do I think of it? Why, I think it's too bad for the revolutionists, Tom, of course."

"No; I mean about the treasure being still on board the ship. What about that?"

"Well, it's likely to stay there, if the divers can't get at it. Now, Mr. Sharp, about the propellers—"

"Wait, dad!" cried Tom earnestly.

"Why, Tom, what's the matter?" asked Mr. Swift in some surprise.

"How soon before we can finish our submarine?" went on Tom, not answering the question.

"About a month. Why?"

"Why? Dad, why can't we have a try for that treasure? It ought to be comparatively easy to find that sunken ship off the coast of Uruguay. In our submarine we can get close up to it, and in the new diving suits you invented we can get at that gold bullion. Three hundred thousand dollars! Think of it, dad! Three hundred thousand dollars! We could easily claim all of it, since the owners have abandoned it, but we would be satisfied with half. Let's hurry up, finish the submarine, and have a try for it."

"But, Tom, you forget that I am to enter my new ship in the trials for the prize offered by the United States Government."

"How much is the prize if you win it?" asked Tom.

"Fifty thousand dollars."

"Well, here's a chance to make three times that much at least, and maybe more. Dad, let the Government prize go, and try for the treasure. Will you?"

Tom looked eagerly at his father, his eyes shining with anticipation. Mr. Swift was not a quick thinker, but the idea his son had proposed made an impression on him. He reached out his hand for the paper in which the young inventor had seen the account of the sunken treasure. Slowly he read it through. Then he passed it to Mr. Sharp.

"What do you think of it?" he asked of the aeronaut

"There's a possibility," remarked the balloonist "We might try for it. We can easily go three miles down, and it doesn't lie as deeply as that, if this account is true. Yes, we might try for it. But we'd have to omit the Government contests."

"Will you, dad?" asked Tom again.

Mr. Swift considered a moment longer.

"Yes, Tom, I will," he finally decided. "Going after the treasure will be likely to afford us a better test of the submarine than would any Government tests. We'll try to locate the sunken Boldero."

"Hurrah!" cried the lad, taking the paper from Mr. Sharp and waving it in the air. "That's the stuff! Now for a search for the submarine treasure!"

CHAPTER TWO

FINISHING THE SUBMARINE

"What's the matter?" cried Mrs. Baggert, the housekeeper, hurrying in from the kitchen, where she was washing the dishes. "Have you seen some of those scoundrels who robbed you, Mr. Swift? If you have, the police down here ought to—"

"No, it's nothing like that," explained Mr. Swift. "Tom has merely discovered in the paper an account of a sunken treasure ship, and he wants us to go after it, down under the ocean."

"Oh, dear! Some more of Captain Kidd's hidden hoard, I suppose?" ventured the housekeeper. "Don't you bother with it, Mr. Swift. I had a cousin once, and he got set in the notion that he knew where that pirate's treasure was. He spent all the money he had and all he could borrow digging for it, and he never found a penny. Don't waste your time on such foolishness. It's bad enough to be building airships and submarines without going after treasure." Mrs. Baggert spoke with the freedom of an old friend rather than a hired housekeeper, but she had been in the family ever since Tom's mother died, when he was a baby, and she had many privileges.

"Oh, this isn't any of Kidd's treasure," Tom assured her. "If we get it, Mrs. Baggert, I'll buy you a diamond ring."

"Humph!" she exclaimed, as Tom began to hug her in boyish fashion. "I guess I'll have to buy all the diamond rings I want, if I have to depend on your treasure for them," and she went back to the kitchen.

"Well," went on Mr. Swift after a pause, "if we are going into the treasure-hunting business, Tom, we'll have to get right to work. In the first place, we must find out more about this ship, and just where it was sunk."

"I can do that part," said Mr. Sharp. "I know some sea captains, and they can put me on the track of locating the exact spot. In fact, it might not be a bad idea to take an expert navigator with us. I can manage in the air all right, but I confess that working out a location under water is beyond me."

"Yes, an old sea captain wouldn't be a bad idea, by any means," conceded Mr. Swift. "Well, if you'll attend to that detail, Mr. Sharp, Tom, Mr. Jackson and I will finish the submarine. Most of the work is done, however, and it only remains to install the engine and motors. Now, in regard to the negative and positive electric plates, I'd like your opinion, Tom."

For Tom Swift was an inventor, second in ability only to his father, and his advice was often sought by his parent on matters of electrical construction, for the lad had made a specialty of that branch of science.

While father and son were deep in a discussion of the apparatus of the submarine, there will be an opportunity to make the reader a little better acquainted with them. Those of you who have read the previous volumes of this series do not need to be told who Tom Swift is. Others, however, may be glad to have a proper introduction to him.

Tom Swift lived with his father, Barton Swift, in the village of Shopton, New York. The Swift home was on the outskirts of the town, and the large house was surrounded by a number of machine shops, in which father and son, aided by Garret Jackson, the engineer, did their experimental and constructive work. Their house was not far from Lake Carlopa, a fairly large body of water, on which Tom often speeded his motor-boat.

In the first volume of this series, entitled "Tom Swift and His Motor-Cycle," it was told how be became acquainted with Mr. Wakefield Damon, who suffered an accident while riding one of the speedy machines. The accident disgusted Mr. Damon with motor-cycles, and Tom secured it for a low price. He had many adventures on it, chief among which was being knocked senseless and robbed of a valuable patent model belonging to his father, which he was taking to Albany. The attack was committed by a gang known as the Happy Harry gang, who were acting at the instigation of a syndicate of rich men, who wanted to secure control of a certain patent turbine engine which Mr. Swift had invented.

Tom set out in pursuit of the thieves, after recovering from their attack, and had a strenuous time before he located them.

In the second volume, entitled "Tom Swift and His Motor-Boat," there was related our hero's adventures in a fine craft which was recovered from the thieves and sold at auction. There was a mystery connected with the boat, and for a long time Tom could not solve it. He was aided, however, by his chum, Ned Newton, who worked in the Shopton Bank, and also by Mr. Damon and Eradicate Sampson, an aged colored whitewasher, who formed quite an attachment for Tom.

In his motor-boat Tom had more than one race with Andy Foger, a rich lad of Shopton, who was a sort of bully. He had red hair and squinty eyes, and was as mean in character as he was in looks. He and his cronies, Sam Snedecker and Pete Bailey, made trouble for Tom, chiefly because Tom managed to beat Andy twice in boat races.

It was while in his motor-boat, Arrow, that Tom formed the acquaintance of John Sharp, a veteran balloonist. While coming down Lake Carlopa on the way to the Swift home, which had been entered by thieves, Tom, his father and Ned Newton, saw a balloon on fire over the lake. Hanging from a trapeze on it was Mr. Sharp, who had made an ascension from a fair ground. By hard work on the part of Tom and his friends the aeronaut was saved, and took up his residence with the Swifts.

His advent was most auspicious, for Tom and his father were then engaged in perfecting an airship, and Mr. Sharp was able to lend them his skill, so that the craft was soon constructed.

In the third volume, called "Tom Swift and His Airship," there was set down the doings of the young inventor, Mr. Sharp and Mr. Damon on a trip above the clouds. They undertook it merely for pleasure, but they encountered considerable danger, before they completed it, for they nearly fell into a blazing forest once, and were later fired at by a crowd of excited people. This last act was to effect their capture, for they were taken for a gang of bank robbers, and this was due directly to Andy Foger.

The morning after Tom and his friends started on their trip in the air, the Shopton Bank was found to have been looted of seventy-five thousand dollars. Andy Foger at once told the police that Tom Swift had taken the money, and when asked how he knew this, he said he had seen Tom hanging around the bank the night before the vault was burst open, and that the young inventor had some burglar tools in his possession. Warrants were at once sworn out for Tom and Mr. Damon, who was also accused of being one of the robbers, and a reward of five thousand dollars was offered.

Tom, Mr. Damon and Mr. Sharp sailed on, all unaware of this, and unable to account for being fired upon, until they accidentally read in the paper an account of their supposed misdeeds. They lost no time in starting back home, and on, the way got on the track of the real bank robbers, who were members of the Happy Harry gang.

How the robbers were captured in an exciting raid, how Tom recovered most of the stolen money, and how he gave Andy Foger a deserved thrashing for giving a false clue was told of, and there was an account of a race in which the *Red Cloud* (as the airship was called) took part, as well as details of how Tom and his friends secured the reward, which Andy Foger hoped to collect.

Those of you who care to know how the *Red Cloud* was constructed, and how she behaved in the air, even during accidents and when struck by lightning, may learn by reading the third volume, for the airship was one of the most successful ever constructed.

When the craft was finished, and the navigators were ready to start on their first long trip, Mr. Swift was asked to go with them. He declined, but would not tell why, until Tom, pressing him for an answer, learned that his father was planning a submarine boat, which he hoped to enter in some trials for Government prizes. Mr. Swift remained at home to work on this submarine, while his son and Mr. Sharp were sailing above the clouds.

On their return, however, and after the bank mystery had been cleared up, Tom and Mr. Sharp, aided Mr. Swift in completing the submarine, until, when the present story opens, it needed but little additional work to make the craft ready for the water.

Of course it had to be built near the sea, as it would have been impossible to transport it overland from Shopton. So, before the keel was laid, Mr. Swift rented a large cottage at a seaside place on the New Jersey coast and there, after, erecting a large shed, the work on the *Advance*, as the under-water ship was called, was begun.

It was soon to be launched in a large creek that extended in from the ocean and had plenty of water at high tide. Tom and Mr. Sharp made several trips back and forth from Shopton in their airship, to see that all was safe at home and occasionally to get needed tools and supplies from the shops, for not all the apparatus could be moved from Shopton to the coast.

It was when returning from one of these trips that Tom brought with him the paper containing an account of the wreck of the Boldero and the sinking of the treasure she carried.

Until late that night the three fortune-hunters discussed various matters.

"We'll hurry work on the ship," said Mr. Swift it length. "Tom, I wonder if your friend, Mr. Damon, would care to try how it seems under Water? He stood the air trip fairly well."

"I'll write and ask him," answered the lad. "I'm sure he'll go."

Securing, a few days later, the assistance of two mechanics, whom he knew he could trust, for as yet the construction of the *Advance* was a secret, Mr. Swift prepared to rush work on the submarine, and for the next three weeks there were busy times in the shed next to the seaside cottage. So busy, in fact, were Tom and Mr. Sharp, that they only found opportunity for one trip in the airship, and that was to get some supplies from the shops at home.

"Well," remarked Mr. Swift one night, at the close of a hard day's work, "another week will see our craft completed. Then we will put it in the water and see how it floats, and whether it submerges as I hope it does. But come on, Tom. I want to lock up. I'm very tired tonight."

"All right, dad," answered the young inventor coming from the darkened rear of the shop. "I just want to—"

Ne paused suddenly, and appeared to be listening. Then he moved softly back to where he had come from.

"What's the matter?" asked his father in a whisper. "What's up, Tom?"

The lad did not answer Mr. Swift, with a worried look on his face, followed his son. Mr. Sharp stood in the door of the shop.

"I thought I heard some one moving around back here," went on Tom quietly.

"Some one in this shop!" exclaimed the aged inventor excitedly. "Some one trying to steal my ideas again! Mr. Sharp, come here! Bring that rifle! We'll teach these scoundrels a lesson!"

Tom quickly darted hack to the extreme rear of the building. There was a scuffle, and the next minute Tom cried out:

"What are you doing here?"

"Ha! I beg your pardon," replied a voice. "I am looking for Mr. Barton Swift."

"My father," remarked Tom. "But that's a queer place to look for him. He's up front. Father, here's a man who wishes to see you," he called.

"Yes, I strolled in, and seeing no one about I went to the rear of the place," the voice went on. "I hope I haven't transgressed."

"We were busy on the other side of the shop, I guess," replied Tom, and he looked suspiciously at the man who emerged from the darkness into the light from a window. "I beg your pardon for grabbing you the way I did," went on the lad, "but I thought you were one of a gang of men we've been having trouble with."

"Oh, that's all right," continued the man easily. "I know Mr. Swift, and I think he will remember me. Ah, Mr. Swift, how do you do?" he added quickly, catching sight of Tom's father, who, with Mr. Sharp, was coming to meet the lad.

"Addison Berg!" exclaimed the aged inventor as he saw the man's face more plainly. "What are you doing here?"

"I came to see you," replied the man. "May I have a talk with you privately?"

"I—I suppose so," assented Mr. Swift nervously. "Come into the house."

Mr. Berg left Tom's side and advanced to where Mr. Swift was standing. Together the two emerged from the now fast darkening shop and went toward the house.

"Who is he?" asked Mr. Sharp of the young inventor in a whisper.

"I don't know," replied the lad; "but, whoever he is, dad seems afraid of him. I'm going to keep my eyes open."

CHAPTER THREE

MR. BERG IS ASTONISHED

Following his father and the stranger whom the aged inventor had addressed as Mr. Berg, Tom and Mr. Sharp entered the house, the lad having first made sure that Garret Jackson was on guard in the shop that contained the sub marine.

"Now," said Mr. Swift to the newcomer, "I am at your service. What is it you wish?"

"In the first place, let me apologize for having startled you and your friends," began the man. "I had no idea of sneaking into your workshop, but I had just arrived here, and seeing the doors open I went in. I heard no one about, and I wandered to the back of the place. There I happened to stumble over a board—"

"And I heard you," interrupted Tom.

"Is this one of your employees?" asked Mr. Berg in rather frigid tones.

"That is my son," replied Mr. Swift.

"Oh, I beg your pardon." The man's manner changed quickly. "Well, I guess you did hear me, young man. I didn't intend to hark my shins the way I did, either. You must have taken me for a burglar or a sneak thief."

"I have been very much bothered by a gang of unscrupulous men," said Mr. Swift, "and I suppose Tom thought it was some of them sneaking around again."

"That's what I did," added the lad. "I wasn't going to have any one steal the secret of the submarine if I could help it."

"Quite right! Quite right!" exclaimed Mr. Berg. "But my purpose was an open one. As you know, Mr. Swift, I represent the firm of Bentley & Eagert, builders of submarine boats and torpedoes. They heard that you were constructing a craft to take part in the competitive prize tests of the United States Government, and they asked me to come and see you to learn when your ship would be ready. Ours is completed, but we recognize that it will be for the best interests of all concerned if there are a number of contestants, and my firm did not want to send in their entry until they knew that you were about finished with your ship. How about it? Are you ready to compete?"

"Yes," said Mr. Swift slowly. "We are about ready. My craft needs a few finishing touches, and then it will be ready to launch."

"Then we may expect a good contest on your part," suggested

Mr. Berg.

"Well," began the aged inventor, "I don't know about that."

"What's that?" exclaimed Mr. Berg.

"I said I wasn't quite sure that we would compete," went on Mr. Swift. "You see, when I first got this idea for a submarine boat I had it in mind to try for the Government prize of fifty thousand dollars."

"That's what we want, too," interrupted Mr. Berg with a smile.

"But," went on Tom's father, "since then certain matters have come up, and I think, on the whole, that we'll not compete for the prize after all."

"Not compete for the prize?" almost shouted the agent for Bentley & Eagert. "Why, the idea! You ought to compete. It is good for the trade. We think we have a very fine craft, and probably we would beat you in the tests, but—"

"I wouldn't be too sure of that," put in Tom. "You have only seen the outside of our boat. The inside is better yet."

"Ah, I have no doubt of that," spoke Mr. Berg, "but we have been at the business longer than you have, and have had more experience. Still we welcome competition. But I am very much surprised that you are not going to compete for the prize, Mr. Swift. Very much surprised, indeed! You see, I came down from Philadelphia to arrange so that we could both enter our ships at the same time. I understand there is another firm of submarine boat builders who are going to try for the prize, and I want to arrange a date that will he satisfactory to all. I am greatly astonished that you are not going to compete."

"Well, we were going to," said Mr. Swift, "only we have changed our minds, that's all. My son and I have other plans."

"May I ask what they are?" questioned Mr. Berg.

"You may," exclaimed Tom quickly; "but I don't believe we can tell you. They're a secret," he added more cordially.

"Oh, I see," retorted Mr. Berg. "Well, of course I don't wish to penetrate any of your secrets, but I hoped we could contest together for the Government prize. It is worth trying for I assure you—fifty thousand dollars. Besides, there is the possibility of selling a number of submarines to the United States. It's a fine prize."

"But the one we are after is a bigger one," Cried Tom impetuously, and the moment he had spoken the wished he could recall the words.

"Eh? What's that?" exclaimed Mr. Berg. "You don't mean to say another government has offered a larger prize? If I had known that I would not have let my firm enter into the competition for the bonus offered by the United States. Please tell me."

"I'm sorry," went on Tom more soberly. "I shouldn't have spoken. Mr. Berg, the plans of my father and myself are such that we can't reveal them now. We are going to try for a prize, but not in competition with you. It's an entirely different matter."

"Well, I guess you'll find that the firm of Bentley & Eagert are capable of trying for any prizes that are offered," boasted the agent. "We may be competitors yet."

"I don't believe so," replied Mr. Swift

"We may," repeated Mr. Berg. "And if we do, please remember that we will show no mercy. Our boats are the best."

"And may the best boat win," interjected Mr. Sharp. "That's all we ask. A fair field and no favors."

"Of course," spoke the agent coldly. "Is this another son of yours?" he asked.

"No but a good friend," replied the aged inventor. "No, Mr. Berg, we won't compete this time. You may tell your firm so."

"Very good," was the other's stiff reply. "Then I will bid you good night. We shall carry off the Government prize, but permit me to add that I am very much astonished, very much indeed, that you do not try for the prize. From what I have seen of your submarine you have a very good one, almost as good, in some respects, as ours. I bid you good night," and with a bow the man left the room and hurried away from the house.

CHAPTER FOUR

TOM IS IMPRISONED

"Well, I must say he's a cool one," remarked Tom, as the echoes of Mr. Berg's steps died away. "The idea of thinking his boat better than ours! I don't like that man, dad. I'm suspicious of him. Do you think he came here to steal some of our ideas?"

"No, I hardly believe so, my son. But how did you discover him?"

"Just as you saw, dad. I heard a noise and went back there to investigate. I found him sneaking around, looking at the electric propeller plates. I went to grab him just as he stumbled over a hoard. At first I thought it was one of the old gang. I'm almost sure he was trying to discover something."

"No, Tom. The firm he works for are good business men, and they would not countenance anything like that. They are heartless competitors, however, and if they saw a legitimate chance to get ahead of me and take advantage, they would do it. But they would not sneak in to steal my ideas. I feel sure of that. Besides, they have a certain type of submarine which they think is the best ever invented, and they would hardly change at this late day. They feel sure of winning the Government prize, and I'm just as glad we're not going to have a contest."

"Do you think our boat is better than theirs?"

"Much better, in many respects."

"I don't like that man Berg, though," went on Tom.

"Nor do I," added his father. "There is something strange about him. He was very anxious that I should compete. Probably he thought his firm's boat would go so far ahead of ours that they would get an extra bonus. But I'm glad he didn't see our new method of propulsion. That is the principal improvement in the *Advance* over other types of submarines. Well, another week and we will be ready for the test."

"Have you known Mr. Berg long, dad?"

"Not very. I met him in Washington when I was in the patent office. He was taking out papers on a submarine for his firm at the same time I got mine for the *Advance*. It is rather curious that he should come all the way here from Philadelphia, merely to see if I was going to compete. There is something strange about it, something that I can't understand."

The time was to come when Mr. Swift and his son were to get at the bottom of Mr. Berg's reasons, and they learned to their sorrow that he had penetrated some of their secrets.

Before going to bed that night Tom and Mr. Sharp paid a visit to the shed where the submarine was resting on the ways, ready for launching. They found Mr. Jackson on guard and the engineer said that no one had been around. Nor was anything found disturbed.

"It certainly is a great machine," remarked the lad as he looked up at the cigar-shaped bulk towering over his head. "Dad has outdone himself this trip."

"It looks all right," commented Mr. Sharp. "Whether it will work is another question."

"Yes, we can't tell until it's in the water," con ceded Tom. "But I hope it does. Dad has spent much time and money on it."

The *Advance* was, as her name indicated, much in advance of previous submarines. There was not so much difference in outward construction as there was in the means of propulsion and in the manner in which the interior and the machinery were arranged.

The submarine planned by Mr. Swift and Tom jointly, and constructed by them, with the aid of Mr. Sharp and Mr. Jackson, was shaped like a Cigar, over one hundred feet long and twenty feet in diameter at the thickest part. It was divided into many compartments, all water-tight, so that if one or even three were flooded the ship would still be useable.

Buoyancy was provided for by having several tanks for the introduction of compressed air, and there was an emergency arrangement so that a collapsible aluminum container could be distended and filled with a powerful gas. This was to be used if, by any means, the ship was disabled on the bottom of the ocean. The container could be expanded and filled, and would send the *Advance* to the surface.

Another peculiar feature was that the engine-room, dynamos and other apparatus were all contained amidships. This gave stability to the craft, and also enabled the same engine to operate both shafts and propellers, as well as both the negative forward electrical plates, and the positive rear ones.

These plates were a new idea in submarine construction, and were the outcome of an idea of Mr. Swift, with some suggestions from his son.

The aged inventor did not want to depend on the usual screw propellers for his craft, nor did he want to use a jet of compressed air, shooting out from a rear tube, nor yet a jet of water, by means of which the creature called the squid shoots himself along. Mr. Swift planned to send the *Advance* along under water by means of electricity.

Certain peculiar plates were built at the forward and aft blunt noses of the submarine. Into the forward plate a negative charge of electricity was sent, and into the one at the rear a positive charge, just as one end of a horseshoe magnet is positive and will repel the north end of a compass needle, while the other pole of a magnet is negative and will attract it. In electricity like repels like, while negative and positive have a mutual attraction for each other.

Mr. Swift figured out that if he could send a powerful current of negative electricity into the forward plate it would pull the boat along, for water is a good conductor of electricity, while if a positive charge was sent into the rear plate it would serve to push the submarine along, and he would thus get a pulling and pushing motion, just as a forward and aft propeller works on some ferry boats.

But the inventor did not depend on these plates alone. There were auxiliary forward and aft propellers of the regular type, so that if the electrical plates did not work, or got out of order, the screws would serve to send the *Advance* along.

There was much machinery in the submarine There were gasolene motors, since space was too cramped to allow the carrying of coal for boilers. There were dynamos, motors and powerful pumps. Some of these were for air, and some for water. To sink the submarine below the surface large tanks were filled with water. To insure a more sudden descent, deflecting rudders were also used, similar to those on an airship. There were also special air pumps, and one for the powerful gas, which was manufactured on board.

Forward from the engine-room was a cabin, where meals could be served, and where the travelers could remain in the daytime. There was also a small cooking galley, or kitchen, there. Back of the engine-room were the sleeping quarters and the storerooms. The submarine was steered from the forward compartment, and here were also levers, wheels and valves that controlled all the machinery, while a number of dials showed in which direction they were going, how deep they were, and at what speed they were moving, as well as what the ocean pressure was.

On top, forward, was a small conning, or observation tower, with auxiliary and steering and controlling apparatus there. This was to be used when the ship was moving along on the surface of the ocean, or merely with the deck awash. There was a small flat deck surrounding the conning tower and this was available when the craft was on the surface.

There was provision made for leaving the ship when it was on the bed of the ocean. When it was desired to do this the occupants put on diving suits, which were provided with portable oxygen tanks. Then they entered a chamber into which water was admitted until it was equal in pressure to that outside. Then a steel door was opened, and they could step out. To re-enter the ship the operation was reversed. This was not a new feature. In fact, many submarines today use it.

At certain places there were thick bull's-eye windows, by means of which the under-water travelers could look out into the ocean through which they were moving. As a defense against the attacks of submarine monsters there was a steel, pointed ram, like a big harpoon. There were also a bow and a stern electrical gun, of which more will be told later.

In addition to ample sleeping accommodations, there were many conveniences aboard the *Advance*. Plenty of fresh water could be carried, and there was an apparatus for distilling more from the sea water that surrounded the travelers. Compressed air was carried in large tanks, and oxygen could be made as needed. In short, nothing that could add to the comfort or safety of the travelers had been omitted. There was a powerful crane and windlass, which had been installed when Mr. Swift thought his boat might be bought by the Government. This was to be used for raising wrecks or recovering objects from the bottom of the ocean. Ample stores and provisions were to be carried and, once the travelers were shut up in the *Advance*, they could exist for a month below the surface, providing no accident occurred.

All these things Tom and Mr. Sharp thought of as they looked over the ship before turning in for the night. The craft was made immensely strong to withstand powerful pressure at the bottom of the ocean. The submarine could penetrate to a depth of about three miles. Below that it was dangerous to go, as the awful force would crush the plates, powerful as they were.

"Well, we'll rush things tomorrow and the next day," observed Tom as he prepared to leave the building. "Then we'll soon see if it works."

For the next week there were busy times in the shop near the ocean. Great secrecy was maintained, and though curiosity seekers did stroll along now and then, they received little satisfaction. At first Mr. Swift thought that the visit of Mr. Berg would have unpleasant results, for he feared that the agent would talk about the craft, of which he had so unexpectedly gotten a sight. But nothing seemed to follow from his chance inspection, and it was forgotten.

It was one evening, about a week later, that Tom was alone in the shop. The two mechanics that had been hired to help out in the rush had been let go, and the ship needed but a few adjustments to make it ready for the sea.

"I think I'll just take another look at the water tank valves," said Tom to himself as he prepared to enter the big compartments which received the water ballast. "I want to be sure they work properly and quickly. We've got to depend on them to make us sink when we want to, and, what's more important, to rise to the surface in a hurry. I've got time enough to look them over before dad and Mr. Sharp get back."

Tom entered the starboard tank by means of an emergency sliding door between the big compartments and the main part of the ship. This was closed by a worm and screw gear, and once the ship was in the water would seldom be used.

The young inventor proceeded with his task, carefully inspecting the valves by the light of a lantern he carried. The apparatus seemed to be all right, and Tom was about to leave when a peculiar noise attracted his attention. It was the sound of metal scraping on metal, and the lad's quick and well-trained ear told him it was somewhere about the ship.

He turned to leave the tank, but as he wheeled around his light flashed on a solid wall of steel back of him. The emergency outlet had been closed! He was a prisoner in the water compartment, and he knew, from past experience, that shout as he would, his voice could not be heard ten feet away. His father and Mr. Sharp, as he was aware, had gone to a nearby city for some tools, and Mr. Jackson, the engineer, was temporarily away. Mrs. Baggert, in the house, could not hear his cries.

"I'm locked in!" cried Tom aloud. "The worm gear must have shut of itself. But I don't see how that could be. I've got to get out mighty soon, though, or I'll smother. This tank is airtight, and it won't take me long to breath up all the oxygen there is here. I must get that slide open."

He sought to grasp the steel plate that closed the emergency opening. His fingers slipped over the smooth, polished surface. He was hermetically sealed up—a captive! Blankly he set his lantern down and leaned hopelessly against the wall of the tank.

"I've got to get out," he murmured.

As if in answer to him he heard a voice on the outside, crying:

"There, Tom Swift! I guess I've gotten even with you now! Maybe next time you won't take a reward away from me, and lick me into the bargain. I've got you shut up good and tight, and you'll stay there until I get ready to let you out."

"Andy Foger!" gasped Tom. "Andy Foger sneaked in here and

turned the gear. But how did he get to this part of the coast? Andy Foger, you let me out!" shouted the young inventor; and as Andy's mocking laugh came to him faintly through the steel sides of the submarine, the imprisoned lad beat desperately with his hands on the smooth sides of the tank, vainly wondering how his enemy had discovered him.

CHAPTER FIVE

MR. BERG IS SUSPICIOUS

Not for long did the young inventor endeavor to break his way out of the water-ballast tank by striking the heavy sides of it. Tom realized that this was worse than useless. He listened intently, but could hear nothing. Even the retreating footsteps of Andy Foger were inaudible.

"This certainly is a pickle!" exclaimed Tom aloud. "I can't understand how he ever got here. He must have traced us after we went to Shopton in the airship the last time. Then he sneaked in here. Probably he saw me enter, but how could he knew enough to work the worm gear and close the door? Andy has had some experience with machinery, though, and one of the vaults in the bank where his father is a director closed just like this tank. That's very likely how he learned about it. But I've got to do something else besides thinking of that sneak, Andy. I've got to get out of here. Let's see if I can work the gear from inside."

Before he started, almost, Tom knew that it would be impossible. The tank was made to close from the interior of the submarine, and the heavy door, built to withstand the pressure of tons of water, could not be forced except by the proper means.

"No use trying that," concluded the lad, after a tiring attempt to force back the sliding door with his hands. "I've got to call for help."

He shouted until the vibrations in the confined space made his ears ring, and the mere exertion of raising his voice to the highest pitch made his heart beat quickly. Yet there came no response. He hardly expected that there would be any, for with his father and Mr. Sharp away, the engineer absent on an errand, and Mrs. Baggert in the house some distance off, there was no one to hear his calls for help, even if they had been capable of penetrating farther than the extent of the shed, where the under-water craft had been constructed.

"I've got to wait until some of them come out here," thought Tom. "They'll be sure to release me and make a search. Then it will be easy enough to call to them and tell them where I am, once they are inside the shed. But—" He paused, for a horrible fear came over him. "Suppose they should come—too late?" The tank was airtight. There was enough air in it to last for some time, but, sooner or later, it would no longer support life. Already, Tom thought, it seemed oppressive, though probably that was his imagination.

"I must get out!" he repeated frantically. "I'll die in here soon."

Again he tried to shove back the steel door. Then he repeated his cries until be was weary. No one answered him. He fancied once he could hear footsteps in the shed, and thought, perhaps, it was Andy, come back to gloat over him. Then Tom knew the red-haired coward would not dare venture back. We must do Andy the justice to say that he never realized that he was endangering Tom's life. The bully had no idea the tank was airtight when he closed it. He had seen Tom enter and a sudden whim came to him to revenge himself.

But that did not help the young inventor any. There was no doubt about it now—the air was becoming close. Tom had been imprisoned nearly two hours, and as he was a healthy, strong lad, he required plenty of oxygen. There was certainly less than there had been in the tank. His head began to buzz, and there was a ringing in his ears.

Once more he fell upon his knees, and his fingers sought the small projections of the gear on the inside of the door He could no more budge the mechanism than a child could open a burglar-proof vault.

"It's no use," he moaned, and he sprawled at full length on the floor of the tank, for there the air was purer. As he did so his fingers touched something. He started as they closed around the handle of a big monkey wrench. It was one he had brought into the place with him. Imbued with new hope be struck a match and lighted his lantern, which he had allowed to go out as it burned up too much of the oxygen. By the gleam of it he looked to see if there were any bolts or nuts he could loosen with the wrench, in order to slide the door back. It needed but a glance to show him the futility of this.

"It's no go," he murmured, and he let the wrench fall to the floor. There was a ringing, clanging sound, and as it smote his ears Tom sprang up with an exclamation.

"That's the thing!" he cried. "I wonder I didn't think of it before. I can signal for help by pounding on the sides of the tank with the wrench. The blows will carry a good deal farther than my voice would." Every one knows how far the noise of a boiler shop, with hammers falling on steel plates, can be heard; much farther than can a human voice.

Tom began a lusty tattoo on the metal sides of the tank. At first he merely rattled out blow after blow, and then, as another thought came to him, he adopted a certain plan. Some time previous, when he and Mr. Sharp had planned their trip in the air, the two had adopted a code of signals. As it was difficult in a high wind to shout from one end of the airship to the other, the young inventor would sometimes pound on the pipe which ran from the pilot house of the *Red Cloud* to the engine-room. By a combination of numbers, simple messages could be conveyed. The code included a call for help. Forty-seven was the number, but there had never been any occasion to use it.

Tom remembered this now. At once he ceased his indiscriminate hammering, and began to beat out regularly— one, two, three, four—then a pause, and seven blows would be given. Over and over again he rang out this number—forty seven—the call for help.

"If Mr. Sharp only comes back he will hear that, even in the house," thought poor Tom "Maybe Garret or Mrs. Baggert will hear it, too, but they won't know what it means. They'll think I'm just working on the submarine."

It seemed several hours to Tom that he pounded out that cry for aid, but, as he afterward learned, it was only a little over an hour. Signal after signal he sent vibrating from the steel sides of the tank. When one arm tired he would use the other. He grew weary, his head was aching, and there was a ringing in his ears; a ringing that seemed as if ten thousand bells were jangling out their peals, and he could barely distinguish his own pounding.

Signal after signal he sounded. It was becoming like a dream to him, when suddenly, as he paused for a rest, he heard his name called faintly, as if far away.

"Tom! Tom! Where are you?"

It was the voice of Mr. Sharp. Then followed the tones of the aged inventor.

"My poor boy! Tom, are you still alive?"

"Yes, dad! In the starboard tank!" the lad gasped out, and then he lost his senses. When he revived he was lying on a pile of bagging in the submarine shop, and his father and the aeronaut were bending over him.

"Are you all right, Tom?" asked Mr. Swift.

"Yes—I—I guess so," was the hesitating answer. "Yes," the lad added, as the fresh air cleared his head. "I'll be all right pretty soon. Have you seen Andy Foger?"

"Did he shut you in there?" demanded Mr. Swift.

Tom nodded.

"I'll have him arrested!" declared Mr. Swift "I'll go to town as soon as you're in good shape again and notify the police."

"No, don't," pleaded Tom. "I'll take care of Andy myself. I don't really believe he knew how serious it was. I'll settle with him later, though."

"Well, it came mighty near being serious," remarked Mr. Sharp grimly. "Your father and I came back a little sooner than we expected, and as soon as I got near the house I heard your signal. I knew what it was in a moment. There were Mrs. Baggert and Garret talking away, and when I asked them why they didn't answer your call they said they thought you were merely tinkering with the machinery. But I knew better. It's the first time we ever had a use for 'forty-seven,' Tom."

"And I hope it will be the last," replied the young inventor with a faint smile. "But I'd like to know what Andy Foger is doing in this neighborhood."

Tom was soon himself again and able to go to the house, where he found Mrs. Baggert brewing a big basin of catnip tea, under the impression that it would in some way be good for his. She could not forgive herself for not having answered his signal, and as for Mr. Jackson, he had started for a doctor as soon as he learned that Tom was shut up in the tank. The services of the medical man were canceled by telephone, as there was no need for him, and the engineer came back to the house.

Tom was fully himself the next day, and aided his father and Mr. Sharp in putting the finishing touches to the *Advance*. It was found that some alteration was required in the auxiliary propellers, and this, much to the regret of the young inventor, would necessitate postponing the trial a few days.

"But we'll have her in the water next Friday." promised Mr. Swift.

"Aren't you superstitious about Friday?" asked the balloonist.

"Not a bit of it," replied the aged inventor. "Tom," he added, "I wish you would go in the house and get me the roll of blueprints you'll find on my desk."

As the lad neared the cottage he saw, standing in front of the place, a small automobile. A man had just descended from it, and it needed but a glance to show that he was Mr. Addison Berg.

"Ah, good morning, Mr. Swift," greeted Mr. Berg. "I wish to see your father, but as I don't wish to lay myself open to suspicions by entering the shop, perhaps you will ask him to step here."

"Certainly," answered the lad, wondering why the agent had returned. Getting the blueprints, and asking Mr. Berg to sit down on the porch, Tom delivered the message.

"You come back with me, Tom," said his father. "I want you to be a witness to what he says. I'm not going to get into trouble with these people."

Mr. Berg came to the point at once.

"Mr. Swift," he said, "I wish you would reconsider your determination not to enter the Government trials. I'd like to see you compete. So would my firm."

"There is no use going over that again," replied the aged inventor. "I have another object in view now than trying for the Government prize. What it is I can't say, but it may develop in time—if we are successful," and he looked at his son, smiling the while.

Mr. Berg tried to argue, but it was of no avail Then he changed his manner, and said:

"Well, since you won't, you won't, I suppose. I'll go back and report to my firm. Have you anything special to do this morning?" he went on to Tom.

"Well, I can always find something to keep me busy," replied the lad, "but as for anything special—"

"I thought perhaps you'd like to go for a trip in my auto," interrupted Mr. Berg. "I had asked a young man who is stopping at the same hotel where I am to accompany me, but he has unexpectedly left, and I don't like to go alone. His name was—let me see. I have a wretched memory for names, but it was something like Roger or Moger."

"Foger!" cried Tom. "Was it Andy Foger?"

"Yes, that was it. Why, do you know him?" asked Mr. Berg in some surprise.

"I should say so," replied Tom. "He was the cause of what might have resulted in something serious for me," and the lad explained about being imprisoned in the tank.

"You don't tell me!" cried Mr. Berg. "I had no idea he was that kind of a lad. You see, his father is one of the directors of the firm by whom I am employed. Andy came from home to spend a few weeks at the seaside, and stopped at the same hotel that I did. He went off yesterday afternoon, and I haven't seen him since, though he promised to go for a ride with me. He must have come over here and entered your shop unobserved. I remember now he asked me where the submarine was being built that was going to compete with our firm's, and I told him. I didn't think he was that kind of a lad. Well, since he's probably gone back home, perhaps you will come for a ride with me, Tom."

"I'm afraid I can't go, thank you," answered the lad. "We are very busy getting our submarine in shape for a trial. But I can imagine why Andy left so hurriedly. He probably learned that a doctor had been summoned for me, though, as it happened, I didn't need one. But Andy probably got frightened at what he had done, and left. I'll make him more sorry, when I meet him."

"Don't blame you a bit," commented Mr. Berg. "Well, I must be getting back."

He hastened out to his auto, while Tom and his father watched the agent.

"Tom, never trust that man," advised the aged inventor solemnly.

"Just what I was about to remark," said his son. "Well, let's get back to work. Queer that he should come here again, and it's queer about Andy Foger."

Father and son returned to the machine shop, while Mr. Berg puffed away in his auto. A little later, Tom having occasion to go to a building near the boundary line of the cottage property which his father had hired for the season, saw, through the hedge that bordered it, an automobile standing in the road. A second glance showed him that it was Mr. Berg's machine. Something had gone wrong with it, and the agent had alighted to make an adjustment.

The young inventor was close to the man, though the latter was unaware of his presence.

"Hang it all!" Tom heard Mr. Berg exclaim to himself. "I wonder what they can be up to? They won't enter the Government contests, and they won't say why. I believe they're up to some game, and I've got to find out what it is. I wonder if I couldn't use this Foger chap?"

"He seems to have it in for this Tom Swift," Mr. Berg went on, still talking to himself, though not so low but that Tom could hear him. "I think I'll try it. I'll get Andy Foger to sneak around and find out what the game is. He'll do it, I know."

By this time the auto was in working order again, and the agent took his seat and started off.

"So that's how matters lie, eh?" thought Tom. "Well, Mr. Berg, we'll be doubly on the lookout for you after this. As for Andy Foger, I think I'll make him wish he'd never locked me in that tank. So you expect to find out our 'game,' eh, Mr. Berg? Well, when you do know it, I think it will astonish you. I only hope you don't learn what it is until we get at that sunken treasure, though."

But alas for Tom's hopes. Mr. Berg did learn of the object of the treasure-seekers, and sought to defeat them, as we shall learn as our story proceeds.

CHAPTER SIX

TURNING THE TABLES

When the young inventor informed his father what he had overheard Mr. Berg saying, the aged inventor was not as much worried as his son anticipated.

"All we'll have to do, Tom," he said, "is to keep quiet about where we are going. Once we have the *Advance* afloat, and try her out, we can start on our voyage for the South American Coast and search for the sunken treasure. When we begin our voyage under water I defy any one to tell where we are going, or what our plans are. No, I don't believe we need worry about Mr. Berg, though he probably means mischief."

"Well, I'm going to keep my eyes open for him and Andy Foger," declared Tom.

The days that followed were filled with work. Not only were there many unexpected things to do about the submarine, but Mr. Sharp was kept busy making inquiries about the sunken treasure ship. These inquiries had to be made carefully, as the adventurers did not want their plans talked of, and nothing circulates more quickly than rumors of an expedition after treasure of any kind.

"What about the old sea captain you were going to get to go with us?" asked Mr. Swift of the balloonist one afternoon. "Have you succeeded in finding one yet?"

"Yes; I am in communication with a man think will be just the person for us. His name is Captain Alden Weston, and he has sailed all over the world. He has also taken part in more than one revolution, and, in fact, is a soldier of fortune. I do not know him personally, but a friend of mine knows him, and says he will serve us faithfully. I have written to him, and he will he here in a few days."

"That's good. Now about the location of the wreck itself. Have you been able to learn any more details?"

"Well, not many. You see, the Boldero was abandoned in a storm, and the captain did not take very careful observations. As nearly as it can be figured out the treasure ship went to the bottom in latitude forty-five degrees south, and longitude twenty-seven east from Washington. That's a pretty indefinite location, but I hope, once we get off the Uruguay coast, we can better it. We can anchor or lay outside the harbor, and in the small boat we carry go ashore and possibly gain more details. For it was at Montevideo that the shipwrecked passengers and sailors landed."

"Does Captain Weston know our object?" inquired Tom.

"No, and I don't propose to tell him until we are ready to start," replied Mr. Sharp. "I don't know just how he'll consider a submarine trip after treasure, but if I spring it on him suddenly he's less likely to back out. Oh, I think he'll go."

Somewhat unexpectedly the next day it was discovered that certain tools and appliances were needed for the submarine, and they had been left in the house at Shopton, where Eradicate Sampson was in charge as caretaker during the absence of Mr. Swift and his son and the housekeeper.

"Well, I suppose we'll have to go back after them," remarked Tom. "We'll take the airship, dad, and make a two-days' trip of it. Is there anything else you want?"

"Well, you might bring a bundle of papers you'll find in the lower right hand drawer of my desk. They contain some memoranda I need."

Tom and Mr. Sharp had become so used to traveling in the airship that it seemed no novelty to them, though they attracted much attention wherever they went. They soon had the *Red Cloud* in readiness for a flight, and rising in the air above the shop that contained the powerful submarine, a craft utterly different in type from the aeroplane, the nose of the airship was pointed toward Shopton.

They made a good flight and landed near the big shed where the bird of the air was kept. It was early evening when they got to the Swift homestead, and Eradicate Sampson was glad to see them.

Eradicate was a good cook, and soon had a meal ready for the travelers. Then, while Mr. Sharp selected the tools and other things needed, and put them in the airship ready for the start back the next morning, Tom concluded he would take a stroll into Shopton, to see if he could see his friend, Ned Newton. It was early evening, and the close of a beautiful day, a sharp shower in the morning having cooled the air.

Tom was greeted by a number of acquaintances as he strolled along, for, since the episode of the bank robbery, when he had so unexpectedly returned with the thieves and the cash, the lad was better known than ever.

"I guess Ned must be home" thought our hero as he looked in vain for his chum among the throng on the streets. "I've got time to take a stroll down to his house."

Tom was about to cross the street when he was startled by the sound of an automobile horn loudly blown just at his side. Then a voice called:

"Hey, there! Git out of the way if you don't want to be run over!"

He looked up, and saw a car careening along. At the wheel was the red-haired bully, Andy Foger, and in the tonneau were Sam Snedecker and Pete Bailey.

"Git out of the way," added Sam, and he grinned maliciously at Tom.

The latter stepped back, well out of the path of the car, which was not moving very fast. Just in front of Tom was a puddle of muddy water. There was no necessity for Andy steering into it, but he saw his opportunity, and a moment later one of the big pneumatic tires had plunged into the dirty fluid, spattering it all over Tom, some even going as high as his face.

"Ha! ha!" laughed Andy. "Maybe you'll get out of my way next time, Tom Swift."

The young inventor was almost speechless from righteous anger. He wiped the mud from his face, glanced down at his clothes, which were all but ruined, and called out:

"Hold on there, Andy Foger! I want to see you!" for he thought of the time when Andy had shut him in the tank.

"Ta! ta!" shouted Pete Bailey.

"See you later," added Sam.

"Better go home and take a bath, and then sail away in your submarine," went on Andy. "I'll bet it will sink."

Before Tom could reply the auto had turned a corner. Disgusted and angry, he tried to sop up some of the muddy water with his handkerchief. While thus engaged he heard his name called, and looked up to see Ned Newton.

"What's the matter? Fall down?" asked his chum.

"Andy Foger," replied Tom.

"That's enough," retorted Ned. "I can guess the rest. We'll have to tar and feather him some day, and ride him out of town on a rail. I'd kick him myself, only his father is a director in the bank where I work, and I'd be fired if I did. Can't afford any such pleasure. But some day I'll give Andy a good trouncing, and then resign before they can discharge me. But I'll be looking for another job before I do that. Come on to my house, Tom, and I'll help you clean up."

Tom was a little more presentable when he left his chum's residence, after spending the evening there, but he was still burning for revenge against Andy and his cronies. He had half a notion to go to Andy's house and tell Mr. Foger how nearly serious the bully's prank at the sub marine had been, but be concluded that Mr. Foger could only uphold his son. "No, I'll settle with him myself," decided Tom.

Bidding Eradicate keep a watchful eye about the house, and

leaving word for Mr. Damon to be sure to come to the coast if he again called at the Shopton house, Tom and Mr. Sharp prepared to make their return trip early the next morning.

The gas tank was filled and the *Red Cloud* arose in the air. Then, with the propellers moving at moderate speed, the nose of the craft was pointed toward the New Jersey coast.

A few miles out from Shopton, finding there was a contrary wind in the upper regions where they were traveling, Mr. Sharp descended several hundred feet. They were moving over a sparsely settled part of the country, and looking down, Tom saw, speeding along a highway, an automobile.

"I wonder who's in it?" he remarked, taking down a telescope and peering over the window ledge of the cabin. The next moment he uttered a startled exclamation.

"Andy Foger, Sam Snedecker and Pete Bailey!" he cried. "Oh, I wish I had a bucket of water to empty on them."

"I know a better way to get even with them than that," said Mr. Sharp.

"How?" asked Tom eagerly.

"I'll show you," replied the balloonist. "It's a trick I once played on a fellow who did me an injury. Here, you steer for a minute until I get the thing fixed, then I'll take charge."

Mr. Sharp went to the storeroom and came back with a long, stout rope and a small anchor of four prongs. It was carried to be used in emergencies, but so far had never been called into requisition. Fastening the grapple to the cable, the balloonist said:

"Now, Tom, they haven't seen you. You stand in the stern and pay out the rope. I'll steer the airship, and what I want you to do is to catch the anchor in the rear of their car. Then I'll show you some fun."

Tom followed instructions. Slowly he lowered the rope with the dangling grapple. The airship was also sent down, as the cable was not quite long enough to reach the earth from the height at which they were. The engine was run at slow speed, so that the noise would not attract the attention of the three cronies who were speeding along, all unconscious of the craft in the air over their heads. The *Red Cloud* was moving in the same direction as was the automobile.

The anchor was now close to the rear of Andy's car. Suddenly it caught on the tonneau and Tom called that fact to Mr. Sharp.

"Fasten the rope at the cleat," directed the balloonist.

Tom did so, and a moment later the aeronaut sent the airship up by turning more gas into the container. At the same time he reversed the engine and the *Red Cloud* began pulling the touring car backward, also lifting the rear wheels clear from the earth.

A startled cry from the occupants of the machine told Tom and his friend that Andy and his cronies were aware something was wrong. A moment later Andy, looking up, saw the airship hovering in the air above him. Then he saw the rope fast to his auto. The airship was not rising now, or the auto would have been turned over, but it was slowly pulling it backward, in spite of the fact that the motor of the car was still going.

"Here! You let go of me!" cried Andy. "I'll have you arrested if you damage my car."

"Come up here and cut the rope." called Tom leaning over and looking down. He could enjoy the bully's discomfiture. As for Sam and Pete, they were much frightened, and cowered down on the floor of the tonneau.

"Maybe you'll shut me in the tank again and splash mud on me!" shouted Tom.

The rear wheels of the auto were lifted still higher from the ground, as Mr. Sharp turned on a little more gas. Andy was not proof against this.

"Oh! oh!" he cried. "Please let me down, Tom. I'm awful sorry for what I did! I'll never do it again! Please, please let me down! Don't You'll tip me over!"

He had shut off his motor now, and was frantically clinging to the steering wheel.

"Do you admit that you're a sneak and a coward?" asked Tom, "rubbing it in."

"Yes, yes! Oh, please let me down!"

"Shall we?" asked Tom of Mr. Sharp.

"Yes," replied the balloonist. "We can afford to lose the rope and anchor for the sake of turning the tables. Cut the cable."

Tom saw what was intended. Using a little hatchet, he severed the rope with a single blow. With a crash that could be heard up in the air where the *Red Cloud* hovered, the rear wheels of the auto dropped to the ground. Then came two loud reports.

"Both tires busted!" commented Mr. Sharp dryly, and Tom, looking down, saw the trio of lads ruefully contemplating the collapsed rubber of the rear wheels. The tables had been effectually turned on Andy Foger. His auto was disabled, and the airship, with a graceful sweep, mounted higher and higher, continuing on its way to the coast.

CHAPTER SEVEN

MR. DAMON WILL GO

"Well, I guess they've had their lesson," remarked Tom, as he took an observation through the telescope and saw Andy and his cronies hard at work trying to repair the ruptured tires. "That certainly was a corking good trick."

"Yes," admitted Mr. Sharp modestly. "I once did something similar, only it was a horse and wagon instead of an auto. But let's try for another speed record. The conditions are just right."

They arrived at the coast much sooner than they had dared to hope, the *Red Cloud* proving herself a veritable wonder.

The remainder of that day, and part of the next, was spent in working on the submarine.

"We'll launch her day after tomorrow," declared Mr. Swift enthusiastically. "Then to see whether my calculations are right or wrong."

"It won't be your fault if it doesn't work," said his son. "You certainly have done your best."

"And so have you and Mr. Sharp and the others, for that matter. Well, I have no doubt but that everything will be all right, Tom."

"There!" exclaimed Mr. Sharp the next morning, as he was adjusting a certain gage. "I knew I'd forget something. That special brand of lubricating oil. I meant to bring it from Shopton, and I didn't."

"Maybe I can get it in Atlantis," suggested Tom, naming the coast city nearest to them. "I'll take a walk over. It isn't far."

"Will you? I'll be glad to have you," resumed the balloonist. "A gallon will be all we'll need."

Tom was soon on his way. He had to walk, as the roads were too poor to permit him to use the motor-cycle, and the airship attracted too much attention to use on a short trip. He was strolling along, when from the other side of a row of sand dunes, that lined the uncertain road to Atlantis, he heard some one speaking. At first the tones were not distinct, but as the lad drew nearer to the voice he heard an exclamation.

"Bless my gold-headed cane! I believe I'm lost. He said it was out this way somewhere, bet I don't see anything of it. If I had that Eradicate Sampson here now I'd—bless my shoelaces I don't know what I would do to him."

"Mr. Damon! Mr. Damon!" cried Tom. "Is that you?"

"Me? Of course it's me! Who else would it be?" answered the voice. "But who are you. Why, bless my liver! If it isn't Tom Swift!" he cried. "Oh, but I'm glad to see you! I was afraid I was ship-wrecked! Bless my gaiters, how are you, anyhow? How is your father? How is Mr. Sharp, and all the rest of them?"

"Pretty well. And you?"

"Me? Oh, I'm all right; only a trifle nervous. I called at your house in Shopton yesterday, and Eradicate told me, as well as he could, where you were located. I had nothing to do, so I thought I'd take a run down here. But what's this I hear about you? Are you going on a voyage?"

"Yes."

"In the air? May I go along again? I certainly enjoyed my other trip in the *Red Cloud*. What is, all but the fire and being shot at. May I go?"

"We're going on a different sort of trip this time," said the youth.

"Where?"

"Under water."

"Under water? Bless my sponge bath! You don't mean it!"

"Yes. Dad has completed the submarine he was working on when we were off in the airship, and it will be launched the day after tomorrow."

"Oh, that's so. I'd forgotten about it. He's going to try for the Government prize, isn't he? But tell me more about it. Bless my scarf-pin, but I'm glad I met you! Going into town, I take it. Well, I just came from there, but I'll walk back with you. Do you think—is there any possibility—that I could go with you? Of course, I don't want to crowd you, but—"

"Oh, there'll be plenty of room," replied the young inventor. "In fact, more room than we had in the airship. We were talking only the other day about the possibility of you going with us, but we didn't think you'd risk it."

"Risk it? Bless my liver! Of course I'll risk' it! It can't be as bad as sailing in the air. You can't fall, that's certain."

"No; but maybe you can't rise," remarked Tom grimly.

"Oh, we won't think of that. Of course, I'd like to go. I fully expected to be killed in the *Red Cloud*, but as I wasn't I'm ready to take a chance in the water. On the whole, I think I prefer to be buried at sea, anyhow. Now, then, will you take me?"

"I think I can safely promise," answered Tom with a smile at his friend's enthusiasm.

The two were approaching the city, having walked along as they talked. There were still some sand dunes near the road, and they kept on the side of these, nearest the beach, where they could watch the breakers.

"But you haven't told me where you are going," went on Mr. Damon, after blessing a few dozen objects. "Where do the Government trials take place?"

"Well," replied the lad, "to be frank with you, we have abandoned our intention of trying for the Government prize."

"Not going to try for it? Bless my slippers! Why not? Isn't fifty thousand dollars worth striving for? And, with the kind of a submarine you say you have, you ought to be able to win."

"Yes, probably we could win," admitted the young inventor, "but we are going to try for a better prize."

"A better one? I don't understand."

"Sunken treasure," explained Tom. "There's a ship sunk off the coast of Uruguay, with three hundred thousand dollars in gold bullion aboard. Dad and I are going to try to recover that in our submarine. We're going to start day after tomorrow, and, if you like, you may go along."

"Go along! Of course I'll go along!" cried the eccentric man. "But I never heard of such a thing. Sunken treasure! Three hundred thousand dollars in gold! My, what a lot of money! And to go after it in a submarine! It's as good as a story!"

"Yes, we hope to recover all the treasure," said the lad. "We ought to be able to claim at least half of it."

"Bless my pocketbook!" cried Mr. Damon, but Tom did not hear him. At that instant his attention was attracted by seeing two men emerge from behind the sand dune near which he and Mr. Damon had halted momentarily, when the youth explained about the treasure. The man looked sharply at Tom. A moment later the first man was joined by another, and at the sight of him our hero could not repress an exclamation of alarm. For the second man was none other than Addison Berg.

The latter glanced quickly at Tom, and then, with a hasty word to his companion, the two swung around and made off in the opposite direction to that in which they had been walking.

"What's the matter?" asked Mr. Damon, seeing the young inventor was strangely affected.

"That—that man," stammered the lad.

"You don't mean to tell me that was one the Happy Harry gang, do you?"

"No. But one, or both of those men, may prove to be worse. That second man was Addison Berg, and he's agent for a firm of submarine boat builders who are rivals of dad's. Berg has been trying to find out why we abandoned our intention of competing for the Government prize."

"I hope you didn't tell him."

"I didn't intend to," replied Tom, smiling grimly, "but I'm afraid I have, however He certainly overheard what I said. I spoke too loud. Yes, he must have heard me. That's why he hurried off so."

"Possibly no harm is done. You didn't give the location of the sunken ship."

"No; but I guess from what I said it will be easy enough to find. Well, if we're going to have a fight for the possession of that sunken gold, I'm ready for it. The *Advance* is well equipped for a battle. I must tell dad of this. It's my fault."

"And partly mine, for asking you such leading questions in a public place," declared Mr. Damon. "Bless my coat-tails, but I'm sorry! Maybe, after all, those men were so interested in what they themselves were saying that they didn't understand what you said."

But if there had been any doubts on this score they would have been dissolved had Tom and his friend been able to see the actions of Mr. Berg and his companion a little later. The plans of the treasure-hunters had been revealed to their ears.

CHAPTER EIGHT

ANOTHER TREASURE EXPEDITION

While Tom and Mr. Damon continued on to Atlantis after the oil, the young inventor lamenting from time to time that his remarks about the real destination of the *Advance* had been overheard by Mr. Berg, the latter and his companion were hastening back along the path that ran on one side of the sand dunes.

"What's your hurry?" asked Mr. Maxwell, who was with the submarine agent. "You turned around as if you were shot when you saw that man and the lad. There didn't appear to be any cause for such a hurry. From what I could hear they were talking about a submarine. You're in the same business. You might be friends."

"Yes, we might," admitted Mr. Berg with a peculiar smile; "but, unless I'm very much mistaken, we're going to be rivals."

"Rivals? What do you mean?"

"I can't tell you now. Perhaps I may later. But if you don't mind, walk a little faster, please. I want to get to a long-distance telephone."

"What for?"

"I have just overheard something that I wish to communicate to my employers, Bentley & Eagert."

"Overheard something? I don't see what it could be, unless that lad—"

"You'll learn in good time," went on the submarine agent. "But I must telephone at once."

A little later the two men had reached a trolley line that ran into Atlantis, and they arrived at the city before Mr. Damon and Tom got there, as the latter had to go by a circuitous route. Mr. Berg lost no time in calling up his firm by telephone.

"I have had another talk with Mr. Swift," he reported to Mr. Bentley, who came to the instrument in Philadelphia.

"Well, what does he say?" was the impatient question. "I can't understand his not wanting to try for the Government prize. It is astonishing. You said you were going to discover the reason, Mr Berg, but you haven't done so."

"I have."

"What is it?"

"Well, the reason Mr. Swift and his son don't care to try for the fifty thousand dollar prize is that they are after one of three hundred thousand dollars."

"Three hundred thousand dollars!" cried Mr. Bentley. "What government is going to offer such a prize as that for submarines, when they are getting almost as common as airships? We ought to have a try for that ourselves. What government is it?"

"No government at all. But I think we ought to have a try for it, Mr. Bentley."

"Explain."

"Well, I have just learned, most accidentally, that the Swifts are going after sunken treasure—three hundred thousand dollars in gold bullion."

"Sunken treasure? Where?

"I don't know exactly, but off the coast of Uruguay," and Mr. Berg rapidly related what he had overheard Tom tell Mr. Damon. Mr. Bentley was much excited and impatient for more details, but his agent could not give them to him.

"Well," concluded the senior member of the firm of submarine boat builders, "if the Swifts are going after treasure, so can we. Come to Philadelphia at once, Mr. Berg, and we'll talk this matter over. There is no time to lose. We can afford to forego the Government prize for the chance of getting a much larger one. We have as much right to search for the sunken gold as the Swifts have. Come here at once, and we will make our plans."

"All right," agreed the agent with a smile as he hung up the receiver. "I guess," he murmured to himself, "that you won't be so high and mighty with me after this, Tom Swift. We'll see who has the best boat, after all. We'll have a contest and a competition, but not for a government prize. It will be for the sunken gold."

It was easy to see that Mr. Berg was much pleased with himself.

Meanwhile, Tom and Mr. Damon had reached Atlantis, and had purchased the oil. They started back, but Tom took a street leading toward the center of the place, instead of striking for the beach path, along which they had come.

"Where are you going?" asked Mr. Damon.

"I want to see if that Andy Foger has come back here," replied the lad, and he told of having been shut in the tank by the bully.

"I've never properly punished him for that trick," he went on, "though we did manage to burst his auto tires. I'm curious to know how he knew enough to turn that gear and shut the tank door. He must have been loitering near the shop, seen me go in the submarine alone, watched his chance and sneaked in after me. But I'd like to get a complete explanation, and if I once got hold of Andy I could make him talk," and Tom clenched his fist in a manner that augured no good for the squint-eyed lad. "He was stopping at the same hotel with Mr. Berg, and be hurried away after the trick he played on me. I next saw him in Shopton, but I thought perhaps he might have come back here. I'm going to inquire at the hotel," he added.

Andy's name was not on the register since his hasty flight, however, and Tom, after inquiring from the clerk and learning that Mr. Berg was still a guest at the hostelry, rejoined Mr. Damon.

"Bless my hat!" exclaimed that eccentric individual as they started back to the lonely beach where the submarine was awaiting her advent into the water. "The more I think of the trip I'm going to take, the more I like it."

"I hope you will," remarked Tom. "It will be a new experience for all of us. There's only one thing worrying me, and that is about Mr. Berg having overheard what I said."

"Oh, don't worry about that. Can't we slip away and leave no trace in the water?"

"I hope so, but I must tell dad and Mr. Sharp about what happened."

The aged inventor was not a little alarmed at what his son related, but he agreed with Mr. Damon, whom he heartily welcomed, that little was to be apprehended from Berg and his employers.

"They know we're after a sunken wreck, but that's all they do know," said Tom's father. "We are only waiting for the arrival of Captain Alden Weston, and then we will go. Even if Bentley & Eagert make a try for the treasure we'll have the start of them, and this will be a case of first come, first served. Don't worry, Tom. I'm glad you're going, Mr Damon. Come, I will show you our submarine."

As father and son, with their guest, were going to the machine shop, Mr. Sharp met them. He had a letter in his hand.

"Good news!" the balloonist cried. "Captain Weston will be with us tomorrow. He will arrive at the Beach Hotel in Atlantis, and wants one of us to meet him there. He has considerable information about the wreck."

"The Beach Hotel," murmured Tom. "That is where Mr. Berg is stopping. I hope he doesn't worm any of our secret from Captain Weston," and it was with a feeling of uneasiness that the young inventor continued after his father and Mr. Damon to where the submarine was.

CHAPTER NINE

CAPTAIN WESTON'S ADVENT

"Bless my water ballast, but that certainly is a fine boat!" cried Mr. Damon, when he had been shown over the new craft. "I think I shall feel even safer in that than in the *Red Cloud*."

"Oh, don't go back on the airship!" exclaimed Mr Sharp. "I was counting on taking you on another trip."

"Well, maybe after we get back from under the ocean," agreed Mr. Damon. "I particularly like the cabin arrangements of the *Advance*. I think I shall enjoy myself."

He would be hard to please who could not take pleasure from a trip in the submarine. The cabin was particularly fine, and the sleeping arrangements were good.

More supplies could be carried than was possible on the airship, and there was more room in which to cook and serve food. Mr. Damon was fond of good living, and the kitchen pleased him as much as anything else.

Early the next morning Tom set out for Atlantis, to meet Captain Weston at the hotel. The young inventor inquired of the clerk whether the seafaring man had arrived, and was told that he had come the previous evening.

"Is he in his room?" asked Tom.

"No," answered the clerk with a peculiar grin. "He's an odd character. Wouldn't go to bed last night until we had every window in his room open, though it was blowing quite hard, and likely to storm. The captain said he was used to plenty of fresh air. Well, I guess he got it, all right."

"Where is he now?" asked the youth, wondering what sort of an individual he was to meet.

"Oh, he was up before sunrise, so some of the scrubwomen told me. They met him coming from his room, and he went right down to the beach with a big telescope he always carries with him. He hasn't come back yet. Probably he's down on the sand."

"Hasn't he had breakfast?"

"No. He left word he didn't want to eat until about four bells, whatever time that is."

"It's ten o'clock," replied Tom, who had been studying up on sea terms lately. "Eight bells is eight o'clock in the morning, or four in the afternoon or eight at night, according to the time of day. Then there's one bell for every half hour, so four bells this morning would be ten o'clock in this watch, I suppose."

"Oh, that's the way it goes, eh?" asked the clerk. "I never could get it through my head. What is twelve o'clock noon?"

"That's eight bells, too; so is twelve o'clock midnight. Eight bells is as high as they go on a ship. But I guess I'll go down and see if I can meet the captain. It will soon be ten o'clock, or four bells, and he must be hungry for breakfast. By the way, is that Mr. Berg still here?"

"No; he went away early this morning. He and Captain Weston seemed to strike up quite an acquaintance, the night clerk told me. They sat and smoked together until long after midnight, or eight bells," and the clerk smiled as he glanced down at the big diamond ring on his little finger.

"They did?" fairly exploded Tom, for he had visions of what the wily Mr. Berg might worm out of the simple captain.

"Yes. Why, isn't the captain a proper man to make friends with?" and the clerk looked at Tom curiously.

"Oh, yes, of course," was the hasty answer. "I guess I'll go and see if I can find him—the captain, I mean."

Tom hardly knew what to think. He wished his father, or Mr. Sharp, had thought to warn Captain Weston against talking of the wreck. It might be too late now.

The young inventor hurried to the beach, which was not far from the hotel. He saw a solitary figure pacing up and down, and from the fact that the man stopped, every now and then, and gazed seaward through a large telescope, the lad concluded it was the captain for whom he was in search. He approached, his footsteps making no sound on the sand. The man was still gazing through the glass.

"Captain Weston?" spoke Tom.

Without a show of haste, though the voice must have startled him, the captain turned. Slowly he lowered the telescope, and then he replied softly:

"That's my name. Who are you, if I may ask?"

Tom was struck, more than by anything else, by the gentle voice of the seaman. He had prepared himself, from the description of Mr. Sharp, to meet a gruff, bewhiskered individual, with a voice like a crosscut saw, and a rolling gait. Instead he saw a man of medium size, with a smooth face, merry blue eyes, and the softest voice and gentlest manner imaginable. Tom was very much disappointed. He had looked for a regular sea-dog, and he met a landsman, as he said afterward. But it was not long before our hero changed his mind regarding Captain Weston.

"I'm Tom Swift," the owner of that name said, "and I have been sent to show you the way to where our ship is ready to launch." The young inventor refrained from mentioning submarine, as it was the wish of Mr Sharp to disclose this feature of the voyage to the sailor himself.

"Ha, I thought as much," resumed the captain quietly. "It's a fine day, if I may be permitted to say so," and he seemed to hesitate, as if there was some doubt whether or not he might make that observation.

"It certainly is," agreed the lad. Then, with a smile he added: "It is nearly eight bells."

"Ha!" exclaimed the captain, also smiling, but even his manner of saying "Ha!" was less demonstrative than that of most persons. "I believe I am getting hungry, if I may be allowed the remark," and again he seemed asking Tom's pardon for mentioning the fact.

"Perhaps you will come back to the cabin and have a little breakfast with me," he went on. "I don't know what sort of a galley or cook they have aboard the Beach Hotel, but it can't be much worse than some I've tackled."

"No, thank you," answered the youth. "I've had my breakfast. But I'll wait for you, and then I'd like to get back. Dad and Mr. Sharp are anxious to meet you."

"And I am anxious to meet them, if you don't mind me mentioning it," was the reply, as the captain once more put the spyglass to his eye and took an observation. "Not many sails in sight this morning," he added. "But the weather is fine, and we ought to get off in good shape to hunt for the treasure about which Mr. Sharp wrote me. I believe we are going after treasure," he said; "that is, if you don't mind talking about it."

"Not in the least," replied Tom quickly, thinking this a good opportunity for broaching a subject that was worrying him. "Did you meet a Mr. Berg here last night, Captain Weston?" he went on.

"Yes. Mr. Berg and I had quite a talk. He is a well-informed man."

"Did he mention the sunken treasure?" asked the lad, eager to find out if his suspicions were true.

"Yes, he did, if you'll excuse me putting it so plainly," answered the seaman, as if Tom might be offended at so direct a reply. But the young inventor was soon to learn that this was only an odd habit with the seaman.

"Did he want to know where the wreck of the Boldero was located?" continued the lad. "That is, did he try to discover if you knew anything about it?"

"Yes," said Mr. Weston, "he did. He pumped me, if you are acquainted with that term, and are not offended by it. You see, when I arrived here I made inquiries as to where your father's place was located. Mr. Berg overheard me, and introduced himself as agent for a shipbuilding concern. He was very friendly, and when he said he knew you and your parent, I thought he was all right."

Tom's heart sank. His worst fears were to be realized, he thought.

"Yes, he and I talked considerable, if I may be permitted to say so," went on the captain. "He seemed to know about the wreck of the Boldero, and that she had three hundred thousand dollars in gold aboard. The only thing he didn't know was where the wreck was located. He knew it was off Uruguay somewhere, but just where he couldn't say. So he asked me if I knew, since he must have concluded that I was going with you on the gold-hunting expedition."

"And you do know, don't you?" asked Tom eagerly.

"Well, I have it pretty accurately charted out, if you will allow me that expression," was the calm answer. "I took pains to look it up at the request of Mr. Sharp."

"And he wanted to worm that information out of you?" inquired the youth excitedly.

"Yes, I'm afraid he did."

"Did you give him the location?"

"Well," remarked the captain, as he took another observation before closing up the telescope, "you see, while we were talking, I happened to drop a copy of a map I'd made, showing the location of the wreck. Mr. Berg picked it up to hand to me, and he looked at it."

"Oh!" cried Tom. "Then he knows just where the treasure is, and he may get to it ahead of us. It's too bad."

"Yes," continued the seaman calmly, "Mr. Berg picked up that map, and he looked very closely at the latitude and longitude I had marked as the location of the wreck."

"Then he won't have any trouble finding it," murmured our hero.

"Eh? What's that?" asked the captain, "if I may be permitted to request you to repeat what you said."

"I say he won't have any trouble locating the sunken Boldero," repeated Tom.

"Oh, but I think he will, if he depends on that map," was the unexpected reply. "You see," explained Mr. Weston, "I'm not so simple as I look. I sensed what Mr. Berg was after, the minute he began to talk to me. So I fixed up a little game on him. The map which I dropped on purpose, not accidentally, where he would see it, did have the location of the wreck marked. Only it didn't happen to be the right location. It was about five hundred miles out of the way, and I rather guess if Mr. Berg and his friends go there for treasure they'll find considerable depth of water and quite a lonesome spot. Oh, no, I'm not as easy as I look, if you don't mind me mentioning that fact; and when a scoundrel sets out to get the best of me, I generally try to turn the tables on him. I've seen such men as Mr. Berg before. I'm afraid, I'm very much afraid, the sight he had of the fake map I made won't do him much good. Well, I declare, it's past four bells. Let's go to breakfast, if you don't mind me asking you," and with that the captain started off up the beach, Tom following, his ideas all a whirl at the unlooked-for outcome of the interview.

CHAPTER TEN

TRIAL OF THE SUBMARINE

Tom felt such a relief at hearing of Captain Weston's ruse that his appetite, sharpened by an early breakfast and the sea air, came to him with a rush, and he had a second morning meal with the odd sea captain, who chuckled heartily when he thought of how Mr Berg had been deceived.

"Yes," resumed Captain Weston, over his bacon and eggs, "I sized him up for a slick article as soon as I laid eyes on him. But he evidently misjudged me, if I may be permitted that term. Oh, well, we may meet again, after we secure the treasure, and then I can show him the real map of the location of the wreck."

"Then you have it?" inquired the lad eagerly.

Captain Weston nodded, before hiding his face behind a large cup of coffee; his third, by the way.

"Let me see it?" asked Tom quickly. The captain set down his cup. He looked carefully about the hotel dining-room. There were several guests, who, like himself, were having a late breakfast.

"It's a good plan," the sailor said slowly, "when you're going into unknown waters, and don't want to leave a wake for the other fellow to follow, to keep your charts locked up. If it's all the same to you," he added diffidently, "I'd rather wait until we get to where your father and Mr. Sharp are before displaying the real map. I've no objection to showing you the one Mr. Berg saw," and again he chuckled.

The young inventor blushed at his indiscretion. He felt that the news of the search for the treasure had leaked out through him, though he was the one to get on the trail of it by seeing the article in the paper. Now he had nearly been guilty of another break. He realized that he must be more cautious. The captain saw his confusion, and said:

"I know how it is. You're eager to get under way. I don't blame you. I was the same myself when I was your age. But we'll soon be at your place, and then I'll tell you all I know. Sufficient now, to say that I believe I have located the wreck within a few miles. I got on the track of a sailor who had met one of the shipwrecked crew of the Boldero, and he gave me valuable information. Now tell me about the craft we are going in. A good deal depends on that."

Tom hardly knew what to answer. He recalled what Mr. Sharp had said about not wanting to tell Captain Weston, until the last moment, that they were going in a submarine, for fear the old seaman (for he was old in point of service though not in years) might not care to risk an under-water trip. Therefore Tom hesitated. Seeing it, Captain Weston remarked quietly:

"I mean, what type is your submarine? Does it go by compressed air, or water power?"

"How do you know it's a submarine?" asked the young inventor quickly, and in some confusion.

"Easy enough. When Mr. Berg thought he was pumping me, I was getting a lot of information from him. He told me about the submarine his firm was building, and, naturally, he mentioned yours. One thing led to another until I got a pretty good idea of your craft. What do you call it?"

"The *Advance.*"

"Good name. I like it, if you don't mind speaking of it."

"We were afraid you wouldn't like it," commented Tom.

"What, the name?"

"No, the idea of going in a submarine."

"Oh," and Captain Weston laughed. "Well, it takes more than that to frighten me, if you'll excuse the expression. I've always had a hankering to go under the surface, after so many years spent on top. Once or twice I came near going under, whether I wanted to or not, in wrecks, but I think I prefer your way. Now, if you're all done, and don't mind me speaking of it, I think we'll start for your place. We must hustle, for Berg may yet get on our trail, even if he has got the wrong route," and he laughed again.

It was no small relief to Mr Swift and Mr. Sharp to learn that Captain Weston had no objections to a submarine, as they feared he might have. The captain, in his diffident manner, made friends at once with the treasure-hunters, and he and Mr. Damon struck up quite an acquaintance. Tom told of his meeting with the seaman, and the latter related, with much gusto, the story of how he had fooled Mr. Berg.

"Well, perhaps you'd like to come and take a look at the craft that is to be our home while we're beneath the water," suggested Mr. Swift and the sailor assenting, the aged inventor, with much pride, assisted by Tom, pointed out on the *Advance* the features of interest. Captain Weston gave hearty approval, making one or two minor suggestions, which were carried out.

"And so you launch her tomorrow," he concluded, when he had completed the inspection "Well, I hope it's a success, if I may be permitted to say so."

There were busy times around the machine shop next day. So

much secrecy had been maintained that none of the residents, or visitors to the coast resort, were aware that in their midst was such a wonderful craft as the submarine. The last touches were put on the under-water ship; the ways, leading from the shop to the creek, were well greased, and all was in readiness for the launching. The tide would soon be at flood, and then the boat would slide down the timbers (at least, that was the hope of all), and would float in the element meant to receive her. It was decided that no one should be aboard when the launching took place, as there was an element of risk attached, since it was not known just how buoyant the craft was. It was expected she would float, until the filled tanks took her to the bottom, but there was no telling.

"It will be flood tide now in ten minutes," remarked Captain Weston quietly, looking at his watch. Then he took an observation through the telescope. "No hostile ships hanging in the offing," he reported. "All is favorable, if you don't mind me saying so," and he seemed afraid lest his remark might give offense.

"Get ready," ordered Mr. Swift. "Tom, see that the ropes are all clear," for it had been decided to ease the *Advance* down into the water by means of strong cables and windlasses, as the creek was so narrow that the submarine, if launched in the usual way, would poke her nose into the opposite mud bank and stick there.

"All clear," reported the young inventor.

"High tide!" exclaimed the captain a moment later, snapping shut his watch.

"Let go!" ordered Mr. Swift, and the various windlasses manned by the inventor, Tom and the others began to unwind their ropes. Slowly the ship slid along the greased ways. Slowly she approached the water. How anxiously they all watched her! Nearer and nearer her blunt nose, with the electric propulsion plate and the auxiliary propeller, came to the creek, the waters of which were quiet now, awaiting the turn of the tide.

Now little waves lapped the steel sides. It was the first contact of the *Advance* with her native element.

"Pay out the rope faster!" cried Mr. Swift.

The windlasses were turned more quickly Foot by foot the craft slid along until, with a final rush, the stern left the ways and the submarine was afloat. Now would come the test. Would she ride on an even keel, or sink out of sight, or turn turtle? They all ran to the water's edge, Tom in the lead.

"Hurrah!" suddenly yelled the lad, trying to stand on his head. "She floats! She's a success! Come on! Let's get aboard!"

For, true enough, the *Advance* was riding like a duck on the

water. She had been proportioned just right, and her lines were perfect. She rode as majestically as did any ship destined to sail on the
surface, and not intended to do double duty.

"Come on, we must moor her to the pier," directed Mr. Sharp.
"The tide will turn in a few minutes and take her out to sea."

He and Tom entered a small boat, and soon the submarine was
tied to a small dock that had been built for the purpose.

"Now to try the engine," suggested Mr. Swift, who was almost
trembling with eagerness; for the completion of the ship meant
much to him.

"One moment," begged Captain Weston. "If you don't mind,
I'll take an observation," he went on, and he swept the horizon with
his telescope. "All clear," he reported. "I think we may go aboard
and make a trial trip."

Little time was lost in entering the cabin and engine-room,
Garret Jackson accompanying the party to aid with the machinery.
It did not take long to start the motors, dynamos and the big
gasolene engine that was the vital part of the craft. A little water was
admitted to the tanks for ballast, since the food and other supplies
were not yet on board. The *Advance* now floated with the deck aft of
the conning tower showing about two feet above the surface of the
creek. Mr. Swift and Tom entered the pilot house.

"Start the engines," ordered the aged inventor, "and we'll try
my new system of positive and negative electrical propulsion."

There was a hum and whir in the body of the ship beneath the
feet of Tom and his father. Captain Weston stood on the little deck
near the conning tower.

"All ready?" asked the youth through the speaking tube to Mr.
Sharp and Mr. Jackson in the engine-room.

"All ready," came the answer.

Tom threw over the connecting lever, while his father grasped
the steering wheel. The *Advance* shot forward, moving swiftly
along, about half submerged.

"She goes! She goes!" cried Tom

"She certainly does, if I may be permitted to say so," was the
calm contribution of Captain Weston. "I congratulate you."

Faster and faster went the new craft. Mr. Swift headed her
toward the open sea, but stopped just before passing out of the
creek, as he was not yet ready to venture into deep water.

"I want to test the auxiliary propellers," he said. After a little
longer trial of the electric propulsion plates, which were found to
work satisfactorily, sending the submarine up and down the creek
at a fast rate, the screws, such as are used on most submarines, were

put into gear. They did well, but were not equal to the plates, nor was so much expected of them.

"I am perfectly satisfied," announced Mr. Swift as he once more headed the boat to sea. "I think, Captain Weston, you had better go below now."

"Why so?"

"Because I am going to completely submerge the craft. Tom, close the conning tower door. Perhaps you will come in here with us, Captain Weston, though it will be rather a tight fit."

"Thank you, I will. I want to see how it feels to be in a pilot house under water."

Tom closed the water-tight door of the conning tower. Word was sent through the tube to the engine-room that a more severe test of the ship was about to be made. The craft was now outside the line of breakers and in the open sea.

"Is everything ready, Tom?" asked his father in a quiet voice.

"Everything," replied the lad nervously, for the anticipation of being about to sink below the surface was telling on them all, even on the calm, old sea captain.

"Then open the tanks and admit the water," ordered Mr. Swift.

His son turned a valve and adjusted some levers. There was a hissing sound, and the *Advance* began sinking. She was about to dive beneath the surface of the ocean, and those aboard her were destined to go through a terrible experience before she rose again.

CHAPTER ELEVEN

ON THE OCEAN BED

Lower and lower sank the submarine. There was a swirling and foaming of the water as she went down, caused by the air bubbles which the craft carried with her in her descent. Only the top of the conning tower was out of water now, the ocean having closed over the deck and the rounded back of the boat. Had any one been watching they would have imagined that an accident was taking place.

In the pilot house, with its thick glass windows, Tom, his father and Captain Weston looked over the surface of the ocean, which every minute was coming nearer and nearer to them.

"We'll be all under in a few seconds," spoke Tom in a solemn voice, as he listened to the water hissing into the tanks.

"Yes, and then we can see what sort of progress we will make," added Mr. Swift. "Everything is going fine, though," he went on cheerfully. "I believe I have a good boat."

"There is no doubt of it in my mind," remarked Captain Weston, and Tom felt a little disappointed that the sailor did not shout out some such expression as "Shiver my timbers!" or "Keel-haul the main braces, there, you lubber!" But Captain Weston was not that kind of a sailor, though his usually quiet demeanor could be quickly dropped on necessity, as Tom learned later.

A few minutes more and the waters closed over the top of the conning tower. The *Advance* was completely submerged. Through the thick glass windows of the pilot house the occupants looked out into the greenish water that swirled about them; but it could not enter. Then, as the boat went lower, the light from above gradually died out, and the semi-darkness gave place to gloom.

"Turn on the electrics and the searchlight, Tom," directed his father.

There was the click of a switch, and the conning tower was flooded with light. But as this had the effect of preventing the three from peering out into the water, just as one in a lighted room cannot look out into the night, Tom shut them off and switched on the great searchlight. This projected its powerful beams straight ahead and there, under the ocean, was a pathway of illumination for the treasure-seekers.

"Fine!" cried Captain Weston, with more enthusiasm than he had yet manifested. "That's great, if you don't mind me mentioning it. How deep are we?"

Tom glanced at a gage on the side of the pilot tower.

"Only about sixty feet," he answered.

"Then don't go any deeper!" cried the captain hastily. "I know these waters around here, and that's about all the depth you've got. You'll be on the bottom in a minute."

"I intend to get on the bottom after a while," said Mr. Swift, "but not here. I want to try for a greater distance under water before I come to rest on the ocean's bed. But I think we are deep enough for a test. Tom, close the tank intake pipes and we'll see how the *Advance* will progress when fully submerged."

The hissing stopped, and then, wishing to see how the motors and other machinery would work, the aged inventor and his son, accompanied by Captain Weston, descended from the conning tower, by means of an inner stairway, to the interior of the ship. The submarine could be steered and managed from below or above. She was now floating about sixty-five feet below the surface of the bay.

"Well, how do you like it?" asked Tom of Mr. Damon, as he saw his friend in an easy chair in the living-room or main cabin of the craft, looking out of one of the plate-glass windows on the side.

"Bless my spectacles, it's the most wonderful thing I ever dreamed of!" cried the queer character, as he peered at the mass of water before him. "To think that I'm away down under the surface, and yet as dry as a bone. Bless my necktie, but it's great! What are we going to do now?"

"Go forward," replied the young inventor.

"Perhaps I had better make an observation," suggested Captain Weston, taking his telescope from under his arm, where he had carried it since entering the craft, and opening it. "We may run afoul of something, if you don't mind me mentioning such a disagreeable subject." Then, as he thought of the impossibility of using his glass under water, he closed it.

"I shall have little use for this here, I'm afraid," he remarked with a smile. "Well, there's some consolation. We're not likely to meet many ships in this part of the ocean. Other vessels are fond enough of remaining on the surface. I fancy we shall have the depths to ourselves, unless we meet a Government submarine, and they are hardly able to go as deep as we can. No, I guess we won't run into anything and I can put this glass away."

"Unless we run into Berg and his crowd," suggested Tom in a low voice.

"Ha! ha!" laughed Captain Weston, for he did not want Mr. Swift to worry over the unscrupulous agent. "No, I don't believe we'll meet them, Tom. I guess Berg is trying to work out the longitude and latitude I gave him. I wish I could see his face when he realizes that he's been deceived by that fake map."

"Well, I hope he doesn't discover it too soon and trail us," went on the lad. "But they're going to start the machinery now. I suppose you and I had better take charge of the steering of the craft. Dad will want to be in the engine-room."

"All right," replied the captain, and he moved forward with the lad to a small compartment, shut off from the living-room, that served as a pilot house when the conning tower was not used. The same levers, wheels and valves were there as up above, and the submarine could be managed as well from there as from the other place.

"Is everything all right?" asked Mr Swift as he went into the engine-room, where Garret Jackson and Mr. Sharp were busy with oil cans.

"Everything," replied the balloonist. "Are you going to start now?"

"Yes, we're deep enough for a speed trial. We'll go out to sea, however, and try for a lower depth record, as soon as there's enough water. Start the engine."

A moment later the powerful electric currents were flowing into the forward and aft plates, and the *Advance* began to gather way, forging through the water.

"Straight ahead, out to sea, Tom," called his father to him.

"Aye, aye, sir," responded the youth.

"Ha! Quite seaman-like, if you don't mind a reference to it," commented Captain Weston with a smile. "Mind your helm, boy, for you don't want to poke her nose into a mud bank, or run up on a shoal."

"Suppose you steer?" suggested the lad. "I'd rather take lessons for a while."

"All right. Perhaps it will be safer. I know these waters from the top, though I can't say as much for the bottom. However, I know where the shoals are."

The powerful searchlight was turned, so as to send its beams along the path which the submarine was to follow, and then, as she gathered speed, she shot ahead, gliding through the waters like a fish.

Mr. Damon divided his time between the forward pilot-room, the living-apartment, and the place where Mr. Swift, Garret Jackson and Mr. Sharp were working over the engines. Every few minutes he would bless some part of himself, his clothing, or the ship. Finally the old man settled down to look through the plate-glass windows in the main apartment.

On and on went the submarine. She behaved perfectly, and was under excellent control. Some times Tom, at the request of his father, would send her toward the surface by means of the deflecting rudder. Then she would dive to the bottom again. Once, as a test, she was sent obliquely to the surface, her tower just emerging, and then she darted downward again, like a porpoise that had come up to roll over, and suddenly concluded to seek the depths. In fact, had any one seen the maneuver they would have imagined the craft was a big fish disporting itself.

Captain Weston remained at Tom's side, giving him instructions, and watching the compass in order to direct the steering so as to avoid collisions. For an hour or more the craft was sent almost straight ahead at medium speed. Then Mr. Swift, joining his son and the captain, remarked:

"How about depth of water here, Captain Weston?"

"You've got more than a mile."

"Good! Then I'm going down to the bottom of the sea! Tom, fill the tanks still more.

"Aye, aye, sir," answered the lad gaily. "Now for a new experience!"

"And use the deflecting rudder, also," advised his father. "That will hasten matters."

Five minutes later there was a slight jar noticeable.

"Bless my soul! What's that?" cried Mr. Damon. "Have we hit something?"

"Yes," answered Tom with a smile.

"What, for gracious sake?"

"The bottom of the sea. We're on the bed of the ocean."

CHAPTER TWELVE

FOR A BREATH OF AIR

They could hardly realize it, yet the depth-gage told the story. It registered a distance below the surface of the ocean of five thousand seven hundred feet—a little over a mile. The *Advance* had actually come to rest on the bottom of the Atlantic.

"Hurrah!" cried Tom. "Let's get on the diving suits, dad, and walk about on land under water for a change."

"No," said Mr. Swift soberly. "We will hardly have time for that now. Besides, the suits are not yet fitted with the automatic air-tanks, and we can't use them. There are still some things to do before we start on our treasure cruise. But I want to see how the plates are standing this pressure."

The *Advance* was made with a triple hull, the spaces between the layers of plates being filled with a secret material, capable of withstanding enormous pressure, as were also the plates themselves. Mr. Swift, aided by Mr. Jackson and Captain Weston, made a thorough examination, and found that not a drop of water had leaked in, nor was there the least sign that any of the plates had given way under the terrific strain.

"She's as tight as a drum, if you will allow me to make that comparison," remarked Captain Weston modestly. "I couldn't ask for a dryer ship."

"Well, let's take a look around by means the searchlight and the observation windows, and then we'll go back," suggested Mr. Swift. "It will take about two days to get the stores and provisions aboard and rig up the diving suits; then we will start for the sunken treasure."

There were several powerful searchlights on the *Advance*, so arranged that the bow, stern or either side could be illuminated independently. There were also observation windows near each light.

In turn the powerful rays were cast first at the bow and then aft. In the gleams could be seen the sandy bed of the ocean, covered with shells of various kinds. Great crabs walked around on their long, jointed legs, and Tom saw some lobsters that would have brought joy to the heart of a fisherman.

"Look at the big fish!" cried Mr. Damon suddenly, and he pointed to some dark, shadowy forms that swam up to the glass windows, evidently puzzled by the light.

"Porpoises," declared Captain Weston briefly, "a whole school of them."

The fish seemed suddenly to multiply, and soon those in the submarine felt curious tremors running through the whole craft.

"The fish are rubbing up against it," cried Tom. "They must think we came down here to allow them to scratch their backs on the steel plates."

For some time they remained on the bottom, watching the wonderful sight of the fishes that swam all about them.

"Well, I think we may as well rise," announced Mr. Swift, after they had been on the bottom about an hour, moving here and there. "We didn't bring any provisions, and I'm getting hungry, though I don't know how the others of you feel about it."

"Bless my dinner-plate, I could eat, too!" cried Mr. Damon. "Go up, by all means. We'll get enough of under-water travel once we start for the treasure."

"Send her up, Tom," called his father. "I Want to make a few notes on some needed changes and improvements."

Tom entered the lower pilot house, and turned the valve that opened the tanks. He also pulled the lever that started the pumps, so that the water ballast would be more quickly emptied, as that would render the submarine buoyant, and she would quickly shoot to the surface. To the surprise of the lad, however, there followed no outrushing of the water. The *Advance* remained stationary on the ocean bed. Mr. Swift looked up from his notes.

"Didn't you hear me ask you to send her up, Tom?" he inquired mildly.

"I did, dad, but something seems to be the matter," was the reply.

"Matter? What do you mean?" and the aged inventor hastened to where his son and Captain Weston were at the wheels, valves and levers.

"Why, the tanks won't empty, and the pumps don't seem to work."

"Let me try," suggested Mr. Swift, and he pulled the various handles. There was no corresponding action of the machinery.

"That's odd," he remarked in a curious voice "Perhaps something has gone wrong with the connections. Go look in the engine-room, and ask Mr. Sharp if everything is all right there."

Tom made a quick trip, returning to report that the dynamos, motors and gas engine were running perfectly.

"Try to work the tank levers and pumps from the conning tower," suggested Captain Weston. "Sometimes I've known the steam steering gear to play tricks like that."

Tom hurried up the circular stairway into the tower. He pulled the levers and shifted the valves and wheels there. But there was no emptying of the water tanks. The weight and pressure of water in them still held the submarine on the bottom of the sea, more than a mile from the surface. The pumps in the engine-room were working at top speed, but there was evidently something wrong in the connections. Mr. Swift quickly came to this conclusion.

"We must repair it at once," he said. "Tom, come to the engine-room. You and I, with Mr. Jackson and Mr. Sharp, will soon have it in shape again."

"Is there any danger?" asked Mr. Damon in a perturbed voice. "Bless my soul, it's unlucky to have an accident on our trial trip."

"Oh, we must expect accidents," declared Mr. Swift with a smile. "This is nothing."

But it proved to be more difficult than he had imagined to re-establish the connection between the pumps and the tanks. The valves, too, had clogged or jammed, and as the pressure outside the ship was so great, the water would not run out of itself. It must be forced.

For an hour or more the inventor, his son and the others, worked away. They could accomplish nothing. Tom looked anxiously at his parent when the latter paused in his efforts.

"Don't worry," advised the aged inventor. "It's got to come right sooner or later."

Just then Mr. Damon, who had been wandering about the ship, entered the engine-room.

"Do you know," he said, "you ought to open a window, or something."

"Why, what's the matter?" asked Tom quickly, looking to see if the odd man was joking.

"Well, of course I don't exactly mean a window," explained Mr. Damon, "but we need fresh air."

"Fresh air!" There was a startled note in Mr. Swift's voice as he repeated the words.

"Yes, I can hardly breathe in the living-room, and it's not much better here."

"Why, there ought to be plenty of fresh air," went on the inventor. "It is renewed automatically."

Tom jumped up and looked at an indicator. He uttered a startled cry.

"The air hasn't been changed in the last hour!" he exclaimed. "It is bad. There's not enough oxygen in it. I notice it, now that I've stopped working. The gage indicates it, too. The automatic air-changer must have stopped working. I'll fix it."

He hurried to the machine which was depended on to supply fresh air to the submarine.

"Why, the air tanks are empty!" the young inventor cried. "We haven't any more air except what is in the ship now!"

"And we're rapidly breathing that up," added Captain Weston solemnly.

"Can't you make more?" cried Mr. Damon. "I thought you said you could make oxygen aboard the ship."

"We can," answered Mr. Swift, "but I did not bring along a supply of the necessary chemicals. I did not think we would be submerged long enough for that. But there should have been enough in the reserve tank to last several days. How about it, Tom?"

"It's all leaked out, or else it wasn't filled," was the despairing answer. "All the air we have is what's in the ship, and we can't make more."

The treasure-seekers looked at each other. It was an awful situation.

"Then the only thing to do is to fix the machinery and rise to the surface," said Mr. Sharp simply. "We can have all the air we want, then."

"Yes, but the machinery doesn't seem possible of being fixed," spoke Tom in a low voice.

"We must do it!" cried his father.

They set to work again with fierce energy, laboring for their very lives. They all knew that they could not long remain in the ship without oxygen. Nor could they desert it to go to the surface, for the moment they left the protection of the thick steel sides the terrible pressure of the water would kill them. Nor were the diving suits available. They must stay in the craft and die a miserable death—unless the machinery could be repaired and the *Advance* sent to the surface. The emergency expanding lifting tank was not yet in working order.

More frantically they toiled, trying every device that was suggested to the mechanical minds of Tom, his father, Mr. Sharp or Mr. Jackson, to make the pumps work. But something was wrong. More and more foul grew the air. They were fairly gasping now. It was difficult to breathe, to say nothing of working, in that atmosphere. The thought of their terrible position was in the minds of all.

"Oh, for one breath of fresh air!" cried Mr. Damon, who seemed to suffer more than any of the others. Grim death was hovering around them, imprisoned as they were on the ocean's bed, over a mile from the surface.

CHAPTER THIRTEEN

OFF FOR THE TREASURE

Suddenly Tom, after a moment's pause, seized a wrench and began loosening some nuts.

"What are you doing?" asked his father faintly, for he was being weakened by the vitiated atmosphere.

"I'm going to take this valve apart," replied his son. "We haven't looked there for the trouble. Maybe it's out of order."

He attacked the valve with energy, but his hands soon lagged. The lack of oxygen was telling on him. He could no longer work quickly.

"I'll help," murmured Mr. Sharp thickly. He took a wrench, but no sooner had he loosened one nut than he toppled over. "I'm all in," he murmured feebly.

"Is he dead?" cried Mr. Damon, himself gasping.

"No, only fainted. But he soon will be dead, and so will all of us, if we don't get fresh air," remarked Captain Weston. "Lie down on the floor, every one. There is a little fairly good air there. It's heavier than the air we've breathed, and we can exist on it for a little longer. Poor Sharp was so used to breathing the rarified air of high altitudes that he can't stand this heavy atmosphere."

Mr. Damon was gasping worse than ever, and so was Mr. Swift. The balloonist lay an inert heap on the floor, with Captain Weston trying to force a few drops of stimulant down his throat.

With a fierce determination in his heart, but with fingers that almost refused to do his bidding, Tom once more sought to open the big valve. He felt sure the trouble was located there, as they had tried to locate it in every other place without avail.

"I'll help," said Mr. Jackson in a whisper. He, too, was hardly able to move.

More and more devoid of oxygen grew the air. It gave Tom a sense as if his head was filled, and ready to burst with every breath he drew. Still he struggled to loosen the nuts. There were but four more now, and he took off three while Mr. Jackson removed one. The young inventor lifted off the valve cover, though it felt like a ton weight to him. He gave a glance inside.

"Here's the trouble!" he murmured. "The valve's clogged. No wonder it wouldn't work. The pumps couldn't force the water out."

It was the work of only a minute to adjust the valve. Then Tom and the engineer managed to get the cover back on.

How they inserted the bolts and screwed the nuts in place they never could remember clearly afterward, but they managed it somehow, with shaking, trembling hands and eyes that grew more and more dim.

"Now start the pumps!" cried Tom faintly. "The tanks will be emptied, and we can get to the surface."

Mr. Sharp was still unconscious, nor was Mr. Swift able to help. He lay with his eyes closed. Garret Jackson, however, managed to crawl to the engine-room, and soon the clank of machinery told Tom that the pumps were in motion. The lad staggered to the pilot house and threw the levers over. An instant later there was the hissing of water as it rushed from the ballast tanks. The submarine shivered, as though disliking to leave the bottom of the sea, and then slowly rose. As the pumps worked more rapidly, and the sea was sent from the tank in great volumes, the boat fairly shot to the surface. Tom was ready to open the conning tower and let in fresh air as soon as the top was above the surface.

With a bound the *Advance* reached the top. Tom frantically worked the worm gear that opened the tower. In rushed the fresh, life-giving air, and the treasure-hunters filled their lungs with it.

And it was only just in time, for Mr. Sharp was almost gone. He quickly revived, as did the others, when they could breathe as much as they wished of the glorious oxygen.

"That was a close call," commented Mr. Swift. "We'll not go below again until I have provided for all emergencies. I should have seen to the air tanks and the expanding one before going below. We'll sail home on the surface now."

The submarine was put about and headed for her dock. On the way she passed a small steamer, and the passengers looked down in wonder at the strange craft.

When the *Advance* reached the secluded creek where she had been launched, her passengers had fully recovered from their terrible experience, though the nerves of Mr. Swift and Mr. Damon were not at ease for some days thereafter.

"I should never have made a submerged test without making sure that we had a reserve supply of air," remarked the aged inventor. "I will not be caught that way again. But I can't understand how the pump valve got out of order."

"Maybe some one tampered with it," suggested Mr. Damon. "Could Andy Foger, any of the Happy Harry gang, or the rival gold-seekers have done it?"

"I hardly think so," answered Tom. "The place has been too carefully guarded since Berg and Andy once sneaked in. I think it was just an accident, but I have thought of a plan whereby such accidents can be avoided in the future. It needs a simple device."

"Better patent it," suggested Mr. Sharp with a smile.

"Maybe I will," replied the young inventor. "But not now. We haven't time, if we intend to get fitted out for our trip."

"No; I should say the sooner we started the better," remarked Captain Weston. "That is, if you don't mind me speaking about it," he added gently, and the others smiled, for his diffident comments were only a matter of habit.

The first act of the adventurers, after tying the submarine at the dock, was to proceed with the loading of the food and supplies. Tom and Mr. Damon looked to this, while Mr. Swift and Mr. Sharp made some necessary changes to the machinery. The next day the young inventor attached his device to the pump valve, and the loading of the craft was continued.

All was in readiness for the gold-seeking expedition a week later. Captain Weston had carefully charted the route they were to follow, and it was decided to move along on the surface for the first day, so as to get well out to sea before submerging the craft. Then it would sink below the surface, and run along under the water until the wreck was reached, rising at times, as needed, to renew the air supply.

With sufficient stores and provisions aboard to last several months, if necessary, though they did not expect to be gone more than sixty days at most, the adventurers arose early one morning and went down to the dock. Mr. Jackson was not to accompany them. He did not care about a submarine trip, he said, and Mr. Swift desired him to remain at the seaside cottage and guard the shops, which contained much valuable machinery. The airship was also left there.

"Well, are we all ready?" asked Mr. Swift of the little party of gold-seekers, as they were about to enter the conning tower hatchway of the submarine.

"All ready, dad," responded his son.

"Then let's get aboard," proposed Captain Weston. "But first let me take an observation."

He swept the horizon with his telescope, and Tom noticed that the sailor kept it fixed on one particular spot for some time.

"Did you see anything?" asked the lad.

"Well, there is a boat lying off there," was the answer. "And some one is observing us through a glass. But I don't believe it matters. Probably they're only trying to see what sort of an odd fish we are."

"All aboard, then," ordered Mr. Swift, and they went into the submarine. Tom and his father, with Captain Weston, remained in the conning tower. The signal was given, the electricity flowed into the forward and aft plates, and the *Advance* shot ahead on the surface.

The sailor raised his telescope once more and peered through a window in the tower. He uttered an exclamation.

"What's the matter?" asked Tom.

"That other ship—a small steamer—is weighing anchor and seems to be heading this way," was the reply.

"Maybe it's some one hired by Berg to follow us and trace our movements," suggested Tom.

"If it is we'll fool them," added his father. "Just keep an eye on them, captain, and I think we can show them a trick or two in a few minutes."

Faster shot the *Advance* through the water. She had started on her way to get the gold from the sunken wreck, but already enemies were on the trail of the adventurers, for the ship the sailor had noticed was steaming after them.

CHAPTER FOURTEEN

IN THE DIVING SUITS

There was no doubt that the steamer was coming after the submarine. Several observations Captain Weston made confirmed this, and he reported the fact to Mr. Swift.

"Well, we'll change our plans, then," said the inventor. "Instead of sailing on the surface we'll go below. But first let them get near so they may have the benefit of seeing what we do. Tom, go below, please, and tell Mr. Sharp to get every thing in readiness for a quick descent. We'll slow up a bit now, and let them get nearer to us."

The speed of the submarine was reduced, and in a short time the strange steamer had overhauled her, coming to within hailing distance.

Mr. Swift signaled for the machinery to stop and the submarine came to a halt on the surface, bobbing about like a half-submerged bottle. The inventor opened a bull's-eye in the tower, and called to a man on the bridge of the steamer:

"What are you following us for?"

"Following you?" repeated the man, for the strange vessel had also come to a stop. "We're not following you."

"It looks like it," replied Mr. Swift. "You'd better give it up."

"I guess the waters are free," was the quick retort. "We'll follow you if we like."

"Will you? Then come on!" cried the inventor as he quickly closed the heavy glass window and pulled a lever. An instant later the submarine began to sink, and Mr. Swift could not help laughing as, just before the tower went under water, he had a glimpse of the astonished face of the man on the bridge. The latter had evidently not expected such a move as that.

Lower and lower in the water went the craft, until it was about two hundred feet below the surface. Then Mr. Swift left the conning tower, descended to the main part of the ship, and asked Tom and Captain Weston to take charge of the pilot house.

"Send her ahead, Tom," his father said. "That fellow up above is rubbing his eyes yet, wondering where we are, I suppose."

Forward shot the *Advance* under water, the powerful electrical plates pulling and pushing her on the way to secure the sunken gold.

All that morning a fairly moderate rate of speed was maintained, as it was thought best not to run the new machinery too fast.

Dinner was eaten about a quarter of a mile below the surface, but no one inside the submarine would ever have known it. Electric lights made the place as brilliant as could be desired, and the food, which Tom and Mr. Damon prepared, was equal to any that could have been served on land. After the meal they opened the shutters over the windows in the sides of the craft, and looked at the myriads of fishes swimming past, as the creatures were disclosed in the glare of the searchlight.

That night they were several hundred miles on their journey, for the craft was speedy, and leaving Tom and Captain Weston to take the first watch, the others went to bed.

"Bless my soul, but it does seem odd, though, to go to bed under water, like a fish," remarked Mr. Damon. "If my wife knew this she would worry to death. She thinks I'm off automobiling. But this isn't half as dangerous as riding in a car that's always getting out of order. A submarine for mine, every time."

"Wait until we get to the end of this trip," advised Tom. "I guess you'll find almost as many things can happen in a submarine as can in an auto," and future events were to prove the young inventor to be right.

Everything worked well that night, and the ship made good progress. They rose to the surface the next morning to make sure of their position, and to get fresh air, though they did not really need the latter, as the reserve supply had not been drawn on, and was sufficient for several days, now that the oxygen machine had been put in running order.

On the second day the ship was sent to the bottom and halted there, as Mr. Swift wished to try the new diving suits. These were made of a new, light, but very strong metal to withstand the pressure of a great depth.

Tom, Mr. Sharp and Captain Weston donned the suits, the others agreeing to wait until they saw how the first trial resulted. Then, too, it was necessary for some one acquainted with the machinery to remain in the ship to operate the door and water chamber through which the divers had to pass to get out.

The usual plan, with some changes, was followed in letting the three out of the boat, and on to the bottom of the sea. They entered a chamber in the side of the submarine, water was gradually admitted until it equaled in pressure that outside, then an outer door was opened by means of levers, and they could step out

It was a curious sensation to Tom and the others to feel that they were actually walking along the bed of the ocean. All around them was the water, and as they turned on the small electric lights in their helmets, which lights were fed by storage batteries fastened to the diving suits, they saw the fish, big and little, swarm up to them, doubtless astonished at the odd creatures which had entered their domain. On the sand of the bottom, and in and out among the shells and rocks, crawled great spider crabs, big eels and other odd creatures seldom seen on the surface of the water. The three divers found no difficulty in breathing, as there were air tanks fastened to their shoulders, and a constant supply of oxygen was fed through pipes into the helmets. The pressure of water did not bother them, and after the first sensation Tom began to enjoy the novelty of it. At first the inability to speak to his companions seemed odd, but he soon got so he could make signs and motions, and be understood.

They walked about for some time, and once the lad came upon a part of a wrecked vessel buried deep in the sand. There was no telling what ship it was, nor how long it had been there, and after silently viewing it, they continued on

"It was great!" were the first words Tom uttered when he and the others were once more inside the submarine and had removed the suits. "If we can only walk around the wreck of the Boldero that way, we'll have all the gold out of her in no time. There are no life-lines nor air-hose to bother with in these diving suits."

"They certainly are a success," conceded Mr. Sharp.

"Bless my topknot!" cried Mr. Damon. "I'll try it next time. I've always wanted to be a diver, and now I have the chance."

The trip was resumed after the diving chamber had been closed, and on the third day Captain Weston announced, after a look at his chart, that they were nearing the Bahama Islands.

"We'll have to be careful not to run into any of the small keys," he said, that being the name for the many little points of land, hardly large enough to be dignified by the name of island. "We must keep a constant lookout."

Fortune favored them, though once, when Tom was steering, he narrowly avoided ramming a coral reef with the submarine. The searchlight showed it to him just in time, and he sheered off with a thumping in his heart.

The course was changed from south to east, so as to get ready to swing out of the way of the big shoulder of South America where Brazil takes up so much room, and as they went farther and farther toward the equator, they noticed that the waters teemed more and more with fish, some beautiful, some ugly and fear-inspiring, and some such monsters that it made one shudder to look at them, even through the thick glass of the bulls-eye windows.

CHAPTER FIFTEEN

AT THE TROPICAL ISLAND

It was on the evening of the fourth day later that Captain Weston, who was steering the craft, suddenly called out:

"Land ho!"

"Where away?" inquired Tom quickly, for he had read that this was the proper response to make.

"Dead ahead," answered the sailor with a smile. "Shall we make for it, if I may be allowed the question?"

"What land is it likely to be?" Mr. Swift wanted to know.

"Oh, some small tropical island," replied the seafaring man. "It isn't down on the charts. Probably it's too small to note. I should say it was a coral island, but we may be able to find a Spring of fresh water there, and some fruit."

"Then we'll land there," decided the inventor. "We can use some fresh water, though our distilling and ice apparatus does very well."

They made the island just at dusk, and anchored in a little lagoon, where there was a good depth of water.

"Now for shore!" cried Tom, as the submarine swung around on the chain. "It looks like a fine place. I hope there are cocoanuts and oranges here. Shall I get out the electric launch, dad?"

"Yes, you may, and we'll all go ashore. It will do us good to stretch our legs a bit."

Carried in a sort of pocket on the deck of the submarine was a small electric boat, capable of holding six. It could be slid from the pocket, or depression, into the water without the use of davits, and, with Mr. Sharp to aid him, Tom soon had the little craft afloat. The batteries were already charged, and just as the sun was going down the gold-seekers entered the launch and were soon on shore.

They found a good spring of water close at hand, and Tom's wish regarding the cocoanuts was realized, though there were no oranges. The lad took several of the delicious nuts, and breaking them open poured the milk into a collapsible cup he carried, drinking it eagerly. The others followed his example, and pronounced it the best beverage they had tasted in a long time.

The island was a typical tropical one, not very large, and it did not appear to have been often visited by man. There were no animals to be seen, but myriads of birds flew here and there amid the trees, the trailing vines and streamers of moss.

"Let's spend a day here tomorrow and explore it," proposed Tom, and his father nodded an assent. They went back to the submarine as night was beginning to gather, and in the cabin, after supper, talked over the happenings of their trip so far.

"Do you think we'll have any trouble getting the gold out of the wrecked vessel?" asked Tom of Captain Weston, after a pause.

"Well, it's hard to say. I couldn't learn just how the wreck lays, whether it's on a sandy or a rocky bottom. If the latter, it won't be so hard, but if the sand has worked in and partly covered it, we'll have some difficulties, if I may be permitted to say so. However, don't borrow trouble. We're not there yet, though at the rate we're traveling it won't be long before we arrive."

No watch was set that night, as it was not considered necessary. Tom was the first to arise in the morning, and he went out on the deck for a breath of fresh air before breakfast.

He looked off at the beautiful little island, and as his eye took in all of the little lagoon where the submarine was anchored he uttered a startled cry.

And well he might, for, not a hundred yards away, and nearer to the island than was the *Advance*, floated another craft—another craft, almost similar in shape and size to the one built by the Swifts. Tom rubbed his eyes to make sure he was not seeing double. No, there could be no mistake about it. There was another submarine at the tropical island.

As he looked, some one emerged from the conning tower of the second craft. The figure seemed strangely familiar. Tom knew in a moment who it was—Addison Berg. The agent saw the lad, too, and taking off his cap and making a mocking bow, he called out:

"Good morning! Have you got the gold yet?"

Tom did not know what to answer. Seeing the other submarine, at an island where he had supposed they would not be disturbed, was disconcerting enough, but to be greeted by Berg was altogether too much, Tom thought. His fears that the rival boat builders would follow had not been without foundation.

"Rather surprised to see us, aren't you?" went on Mr. Berg, smiling.

"Rather," admitted Tom, choking over the word.

"Thought you'd be," continued Berg. "We didn't expect to meet you so soon, but we're glad we did. I don't altogether like hunting for sunken treasure, with such indefinite directions as I have."

"You—are going to—" stammered Tom, and then he concluded it would be best not to say anything. But his talk had been heard inside the submarine. His father came to the foot of the conning tower stairway.

"To whom are you speaking, Tom?" he asked.

"They're here, dad," was the youth's answer.

"Here? Who are here?"

"Berg and his employers. They've followed us, dad."

CHAPTER SIXTEEN

"WE'LL RACE YOU FOR IT"

Mr. Swift hurried up on deck. He was accompanied by Captain Weston. At the sight of Tom's father, Mr. Berg, who had been joined by' two other men, called out:

"You see we also concluded to give up the trial for the Government prize, Mr. Swift. We decided there was more money in something else. But we still will have a good chance to try the merits of our respective boats. We hurried and got ours fitted up almost as soon as you did yours, and I think we have the better craft."

"I don't care to enter into any competition with you," said Mr. Swift coldly.

"Ah, but I'm afraid you'll have to, whether you want to or not," was the insolent reply.

"What's that? Do you mean to force this matter upon me?"

"I'm afraid I'll have to—my employers and I, that is. You see, we managed to pick up your trail after you left the Jersey coast, having an idea where you were bound, and we don't intend to lose you now."

"Do you mean to follow us?" asked Captain Weston softly.

"Well, you can put it that way if you like," answered one of the two men with Mr. Berg.

"I forbid it!" cried Mr. Swift hotly. "You have no right to sneak after us."

"I guess the ocean is free," continued the rascally agent.

"Why do you persist in keeping after us?" inquired the aged inventor, thinking it well to ascertain, if possible, just how much the men knew.

"Because we're after that treasure as well as you," was the bold reply. "You have no exclusive right to it. The sunken ship is awaiting the first comer, and whoever gets there first can take the gold from the wreck. We intend to be there first, but we'll be fair with you."

"Fair? What do you mean?" demanded Tom.

"This: We'll race you for it. The first one to arrive will have the right to search the wreck for the gold bullion. Is that fair? Do you agree to it?"

"We agree to nothing with you," interrupted Captain Weston, his usual diffident manner all gone. "I happen to be in partial command of this craft, and I warn you that if I find you interfering with us it won't be healthy for you. I'm not fond of fighting, but when I begin I don't like to stop," and he smiled grimly. "You'd better not follow us."

"We'll do as we please," shouted the third member of the trio on the deck of the other boat, which, as Tom could see, was named the *Wonder*. "We intend to get that gold if we can."

"All right. I've warned you," went on the sailor, and then, motioning to Tom and his father to follow, he went below.

"Well, what's to be done?" asked Mr. Swift when they were seated in the living-room, and had informed the others of the presence of the rival submarine.

"The only thing I see to do is to sneak away unobserved, go as deep as possible, and make all haste for the wreck," advised the captain. "They will depend on us, for they have evidently no chart of the wreck, though of course the general location of it may be known to them from reading the papers. I hoped I had thrown them off the track by the false chart I dropped, but it seems they were too smart for us."

"Have they a right to follow us?" asked Tom.

"Legally, but not morally. We can't prevent them, I'm afraid. The only thing to do is to get there ahead of them. It will be a race for the sunken treasure, and we must get there first."

"What do you propose doing, captain?" asked Mr. Damon. "Bless my shirt-studs, but can't we pull their ship up on the island and leave it there?"

"I'm afraid such high-handed proceedings would hardly answer," replied Mr. Swift. "No, as Captain Weston says, we must get there ahead of them. What do you think will be the best scheme, captain?"

"Well, there's no need for us to forego our plan to get fresh water. Suppose we go to the island, that is, some of us, leaving a guard on board here. We'll fill our tanks with fresh water, and at night we'll quietly sink below the surface and speed away."

They all voted that an excellent idea, and little time was lost putting it into operation.

All the remainder of that day not a sign of life was visible about the *Wonder*. She lay inert on the surface of the lagoon, not far away from the *Advance*; but, though no one showed himself on the deck, Tom and his friends had no doubt but that their enemies were closely watching them.

As dusk settled down over The tropical sea, and as the shadows of the trees on the little island lengthened, those on board the *Advance* closed the Conning tower. No lights were turned on, as they did not want their movements to be seen, but Tom, his father and Mr. Sharp took their positions near the various machines and apparatus, ready to open the tanks and let the submarine sink to the bottom, as soon as it was possible to do this unobserved.

"Luckily there's no moon," remarked Captain Weston, as he took his place beside Tom. "Once below the surface and we can defy them to find us. It is odd how they traced us, but I suppose that steamer gave them the clue."

It rapidly grew dark, as it always does in the tropics, and when a cautious observation from the conning tower did not disclose the outlines of the other boat, those aboard the *Advance* rightly concluded that their rivals were unable to see them.

"Send her down, Tom," called his father, and with a hiss the water entered the tanks. The submarine quickly sank below the surface, aided by the deflecting rudder.

But alas for the hopes of the gold-seekers. No sooner was she completely submerged, with the engine started so as to send her out of the lagoon and to the open sea, than the waters all about were made brilliant by the phosphorescent phenomenon. In southern waters this frequently occurs. Millions of tiny creatures, which, it is said, swarm in the warm currents, give an appearance of fire to the ocean, and any object moving through it can plainly be seen. It was so with the *Advance*. The motion she made in shooting forward, and the undulations caused by her submersion, seemed to start into activity the dormant phosphorus, and the submarine was afloat in a sea of fire.

"Quick!" cried Tom. "Speed her up! Maybe we can get out of this patch of water before they see us."

But it was too late. Above them they could hear the electric siren of the *Wonder* as it was blown to let them know that their escape had been noticed. A moment later the water, which acted as a sort of sounding-board, or telephone, brought to the ears of Tom Swift and his friends the noise of the engines of the other craft in operation. She was coming after them. The race for the possession of three hundred thousand dollars in gold was already under way. Fate seemed against those on board the *Advance*.

CHAPTER SEVENTEEN

THE RACE

Directed by Captain Weston, who glanced at the compass and told him which way to steer to clear the outer coral reef, Tom sent the submarine ahead, signaling for full speed to the engine-room, where his father and Mr. Sharp were. The big dynamos purred like great cats, as they sent the electrical energy into the forward and aft plates, pulling and pushing the *Advance* forward. On and on she rushed under water, but ever as she shot ahead the disturbance in the phosphorescent water showed her position plainly. She would be easy to follow.

"Can't you get any more speed out of her?" asked the captain of the lad.

"Yes," was the quick reply; "by using the auxiliary screws I think we can. I'll try it."

He signaled for the propellers, forward and aft, to be put in operation, and the motor moving the twin screws was turned on. At once there was a perceptible increase to the speed of the *Advance*.

"Are we leaving them behind?" asked Tom anxiously, as he glanced at the speed gage, and noted that the submarine was now about five hundred feet below the surface.

"Hard to tell," replied the Captain. "You'd have to take an observation to make sure."

"I'll do it," cried the youth. "You steer, please, and I'll go in the conning tower. I can look forward and aft there, as well as straight up. Maybe I can see the *Wonder*."

Springing up the circular ladder leading into the tower, Tom glanced through the windows all about the small pilot house. He saw a curious sight. It was as if the submarine was in a sea of yellowish liquid fire. She was immersed in water which glowed with the flames that contained no heat. So light was it, in fact, that there was no need of the incandescents in the tower. The young inventor could have seen to read a paper by the illumination of the phosphorus. But he had something else to do than observe this phenomenon. He wanted to see if he could catch sight of the rival submarine.

At first he could make out nothing save the swirl and boiling of the sea, caused by the progress of the *Advance* through it. But suddenly, as he looked up, he was aware of some great, black body a little to the rear and about ten feet above his craft.

"A shark!" he exclaimed aloud. "An immense one, too."

But the closer he looked the less it seemed like a shark. The position of the black object changed. It appeared to settle down, to be approaching the top of the conning tower. Then, with a suddenness that unnerved him for the time being, Tom recognized what it was; it was the underside of a ship. He could see the plates riveted together, and then, as be noted the rounded, cylindrical shape, he knew that it was a submarine. It was the *Wonder.* She was close at hand and was creeping up on the *Advance.* But, what was more dangerous, she seemed to be slowly settling in the water. Another moment and her great screws might crash into the Conning tower of the Swifts' boat and shave it off. Then the water would rush in, drowning the treasure-seekers like rats in a trap.

With a quick motion Tom yanked over the lever that allowed more water to flow into the ballast tanks. The effect was at once apparent. The *Advance* shot down toward the bottom of the sea. At the same time the young inventor signaled to Captain Weston to notify those in the engine-room to put on a little more speed. The *Advance* fairly leaped ahead, and the lad, looking up through the bull's-eye in the roof of the conning tower, had the satisfaction of seeing the rival submarine left behind.

The youth hurried down into the interior of the ship to tell what he had seen, and explain the reason for opening the ballast tanks. He found his father and Mr. Sharp somewhat excited over the unexpected maneuver of the craft.

"So they're still following us," murmured Mr. Swift. "I don't see why we can't shake them off."

"It's on account of this luminous water," explained Captain Weston. "Once we are clear of that it will be easy, I think, to give them the slip. That is, if we can get out of their sight long enough. Of course, if they keep close after us, they can pick us up with their searchlight, for I suppose they carry one."

"Yes," admitted the aged inventor, "they have as strong a one as we have. In fact, their ship is second only to this one in speed and power. I know, for Bentley & Eagert showed me some of the plans before they started it, and asked my opinion. This was before I had the notion of building a submarine. Yes, I am afraid we'll have trouble getting away from them."

"I can't understand this phosphorescent glow keeping up so long," remarked Captain Weston. "I've seen it in this locality several times, but it never covered such an extent of the ocean in my time. There must be changed conditions here now."

For an hour or more the race was kept up, and the two submarines forged ahead through the glowing sea. The *Wonder* remained slightly above and to the rear of the other, the better to keep sight of her, and though the *Advance* was run to her limit of speed, her rival could not be shaken off. Clearly the *Wonder* was a speedy craft.

"It's too bad that we've got to fight them, as well as run the risk of lots of other troubles which are always present when sailing under water," observed Mr Damon, who wandered about the submarine like the nervous person he was. "Bless my shirt-studs! Can't we blow them up, or cripple them in some way? They have no right to go after our treasure."

"Well, I guess they've got as much right as we have," declared Tom. "It goes to whoever reaches the wreck first. But what I don't like is their mean, sneaking way of doing it. If they went off on their own hook and looked for it I wouldn't say a word. But they expect us to lead them to the wreck, and then they'll rob us if they can. That's not fair."

"Indeed, it isn't," agreed Captain Weston, "if I may be allowed the expression. We ought to find some way of stopping them. But, if I'm not mistaken," he added quickly, looking from one of the port bull's-eyes, "the phosphorescent glow is lessening. I believe we are running beyond that part of the ocean."

There was no doubt of it, the glow was growing less and less, and ten minutes later the *Advance* was speeding along through a sea as black as night. Then, to avoid running into some wreck, it was necessary to turn on the searchlight.

"Are they still after us?" asked Mr. Swift of his son, as he emerged from the engine-room, where he had gone to make some adjustments to the machinery, with the hope of increasing the speed.

"I'll go look," volunteered the lad. He climbed up into the conning tower again, and for a moment, as he gazed back into the black waters swirling all about, he hoped that they had lost the *Wonder*. But a moment later his heart sank as he caught sight, through the liquid element, of the flickering gleams of another searchlight, the rays undulating through the sea.

"Still following," murmured the young inventor. "They're not going to give up. But we must make 'em—that's all."

He went down to report what he had seen, and a consultation was held. Captain Weston carefully studied the charts of that part of the ocean, and finding that there was a great depth of water at hand, proposed a series of evolutions.

"We can go up and down, shoot first to one side and then to the other," he explained. "We can even drop down to the bottom and rest there for a while. Perhaps, in that way, we can shake them off."

They tried it. The *Advance* was sent up until her conning tower was out of the water, and then she was suddenly forced down until she was but a few feet from the bottom. She darted to the left, to the right, and even doubled and went back over the course she had taken. But all to no purpose. The *Wonder* proved fully as speedy, and those in her seemed to know just how to handle the submarine, so that every evolution of the *Advance* was duplicated. Her rival could not be shaken off.

All night this was kept up, and when morning came, though only the clocks told it, for eternal night was below the surface, the rival gold-seekers were still on the trail.

"They won't give up," declared Mr. Swift hopelessly.

"No, we've got to race them for it, just as Berg proposed," admitted Tom. "But if they want a straightaway race we'll give it to 'em Let's run her to the limit, dad."

"That's what we've been doing, Tom."

"No, not exactly, for we've been submerged a little too much to get the best speed out of our craft. Let's go a little nearer the surface, and give them the best race they'll ever have."

Then the race began; and such a contest of speed as it was! With her propellers working to the limit, and every volt of electricity that was available forced into the forward and aft plates, the *Advance* surged through the water, about ten feet below the surface. But the *Wonder* kept after her, giving her knot for knot. The course of the leading submarine was easy to trace now, in the morning light which penetrated ten feet down.

"No use," remarked Tom again, when, after two hours, the *Wonder* was still close behind them. "Our only chance is that they may have a breakdown."

"Or run out of air, or something like that," added Captain Weston. "They are crowding us pretty close. I had no idea they could keep up this speed. If they don't look out," he went on as he looked from one of the aft observation windows, "they'll foul us, and—"

His remarks were interrupted by a jar to the *Advance*. She seemed to shiver and careened to one side. Then came another bump.

"Slow down!" cried the captain, rushing toward the pilot house.

"What's the matter?" asked Tom, as he threw the engines and electrical machines out of gear. "Have we hit anything?"

"No. Something has hit us," cried the captain. "Their submarine has rammed us."

"Rammed us!" repeated Mr. Swift. "Tom, run out the electric cannon! They're trying to sink us! We'll have to fight them. Run out the stern electric gun and we'll make them wish they'd not followed us."

CHAPTER EIGHTEEN

THE ELECTRIC GUN

There was much excitement aboard the *Advance*. The submarine came to a stop in the water, while the treasure-seekers waited anxiously for what was to follow. Would they be rammed again? This time, stationary as they were, and with the other boat coming swiftly on, a hole might be stove through the *Advance*, in spite of her powerful sides.

They had not long to wait. Again there came a jar, and once more the Swifts' boat careened. But the blow was a glancing one and, fortunately, did little damage.

"They certainly must be trying to sink us," agreed Captain Weston. "Come, Tom, we'll take a look from the stern and see what they're up to."

"And get the stern electric gun ready to fire," repeated Mr. Swift. "We must protect ourselves. Mr. Sharp and I will go to the bow. There is no telling what they may do. They're desperate, and may ram us from in front."

Tom and the captain hurried aft. Through the thick plate-glass windows they could see the blunt nose of the *Wonder* not far away, the rival submarine having come to a halt. There she lay, black and silent, like some monster fish waiting to devour its victim.

"There doesn't appear to be much damage done back here," observed Tom. "No leaks. Guess they didn't puncture us."

"Perhaps it was due to an accident that they rammed us," suggested the captain.

"Well, they wouldn't have done it if they hadn't followed us so close," was the opinion of the young inventor. "They're taking too many chances. We've got to stop 'em."

"What is this electric gun your father speaks of?"

"Why, it's a regular electric cannon. It fires a solid ball, weighing about twenty-five pounds, but instead of powder, which would hardly do under water, and instead of compressed air, which is used in the torpedo tubes of the Government submarines, we use a current of electricity. It forces the cannon ball out with great energy."

"I wonder what they will do next?" observed the captain, peering through a bull'seye.

"We can soon tell," replied the youth. "We'll go ahead, and if they try to follow I'm going to fire on them."

"Suppose you sink them?"

"I won't fire to do that; only to disable them. They brought it on themselves. We can't risk having them damage us. Help me with the cannon, will you please, captain?"

The electric cannon was a long, steel tube in the after part of the submarine. It projected a slight distance from the sides of the ship, and by an ingenious arrangement could he swung around in a ball and socket joint, thus enabling it to shoot in almost any direction.

It was the work of but a few minutes to get it ready and, with the muzzle pointing toward the *Wonder*, Tom adjusted the electric wires and inserted the solid shot.

"Now we're prepared for them!" he cried. "I think a good plan will be to start ahead, and if they try to follow to fire on them. They've brought it on themselves."

"Correct," spoke Captain Weston.

Tom hurried forward to tell his father of this plan.

"We'll do it!" cried Mr. Swift. "Go ahead, Mr. Sharp, and we'll see if those scoundrels will follow."

The young inventor returned on the run to the electric cannon. There was a whir of machinery, and the *Advance* moved forward. She increased her speed, and the two watchers in the stern looked anxiously out of the windows to see what their rivals would do.

For a moment no movement was noticeable on the part of the *Wonder*. Then, as those aboard her appeared to realize that the craft on which they depended to pilot them to the sunken treasure was slipping away, word was given to follow. The ship of Berg and his employers shot after the *Advance*.

"Here they come!" cried Captain Weston. "They're going to ram us again!"

"Then I'm going to fire on them!" declared Tom savagely.

On came the *Wonder*, nearer and nearer. Her speed was rapidly increasing. Suddenly she bumped the *Advance*, and then, as if it was an unavoidable accident, the rear submarine sheered off to one side.

"They're certainly at it again!" cried Tom, and peering from the bull's-eye he saw the *Wonder* shoot past the mouth of the electric cannon. "Here it goes!" he added.

He shoved over the lever, making the proper connection. There was no corresponding report, for the cannon was noiseless, but there was a slight jar as the projectile left the muzzle. The *Wonder* could be seen to heel over.

"You hit her! You hit her!" cried Captain Weston. "A good shot!"

"I was afraid she was past me when I pulled the lever," explained Tom. "She went like a flash."

"No, you caught her on the rudder," declared the captain. "I think you've put her out of business. Yes, they're rising to the surface."

The lad rapidly inserted another ball, and recharged the cannon. Then he peered out into the water, illuminated by the light of day overhead, as they were not far down. He could see the *Wonder* rising to the surface. Clearly something had happened.

"Maybe they're going to drop down on us from above, and try to sink us," suggested the youth, while he stood ready to fire again. "If they do—"

His words were interrupted by a slight jar throughout the submarine.

"What was that?" cried the captain.

"Dad fired the bow gun at them, but I don't believe he hit them," answered the young inventor.

"I wonder what damage I did? Guess we'll go to the surface to find out."

Clearly the *Wonder* had given up the fight for the time being. In fact, she had no weapon with which to respond to a fusillade from her rival. Tom hastened forward and informed his father of what had happened.

"If her steering gear is out of order, we may have a chance to slip away," said Mr. Swift "We'll go up and see what we can learn."

A few minutes later Tom, his father and Captain Weston stepped from the conning tower, which was out of water, on to the little flat deck a short distance away lay the *Wonder*, and on her deck was Berg and a number of men, evidently members of the crew.

"Why did you fire on us?" shouted the agent angrily.

"Why did you follow us?" retorted Torn.

"Well, you've broken our rudder and disabled us," went on Berg, not answering the question. "You'll suffer for this! I'll have you arrested."

"You only got what you deserved," added Mr. Swift. "You were acting illegally, following us, and you tried to sink us by ramming my craft before we retaliated by firing on you."

"It was an accident, ramming you," said Berg. "We couldn't help it. I now demand that you help us make repairs."

"Well, you've got nerve!" cried Captain Weston, his eyes flashing. "I'd like to have a personal interview with you for about ten minutes. Maybe something besides your ship would need repairs then."

Berg turned away, scowling, but did not reply. He began directing the crew what to do about the broken rudder.

"Come on," proposed Tom in a low voice, for sounds carry very easily over water. "Let's go below and skip out while we have a chance. They can't follow now, and we can get to the sunken treasure ahead of them."

"Good advice," commented his father. "Come, Captain Weston, we'll go below and close the conning tower."

Five minutes later the *Advance* sank from sight, the last glimpse Tom had of Berg and his men being a sight of them standing on the deck of their floating boat, gazing in the direction of their successful rival. The *Wonder* was left behind, while Tom and his friends were soon once more speeding toward the treasure wreck.

CHAPTER NINETEEN

CAPTURED

"Down deep," advised Captain Weston, as he stood beside Tom and Mr. Swift in the pilot house. "As far as you can manage her, and then forward. We'll take no more chances with these fellows."

"The only trouble is," replied the young inventor, "that the deeper we go the slower we have to travel. The water is so dense that it holds us back."

"Well, there is no special need of hurrying now," went on the sailor. "No one is following you, and two or three days difference in reaching the wreck will not amount to anything."

"Unless they repair their rudder, and take after us again," suggested Mr. Swift.

"They're not very likely to do that," was the captain's opinion. "It was more by luck than good management that they picked us up before. Now, having to delay, as they will, to repair their steering gear, while we can go as deep as we please and speed ahead, it is practically impossible for them to catch up to us. No, I think we have nothing to fear from them."

But though danger from Berg and his crowd was somewhat remote, perils of another sort were hovering around the treasure-seekers, and they were soon to experience them.

It was much different from sailing along in the airship, Tom thought, for there was no blue sky and fleecy clouds to see, and they could not look down and observe, far below them, cities and villages. Nor could they breathe the bracing atmosphere of the upper regions.

But if there was lack of the rarefied air of the clouds, there was no lack of fresh atmosphere. The big tanks carried a large supply, and whenever more was needed the oxygen machine would supply it.

As there was no need, however, of remaining under water for any great stretch of time, it was their practice to rise every day and renew the air supply, also to float along on the surface for a while, or speed along, with only the conning tower out, in order to afford a view, and to enable Captain Weston to take observations. But care was always exercised to make sure no ships were in sight when emerging on the surface, for the gold-seekers did not want to be hailed and questioned by inquisitive persons.

It was about four days after the disabling of the rival submarine, and the *Advance* was speeding along about a mile and a half under water. Tom was in the pilot house with Captain Weston, Mr. Damon was at his favorite pastime of looking out of the glass side windows into the ocean and its wonders, and Mr. Swift and the balloonists were, as usual, in the engine-room.

"How near do you calculate we are to the sunken wreck?" asked Tom of his companion.

"Well, at the calculation we made yesterday, we are within about a thousand miles of it now. We ought to reach it in about four more days, if we don't have any accidents."

"And how deep do you think it is?" went on the lad.

"Well, I'm afraid it's pretty close to two miles, if not more. It's quite a depth, and of course impossible for ordinary divers to reach. But it will be possible in this submarine and in the strong diving suits your father has invented for us to get to it. Yes, I don't anticipate much trouble in getting out the gold, once we reach the wreck of course—"

The captain's remark was not finished. From the engine-room there came a startled shout:

"Tom! Tom! Your father is hurt! Come here, quick!"

"Take the wheel!" cried the lad to the captain. "I must go to my father." It was Mr. Sharp's voice he had heard.

Racing to the engine-room, Tom saw his parent doubled up over a dynamo, while to one side, his hand on a copper switch, stood Mr. Sharp.

"What's the matter?" shouted the lad.

"He's held there by a current of electricity," replied the balloonist. "The wires are crossed."

"Why don't you shut off the current?" demanded the youth, as he prepared to pull his parent from the whirring machine. Then he hesitated, for he feared he, too, would be glued fast by the terrible current, and so be unable to help Mr. Swift.

"I'm held fast here, too," replied the balloonist. "I started to cut out the current at this switch, but there's a short circuit somewhere, and I can't let go, either. Quick, shut off all power at the main switchboard forward."

Tom realized that this was the only thing to do. He ran forward and with a yank cut out all the electric wires. With a sigh of relief Mr. Sharp pulled his hands from the copper where he had been held fast as if by some powerful magnet, his muscles cramped by the current. Fortunately the electricity was of low voltage, and he was not burned. The body of Mr. Swift toppled backward from the dynamo, as Tom sprang to reach his father.

"He's dead!" he cried, as he saw the pale face and the closed eyes.

"No, only badly shocked, I hope," spoke Mr. Sharp. "But we must get him to the fresh air at once. Start the tank pumps. We'll rise to the surface."

The youth needed no second bidding. Once more turning on the electric current, he set the powerful pumps in motion and the submarine began to rise. Then, aided by Captain Weston and Mr. Damon, the young inventor carried his father to a couch in the main cabin. Mr. Sharp took charge of the machinery.

Restoratives were applied, and there was a flutter of the eyelids of the aged inventor.

"I think he'll come around all right," said the sailor kindly, as he saw Tom's grief. "Fresh air will be the thing for him. We'll be on the surface in a minute."

Up shot the *Advance*, while Mr. Sharp stood ready to open the conning tower as soon as it should be out of water. Mr. Swift seemed to be rapidly reviving. With a bound the submarine, forced upward from the great depth, fairly shot out of the water. There was a clanking sound as the aeronaut opened the airtight door of the tower, and a breath of fresh air came in.

"Can you walk, dad, or shall we carry you?" asked Tom solitiously.

"Oh, I—I'm feeling better now," was the inventor's reply. "I'll soon be all right when I get out on deck. My foot slipped as I was adjusting a wire that had gotten out of order, and I fell so that I received a large part of the current. I'm glad I was not burned. Was Mr. Sharp hurt? I saw him run to the switch, just before I lost consciousness."

"No, I'm all right," answered the balloonist. "But allow us to get you out to the fresh air. You'll feel much better then."

Mr. Swift managed to walk slowly to the ladder leading to the conning tower, and thence to the deck. The others followed him. As all emerged from the submarine they uttered a cry of astonishment.

There, not one hundred yards away, was a great warship, flying a flag which, in a moment. Tom recognized as that of Brazil. The cruiser was lying off a small island, and all about were small boats, filled with natives, who seemed to be bringing supplies from land to the ship. At the unexpected sight of the submarine, bobbing up from the bottom of the ocean, the natives uttered cries of fright. The attention of those on the warship was attracted, and the bridge and rails were lined with curious officers and men.

"It's a good thing we didn't come up under that ship," observed

Tom. "They would have thought we were trying to torpedo her. Do you feel better, dad?" he asked, his wonder over the sight of the big vessel temporarily eclipsed in his anxiety for his parent.

"Oh, yes, much better. I'm all right now. But I wish we hadn't disclosed ourselves to these people. They may demand to know where we are going, and Brazil is too near Uruguay to make it safe to tell our errand. They may guess it, however, from having read of the wreck, and our departure."

"Oh, I guess it will be all right," replied Captain Weston. "We can tell them we are on a pleasure trip. That's true enough. It would give us great pleasure to find that gold."

"There's a boat, with some officers in it, to judge by the amount of gold lace on them, putting off from the ship," remarked Mr. Sharp.

"Ha! Yes! Evidently they intend to pay us a formal visit," observed Mr. Damon. "Bless my gaiters, though. I'm not dressed to receive company. I think I'll put on my dress suit."

"It's too late," advised Tom. "They'll be here in a minute."

Urged on by the lusty arms of the Brazilian sailors, the boat, containing several officers, neared the floating submarine rapidly.

"Ahoy there!" called an officer in the bow, his accent betraying his unfamiliarity with the English language. "What craft are you?"

"Submarine, *Advance*, from New Jersey," replied Tom. "Who are you?"

"Brazilian cruiser San Paulo," was the reply. "Where are you bound?" went on the officer.

"On pleasure," answered Captain Weston quickly. "But why do you ask? We are an American ship, sailing under American colors. Is this Brazilian territory?"

"This island is—yes," came back the answer, and by this time the small boat was at the side of the submarine. Before the adventurers could have protested, had they a desire to do so, there were a number of officers and the crew of the San Paulo on the small deck.

With a flourish, the officer who had done the questioning drew his sword. Waving it in the air with a dramatic gesture, he exclaimed:

"You're our prisoners! Resist and my men shall cut you down like dogs! Seize them, men!"

The sailors sprang forward, each one stationing himself at the side of one of our friends, and grasping an arm.

"What does this mean?" cried Captain Weston indignantly. "If this is a joke, you're carrying it too far. If you're in earnest, let me warn you against interfering with Americans!"

"We know what we are doing," was the answer from the officer.

The sailor who had hold of Captain Weston endeavored to secure a tighter grip. The captain turned suddenly, and seizing the man about the waist, with an exercise of tremendous strength hurled him over his head and into the sea, the man making a great splash.

"That's the way I'll treat any one else who dares lay a hand on me!" shouted the captain, who was transformed from a mild-mannered individual into an angry, modern giant. There was a gasp of astonishment at his feat, as the ducked sailor crawled back into the small boat. And he did not again venture on the deck of the submarine.

"Seize them, men!" cried the gold-laced officer again, and this time he and his fellows, including the crew, crowded so closely around Tom and his friends that they could do nothing. Even Captain Weston found it impossible to offer any resistance, for three men grabbed hold of him but his spirit was still a fighting one, and he struggled desperately but uselessly.

"How dare you do this?" he cried.

"Yes," added Tom, "what right have you to interfere with us?"

"Every right," declared the gold-laced officer.

"You are in Brazilian territory, and I arrest you."

"What for?" demanded Mr. Sharp.

"Because your ship is an American submarine, and we have received word that you intend to damage our shipping, and may try to torpedo our warships. I believe you tried to disable us a little while ago, but failed. We consider that an act of war and you will be treated accordingly. Take them on board the San Paulo," the officer Went on, turning to his aides. "We'll try them by court-marital here. Some of you remain and guard this submarine. We will teach these filibustering Americans a lesson."

CHAPTER TWENTY

DOOMED TO DEATH

There was no room on the small deck of the submarine to make a stand against the officers and crew of the Brazilian warship. In fact, the capture of the gold-seekers had been effected so suddenly that their astonishment almost deprived them of the power to think clearly.

At another command from the officer, who was addressed as Admiral Fanchetti, several of the sailors began to lead Tom and his friends toward the small boat.

"Do you feel all right, father?" inquired the lad anxiously, as he looked at his parent. "These scoundrels have no right to treat us so."

"Yes, Tom, I'm all right as far as the electric shock is concerned, but I don't like to be handled in this fashion."

"We ought not to submit!" burst out Mr. Damon. "Bless the stars and stripes! We ought to fight."

"There's no chance," said Mr. Sharp. "We are right under the guns of the ship. They could sink us with one shot. I guess we'll have to give in for the time being."

"It is most unpleasant, if I may be allowed the expression," commented Captain Weston mildly. He seemed to have lost his sudden anger, but there was a steely glint in his eyes, and a grim, set look around his month that showed his temper was kept under control only by an effort. It boded no good to the sailors who had hold of the doughty captain if he should once get loose, and it was noticed that they were on their guard.

As for Tom, he submitted quietly to the two Brazilians who had hold of either arm, and Mr. Swift was held by only one, for it was seen that he was feeble.

"Into the boat with them!" cried Admiral Fanchetti. "And guard them well, Lieutenant Drascalo, for I heard them plotting to escape," and the admiral signaled to a younger officer, who was in charge of the men guarding the prisoners.

"Lieutenant Drascalo, eh?" murmured Mr. Damon. "I think they made a mistake naming him. It ought to be Rascalo. He looks like a rascal."

"Silenceo!" exclaimed the lieutenant, scowling at the odd character'.

"Bless my spark plug! He's a regular fire-eater!" went on Mr. Damon, who appeared to have fully recovered his spirits.

"Silenceo!" cried the lieutenant, scowling again, but Mr. Damon did not appear to mind.

Admiral Fanchetti and several others of the gold-laced officers remained aboard the submarine, while Tom and his friends were hustled into the small boat and rowed toward the warship.

"I hope they don't damage our craft," murmured the young inventor, as he saw the admiral enter the conning tower.

"If they do, we'll complain to the United States consul and demand damages," said Mr. Swift.

"I'm afraid we won't have a chance to communicate with the consul," remarked Captain Weston.

"What do you mean?" asked Mr. Damon. "Bless my shoelaces, but will these scoundrels—"

"Silenceo!" cried Lieutenant Drascalo quickly. "Dogs of Americans, do you wish to insult us?"

"Impossible; you wouldn't appreciate a good, genuine United States insult," murmured Tom under his breath.

"What I mean," went on the captain, "is that these people may carry the proceedings off with a high hand. You heard the admiral speak of a court-martial."

"Would they dare do that?" inquired Mr. Sharp.

"They would dare anything in this part of the world, I'm afraid," resumed Captain Weston. "I think I see their plan, though. This admiral is newly in command; his uniform shows that He wants to make a name for himself, and he seizes on our submarine as an excuse. He can send word to his government that he destroyed a torpedo craft that sought to wreck his ship. Thus he will acquire a reputation."

"But would his government support him in such a hostile act against the United States, a friendly nation?" asked Tom.

"Oh, he would not claim to have acted against the United States as a power. He would say that it was a private submarine, and, as a matter of fact, it is. While we are under the protection of the stars and stripes, our vessel is not a Government one," and Captain Weston spoke the last in a low voice, so the scowling lieutenant could not hear.

"What will they do with us?" inquired Mr. Swift.

"Have some sort of a court-martial, perhaps," went on the captain, "and confiscate our craft Then they will send us back home, I expect for they would not dare harm us."

"But take our submarine!" cried Tom. "The villains—"

"Silenceo!" shouted Lieutenant Drascalo and he drew his sword.

By this time the small boat was under the big guns of the San Paulo, and the prisoners were ordered, in broken English, to mount a companion ladder that hung over the side. In a short time they were on deck, amid a crowd of sailors, and they could see the boat going back to bring off the admiral, who signaled from the submarine. Tom and his friends were taken below to a room that looked like a prison, and there, a little later, they were visited by Admiral Fanchetti and several officers.

"You will be tried at once," said the admiral. "I have examined your submarine and I find she carries two torpedo tubes. It is a wonder you did not sink me at once."

"Those are not torpedo tubes!" cried Tom, unable to keep silent, though Captain Weston motioned him to do so.

"I know torpedo tubes when I see them," declared the admiral. "I consider I had a very narrow escape. Your country is fortunate that mine does not declare war against it for this act. But I take it you are acting privately, for you fly no flag, though you claim to be from the United States."

"There's no place for a flag on the submarine," went on Tom. "What good would it be under water?"

"Silenceo!" cried Lieutenant Drascalo, the admonition to silence seeming to be the only command of which he was capable.

"I shall confiscate your craft for my government," went on the admiral, "and shall punish you as the court-martial may direct. You will be tried at once."

It was in vain for the prisoners to protest. Matters were carried with a high hand. They were allowed a spokesman, and Captain Weston, who understood Spanish, was selected, that language being used. But the defense was a farce, for he was scarcely listened to. Several officers testified before the admiral, who was judge, that they had seen the submarine rise out of the water, almost under the prow of the San Paulo. It was assumed that the *Advance* had tried to wreck the warship, but had failed. It was in vain that Captain Weston and the others told of the reason for their rapid ascent from the ocean depths—that Mr. Swift had been shocked, and needed fresh air. Their story was not believed.

"We have heard enough!" suddenly exclaimed the admiral. "The evidence against you is over-whelming—er—what you Americans call conclusive," and be was speaking then in broken English. "I find you guilty, and the sentence of this court-martial is that you be shot at sunrise, three days hence!"

"Shot!" cried Captain Weston, staggering back at this unexpected sentence. His companions turned white, and Mr. Swift leaned against his son for support.

"Bless my stars! Of all the scoundrelly!" began Mr. Damon.

"Silenceo!" shouted the lieutenant, waving his sword.

"You will be shot," proceeded the admiral. "Is not that the verdict of the honorable court?" he asked, looking at his fellow officers. They all nodded gravely.

"But look here!" objected Captain Weston. "You don't dare do that! We are citizens of the United States, and—"

"I consider you no better than pirates," interrupted the admiral. "You have an armed submarine—a submarine with torpedo tubes. You invade our harbor with it, and come up almost under my ship. You have forfeited your right to the protection of your country, and I have no fear on that score. You will be shot within three days. That is all. Remove the prisoners."

Protests were in vain, and it was equally useless to struggle. The prisoners were taken out on deck, for which they were thankful, for the interior of the ship was close and hot, the weather being intensely disagreeable. They were told to keep within a certain space on deck, and a guard of sailors, all armed, was placed near them. From where they were they could see their submarine floating on the surface of the little bay, with several Brazilians on the small deck. The *Advance* had been anchored, and was surrounded by a flotilla of the native boats, the brown-skinned paddlers gazing curiously at the odd craft.

"Well, this is tough luck!" murmured Tom. "How do you feel, dad?"

"As well as can be expected under the circumstances," was the reply. "What do you think about this, Captain Weston?"

"Not very much, if I may be allowed the expression," was the answer.

"Do you think they will dare carry out that threat?" asked Mr. Sharp.

The captain shrugged his shoulders. "I hope it is only a bluff," he replied, "made to scare us so we will consent to giving up the submarine, which they have no right to confiscate. But these fellows look ugly enough for anything," he went on.

"Then if there's any chance of them attempting to carry it out," spoke Tom, "we've got to do something."

"Bless my gizzard, of course!" exclaimed Mr. Damon. "But what? That's the question. To be shot! Why, that's a terrible threat! The villains—"

"Silenceo!" shouted Lieutenant Drascalo, coming up at that moment.

CHAPTER TWENTY-ONE

THE ESCAPE

Events had happened so quickly that day that the gold-hunters could scarcely comprehend them. It seemed only a short time since Mr. Swift had been discovered lying disabled on the dynamo, and what had transpired since seemed to have taken place in a few minutes, though it was, in reality, several hours. This was made manifest by the feeling of hunger on the part of Tom and his friends.

"I wonder if they're going to starve us, the scoundrels?" asked Mr. Sharp, when the irate lieutenant was beyond hearing. "It's not fair to make us go hungry and shoot us in the bargain."

"That's so, they ought to feed us," put in Tom. As yet neither he nor the others fully realized the meaning of the sentence passed on them.

From where they were on deck they could look off to the little island. From it boats manned by natives were constantly putting off, bringing supplies to the ship. The place appeared to be a sort of calling station for Brazilian warships, where they could get fresh water and fruit and other food.

From the island the gaze of the adventurers wandered to the submarine, which lay not far away. They were chagrined to see several of the bolder natives clambering over the deck.

"I hope they keep out of the interior," commented Tom. "If they get to pulling or hauling on the levers and wheels they may open the tanks and sink her, with the Conning tower open."

"Better that, perhaps, than to have her fall into the hands of a foreign power," commented Captain Weston. "Besides, I don't see that it's going to matter much to us what becomes of her after we're—"

He did not finish, but every one knew what he meant, and a grim silence fell upon the little group.

There came a welcome diversion, however, in the shape of three sailors, bearing trays of food, which were placed on the deck in front of the prisoners, who were sitting or lying in the shade of an awning, for the sun was very hot.

"Ha! Bless my napkin-ring!" cried Mr. Damon with something of his former gaiety. "Here's a meal, at all events. They don't intend to starve us. Eat hearty, every one."

"Yes, we need to keep up our strength," observed Captain Weston.

"Why?" inquired Mr. Sharp.

"Because we're going to try to escape!" exclaimed Tom in a low voice, when the sailors who had brought the food had gone. "Isn't that what you mean, captain?"

"Exactly. We'll try to give these villains the slip, and we'll need all our strength and wits to do it. We'll wait until night, and see what we can do."

"But where will we escape to?" asked Mr. Swift. "The island will afford no shelter, and—"

"No, but our submarine will," went on the sailor.

"It's in the possession of the Brazilians," objected Tom.

"Once I get aboard the *Advance* twenty of those brown-skinned villains won't keep me prisoner," declared Captain Weston fiercely. "If we can only slip away from here, get into the small boat, or even swim to the submarine, I'll make those chaps on board her think a hurricane has broken loose."

"Yes, and I'll help," said Mr. Damon.

"And I," added Tom and the balloonist.

"That's the way to talk," commented the captain. "Now let's eat, for I see that rascally lieutenant coming this way, and we mustn't appear to be plotting, or he'll be suspicious."

The day passed slowly, and though the prisoners seemed to be allowed considerable liberty, they soon found that it was only apparent. Once Tom walked some distance from that portion of the deck where he and the others had been told to remain. A sailor with a gun at once ordered him back. Nor could they approach the rails without being directed, harshly enough at times, to move back amidships.

As night approached the gold-seekers were on the alert for any chance that might offer to slip away, or even attack their guard, but the number of Brazilians around them was doubled in the evening, and after supper, which was served to them on deck by the light of swinging lanterns, they were taken below and locked in a stuffy cabin. They looked helplessly at each other.

"Don't give up," advised Captain Weston. "It's a long night. We may be able to get out of here."

But this hope was in vain. Several times he and Tom, thinking the guards outside the cabin were asleep, tried to force the lock of the door with their pocket-knives, which had not been taken from them. But one of the sailors was aroused each time by the noise, and looked in through a barred window, so they had to give it up. Slowly the night passed, and morning found the prisoners pale, tired and discouraged. They were brought up on deck again, for which they were thankful, as in that tropical climate it was stifling below.

During the day they saw Admiral Fanchetti and several of his officers pay a visit to the submarine. They went below through the opened conning tower, and were gone some time.

"I hope they don't disturb any of the machinery," remarked Mr. Swift. "That could easily do great damage."

Admiral Fanchetti seemed much pleased with himself when he returned from his visit to the submarine.

"You have a fine craft," he said to the prisoners. "Or, rather, you had one. My government now owns it. It seems a pity to shoot such good boat builders, but you are too dangerous to be allowed to go."

If there had been any doubt in the minds of Tom and his friends that the sentence of the court-martial was only for effect, it was dispelled that day. A firing squad was told off in plain view of them, and the men were put through their evolutions by Lieutenant Drascalo, who had them load, aim and fire blank cartridges at an imaginary line of prisoners. Tom could not repress a shudder as he noted the leveled rifles, and saw the fire and smoke spurt from the muzzles.

"Thus we shall do to you at sunrise tomorrow," said the lieutenant, grinning, as he once more had his men practice their grim work.

It seemed hotter than ever that day. The sun was fairly broiling, and there was a curious haziness and stillness to the air. It was noticed that the sailors on the San Paulo were busy making fast all loose articles on deck with extra lashings, and hatch coverings were doubly secured.

"What do you suppose they are up to?" asked Tom of Captain Weston.

"I think it is coming on to blow," he replied, "and they don't want to be caught napping. They have fearful storms down in this region at this season of the year, and I think one is about due."

"I hope it doesn't wreck the submarine," spoke Mr. Swift. "They ought to close the hatch of the conning tower, for it won't take much of a sea to make her ship considerable water."

Admiral Fanchetti had thought of this, however, and as the afternoon wore away and the storm signs multiplied, he sent word to close the submarine. He left a few sailors aboard inside on guard.

"It's too hot to eat," observed Tom, when their supper had been brought to them, and the others felt the same way about it. They managed to drink some cocoanut milk, prepared in a palatable fashion by the natives of the island, and then, much to their disgust, they were taken below again and locked in the cabin.

"Whew! But it certainly is hot!" exclaimed Mr. Damon as he sat down on a couch and fanned himself. "This is awful!"

"Yes, something is going to happen pretty soon," observed Captain Weston. "The storm will break shortly, I think."

They sat languidly about the cabin. It was so oppressive that even the thought of the doom that awaited them in the morning could hardly seem worse than the terrible heat. They could hear movements going on about the ship, movements which indicated that preparations were being made for something unusual. There was a rattling of a chain through a hawse hole, and Captain Weston remarked:

"They're putting down another anchor. Admiral Fanchetti had better get away from the island, though, unless he wants to be wrecked. He'll be blown ashore in less than no time. No cable or chain will hold in such storms as they have here."

There came a period of silence, which was suddenly broken by a howl as of some wild beast.

"What's that?" cried Tom, springing up from where he was stretched out on the cabin floor.

"Only the wind," replied the captain. "The storm has arrived."

The howling kept up, and soon the ship began to rock. The wind increased, and a little later there could be heard, through an opened port in the prisoners' cabin, the dash of rain.

"It's a regular hurricane!" exclaimed the captain. "I wonder if the cables will hold?"

"What about the submarine?" asked Mr. Swift anxiously.

"I haven't much fear for her. She lies so low in the water that the wind can't get much hold on her. I don't believe she'll drag her anchor."

Once more came a fierce burst of wind, and a dash of rain, and then, suddenly above the outburst of the elements, there sounded a crash on deck. It was followed by excited cries.

"Something's happened!" yelled Tom. The prisoners gathered in a frightened group in the middle of the cabin. The cries were repeated, and then came a rush of feet just outside the cabin door.

"Our guards! They're leaving!" shouted Tom.

"Right!" exclaimed Captain Weston. "Now's our chance! Come on! If we're going to escape we must do it while the storm is at its height, and all is in confusion. Come on!"

Tom tried the door. It was locked.

"One side!" shouted the captain, and this time he did not pause to say "by your leave." He came at the portal on the run, and his shoulder struck it squarely. There was a splintering and crashing of wood, and the door was burst open.

"Follow me!" cried the valiant sailor, and Tom and the others rushed after him. They could hear the wind howling more loudly than ever, and as they reached the deck the rain dashed into their faces with such violence that they could hardly see. But they were aware that something had occurred. By the light of several lanterns swaying in the terrific blast they saw that one of the auxiliary masts had broken off near the deck.

It had fallen against the chart house, smashing it, and a number of sailors were laboring to clear away the wreckage.

"Fortune favors us!" cried Captain Weston. "Come on! Make for the small boat. It's near the side ladder. We'll lower the boat and pull to the submarine."

There came a flash of lightning, and in its glare Tom saw something that caused him to cry out.

"Look!" he shouted. "The submarine. She's dragged her anchors!"

The *Advance* was much closer to the warship than she had been that afternoon. Captain Weston looked over the side.

"It's the San Paulo that's dragging her anchors, not the submarine!" he shouted. "We're bearing down on her! We must act quickly. Come on, we'll lower the boat!"

In the rush of wind and the dash of rain the prisoners crowded to the accommodation companion ladder, which was still over the side of the big ship. No one seemed to be noticing them, for Admiral Fanchetti was on the bridge, yelling orders for the clearing away of the wreckage. But Lieutenant Drascalo, coming up from below at that moment, caught sight of the fleeing ones. Drawing his sword, he rushed at them, shouting:

"The prisoners! The prisoners! They are escaping!"

Captain Weston leaped toward the lieutenant

"Look out for his sword!" cried Tom. But the doughty sailor did not fear the weapon. Catching up a coil of rope, he cast it at the lieutenant. It struck him in the chest, and he staggered back, lowering his sword.

Captain Weston leaped forward, and with a terrific blow sent Lieutenant Drascalo to the deck.

"There!" cried the sailor. "I guess you won't yell 'Silenceo!' for a while now."

There was a rush of Brazilians toward the group of prisoners. Tom caught one with a blow on the chin, and felled him, while Captain Weston disposed of two more, and Mr. Sharp and Mr. Damon one each. The savage fighting of the Americans was too much for the foreigners, and they drew back.

"Come on!" cried Captain Weston again. "The storm is getting worse. The warship will crash into the submarine in a few minutes. Her anchors aren't holding. I didn't think they would."

He made a dash for the ladder, and a glance showed him that the small boat was in the water at the foot of it. The craft had not been hoisted on the davits.

"Luck's with us at last!" cried Tom, Seeing it also. "Shall I help you, dad?"

"No; I think I'm all right. Go ahead."

There came such a gust of wind that the San Paulo was heeled over, and the wreck of the mast, rolling about, crashed into the side of a deck house, splintering it. A crowd of sailors, led by Admiral Fanchetti, who were again rushing on the escaping prisoners, had to leap back out of the way of the rolling mast.

"Catch them! Don't let them get away!" begged the commander, but the sailors evidently had no desire to close in with the Americans.

Through the rush of wind and rain Tom and his friends staggered down the ladder. It was hard work to maintain one's footing, but they managed it. On account of the high side of the ship the water was comparatively calm under her lee, and, though the small boat was bobbing about, they got aboard. The oars were in place, and in another moment they had shoved off from the landing stage which formed the foot of the accommodation ladder.

"Now for the *Advance*!" murmured Captain Weston.

"Come back! Come back, dogs of Americans!" cried a voice at the rail over their heads, and looking up, Tom saw Lieutenant Drascalo. He had snatched a carbine from a marine, and was pointing it at the recent prisoners. He fired, the flash of the gun and a dazzling chain of lightning coming together. The thunder swallowed up the report of the carbine, but the bullet whistled uncomfortable close to Tom's head. The blackness that followed the lightning shut out the view of everything for a few seconds, and when the next flash came the adventurers saw that they were close to their submarine.

A fusillade of shots sounded from the deck of the warship, but as the marines were poor marksmen at best, and as the swaying of the ship disconcerted them, our friends were in little danger.

There was quite a sea once they were beyond the protection of the side of the warship, but Captain Weston, who was rowing, knew how to manage a boat skillfully, and he soon had the craft alongside the bobbing submarine.

"Get aboard, now, quick!" he cried.

They leaped to the small deck, casting the rowboat adrift. It was the work of but a moment to open the conning tower. As they started to descend they were met by several Brazilians coming up.

"Overboard with 'em!" yelled the captain. "Let them swim ashore or to their ship!"

With almost superhuman strength he tossed one big sailor from the small deck. Another showed fight, but he went to join his companion in the swirling water. A man rushed at Tom, seeking the while to draw his sword, but the young inventor, with a neat left-hander, sent him to join the other two, and the remainder did not wait to try conclusions. They leaped for their lives, and soon all could be seen, in the frequent lightning flashes, swimming toward the warship which was now closer than ever to the submarine.

"Get inside and we'll sink below the surface!" called Tom. "Then we don't care what happens."

They closed the steel door of the conning tower. As they did so they heard the patter of bullets from carbines fired from the San Paulo. Then came a violent tossing of the *Advance*; the waves were becoming higher as they caught the full force of the hurricane. It took but an instant to sever, from within, the cable attached to the anchor, which was one belonging to the warship. The Advance began drifting.

"Open the tanks, Mr. Sharp!" cried Tom. "Captain Weston and I will steer. Once below we'll start the engines."

Amid a crash of thunder and dazzling flashes of lightning, the submarine began to sink. Tom, in the conning tower had a sight of the San Paulo as it drifted nearer and nearer under the influence of the mighty wind. As one bright flash came he saw Admiral Fanchetti and Lieutenant Drascalo leaning over the rail and gazing at the Advance.

A moment later the view faded from sight as the submarine sank below the surface of the troubled sea. She was tossed about for some time until deep enough to escape the surface motion. Waiting until she was far enough down so that her lights would not offer a mark for the guns of the warship, the electrics were switched on.

"We're safe now!" cried Tom, helping his father to his cabin. "They've got too much to attend to themselves to follow us now, even if they could. Shall we go ahead, Captain Weston?"

"I think so, yes, if I may be allowed to express my opinion," was the mild reply, in strange contrast to the strenuous work in which the captain had just been engaged.

Tom signaled to Mr. Sharp in the engine-room, and in a few

seconds the Advance was speeding away from the island and the hostile vessel. Nor, deep as she was now, was there any sign of the hurricane. In the peaceful depths she was once more speeding toward the sunken treasure.

CHAPTER TWENTY-TWO

AT THE WRECK

"Well," remarked Mr. Damon, as the submarine hurled herself forward through the ocean, "I guess that firing party will have something else to do tomorrow morning besides aiming those rifles at us."

"Yes, indeed," agreed Tom. "They'll be lucky if they save their ship. My, how that wind did blow!"

"You're right," put in Captain Weston. "When they get a hurricane down in this region it's no cat's paw. But they were a mighty careless lot of sailors. The idea of leaving the ladder over the side, and the boat in the water."

"It was a good thing for us, though," was Tom's opinion.

"Indeed it was," came from the captain. "But as long as we are safe now I think we'd better take a look about the craft to see if those chaps did any damage. They can't have done much, though, or she wouldn't be running so smoothly. Suppose you go take a look, Tom, and ask your father and Mr. Sharp what they think. I'll steer for a while, until we get well away from the island."

The young inventor found his father and the balloonist busy in the engine-room. Mr. Swift had already begun an inspection of the machinery, and so far found that it had not been injured. A further inspection showed that no damage had been done by the foreign guard that had been in temporary possession of the *Advance*, though the sailors had made free in the cabins, and had broken into the food lockers, helping themselves plentifully. But there was still enough for the gold-seekers.

"You'd never know there was a storm raging up above," observed Tom as he rejoined Captain Weston in the lower pilot house, where he was managing the craft. "It's as still and peaceful here as one could wish."

"Yes, the extreme depths are seldom disturbed by a surface storm. But we are over a mile deep now. I sent her down a little while you were gone, as I think she rides a little more steadily."

All that night they speeded forward, and the next day, rising to the surface to take an observation, they found no traces of the storm, which had blown itself out. They were several hundred miles away from the hostile warship, and there was not a vessel in sight on the broad expanse of blue ocean.

The air tanks were refilled, and after sailing along on the surface for an hour or two, the submarine was again sent below, as Captain Weston sighted through his telescope the smoke of a distant steamer.

"As long as it isn't the *Wonder*, we're all right," said Tom. "Still, we don't want to answer a lot of questions about ourselves and our object."

"No. I fancy the *Wonder* will give up the search," remarked the captain, as the *Advance* was sinking to the depths.

"We must be getting pretty near to the end of our search ourselves," ventured the young inventor.

"We are within five hundred miles of the intersection of the forty-fifth parallel and the twenty-seventh meridian, east from Washington," said the captain. "That's as near as I could locate the wreck. Once we reach that point we will have to search about under water, for I don't fancy the other divers left any buoys to mark the spot."

It was two days later, after uneventful sailing, partly on the surface, and partly submerged, that Captain Weston, taking a noon observation, announced:

"Well, we're here!"

"Do you mean at the wreck?" asked Mr. Swift eagerly.

"We're at the place where she is supposed to lie, in about two miles of water," replied the captain. "We are quite a distance off the coast of Uruguay, about opposite the harbor of Rio de La Plata. From now on we shall have to nose about under water, and trust to luck."

With her air tanks filled to their capacity, and Tom having seen that the oxygen machine and other apparatus was in perfect working order, the submarine was sent below on her search. Though they were in the neighborhood of the wreck, the adventurers might still have to do considerable searching before locating it. Lower and lower they sank into the depths of the sea, down and down, until they were deeper than they had ever gone before. The pressure was tremendous, but the steel sides of the *Advance* withstood it

Then began a search that lasted nearly a week. Back and forth they cruised, around in great circles, with the powerful searchlight focused to disclose the sunken treasure ship. Once Tom, who was observing the path of light in the depths from the conning tower, thought he had seen the remains of the Boldero, for a misty shape loomed up in front of the submarine, and he signaled for a quick stop. It was a wreck, but it had been on the ocean bed for a score of years, and only a few timbers remained of what had been a great ship. Much disappointed, Tom rang for full speed ahead again, and the current was sent into the great electric plates that pulled and pushed the submarine forward.

For two days more nothing happened. They searched around under the green waters, on the alert for the first sign, but they saw nothing. Great fish swam about them, sometimes racing with the *Advance*. The adventurers beheld great ocean caverns, and skirted immense rocks, where dwelt monsters of the deep. Once a great octopus tried to do battle with the submarine and crush it in its snaky arms, but Tom saw the great white body, with saucer-shaped eyes, in the path of light and rammed him with the steel point. The creature died after a struggle.

They were beginning to despair when a full week had passed and they were seemingly as far from the wreck as ever. They went to the surface to enable Captain Weston to take another observation. It only confirmed the other, and showed that they were in the right vicinity. But it was like looking for a needle in a haystack, almost, to and the sunken ship in that depth of water.

"Well, we'll try again," said Mr. Swift, as they sank once more beneath the surface.

It was toward evening, on the second day after this, that Tom, who was on duty in the conning tower, saw a black shape looming up in front of the submarine, the searchlight revealing it to him far enough away so that he could steer to avoid it. He thought at first that it was a great rock, for they were moving along near the bottom, but the peculiar shape of it soon convinced him that this could not be. It came more plainly into view as the submarine approached it more slowly, then suddenly, out of the depths in the illumination from the searchlight, the young inventor saw the steel sides of a steamer. His heart gave a great thump, but he would not call out yet, fearing that it might be some other vessel than the one containing the treasure.

He steered the *Advance* so as to circle it. As he swept past the bows he saw in big letters near the sharp prow the word, Boldero.

"The wreck! The wreck!" he cried, his voice ringing through the craft from end to end. "We've found the wreck at last!"

"Are you sure?" cried his father, hurrying to his son, Captain Weston following.

"Positive," answered the lad. The submarine was slowing up now, and Tom sent her around on the other side. They had a good view of the sunken ship. It seemed to be intact, no gaping holes in her sides, for only her plates had started, allowing her to sink gradually.

"At last," murmured Mr. Swift. "Can it be possible we are about to get the treasure?"

"That's the Boldero, all right," affirmed Captain Weston. "I recognize her, even if the name wasn't on her bow. Go right down on the bottom, Tom, and we'll get out the diving suits and make an examination."

The submarine settled to the ocean bed. Tom glanced at the depth gage. It showed over two miles and a half. Would they be able to venture out into water of such enormous pressure in the comparatively frail diving suits, and wrest the gold from the wreck? It was a serious question.

The *Advance* came to a stop. In front of her loomed the great bulk of the Boldero, vague and shadowy in the flickering gleam of the searchlight As the gold-seekers looked at her through the bull's-eyes of the conning tower, several great forms emerged from beneath the wreck's bows.

"Deep-water sharks!" exclaimed Captain Weston, "and monsters, too. But they can't bother us. Now to get out the gold!"

CHAPTER TWENTY-THREE

ATTACKED BY SHARKS

For a few minutes after reaching the wreck, which had so occupied their thoughts for the past weeks, the adventurers did nothing but gaze at it from the ports of the submarine. The appearance of the deep-water sharks gave them no concern, for they did not imagine the ugly creatures would attack them. The treasure-seekers were more engrossed with the problem of getting out the gold.

"How are we going to get at it?" asked Tom, as he looked at the high sides of the sunken ship, which towered well above the comparatively small *Advance*.

"Why, just go in and get it," suggested Mr. Damon. "Where is gold in a cargo usually kept, Captain Weston? You ought to know, I should think. Bless my pocketbook!"

"Well, I should say that in this case the bullion would be kept in a safe in the captain's cabin," replied the sailor. "Or, if not there, in some after part of the vessel, away from where the crew is quartered. But it is going to be quite a problem to get at it. We can't climb the sides of the wreck, and it will be impossible to lower her ladder over the side. However, I think we had better get into the diving suits and take a closer look. We can walk around her."

"That's my idea," put in Mr. Sharp. "But who will go, and who will stay with the ship?"

"I think Tom and Captain Weston had better go," suggested Mr. Swift. "Then, in case anything happens, Mr. Sharp, you and I will be on board to manage matters."

"You don't think anything will happen, do you, dad?" asked his son with a laugh, but it was not an easy one, for the lad was thinking of the shadowy forms of the ugly sharks.

"Oh, no, but it's best to be prepared," answered his father.

The captain and the young inventor lost no time in donning the diving suits. They each took a heavy metal bar, pointed at one end, to use in assisting them to walk on the bed of the ocean, and as a protection in case the sharks might attack them. Entering the diving chamber, they were shut in, and then water was admitted until the pressure was seen, by gauges, to be the same as that outside the submarine. Then the sliding steel door was opened. At first Tom and the captain could barely move, so great was the pressure of water on their bodies. They would have been crushed but for the protection afforded by the strong diving suits.

In a few minutes they became used to it, and stepped out on the floor of the ocean. They could not, of course, speak to each other, but Tom looked through the glass eyes of his helmet at the captain, and the latter motioned for the lad to follow. The two divers could breathe perfectly, and by means of small, but powerful lights on the helmets, the way was lighted for them as they advanced.

Slowly they approached the wreck, and began a circuit of her. They could see several places where the pressure of the water, and the strain of the storm in which she had foundered, had opened the plates of the ship, but in no case were the openings large enough to admit a person. Captain Weston put his steel bar in one crack, and tried to pry it farther open, but his strength was not equal to the task. He made some peculiar motions, but Tom could not understand them.

They looked for some means by which they could mount to the decks of the Boldero, but none was visible. It was like trying to scale a fifty-foot smooth steel wall. There was no place for a foothold. Again the sailor made some peculiar motions, and the lad puzzled over them. They had gone nearly around the wreck now, and as yet had seen no way in which to get at the gold. As they passed around the bow, which was in a deep shadow from a great rock, they caught sight of the submarine lying a short distance away. Light streamed from many hull's-eyes, and Tom felt a sense of security as he looked at her, for it was lonesome enough in that great depth of water, unable to speak to his companion, who was a few feet in advance.

Suddenly there was a swirling of the water, and Tom was nearly thrown off his feet by the rush of some great body. A long, black shadow passed over his head, and an instant later he saw the form of a great shark launched at Captain Weston. The lad involuntarily cried in alarm, but the result was surprising. He was nearly deafened by his own voice, confined as the sound was in the helmet he wore. But the sailor, too, had felt the movement of the water, and turned just in time. He thrust upward with his pointed bar. But he missed the stroke, and Tom, a moment later, saw the great fish turn over so that its mouth, which is far underneath its snout, could take in the queer shape which the shark evidently thought was a choice morsel. The big fish did actually get the helmet of Captain Weston inside its jaws, but probably it would have found it impossible to crush the strong steel. Still it might have sprung the joints, and water would have entered, which would have been as fatal as though the sailor had been swallowed by the shark. Tom realized this and, moving as fast as he could through the water, he came up behind the monster and drove his steel bar deep into it.

The sea was crimsoned with blood, and the savage creature, opening its mouth, let go of the captain. It turned on Tom, who again harpooned it. Then the fish darted off and began a wild flurry, for it was dying. The rush of water nearly threw Tom off his feet, but he managed to make his way over to his friend, and assist him to rise. A confident look from the sailor showed the lad that Captain Weston was uninjured, though he must have been frightened. As the two turned to make their way back to the submarine, the waters about them seemed alive with the horrible monsters.

It needed but a glance to show what they were, Sharks! Scores of them, long, black ones, with their ugly, undershot mouths. They had been attracted by the blood of the one Tom had killed, but there was not a meal for all of them off the dying creature, and the great fish might turn on the young inventor and his companion.

The two shrank closer toward the wreck. They might get under the prow of that and be safe. But even as they started to move, several of the sea wolves darted quickly at them. Tom glanced at the captain. What could they do? Strong as were the diving suits, a combined attack by the sharks, with their powerful jaws, would do untold damage.

At that moment there seemed some movement on board the submarine. Tom could see his father looking from the conning tower, and the aged inventor seemed to be making some motions. Then Tom understood. Mr. Swift was directing his son and Captain Weston to crouch down. The lad did so, pulling the sailor after him. Then Tom saw the bow electric gun run out, and aimed at the mass of sharks, most of whom were congregated about the dead one. Into the midst of the monsters was fired a number of small projectiles, which could be used in the electric cannon in place of the solid shot. Once more the waters were red with blood, and those sharks which were not killed swirled off. Tom and Captain Weston were saved. They were soon inside the submarine again, telling their thrilling story.

"It's lucky you saw us, dad," remarked the lad, blushing at the praise Mr. Damon bestowed on him for killing the monster which had attacked the captain.

"Oh, I was on the lookout," said the inventor. "But what about getting into the wreck?"

"I think the only way we can do it will be to ram a hole in her side," said Captain Weston. "That was what I tried to tell Tom by motions, but he didn't seem to understand me."

"No," replied the lad, who was still a little nervous from his recent experience. "I thought you meant for us to turn it over, bottom side up," and he laughed.

"Bless my gizzard! Just like a shark," commented Mr. Damon.

"Please don't mention them," begged Tom. "I hope we don't see any more of them."

"Oh, I fancy they have been driven far enough away from this neighborhood now," commented the captain. "But now about the wreck. We may be able to approach it from above. Suppose we try to lower the submarine on it? That will save ripping it open."

This was tried a little later, but would not work. There were strong currents sweeping over the top of the Boldero, caused by a submerged reef near which she had settled. It was a delicate task to sink the submarine on her decks, and with the deep waters swirling about was found to be impossible, even with the use of the electric plates and the auxiliary screws. Once more the *Advance* settled to the ocean bed, near the wreck.

"Well, what's to be done?" asked Tom, as he looked at the high steel sides.

"Ram her, tear a hole, and then use dynamite," decided Captain Weston promptly. "You have some explosive, haven't you, Mr. Swift?"

"Oh, yes. I came prepared for emergencies."

"Then we'll blow up the wreck and get at the gold."

CHAPTER TWENTY-FOUR

RAMMING THE WRECK

Fitted with a long, sharp steel ram in front, the *Advance* was peculiarly adapted for this sort of work. In designing the ship this ram was calculated to be used against hostile vessels in war time, for the submarine was at first, as we know, destined for a Government boat. Now the ram was to serve a good turn.

To make sure that the attempt would be a success, the machinery of the craft was carefully gone over. It was found to be in perfect order, save for a few adjustments which were needed. Then, as it was night, though there was no difference in the appearance of things below the surface, it was decided to turn in, and begin work in the morning. Nor did the gold-seekers go to the surface, for they feared they might encounter a storm.

"We had trouble enough locating the wreck," said Captain Weston, "and if we go up we may be blown off our course. We have air enough to stay below, haven't we, Tom?"

"Plenty," answered the lad, looking at the gages.

After a hearty breakfast the next morning, the submarine crew got ready for their hard task. The craft was backed away as far as was practical, and then, running at full speed, she rammed the wreck. The shock was terrific, and at first it was feared some damage had been done to the *Advance*, but she stood the strain.

"Did we open up much of a hole?" anxiously asked Mr. Swift.

"Pretty good," replied Tom, observing it through the conning tower bull's-eyes, when the submarine had backed off again. "Let's give her another."

Once more the great steel ram hit into the side of the Boldero, and again the submarine shivered from the shock. But there was a bigger hole in the wreck now, and after Captain Weston had viewed it he decided it was large enough to allow a person to enter and place a charge of dynamite so that the treasure ship would be broken up.

Tom and the captain placed the explosive. Then the *Advance* was withdrawn to a safe distance. There was a dull rumble, a great swirling of the water, which was made murky; but when it cleared, and the submarine went back, it was seen that the wreck was effectively broken up. It was in two parts, each one easy of access.

"That's the stuff!" cried Tom. "Now to get at the gold!"

"Yes, get out the diving suits," added Mr. Damon. "Bless my

watch-charm, I think I'll chance it in one myself! Do you think the sharks are all gone, Captain Weston?"

"I think so."

In a short time Tom, the captain, Mr. Sharp and Mr. Damon were attired in the diving suits, Mr. Swift not caring to venture into such a great depth of water. Besides, it was necessary for at least one person to remain in the submarine to operate the diving chamber.

Walking slowly along the bottom of the sea the four gold-seekers approached the wreck. They looked on all sides for a sight of the sharks, but the monster fish seemed to have deserted that part of the ocean. Tom was the first to reach the now disrupted steamer. He found he could easily climb up, for boxes and barrels from the cargo holds were scattered all about by the explosion. Captain Weston soon joined the lad. The sailor motioned Tom to follow him, and being more familiar with ocean craft the captain was permitted to take the lead. He headed aft, seeking to locate the captain's cabin. Nor was he long in finding it. He motioned for the others to enter, that the combined illumination of the lamps in their helmets would make the place bright enough so a search could be made for the gold. Tom suddenly seized the arm of the captain, and pointed to one corner of the cabin. There stood a small safe, and at the sight of it Captain Weston moved toward it. The door was not locked, probably having been left open when the ship was deserted. Swinging it back the interior was revealed.

It was empty. There was no gold bullion in it.

There was no mistaking the dejected air of Captain Weston. The others shared his feelings, but though they all felt like voicing their disappointment, not a word could be spoken. Mr. Sharp, by vigorous motions, indicated to his companions to seek further.

They did so, spending all the rest of the day in the wreck, save for a short interval for dinner. But no gold rewarded their search.

Tom, late that afternoon, wandered away from the others, and found himself in the captain's cabin again, with the empty safe showing dimly in the water that was all about.

"Hang it all!" thought the lad, "we've had all our trouble for nothing! They must have taken the gold with them."

Idly he raised his steel bar, and struck it against the partition back of the safe. To his astonishment the partition seemed to fall inward, revealing a secret compartment. The lad leaned forward to bring the light for his helmet to play on the recess. He saw a number of boxes, piled one upon the other. He had accidentally touched a hidden spring and opened a secret receptacle. But what did it contain?

Tom reached in and tried to lift one of the boxes. He found it beyond his strength. Trembling from excitement, he went in search of the others. He found them delving in the after part of the wreck, but by motions our hero caused them to follow him. Captain Weston showed the excitement he felt as soon as he caught sight of the boxes. He and Mr. Sharp lifted one out, and placed it on the cabin floor. They pried off the top with their bars.

There, packed in layers, were small yellow bars; dull, gleaming, yellow bars! It needed but a glance to show that they were gold bullion. Tom had found the treasure. The lad tried to dance around there in the cabin of the wreck, nearly three miles below the surface of the ocean, but the pressure of water was too much for him. Their trip had been successful.

CHAPTER TWENTY-FIVE

HOME WITH THE GOLD

There was no time to be lost. They were in a treacherous part of the ocean, and strong currents might at any time further break up the wreck, so that they could not come at the gold. It was decided, by means of motions, to at once transfer the treasure to the submarine. As the boxes were too heavy to carry easily, especially as two men, who were required to lift one, could not walk together in the uncertain footing afforded by the wreck, another plan was adopted. The boxes were opened and the bars, a few at a time, were dropped on a firm, sandy place at the side of the wreck. Tom and Captain Weston did this work, while Mr. Sharp and Mr. Damon carried the bullion to the diving chamber of the Advance. They put the yellow bars inside, and when quite a number had been thus shifted, Mr. Swift, closing the chamber, pumped the water out and removed the gold. Then he opened the chamber to the divers again, and the process was repeated, until all the bullion had been secured.

Tom would have been glad to make a further examination of the wreck, for he thought he could get some of the rifles the ship carried, but Captain Weston signed to him not to attempt this.

The lad went to the pilot house, while his father and Mr. Sharp took their places in the engine-room. The gold had been safely stowed in Mr. Swift's cabin.

Tom took a last look at the wreck before he gave the starting signal. As he gazed at the bent and twisted mass of steel that had once been a great ship, he saw something long, black and shadowy moving around from the other side, coming across the bows.

"There's another big shark," he observed to Captain Weston. "They're coming back after us."

The captain did not speak. He was staring at the dark form. Suddenly, from what seemed the pointed nose of it, there gleamed a light, as from some great eye.

"Look at that!" cried Tom. "That's no shark!"

"If you want my opinion," remarked the sailor, "I should say it was the other submarine—that of Berg and his friends—the *Wonder*. They've managed to fix up their craft and are after the gold."

"But they're too late!" cried Tom excitedly. "Let's tell them so."

"No," advised the captain. "We don't want any trouble with them."

Mr. Swift came forward to see why his son had not given the signal to start. He was shown the other submarine, for now that the *Wonder* had turned on several searchlights, there was no doubt as to the identity of the craft.

"Let's get away unobserved if we can," he suggested. "We have had trouble enough."

It was easy to do this, as the *Advance* was hidden behind the wreck, and her lights were glowing but dimly. Then, too, those in the other submarine were so excited over the finding of what they supposed was the wreck containing the treasure, that they paid little attention to anything else.

"I wonder how they'll feel when they find the gold gone?" asked Tom as he pulled the lever starting the pumps.

"Well, we may have a chance to learn, when we get back to civilization," remarked the captain.

The surface was soon reached, and then, under fair skies, and on a calm sea, the voyage home was begun. Part of the time the *Advance* sailed on the top, and part of the time submerged.

They met with but a single accident, and that was when the forward electrical plate broke. But with the aft one still in commission, and the auxiliary screws, they made good time. Just before reaching home they settled down to the bottom and donned the diving suits again, even Mr. Swift taking his turn. Mr. Damon caught some large lobsters, of which he was very fond, or, rather, to be more correct, the lobsters caught him. When he entered the diving chamber there were four fine ones clinging to different parts of his diving suit. Some of them were served for dinner.

The adventurers safely reached the New Jersey coast, and the submarine was docked. Mr. Swift at once communicated with the proper authorities concerning the recovery of the gold. He offered to divide with the actual owners, after he and his friends had been paid for their services, but as the revolutionary party to whom the bullion was intended had gone out of existence, there was no one to officially claim the treasure, so it all went to Tom and his friends, who made an equitable distribution of it. The young inventor did not forget to buy Mrs. Baggert a fine diamond ring, as he had promised.

As for Berg and his employers, they were, it was learned later, greatly chagrined at finding the wreck valueless. They tried to make trouble for Tom and his father, but were not successful.

A few days after arriving at the seacoast cottage, Tom, his father and Mr. Damon went to Shopton in the airship. Captain Weston, Garret Jackson and Mr Sharp remained behind in charge of the submarine. It was decided that the Swifts would keep the craft and not sell it to the Government, as Tom said they might want to go after more treasure some day.

"I must first deposit this gold," said Mr. Swift as the airship landed in front of the shed at his home. "It won't do to keep it in the house over night, even if the Happy Harry gang is in jail."

Tom helped him take it to the bank. As they were making perhaps the largest single deposit ever put in the institution, Ned Newton came out.

"Well, Tom," he cried to his chum, "it seems that you are never going to stop doing things. You've conquered the air, the earth and the water."

"What have you been doing while I've been under water, Ned?" asked the young inventor.

"Oh, the same old thing. Running errands and doing all sorts of work in the bank."

Tom had a sudden idea. He whispered to his father and Mr. Swift nodded. A little later he was closeted with Mr. Prendergast, the bank president. It was not long before Ned and Tom were called in.

"I have some good news for you, Ned," said Mr. Prendergast, while Tom smiled. "Mr. Swift er—ahem—one of our largest depositors, has spoken to me about you, Ned. I find that you have been very faithful. You are hereby appointed assistant cashier, and of course you will get a much larger salary."

Ned could hardly believe it, but he knew then what Tom had whispered to Mr. Swift. The wishes of a depositor who brings much gold bullion to a bank can hardly be ignored.

"Come on out and have some soda," invited Tom, and when Ned looked inquiringly at the president, the latter nodded an assent.

As the two lads were crossing the street to a drug store, something whizzed past them, nearly running them down.

"What sort of an auto was that?" cried Tom.

"That? Oh, that was Andy Foger's new car," answered Ned. "He's been breaking the speed laws every day lately, but no one seems to bother him. It's because his father is rich, I suppose. Andy says he has the fastest car ever built."

"He has, eh?" remarked Tom, while a curious look came into his eyes. "Well, maybe I can build one that will beat his."

And whether the young inventor did or not you can learn by reading the fifth volume of this series, to be called "Tom Swift and His Electric Runabout; Or, The Speediest Car on the Road."

"Well, Tom, I certainly appreciate what you did for me in getting me a better position," remarked Ned as they left the drug store. "I was beginning to think I'd never get promoted. Say, have you anything to do this evening? If you haven't, I wish you'd come over to my house. I've got a lot of pictures I took while you were away."

"Sorry, but I can't," replied Tom.

"Why, are you going to build another airship or submarine?"

"No, but I'm going to see— Oh, what do you want to know for, anyhow?" demanded the young inventor with a blush. "Can't a fellow go see a girl without being cross-questioned?"

"Oh, of course," replied Ned with a laugh. "Give Miss Nestor my regards," and at this Tom blushed still more. But, as he said, that was his own affair.

Made in the USA
Monee, IL
11 October 2020

44539665R00267